JOEL C. ROSENBERG

D1712701

40-DBB-274

THE BEIJING BETRAYAL

A MARCUS RYKER NOVEL

Tyndale House Publishers
Carol Stream, Illinois

Visit Tyndale online at tyndale.com.

Visit Joel C. Rosenberg's website at joelrosenberg.com.

Tyndale and Tyndale's quill logo are registered trademarks of Tyndale House Ministries.

The Beijing Betrayal

For information about special discounts for bulk purchases, please contact Tyndale House Publishers at csresponse@tyndale.com or call 1-855-277-9400.

Library of Congress Cataloging-in-Publication Data

A catalog record for this book is available from the Library of Congress.

ISBN 978-1-4964-3799-0 (hardcover)

Printed in the United States of America

31	30	29	28	27	26	25
7	6	5	4	3	2	1

To my Lynn—my college sweetheart and best friend. Thank you for loving me, believing in me, encouraging me, and running the race with me. Can you believe we actually get to live and work and serve in Jerusalem, the City of the Great King?

CAST OF CHARACTERS

Americans

Marcus Ryker—Diplomatic Security Service/Central Intelligence Agency

Peter Hwang—Diplomatic Security Service/Central Intelligence Agency

Geoff Stone—Diplomatic Security Service/Central Intelligence Agency

Kailea Curtis—Diplomatic Security Service

Jennifer Morris—Central Intelligence Agency

Noah Daniels—Central Intelligence Agency

Donny Callaghan—Central Intelligence Agency

Miguel Navarro—Central Intelligence Agency

Martha Dell—Director of the Central Intelligence Agency

Annie Stewart—Deputy Director, Central Intelligence Agency

Carlos Hernandez—President of the United States

Margaret "Meg" Whitney—Vice President of the United States

Robert Dayton—Secretary of State; former Senator from Iowa

Mickey Clawson—Secretary of Energy

Cal Foster—Secretary of Defense

James Meyers—Chairman of the Joint Chiefs of Staff

Bill McDermott—National Security Advisor

Marjorie Ryker—Marcus Ryker's mother

Kairos

Abu Nakba—Commander of terror group known as *Kairos*

Mohammed Faisal—Senior advisor to Abu Nakba

Omar Nazim—Head of Abu Nakba's security detail

Chinese

Chen Guanzhong—President of the People's Republic of China and
General Secretary of the Chinese Communist Party
Dai Wangshu—Minister of State Security
Li Bai Xiang—Chief of Operations for the Ministry of State Security
Wei Daoming—Junior Officer, Ministry of National Defense

Taiwanese

Yani Lee—President of Taiwan
Ben We-Ming—Vice President
Henry Wang—Defense Minister

Russians

Mikhail Borisovich Petrovsky—President of the Russian Federation
Nikolay Vladimirovich Kropatkin—Former head of the FSB
Oleg Kraskin—Son-in-law of the late President Aleksandr Luganov

Iranians

Yadollah Afshar—Supreme Leader of the Islamic Republic of Iran
Mahmoud Entezam—Commander of the Iranian Revolutionary
Guard Corps

PRELUDE

Taichung

Changhua

Nantou

Yunlin

Taiwan
(Republic of China

Chiayi County
Chiayi

Tainan

Kaohsiung

Tarang

All warfare is based on deception.

SUN TZU, THE ART OF WAR

1

"Someone just fired a missile at the president!"

Instantly, Abu Nakba's head jerked back.

He had just bowed his face toward Mecca to begin his evening prayers when he heard the stunned voice of a CNN anchor on one of the television sets in the other room.

"Father, come quickly—it's started," shouted one of his bodyguards from the living room.

Then the old man heard gasps.

"There has just been an enormous explosion outside the stadium," exclaimed Carolyn Tam, the veteran CNN anchor.

"Mohammed, help me," the old man ordered, grabbing the walking stick with his left hand as Mohammed Faisal, his aide-de-camp, sprang up from his own prayers, grabbed Abu Nakba's right hand, and pulled him to his feet.

Hobbling out of the master bedroom into the rustic, unadorned living room of the mountaintop compound they had finally reached and settled into that very morning, the Kairos founder had no interest in the stunning views of silver snow-covered peaks, all bathed in moonlight. As Faisal helped him into a creaky wooden chair, surrounded by heavily armed bodyguards and Kairos jihadists, the old man's attention was now entirely riveted on the six flat-screen TV sets—connected to satellite dishes on the roof—that had been set up for them before their arrival. Though each was tuned to a different American or European network, each showed the live coverage of the Mass being held that very moment at Soldier Field in Chicago by Pope Pius XIII, with President Andrew Clarke and the First Lady in attendance.

Now they were broadcasting live images of a huge fireball outside the stadium.

Al Jazeera quickly cut to a split screen. On the left side of the screen, Abu Nakba could see confusion in the eyes of the pope and the priests around him, who had just heard the explosion but couldn't see it and clearly didn't know what was happening. On the right side, they showed a Patriot missile battery outside the stadium engulfed in flames and dozens of charred bodies all around it.

The BBC chose a different strategy. They cut to a wide external shot showing not only the destroyed missile battery but panic breaking out among the twenty-five thousand people who moments earlier had been sitting in the parking lot, watching the Mass on jumbo screens, hundreds of whom had just been incinerated.

"*No, no—my God, here comes another,*" shouted the CNN anchor, drawing Abu Nakba's full attention once again.

CNN now showed an extremely wide shot, apparently coming from a crew positioned on the roof of a nearby skyscraper. This not only showed the fireball and thousands of screaming people running for their lives but also the contrail of a second missile emerging from the top of the Willis Tower. But it was veering wildly through the bright morning sky, as though something had knocked it off course. This one didn't strike the stadium but smashed into a makeshift medical center of some sort—a sprawling white tent emblazoned with a large red cross—located on the far side of the parking lot. It, too, suddenly erupted into a massive fireball, instantly obliterating the tent and everyone inside it.

Abu Nakba's men started cheering, but he demanded they be silent. Then he ordered Faisal to turn up the volume on CNN as he leaned forward in his chair.

"The president of the United States and Pope Pius XIII are under attack," said Tam, her voice trembling. *"I repeat—despite the most stringent security ever set up by the Secret Service, the president, the First Lady, the pope, and the hundred thousand people attending this Mass are now under missile attack."*

Then it came, just as Abu Nakba knew it would.

A third SA-7 missile.

Also from the top of the Willis Tower.

And this one scored a direct hit.

The Libyan watched in delight as the missile streaked over the parking lot, barely missed the roof of the stadium, and careened into the east-side bleachers just to the left of the main platform. He was mumbling something, but none of his aides or bodyguards could hear him. Nor were they paying much attention. Like their leader, they were mesmerized by the sight of thousands of Americans being vaporized.

Every network now cut back inside the stadium. Some showed Secret Service agents hustling President Clarke and the First Lady off the stage and into the bowels of the building. Others focused on the pope, who had been knocked off his feet by the blast in the middle of his homily and was not moving. Secret Service agents and members of the Vatican security details raced to his side. Some tried to shield him from the searing heat of the firestorm surging through the east side of Soldier Field. Others tried to administer first aid. And the pope was not the only one down. At least a dozen other bodies lay motionless on the main stage.

Still other networks focused on the mass panic breaking out among the seventy thousand or so people still alive but trapped inside the stadium. Desperate to escape, people were running over one another, shrieking, jumping over rows of empty seats, even trampling those who'd fallen in front of them.

Everything Abu Nakba had trained and prepared and prayed for had come down to this day. But it was not yet over, he knew. Indeed, it had only just begun.

2

Abu Nakba turned to check the clock on the wall in the kitchen.

None of the six networks—even Al Jazeera—had picked up on it yet.

But when they did, his triumph would finally be complete.

As his eyes shifted from screen to screen, he savored the destruction. Even more delicious was the rapidly rising death toll and the fear spreading not just through Soldier Field but the rest of Chicago and all over the United States.

"Hold on, we have a new development," said a breathless Carolyn Tam at CNN Center in Atlanta. *"I'm just being told that a 737 passenger jet has been hijacked from somewhere in either Michigan or Canada. It's not yet clear which. But my producer is telling me that CNN has two federal sources indicating that the jet is heading toward the Windy City."*

A shot of electricity rippled through the old man's system.

It was not a passenger jet, he knew. It was a DHL cargo jet. But it was a 737. It had been hijacked in Grand Rapids, Michigan. It was heading straight for the stadium. And now that the Patriot missile battery positioned outside the stadium had been destroyed, it could not be stopped.

A twisted smile began to appear on the old man's face. He began rocking to and fro in his chair. And though he never closed his eyes—they kept scanning the rapidly changing coverage on all six screens—he began to pray aloud.

Carolyn Tam seemed to be talking to someone off-screen, apparently trying to clarify the information she was getting over her earpiece. Then the image on CNN split between her at the anchor desk in Atlanta on the left side of the screen and the shimmering glow of a barely identifiable object in the blazing blue sky.

"The image we are showing you right now is, we believe, that of a hijacked 737, inbound for Chicago," she explained. *"CNN reporters and producers are trying to ascertain whether U.S. fighter jets have been scrambled and are en route to intercept the plane, but so far, we cannot either confirm or deny that. Most phone lines inside Chicago, and certainly those downtown and in a several-block radius around Soldier Field, are jammed."*

A moment later, with the image of the plane becoming slightly clearer, though very shaky, Tam explained that CNN had just received unconfirmed reports—and she repeated that they were unconfirmed thus far—that the bodies of two pilots and several members of a ground crew had just been found at the Grand Rapids airport.

"I'm being told several had their throats slit," Tam reported. *"The lead pilot was murdered execution style, hog-tied, with a single bullet to the back of the head. We can only guess as to whether this hijacking is related to the missile attacks unfolding here in Chicago, but at this point it would be hard to imagine that the events are not related, and of course this suggests the possibility that this 737 passenger plane is on a kamikaze mission into the city center, and possibly into the stadium itself."*

"Praise Allah," Abu Nakba prayed, almost in a whisper. "Praise be to the Lord of the worlds, the Infinitely Good, the All-Merciful, Master of the Day of Judgment."

He had not expected so many details of his operation to become public so quickly. Yet it did not bother him. To the contrary, he felt certain that such details were dramatically exacerbating the level of fear being felt by any American watching TV at that moment. And this certainty gave him great joy.

With every second that passed, the Boeing 737 MAX jet was getting closer, becoming clearer. Soon, Tam noted its paint job was such a bright yellow that it appeared to be more likely a DHL cargo jet than a civilian airliner carrying passengers.

"It's barely ten miles out now, coming in hot, and yet there are no fighter jets to be seen in any direction," Tam explained. "I cannot imagine the authorities are going to let this plane get any closer to Chicago's huge civilian population, but right now, honestly, I can't see any way they are going to stop it."

This was exactly the point, mused Abu Nakba.

Seconds later, the plane was seven miles out.

Then five.

Then three.

Suddenly, the image of the plane on CNN was zoomed in so tightly Abu Nakba could actually see Zaid Farooq—one of three deputy commanders of Kairos and his chief of intelligence—in the cockpit. The men around him audibly gasped, no one more loudly than Mohammed Faisal, who had long served on Farooq's team. Feelings of profound pride welled up within the Libyan. His eyes began filling with tears. Zaid Farooq was about to make history. They all were. Already so many Americans were dead. But the numbers were about to soar—perhaps to fifty thousand, perhaps even to seventy-five thousand or more—but regardless, exponentially more than the three thousand killed on 9/11.

3

Abu Nakba's gaze shifted to Al Jazeera.

The network was now showing a gorgeous panoramic shot of the 737, scorching in over Lake Michigan, arrayed against the entire Chicago skyline. The arresting image was picked up almost immediately by every other network. One by one, every screen before him displayed the same shot.

In the center of the frame, Abu Nakba could see the stunning silhouette of Willis Tower, the tallest building in the American Midwest. On the right side, he could see the stadium and raging fire and thick black billowing column of smoke rising above it. The plane itself was on the far left side of the screen, arcing over the lake, banking toward the stadium, and making a rapid descent.

Then something suddenly exploded out of one of the upper windows of the tower—the Skydeck. In shock, Abu Nakba realized it was another SA-7 missile. But it wasn't streaking toward the stadium. It was streaking toward the plane. That was impossible, the old man thought.

None of his men would fire at the plane.

Not now.

Not ever.

Not when their greatest victory was mere seconds away.

But then—on all six screens—Abu Nakba watched in absolute horror as the missile slammed through the front windshield of the 737 and exploded on impact. And yet the plane was not destroyed. Not entirely. What was left of the fuselage was now a ball of burning wreckage. But rather than crash into the stadium or the parking lot, it crashed into a high floor of the Willis Tower.

The building rocked violently on impact. Every window on the Skydeck was immediately blown out. Then came the massive fireball as six thousand gallons of aviation fuel set the iconic building ablaze.

Everyone around the Libyan jumped to his feet and began cheering wildly, Mohammed Faisal included. Abu Nakba turned and looked at them in disbelief. But then he realized they didn't know the plan. He had told them nothing about the hijacking, lest Farooq and his men were unable to pull it off. Thus they had no idea the plane was supposed to crash into Soldier Field, not the tower. To them, this was another sign of Allah's favor.

As he turned back and watched the tower begin to burn—and listened to the panic in the voices of Carolyn Tam and her colleagues on CNN—Abu Nakba began to think that this might have been a great blessing after all. Upwards of twenty-five thousand people worked in the building. He knew because the Troika—Farooq included—had at one point war-gamed a plan to take it down. They couldn't all escape before it collapsed, could they?

And yet, the longer he watched, the more sickened he became. CBS News soon cited a source inside the mayor's office, and another from Homeland Security, who said that because of the stadium event and all the traffic and parking problems it had created, most employers inside the tower had given their people the day off. There were very few people in the building at the time of impact, and most were being evacuated without incident.

Sure enough, every screen was soon showing images of people pouring out of the lobby of the Willis Tower.

Before long, aerial firefighting planes—several of them massive air tankers— were streaking overhead. They began dropping flame-suppressing chemicals on the tower to put out the blaze, and with every pass they were showing success.

Then came a shocking new development.

Fox News was the first to report that dozens of people above the 100th floor had been trapped and were unable to evacuate the building because the flames and smoke in the elevator shafts and stairwells below them were too intense. Instead, they had all made their way to the roof and were now being helped—on live worldwide television—to evacuate by climbing into window-washing machines that brought them down the side of the tower to safety.

Roughly twenty minutes or so into the rescue effort, as the smoke finally began to clear just enough to get a decent shot, ABC News started showing live images from their local affiliate's news helicopter. The feed showed a team of federal agents leading the rescue effort. All the color drained from Abu Nakba's face as the camera zeroed in on the lead agent. It was a face he knew. It was the face of Marcus Ryker.

The old man felt violently ill.

He had no idea how it had happened. All he knew was that everything he had worked for, everything his patron had paid for, everything he had devoted his life to achieve, had just been thwarted before his very eyes.

Taichung

Changhua

Nantou

Yunlin   Taiwan
            (Republic of China

Chiayi County
Chiayi

Tainan

Koohsiung

PART
ONE

4

Wei Daoming's hands were shaking.

At the tender age of twenty-nine, he was only a junior officer. But it didn't take a lifetime of battlefield experience to see that war was coming and that it could not be stopped.

Terrified that someone would notice his rising anxiety, he desperately tried to calm his breathing and steady his nerves as his slender fingers hung over the keypad, poised to launch the very missiles that would start the slaughter. He wanted to glance around the war room. He wanted to look into the eyes of the other young military aides around him—and into the eyes of the generals as well. Did anyone else believe this was all a terrible mistake? Or was he alone?

Wei Daoming knew one thing for certain. He was a nobody. Just a cog in China's giant wheel of destiny. He had no right to speak. No opportunity to ask questions. No power to stop what was coming. Questioning wartime orders meant certain death. So he kept his mouth shut. And at precisely 2:13 a.m. local time, Operation Dragon Fire commenced. Without warning. In the dead of night.

While twenty-four million Taiwanese civilians slept peacefully in their beds, 480 Dongfeng-16 ballistic missiles erupted from mobile launchers positioned across China's Fujian province. The short-range, solid-fuel rockets streaked toward Taipei, the capital of Taiwan, and six other major cities, where fully 70 percent of Taiwan's population was located.

Seconds later, the rocket force of the People's Liberation Army launched a thousand more ballistic missiles. Traveling at nearly nine times the speed of sound, the weapons were aimed at Taiwan's air, naval, and army bases, radar stations, missile-defense batteries, and command-and-control centers. And at Taiwan's government buildings, TV and radio stations, hospitals, fuel depots, water-pumping stations, and power stations. Hundreds more missiles rained down on civilian airports, commercial ports, and shipping facilities, as well as the island's industrial infrastructure. They also struck the factories where upwards of 60 percent of the world's semiconductors and 90 percent of the world's most advanced microchips were produced.

Some of the older missiles were shot down by Taiwanese air defenses in the early minutes of the war. Others misfired and landed in the Strait of Taiwan. But the sheer number of incoming missiles and rockets overwhelmed the island's woefully underfunded air-defense system. What's more, a surprising number of Chinese missiles were brand-new and hypersonic, capable of evading the American-built Patriot missile batteries that had been installed to protect the island from just such a scenario.

If all this weren't bad enough, Beijing's cyberattacks fried most of Taiwan's computer networks—both military and civilian—making it difficult, if not impossible, for the island's democratically elected leaders to communicate with each other, much less with their citizens, or send out distress calls to regional allies.

Yet Beijing's brazen sneak attack was just getting started.

Still more missiles—longer range and even more powerful—were soon launched from the Chinese provinces of Shandong and Jiangsu at American air and naval bases in Japan, South Korea, the Philippines, Australia, and Guam. Within minutes, most runways on those bases were destroyed. Hangars filled with prepositioned American fighter jets and bombers were obliterated. So were fuel depots and bunkers storing air-to-air and air-to-ground missiles and other critical munitions. One by one, American destroyers, battleships, and other surface ships positioned across the Pacific were struck, and struck hard, and began to sink.

Further complicating the capacity of Washington and its allies to launch an effective military counteroffensive was the fact that Chinese submarines had just fired dozens of antiship missiles and torpedoes at two U.S. aircraft carrier strike groups patrolling the East China Sea and South China Sea, sinking the USS *Nimitz* almost immediately and severely crippling the USS *Ronald Reagan*.

Chen Guanzhong found himself mesmerized at the images on the big screens.

But the president of the People's Republic of China and general secretary of the Chinese Communist Party was not satisfied.

True, Beijing had the advantage, but they could not hesitate for an instant lest the Americans and their allies recover and deliver an effective counterstrike. So the president ordered Chinese fighter planes to establish full air superiority over the skies of Taiwan. Next he ordered Chinese bombers to begin savagely attacking Taiwan's coastal defenses as the island's active-duty ground forces and reservists mobilized and raced to their positions, bracing for the coming wave of Chinese ground forces. Once this had been achieved, Guanzhong ordered the bulk of China's surface fleet—including troop transports filled with elite PLA commandos—to begin steaming across the one hundred miles of the Strait of Taiwan to unleash a massive maritime invasion on a scale not seen since D-Day at the Normandy beaches of France back in World War II.

The ships were not headed toward Taiwan's northern shores near Taipei, however. Guanzhong's war plan focused instead on establishing beachheads on the southern shores of the island that were far less well defended. While his ground troops would then have to fight their way up the mountains on a long and perilous slog toward the capital, Chinese intelligence had informed Guanzhong that the number of mines, antiship missiles, and other obstacles were far fewer in the south, thus making it easier for him to get enough troops safely on the island before the Americans, Japanese, or anyone else could stop them.

By now, however, the Americans and their Asian allies were in the fight. A massive air battle was underway. The American Navy—what was left of it, anyway—was steaming toward Taiwan. And American missiles were in the sky. Hundreds of them. Thousands, actually. Washington had been caught sleeping, but now they were raining hellfire down on Chinese battleships, frigates, troop transports, and ports.

Taiwanese fighter jets were also launching from previously unknown runways hidden inside mountains and caves. Taiwanese missiles were exploding from well-camouflaged launchpads all over the island, and they were smashing into Chinese military bases and densely populated metropolitan areas as well. Soon Japanese, Korean, and Australian fighter jets and missiles were in the air as well.

The counteroffensive was on, and it was ugly.

That's when Beijing went nuclear.

To the shock of his general staff, Guanzhong suddenly ordered them to launch a decapitation strike against the Taiwanese government.

Wei Daoming heard the order from his seat just ten yards from President Guanzhong. This was insane, he told himself. Wasn't there anyone who could stand between this madman and the murder of millions of innocents? What had happened to the plan to peacefully incorporate the island of Taiwan back into the mainland? Whatever had happened to the mission of joining as one people to celebrate one great and glorious tradition?

Suddenly two Dongfeng-12 medium-range ballistic missiles—each armed with a tactical nuclear warhead—erupted from their launchers, one after the other, arcing over the strait, and slamming into Taiwan's main military command center, burrowed deep inside a mountain range several miles south of the capital. Both scored direct hits, turning the facility into a smoldering crater of molten rock and glass.

But that wasn't all.

Guanzhong quickly ordered a dozen more Dongfeng-12 missiles fired into the heart of Taipei.

Now standing at attention near the back of the war room, Wei Daoming stared helplessly at the huge monitors before him as the missiles lifted off from launchpads not far from Beijing. He watched them gain altitude and then arc over the Strait of Taiwan. His hands shaking with fear and rage, he winced—but forced himself not to look away—as much of the Taiwanese capital disappeared in a nanosecond of blinding heat and light and as images from various satellites and drones showed mushroom clouds rising into the morning sky.

5

Nine hours after it began, Guanzhong ordered the massive war game to an end.

It had been the most elaborate—and expensive—simulation he and his generals had ever conducted. But to the president, it had all been worth it, for one thing was now clear.

Guanzhong now knew that his people would pay a steep price in blood and treasure. But he also knew there was no other way to achieve the objectives for which the great people of China had raised him to power.

After all, Article 2 of China's Anti-Secession Law—passed on May 14, 2005—stated categorically and unapologetically that "there is only one China in the world," that "both the mainland and Taiwan belong to one China," and that "China's sovereignty and territorial integrity allow for no division."

Article 4 stated that "accomplishing the great task of reunifying the motherland is the sacred duty of all Chinese people, the Taiwan compatriots included."

Articles 5, 6, and 7 emphasized Beijing's desire for a "peaceful reunification."

Yet Article 8 was explicit: If the "possibilities for a peaceful reunification should be completely exhausted, the state shall employ *nonpeaceful means* and other necessary measures to protect China's sovereignty and territorial integrity."

It was this law that had driven Guanzhong every day of his professional life. When he had first been appointed as minister of state security. Later as head of intelligence. Then as defense minister and more recently as vice-premier. And now that he had been elevated to the most powerful seat in the land, how could he fail to keep his oath? On that proud day when he had stood before the Politburo, the State Council, and the Central Military Commission in the process of being vetted for the role of president, he had given his word—he had pledged his very honor—to carry out the Anti-Secession Law. Under direct questioning by his colleagues, he had repeatedly vowed to pursue every peaceful path toward reunifying Taiwan with the mainland. But he had also vowed never to allow Taiwan to break away under any circumstances.

Decades of diplomacy had clearly not worked to bring about such a reunification. Nor had economic inducements. Nor political pressure, nor subversion. *What choice, then, do I have but all-out war?* Guanzhong asked himself.

Elections were rapidly approaching in Taiwan. After eight years in office, Taiwan's current president, Yani Lee, was on her way out due to term limits. Ordinarily, this would be no cause for alarm. The problem was that her vice president, a cunning and rebellious man by the name of Ben We-Ming, had emerged as the leading candidate to replace her. Rapidly rising in the polls, he was on track for a decisive victory when the elections were held in just a few months. Yet Ben We-Ming was a traitor of the first order. Only in his midfifties, he was young and handsome and charismatic. He was also the island's most outspoken proponent of independence, of separation from the mainland, of secession.

To be sure, now that the polls showed him surging ahead of his rivals, We-Ming was carefully dialing back his rhetoric, trying to appear as a moderate and not a revolutionary. But such smoke and mirrors—such political parlor tricks and sleight of hand—would never cause Guanzhong or his loyal subjects on the mainland to forget all the egregious statements that We-Ming had made in the past.

The man had bitterly, publicly, and relentlessly denounced Beijing's takeover of Hong Kong.

He had denounced China's treatment of religious minorities, be it the "pernicious and appalling persecution" of Chinese Christians and brutal crackdown of the house church networks, or what he decried as the "cruel and heartless concentration camps" that he kept telling any Western journalist who would listen that Chinese Uighur Muslims had been forced into.

He had lambasted Guanzhong's introduction—and aggressive implementation—of China's Social Credit System and had decried his "brutal and wicked throttling of the Internet" on the "humble and innocent people of China" who "desperately long for the freedom to connect with the free and civilized world."

All of these sins were unforgivable, but worst of all in Guanzhong's eyes was that Ben We-Ming had long championed himself an avowed agitator for Taiwan's independence. He proclaimed himself a "tireless servant in the cause of setting Taiwan free from Beijing's subjection and colonialism." Indeed, from the time he had served as CEO of Taiwan's largest semiconductor factory, then later as mayor of Taipei, and most recently as the island's vice president, Ben We-Ming had repeatedly vowed to be Taiwan's "champion of free and independent choices."

To the seventy-year-old Chinese president, these were treasonous words.

There was no way he could ever allow a traitor on the magnitude of Ben We-Ming to become Taiwan's next president.

The man's rapid and steady rise in the polls was proof to Guanzhong that all hope of a peaceful resolution had run dry.

War, he now saw, was the only way to stop Taiwan from seceding.

The only path to achieving Beijing's One China policy was to exterminate once and for all the foolish separatists who had tried for so many years to lead Taiwan into the cataclysmic darkness of capitalism and democracy and truly end and avenge what the Chinese state media called the "Century of Shame and Humiliation" from the Western world.

Still, conquering Taiwan would by no means be an easy task. The raw numbers before him were ghastly. Guanzhong's minister of defense informed him that between ten thousand and fifteen thousand of China's best and bravest ground and naval forces would likely perish if the real war played out as they had just simulated. Upwards of 155 combat aircraft would be shot down. At least 138 warships—a third of China's entire navy—could be sunk. And tens of thousands of Chinese civilians, particularly those living on or near the coast, would likely be killed by Taiwan's retaliatory missile strikes.

Yet this would not be his fault, Guanzhong told himself. This was the cost of waiting. This was the price China would have to pay for the leaders who had preceded him and had not taken decisive military action sooner. The traitors in Taipei had used their time—and America's money—shrewdly. Their "porcupine strategy" was not complicated, but it would be costly. Beijing could no longer be denied victory, but it would be ugly. Of that Guanzhong now had no doubt.

The other major takeaway from this war game was that not only would Beijing prevail, but the Americans would pay far more dearly than the Chinese. By his generals' best reckoning, the American Navy would lose two entire carrier strike groups and a total of some nine hundred warships. That was nearly half of the entire U.S. fleet. What's more, hundreds of American fighter planes and bombers would be destroyed. Best of all, at least thirty-two hundred American soldiers, sailors, airmen, and Marines—but possibly as many as five thousand or even six thousand—would die trying desperately, but ultimately in vain, to defend their little island ally.

And this was not all.

6

Guanzhong believed there were three keys to Beijing's victory.

First, he had to launch a surprise attack.

Neither the Taiwanese nor the Americans—nor any of their other Asian allies—could know that war was coming. If they knew, or even sensed, that he was preparing to strike, these enemies would mobilize for war. They would pre-position more troops, more antimissile batteries, and more antiship missiles on the island. The Taiwanese would immediately begin laying thousands of mines in their coastal waters and on the beaches. The Americans would order the bulk of the Pacific fleet to begin steaming eastward to counter any possible Chinese first strike.

This could not be allowed, or Beijing's casualties could be double or triple or worse, Guanzhong told himself as he listened to his generals continue their debriefing. Thus, all the threatening and posturing that he had been ordering the PLA to engage in—and to ratchet up—over the past few years had to come to an immediate halt. He knew he would never convince Taipei to lower their guard, but he had to dial down tensions with Washington, Tokyo, and Seoul. He had to convince them that China wasn't ready for war and wouldn't be for another ten to fifteen years at least.

It would not be easy. China was increasingly seen by Americans as their most serious enemy. Anti-China sentiment was growing exponentially in the States. And it now struck Guanzhong that he had to take emergency action—make a bold move—to deceive the American people and America's leaders into thinking that his time frame for taking Taiwan had lengthened dramatically and that his desire for détente with the West was based on a sudden realization that China was not as strong as he wished it to be.

Was this not what Sun Tzu had counseled in his classic military treatise, *The Art of War*? Had he not written, "All warfare is based on deception"? Had this sagacious prophet not been ahead of his time?

That said, deceiving the Americans and then launching a sneak attack was not enough.

The second secret to success was in determining the correct manner of the attack. A classic naval bombardment of the island, followed by a ground invasion, would be a mistake. Launching a massive and overwhelming missile barrage against Taiwan in the first minutes of the war was the far wiser move.

This was an entirely new concept in the annals of Chinese military planning. For decades, Beijing's strategic thinking had involved announcing an enormous naval exercise in and around the Strait of Taiwan. Once the exercise was well underway, and Chinese naval forces had surrounded the entire island, Beijing would then announce a naval blockade. At that point, it would launch hundreds of fighter jets to secure dominance of the skies over Taiwan and declare that no ships or planes could approach Taiwan until the island capitulated and agreed to rejoin the mainland under Beijing's rule.

This incremental approach had been sacrosanct doctrine among China's generals for as long as Guanzhong could remember. But the conventional wisdom, Guanzhong thought, was a terrible mistake. It would take weeks to prepare for a "naval exercise" of sufficient size to pre-position enough of China's naval forces and troop transports to support a full invasion. The troops themselves would have to be called up, mobilized, and placed at ports all along the Strait of Taiwan. That, too, would take weeks, and all that activity would be immediately obvious to every intelligence agency in the world, giving Taipei, Tokyo,

Seoul, Canberra, Manila, and certainly Washington more than enough time to see what was happening, rightly fear an invasion was imminent, and mobilize their defenses.

Previous war games had convinced Guanzhong that he could win with such a strategy, but the war would last for months. The cost to the Chinese people would be extreme, and there was always the possibility that the Americans would find a way to exploit weaknesses in his defenses and fight their way to a draw. This was completely unacceptable to Guanzhong. This new concept of devastating Taiwan with China's massive missile force before ever landing a single soldier on Taiwan's beaches was far better.

The third key to victory was one that Guanzhong had not even considered until just days before this exercise had commenced. Now, however, having watched it play out in real time, the president was completely convinced that this was the ace that would ensure a quick and decisive victory.

He had to go nuclear.

Only by annihilating Taipei's government and military leadership with tactical nuclear weapons could he force Taiwan's survivors to accept that they were suddenly sheep without a shepherd. Then, by raining nuclear warheads down on the center of Taipei, he could break their spirit completely. What's more, by demonstrating to the Americans and the rest of the region and world that he was ready, willing, and able to use nuclear weapons, he could send a chill through the international community—enough to cause them to hesitate before launching a full-scale retaliation. And every minute counted.

True, many, many Taiwanese lives would be lost. That's why his generals were raising questions about the wisdom of going nuclear, suggesting to their commander in chief that a sneak attack using conventional weapons would likely be sufficient to win.

"After all, Your Excellency," they said, "there's obviously no point to retaking the island if we kill off all its people."

But Guanzhong vehemently disagreed.

"We want the island, not its traitors," he insisted. "The scenario we just ran would kill close to a million Taiwanese, but we may want to consider killing two to three times that number."

The generals were aghast, but Guanzhong continued.

"Such an enormous death toll—combined with the decapitation strike—will help us truly pacify the population. Isn't that what happened when the Americans dropped the Bomb on Hiroshima and Nagasaki in World War II? Of course it is. The Americans not only secured victory in the Pacific but terrified the Japanese population into accepting their military occupation. That's our model, gentlemen."

Despite the shock on their faces, Guanzhong went further.

"And let's be honest, after the Americans dropped those atomic bombs, did they not become the dominant military and political force in the Pacific, and the world? Of course they did. And after we deploy the Bomb, we will replace the Americans as the dominant force in the Pacific. Make no mistake: Losing Taiwan will be a terrible blow to the Americans. The whole world will see Washington as weak and ineffectual. That will rattle their allies to their core, leaving them little reason to trust American promises to come to their aid if they are ever attacked, further weakening Washington geopolitically. What's more, we will threaten not to trade with the Americans unless they agree to our new and punishing demands, devastating their economy. Think about it. Most Americans spend little or no time thinking about Taiwan. I bet few could find it on a map. They have little desire to go to war to save an island they know nothing about. But even if their leaders in Washington decide to fight us, they will lose. And when they do, when the smoke clears, every American will realize that they are waking up to a very different world. Losing Taiwan will mark the death knell of American power and prestige forever and mark the dawn of the new Chinese dominance."

At first the generals were stunned. But the longer the president spoke, the more enthusiastic they became, and by the time he concluded his remarks, they erupted in a standing ovation.

"Congratulations, Comrade President," said Dai Wangshu, China's minister of state security. "You have proven that the past half century of China's patient and persistent preparation has been worth it. It has not been easy—not by any measure—but we are finally ready to fulfill China's destiny."

"Exactly," Guanzhong replied, moved by their outpouring of affection. "As the leaders of our esteemed and beloved military, you have done well—very well—today. This war plan is far superior to previous plans. But we're not finished. I have a few more tricks up my sleeve. I'm not ready to share them with you yet, but I promise that I will very soon. For now, make quiet and discreet preparations to execute this precise war plan on or around March 1."

Then Guanzhong turned to Minister Wangshu.

"Come, my friend, take a walk with me. There is something I must discuss with you immediately."

"What is it?" the minister asked. "What can I do to help you?"

"In the weeks prior to this surprise attack on Taiwan, we must not be passive," Guanzhong replied. "We must blindside the Americans so thoroughly that they have no will, much less capacity, to stop us from taking Taiwan, and from there full control of the Pacific."

"How, Your Excellency?"

"There are only a handful of people in the world who know what I'm about to tell you, Dai Wangshu. And one of them is your friend Abu Nakba."

7

It was almost midnight when four white SUVs arrived at Pier 19.

Stopping at the front gate, the driver of the first Chevy Suburban rolled the side window down. No words were exchanged. Instead, the driver handed the night watchman a business card. It was enough.

Without speaking, the guard nodded, handed the card back, and pushed a button on the console next to him. The heavy iron gate began to open. Then he pushed another button, and the steel barricade behind the gate began to lower. Soon the convoy drove onto the pier under the cover of thick darkness. There were no streetlamps. Clouds obscured the moon and stars.

Driving past darkened warehouses and massive tanks storing liquefied natural gas, the convoy came to a halt in front of a building that bore no name, logo, or distinctive markings of any kind.

A dozen men sporting AK-47 submachine guns quickly exited the SUVs and created a protective cordon, scanning the pier and adjacent windows and rooftops for any sign of movement. Seeing none, the lead bodyguard opened the rear door of the second Suburban. "Father, we have arrived."

Abu Nakba said nothing. He simply stretched out his hand so that his lead bodyguard could help him out of the vehicle.

The evening winds coming off the water were brisk. Yet the old man wore only his trademark white tunic, covered by a classic brown Libyan robe, and sandals on his bony feet. No coat. No gloves. No hat. Not even a scarf.

"You must be cold, Father," said the head of the detail. "Please, take my coat, at least until you get inside."

But the old man waved him off. Gripping his ornately carved wooden cane in his right hand, and aided by the bodyguard on his left side, Abu Nakba—now in his eighties—limped his way across the pavement until he reached the open door.

Inside the cavernous warehouse, a wheelchair was waiting. Several aides helped him sit down, then one rolled him to the elevators, where they went down.

When the elevator door opened, Mohammed Faisal was waiting. Now forty-two, Faisal was a former deputy director of Syrian intelligence who several years earlier had been recruited by Hamdi Yaşar to join Kairos, the preeminent terrorist organization in the world, the very one that Abu Nakba had formed after breaking away from Hamas so many years before. In the wake of Yaşar's arrest by the Americans some eight months earlier—together with the capture and killing of so many senior Kairos leaders—Faisal had emerged as Abu Nakba's most trusted counselor.

"Welcome back, Father," said the Syrian as he assumed charge of the wheelchair. "Everything is ready for our guest, just as you asked. And I've been informed that his flight should be on time."

Faisal pushed the old man down several corridors, through a side door, and into a cramped office filled with file cabinets and shelves of books and binders. Then he shut the door behind them.

"May I offer you some tea, Father?" the Syrian asked.

"I don't want tea, Mohammed," Abu Nakba shot back. "I want answers."

"I realize that things have been moving more slowly than we'd hoped," Faisal said, taking his seat.

"Do you need more money?" the old man pressed.

"No, sir—you've been exceedingly generous."

"Then what is the holdup? My patrons are pressing me for results."

"The science is new, Father," Faisal explained. "But I asked you to come all this way because we believe we finally have something to show you."

"When?"

"First thing in the morning," said Faisal. "For now, I've rented a penthouse suite for you and your team so you all can shower, have something to eat, and get a good night's rest."

"No, I want to see it now."

"But, Father, don't you want to—"

"No, Mohammed—I want to see it now."

8

Faisal swallowed hard but nodded.

Then he picked up the phone on his desk, dialed, and said something in Urdu that Abu Nakba did not catch. When he was finished, he hung up and walked over to a tall metal locker in the corner. Opening the door, he pulled out a set of protective gear and helped the old man put it on. Then he returned to the locker, pulled out a second set, and dressed himself. Once this was complete, he closed the locker and wheeled the Libyan out of the office, down the hall, and into a massive underground laboratory.

Along the walls were a series of walk-in freezers and refrigerators and biosafety cabinets. In the center stood stainless steel tables and individual workstations stacked with all manner of test tubes, Bunsen burners, microscopes, centrifuges, and incubators, each covered by fume hoods. Elsewhere in the huge room were MRI machines, CT scanners, and various other medical equipment.

Standing before them at full attention were a dozen scientists. All were Chinese. None wore white lab coats. Rather, they were all wearing hazmat suits, helmets, gloves, and protective footwear. Most appeared to be young, perhaps in their thirties. One older gentleman, probably in his sixties, stood in the center of the group and held a clipboard.

Faisal did not introduce the team. He simply parked the Libyan at one of the workstations, a good ten or twelve yards away from the team but with a clear view of the entire lab. Then he nodded to the lead scientist, the one with the clipboard, and soon three scientists were hustling over to a room on the far side of the lab. They unlocked the door and soon came back out leading three monkeys on leashes. As Abu Nakba looked on, they led the monkeys into one of three large steel boxes that resembled old British phone booths, though significantly wider. Faisal explained that these were hermetically sealed isolation chambers and that each had one rather small window made of thick, tempered protective glass.

One of the scientists now positioned a small digital camera on a tripod in front of the window of the chamber the monkeys had been taken into. The camera was attached to a cable that ran across the floor to an iPad mounted on one of the workstations.

Faisal leaned down and flipped on a computer monitor on the desk of the workstation where the old man was sitting.

Together, they watched a live image of the monkeys being strapped to three stainless steel chairs that had been bolted to the floor of the chamber. Each began screeching wildly until the cacophony filled the lab. Then the chamber door was shut and sealed. No longer could they hear the monkeys, but on the monitor, they could see them desperately trying to break free. Suddenly, from a nozzle emanating from the ceiling of the chamber came a bright red mist.

Mesmerized, Abu Nakba watched as the monkeys strained even more desperately against their restraints, screeching even more frenetically. Then the animals began coughing and gagging. Within minutes, their eyes began to bleed. Soon, blood began dripping—then streaming, then gushing—from their ears and noses. Eventually, each monkey was bleeding from every orifice. Within twenty to thirty minutes, hair and flesh began to melt off their faces and bellies. Yet they were not dead.

The Libyan could not hear them, but he could feel their panic and their suffering. And for the first time in Faisal's recollection, the old man smiled.

"Oh, my son, you've really done it," Abu Nakba sighed. "And it works so much faster than I'd expected."

"Yes, Father, and we believe this is the key. It's not just the lethality; it's the speed that you kept pressing for. I believe we are there."

"Yes, I believe you are. And it works this quickly on humans, as well?"

"It does."

"How many have you tested?"

"How many humans?"

"Yes."

"Yesterday was our nineteenth trial, and it went off without a hitch."

"You've recorded everything for me to review?"

"We have, Father," Faisal replied, handing the old man a thumb drive.

"Now, tell me this: How quickly can you mass-produce it?" Abu Nakba asked.

"How much do you need?"

"Enough to pump it into America's water supplies. Enough to release it into the HVAC systems of American airports and hospitals, churches and synagogues, elementary and secondary schools. Enough to kill millions of Americans before they can figure out what hit them. But my patrons are growing impatient, and I must confess, so am I."

"Give me a factory, and enough labor, and I can have everything you need in sixty days," Faisal replied.

"I'm not sure we have that much time, Mohammed," the old man replied.

"Why not?"

"Two words: Marcus Ryker."

9

Marcus Ryker was a man consumed.

Having been appointed by the president to head up the CIA's top secret task force to hunt down and destroy the Libyan, Marcus had thought of nothing else for the past eight grueling months. Sixteen to eighteen hours a day. Seven days a week. Without a break. Without a vacation. To the neglect of his health. Friendships. Family. Even his fiancée.

But finally, the team had caught a break. Their patience and painstaking attention to detail was paying off. They now had Abu Nakba in their crosshairs.

An air strike would have been far faster and simpler, but the president wouldn't hear of it. They were, after all, talking about a warehouse on the edge of Karachi, the biggest city in Pakistan—the twelfth biggest city in the world— teeming with twenty million souls. What's more, the warehouse was located on a pier next to the biggest liquefied natural gas storage facilities in the region. Even Marcus had to concede that an airstrike was far too risky and could cause far too much collateral damage.

Then there was the Osama bin Laden precedent. The last time the U.S. had targeted a terror master in Pakistan, the American president had opted against the use of laser-guided bombs that would have obliterated bin Laden in a millisecond. Rather, he'd opted for a special-ops mission that would not only kill the al Qaeda leader but bring back ironclad proof that it really was bin Laden in that compound in Abbottabad and that he truly was dead. The American people needed that proof. So did the rest of the world. That's why Barack Obama had ordered a team of America's best and bravest commandos to enter sovereign Pakistani territory to avenge the deaths of nearly three thousand Americans murdered by al Qaeda operatives on 9/11.

Not only had the operation been a stellar success, but the decision had juiced Obama's poll numbers, no doubt helping if not outright securing his reelection in 2012.

Today, President Carlos Hernandez—the country's first Latino chief executive—was following the same playbook, albeit with two critical modifications. Rather than deploying a team of elite Navy SEAL operators, Hernandez was entrusting the mission to an elite team of operators from the Central Intelligence Agency, led by Marcus Ryker, a combat-decorated former Marine and former Secret Service agent who had served on the Presidential Protective Detail. And rather than inserting the operators into Pakistan by air via Black Hawk helicopters, Hernandez was sending them in by sea.

The alarm on Marcus's wristwatch suddenly went off. Forcing his eyes open, Marcus glanced at the dial, glowing green in the pitch black. How could it be time already? Hadn't he collapsed into the bunk just a few hours earlier?

Marcus knew he should be excited. This was, after all, effectively Christmas morning. This was the moment they'd all been working for. The next time he laid his head on a pillow—assuming, of course, that he survived the operation—Abu Nakba would be dead. His Kairos terrorist network would finally be history. The American people would be safer. And Hernandez would have both his trophy and his guarantee of victory in the next election.

But for Marcus, taking down the Libyan wouldn't simply be a professional triumph. It would mean he could finally resign from the CIA. He could finally marry Annie Stewart and start a whole new life with the smartest, kindest, godliest, and most stunningly beautiful woman he'd ever met.

Since Elena, that is.

Yet the thrill of the hunt was long gone. Even the promise of a bright new future outside of the Agency wasn't enough to breathe new life into him. Every muscle in Marcus's scarred body ached. His throat burned. His temples throbbed. Since the attacks in Chicago, Marcus and his team had crisscrossed the globe almost nonstop. They'd taken down a dozen cells from Mexico City to Manila and from Lisbon to Lagos. They'd killed or captured hundreds of Kairos operatives. They'd blown up countless caches of weapons and explosives. They'd also scooped up valuable actionable intelligence with barely enough time between operations to catch their breath or see their loved ones.

Now it was time to go back into harm's way.

Marcus, now in his midforties, was teetering on the edge of burnout. So was every member of his team. He knew the warning signs. He also knew that such physical, emotional, and spiritual exhaustion significantly increased the risk of making mistakes, even fatal ones. Still, he'd promised the president that he'd stay with the Agency until Abu Nakba had met his Maker. Whatever his other myriad flaws, Marcus Ryker was nothing if not a man of his word. So, in the darkness, he silently mouthed the same prayer he always prayed before suiting up for battle. He thanked God for a new day and a new mission. Then he asked the Lord to grant them wisdom, success, and safety as he prayed through his favorite psalms.

"I praise you, Lord, for you are my rock. You've trained my hands for war. You've given my fingers skill for battle. You are my loving ally. You are my fortress, my tower of safety, my rescuer. You are my shield, and today—like every day—I take refuge in you, Lord. But have mercy on me, Father. Breathe new life into me physically, spiritually, and emotionally. And create in me a clean heart, O Lord, and renew a right spirit within me. Cast me not away from your presence, O Lord, and take not your Holy Spirit from me. Restore unto me the joy of your salvation and grant a willing spirit to sustain me. Please, Father; you know I cannot do any of this without you. But in Christ, all things are possible. So into your hands I commit my spirit. In Christ's holy and powerful name, I pray. Amen."

Then, grabbing his rucksack and a clipboard off the wall beside him, Marcus slipped out of his bunk. It was time to execute Operation Silent Vengeance and lead his team into battle one last time.

10

"*Hey, man, it's time,*" Marcus whispered in the darkness.

But Dr. Peter Hwang, snoring up a storm in the bunk above him, didn't stir.

"*Seriously, Saint Pete, it's time,*" Marcus repeated, nudging Pete's arm. "*Let's go. Up and at 'em.*"

"It can't be," Pete groaned. "Gimme another hour."

"Move it, old man," Marcus now ordered at full volume, slapping Pete's side with the clipboard. "Round up the team and meet me in ten."

Pete grunted something inaudible but finally swung his legs around and dangled them off the side of the bunk.

Satisfied his friend wasn't going to drift back off, Marcus pulled on his own boots, stepped into the lav, splashed water on his face, brushed his teeth, and headed to the mess.

Despite all his years in the Marines on multiple combat tours in Afghanistan and Iraq, this was only Marcus's second time on a nuclear-powered submarine. The first had been on the USS *Michigan*, shortly after he'd been drafted into the CIA. That had been an exfil, designed to bring a high-level defector out of

North Korea. But everything had gone wrong. By the time they'd reached him, the general they'd come for was dead and stripped clean of all the top secret files he'd promised to Marcus. Worse, the whole thing was an ambush, and Nick Vinetti—one of Marcus's and Pete's closest friends since they'd all first met at Parris Island—had been killed.

Pete had almost bought it too. He'd been critically wounded, and though he'd eventually recovered, he no longer wanted anything to do with the Agency. Twice he'd tried to retire and find a quieter life. Twice Marcus had persuaded him to stay, promising, *"Just one more, Pete. This is it, this is our last mission, and I need you at my side."*

Fortunately, it had worked last week, but Marcus knew it was not a card he could play again. Of course, he could hardly blame the good doctor for not being eager to suit up. Having been one of the most respected and successful surgeons in the country just a few years earlier, Pete had given it all up to serve his country and watch Marcus's back. But now, exhausted, broke, and divorced, Pete was done. All he wanted was to move far away from Washington, restart his practice, make some serious money, find a nice girl, fall in love, settle down, and perhaps play a little golf on the weekends. *Was that really asking too much?* Pete had pressed, and Marcus could hardly say no.

Now here they were, aboard the USS *Maine*, one of the most advanced ballistic missile submarines in the American arsenal. Operating at a depth of four thousand feet and advancing at a speed of nearly thirty knots, they were thus far undetected and just minutes from their destination. At 560 feet long and nearly twenty thousand tons submerged, the Ohio-class boomer carried a terrifying payload—twenty Trident II ballistic missiles, each equipped with nuclear warheads capable of turning entire cities into glass.

Marcus felt his age as he worked his way through the sub's narrow corridors, passing one crew member after another who looked barely out of their teens. With every step, he was trying—without success—to suppress his memories of that disastrous mission in Tanchon and focus on the mission at hand.

The *Maine*'s cramped and claustrophobic mess hall had six metal tables flanked by straight-backed metal chairs. The room was capable of seating up to thirty-six sailors at a time, though for the moment it was empty. There was no finished ceiling. Instead, large pipes and miles of thick electrical cables were visible overhead, snaking between several rows of fluorescent lights hung from steel beams. A large clock on one wall read 1:36 a.m. Various plaques, awards, and a bulletin board hung on another. At the front of the room was a large flat-screen television monitor. In the back were several stainless-steel coffee urns and stacks of blue mugs with the logo of the *Maine* emblazoned on them.

Marcus had no idea who had made a fresh pot of coffee, but he was grateful. Pouring himself a mug, he took a seat at the last table in the back of the room. He rubbed his bloodshot eyes and set his rucksack and clipboard on the table next to him. He grabbed a pen from the bag and reviewed his final checklist. Everything had been crossed off. He strained to think of anything he might have missed but came up empty. The previous night he had walked his colleagues one last time through the map of Pier 19, the floor plan of the warehouse, and its proximity to the LNG storage facility. He'd gone over all the latest intel. Answered all their questions. And together they'd triple-checked their equipment. There was nothing left to discuss. It was time to move.

"Hey, boss, where is everyone?"

Marcus looked up as his Number Two, Jenny Morris, entered the mess.

"Pete's rounding up the boys. Where's Kai?" Marcus asked, referring to Kailea Curtis, the only other woman on the team.

"I sent her to the radio room to retrieve the latest satellite imagery," Jenny replied. "She should be here soon."

"Good," said Marcus. "Coffee?"

"You've got to be kidding, right?" she said.

"Why not? It's actually good—and strong."

"Ryker, we've got a two-hour ride ahead of us with no opportunity to pull over at a rest stop. You must have a stronger bladder than me."

As Marcus smiled and shook his head, Jenny took the seat across from him. She stared at him as he took another sip and looked over his checklist again.

"You okay?" she finally asked.

More than anyone else on the team, Jenny had taken it upon herself to make sure Marcus was eating decently and getting enough rest, and chided him when he wasn't, which of course was most of the time.

"Like pulverized pepper," he said without looking up.

"How's that?" she asked.

"Fiiiine," he deadpanned.

The lines were banter from an old vaudeville routine, something Marcus's father used to say before his untimely death. Over the years, they had become shorthand between Marcus and Jenny—neither funny nor true.

Jenny snatched the clipboard from him and reviewed each item. As she did, Marcus stared at her. He knew she was running on fumes just like he was. Her brown eyes were bleary and bloodshot. Her brunette hair—pulled back in a ponytail—showed streaks of gray.

To be sure, Jennifer Marie Morris was one of the most impressive officers in the Agency's Clandestine Service. Not only did she have a positive, can-do spirit and routinely did more than she was asked, she was fluent in Russian, Arabic, and Farsi. She'd been the youngest Moscow station chief in CIA history. She'd seen nonstop action at Marcus's side ever since they'd first worked together to get "the Raven"—the son-in-law and assassin of the Russian president—out of Russia. She'd taken a bullet on that mission, lost a great deal of blood, and almost died in Marcus's arms. Still, the moment she'd been physically able to get back in the game, Jenny was at the gun range, running five miles a day again, catching up on cable traffic, and getting back into the swing of serving as both his deputy and consigliere. Aside from Pete, no one on his team had been more loyal or served so sacrificially. But the work and the pace were clearly taking a toll.

"You sure about this one, boss?" Jenny asked, still fixated on the clipboard, her voice scratchy and low.

"What one?" Marcus asked, thinking she was talking about some line item on his checklist.

"This mission," she replied, still staring at the clipboard.

"You're not?" he asked, surprised. "You've seen all the intel. What am I missing?"

"I don't know," she said softly. "It's just that . . ."

Her gaze shifted. She was now staring at the steam coming off his coffee. She said nothing for what seemed like an eternity. But as Marcus brought the mug up for another sip, her eyes met his.

"Spit it out, young lady. I don't have time to guess."

"I don't know—I can't explain it," she said at last, almost in a whisper. "I've just got a bad feeling about this one. Something's not right."

11

One by one, the team entered the mess and took their seats.

They were moving slowly and looking haggard. No one got coffee. Nor did they engage in small talk. Marcus hoped they'd already eaten something, protein bars and the like, since the galley wouldn't open for another hour, and by then they'd be gone.

Kailea Curtis arrived first, looking pale but determined to press on. She approached Marcus and set a thumb drive on the table. Then, nodding to Jenny, she crossed the room and took a seat at the table farthest from them. Slumping down in a chair, she flipped open her briefing book and began reviewing it again, page by page.

The daughter of immigrants from India, Kailea had been born and raised in the Bronx. After serving as an NYPD cop, she'd moved to D.C. and joined the Diplomatic Security Service. Though she had never served in the military and thus lacked combat experience, Kailea's intelligence, instincts, and sheer grit had won Marcus over, and he'd asked her to join his team on a permanent basis.

After Kailea had survived a suicide bombing at Number 10 Downing Street and taken a bullet on the Temple Mount during the U.S.–Israeli–Saudi peace summit, Marcus had fully expected her to retire. Indeed, he'd encouraged it. Instead, Kailea had returned with a vengeance, eager to get back in the field. The firefight on the Israel–Lebanon border the previous year had been her shining hour. Marcus lost count of how many Hezbollah terrorists she'd taken out and how many times she'd saved his life that day. Yet even after they'd been taken hostage, dragged deep behind enemy lines into Lebanon, and tortured without mercy, after they'd made a daring escape and recovered, Kai had once again stunned Marcus by not retiring. Instead, after months in the hospital and many more in rehab, she'd requested a transfer from the DSS to the CIA and insisted that he put her on his team again. He'd readily agreed, and she'd proven once again to be one of Marcus's MVPs.

Donny Callaghan, the former commander of SEAL Team Six, lumbered in next, taking a seat next to Kai. Born in south Boston, Callaghan was a bear—six foot five and nearly 250 pounds—with closely cropped red hair and a bushy red beard. The man had military in his blood. His father had been a West Point grad, served as a tank commander, and risen to become a three-star Army general after serving under General Norman Schwarzkopf in the first Gulf War. But Callaghan—ever the rebel—had rejected the chance to follow in his father's footsteps. Instead, he'd opted for the Navy, graduated from Annapolis, and served with distinction in the SEALs for nearly a decade. No one brought more close-quarters combat skills to the team, and Marcus was grateful to have him on board.

Right behind Callaghan was Geoff Stone, six foot two and 185 pounds, joining Kai and Cally. Though technically still a senior special agent with the DSS, Stone had spent the last several years detailed to the Agency and proven an ideal fit on Marcus's team. Born and raised in Philadelphia, Stone had graduated from West Point, trained as an intelligence specialist, learned conversational Arabic, served as an Army Ranger, and done multiple combat tours in Afghanistan and Iraq. After finishing his service in the Army, he'd been recruited by the State Department to serve in their elite DSS division, rising through the ranks until he was the head of the secretary's protective detail. It was there that he'd crossed paths with Ryker, who at the time was still in the Secret Service and working at the White House. Marcus had liked Stone immediately. Now in his forties, Stone was not only smart, tough, and savvy, but in peak physical condition.

Marcus reached into his rucksack and pulled out his laptop. Powering it up, he inserted the thumb drive Kailea had brought him, then pushed the computer across the table for Jenny to set up the PowerPoint presentation. Then he got up and poured himself another cup of coffee.

As he did, Miguel Navarro entered the mess and took a seat at an empty table in the middle of the room. Five foot eleven and thirty-eight, Navarro was the newbie on the team. Born in Houston to Mexican immigrants, he was fluent in both Spanish and Portuguese. Like Stone, Navarro was a West Pointer and a former Army Ranger—an expert sniper, no less—and had served on the front lines in Afghanistan and Iraq. Wounded by an IED near Fallujah, Navarro had recovered for several months at Walter Reed before being recruited into the CIA's Clandestine Service by Dr. Martha Dell, then the Agency's deputy director. Distinguishing himself on missions in Venezuela, Colombia, Brazil, and Nicaragua, Navarro had eventually been appointed to serve as CIA station chief in Mexico City. That's where Marcus had met him the previous year and been so impressed that he'd prevailed upon Dell, who had recently been promoted to director of the CIA, to transfer Navarro to his team. At first, Dell hadn't agreed, preferring that Navarro stay in Mexico because he was so well-suited for the role. But in the end, Marcus wore her down and got his man.

Arriving next was Noah Daniels, who apologized for being late. He also took a seat in the middle of the room, though at a different table from Navarro. At thirty-six, Noah looked much younger, and it was hard for Marcus not to think of him as a kid. He'd been recruited into the CIA soon after earning his bachelor's degree from MIT and his master's and PhD from Stanford. Marcus had first met him while arranging security for the peace summit in Jerusalem a few years back. Marcus had been wowed—mesmerized, actually—not only by Noah's ability to set up, hack, or crash any computer or phone system in the world, but by the spycraft and shooting skills he'd learned at the Farm.

Last in was the good doctor Hwang, whom Marcus had long ago affectionately dubbed "Saint Pete" when they'd become friends in boot camp on Parris Island as freshly scrubbed and newly minted Marines. That was more than twenty years ago, and Marcus had certainly discovered since then that the nickname didn't exactly fit. A lapsed Catholic, Pete was irreverent and snarky and could occasionally catch even his closest friends off guard with a nasty temper. Pete's wife had left him, and he rarely saw his kids, who mostly wanted nothing to do with him. But Marcus loved this brilliant if quirky first-generation American—raised in Houston by parents who had immigrated from Seoul in the '50s—dearly.

A fresh mug of piping hot brew in his hand, Marcus now addressed his team. "We roll in fifteen," he began. "But before we do, I've got good news and bad."

12

Jenny connected the laptop to the wall-mounted monitor.

A series of images from a KH-11 Keyhole satellite flashed up on the screen behind Marcus as he began to narrate.

"The good news is that we've gotten some very encouraging images overnight," he said as Jenny ran through photos of a port facility on the southern side of Karachi. "This first image was taken at 11:53 p.m. As you can see, a four-vehicle convoy has pulled up in front of the warehouse. In this next image, you can see a dozen heavily armed men taking up positions around the vehicles. And in the next, that's our man stepping out of the second Chevy Suburban."

Marcus asked Jenny to zoom in on the target. The satellite's line of sight had been ideal. The wizened face, distinctive white beard, trademark cane, and soulless eyes of the old man were plain to everyone in the room. There was no question. It was him.

Walid Abdel-Shafi.

Aka, Abu Nakba, the "father of the catastrophe."

Aka, the Libyan.

Marcus was glad to see the team's collective pulse quicken. They were suddenly sitting up straight. Leaning forward. Listening carefully. Shaking off their fatigue. Up until now, the case that the most wanted terrorist on the planet was spending time in this particular section of Karachi was a matter of compelling but certainly not conclusive circumstantial evidence. Now the case was airtight. The intel was real. After eight excruciating months, they finally had this savage cornered.

"Over the past two weeks," Marcus continued, "we've seen a convoy show up at this warehouse every few days. Sometimes made up of four SUVs. Sometimes just two. Never with Abu Nakba before. But always with men believed to work for him. Never the same arrival time, but always in the dead of night. Always coming via different routes. Always to the same destination. Always here. Langley still has no idea why. Nor does DIA. We still don't know what's inside that building or why it's located next to an LNG facility. But none of that really matters right now. The good news is that—for the moment, at least—we know exactly where Abu Nakba is. Now we just have to pray he remains there long enough for us to get to him and take him down."

"So what's the bad news?" Pete asked.

Marcus motioned for Jenny to put the next images on the screen. "Today the Libyan has a special guest," he explained.

The team stared at a photo of a second convoy now on-site. This one was made up of a single black BMW sedan, flanked by three black SUVs. The time stamp in the top right-hand corner indicated the photo was taken at 1:06 a.m.

"We don't have a photo of this person, but Langley suspects he's a very senior-level Pakistani official—a general, a minister perhaps," Marcus continued. "What we do know is that there are now another fifteen heavily armed men on-site. Men we didn't plan for. But this is our chance, and here's how it's going to play out."

For the next few minutes, Marcus laid out the updated battle plan. Then he dismissed the team, and everyone headed to the stern of the sub, where they donned scuba gear, climbed into their "full metal coffins"—as Pete had dubbed them—and embarked on the two-hour-and-seventeen-minute journey to Karachi.

Just as they had done to secretly enter North Korea several years earlier, they were using two Advanced SEAL Delivery Vehicles, both of which looked like long black torpedoes. Powered by a single propeller running off lithium polymer batteries, the highly classified mini submarines were nearly silent. They'd been designed specifically for the U.S. military, but after serious cost overruns the program had been canceled. The few vehicles the Pentagon had could transport four to six of the Navy's best and brightest—or in this case, CIA operatives—and their gear into enemy territory without being seen or heard. The challenge was that they were trapped inside a sardine can for the entire journey while they used their oxygen tanks to breathe and state-of-the-art sonar navigational systems to get them precisely to their target. What's more, the ASDVs were cramped. Windowless. Filled with bone-chilling ocean water. The team's dry suits kept out the water but not the cold. And it was pitch-black. As a SEAL commander had told Marcus, "They're not for the faint of heart, and anyone with even a touch of claustrophobia need not apply."

The Navy was in the process of developing a new, far more sophisticated (and far more expensive) version that was roomier, had a dry interior, and was thus warmer. But those were not yet ready for deployment. For now, this was all they had.

In the first minisub, a SEAL serving on the *Maine* navigated from a console at the front while Marcus, Jenny, Pete, and Callaghan were squeezed together in the back, side by side. In the second sub, another SEAL navigated while Kailea, Noah, Stone, and Navarro rode shotgun with their gear safely tucked away in specially designed waterproof duffel bags.

Once inside, ensconced in thick darkness, Marcus mentally reviewed every square inch of the satellite images. He recalled the men in the protective detail, dressed in business suits and ties suggesting they were government, not military or paramilitary. They weren't sporting Kalashnikov rifles but rather what appeared to be Chinese submachine guns. Regardless, they were creating a serious new wrinkle in an already risky operation.

Marcus's small force had enough on their hands trying to ambush Abu Nakba and his security detail. The last thing he wanted to do was open fire on a Pakistani general, much less a government minister. That would really stir up the hornet's nest. Rather than a lightning-fast strike, they were now facing the very real possibility of getting bogged down in a firefight in one of the most populous cities in one of the most dangerous countries in Central Asia. It could easily bring the entire Karachi police force down on their heads, along with perhaps a paramilitary division or two. What's more, they had no backup and no possibility of extraction by air.

Jenny's worries echoed in his head. The caffeine and the tension were wreaking havoc on his stomach. Marcus tried to pray but couldn't focus. He tried to meditate on Scriptures that he'd memorized over the years, but nothing was coming back. So he focused on Annie instead. He pictured her pacing the floor of the Global Operations Center at Langley, anxiously watching over this complicated operation. Soon, the rhythmic hum of the motor, the sloshing of the water inside their "coffin," and the utter lack of true sleep over the past few months made Marcus so drowsy that before he realized it, he had completely conked out.

Eventually, Marcus sensed they were slowing down. Groggy and with no idea how long he'd been asleep, he glanced at his watch and winced. The glowing dial on his wrist read 5:46 a.m. They were twenty minutes behind schedule. The sun would rise over Karachi in less than ninety minutes. Their already narrow window of opportunity was rapidly closing.

His pulse quickening, Marcus put his right hand out, found Jenny, and gave her a tap. Despite how freezing cold they all felt, however cramped their muscles, it was time to move. Blindly feeling his way forward, Marcus found the hatch on the bottom of the ASDV. He opened it, lowered himself into the Arabian Sea, made sure the rest of his team were with him, and began swimming for shore.

13

Annie Stewart was the highest-ranking employee in the building at the moment.

She was no longer a professional staffer on the Senate Intelligence Committee. She was now the Deputy Director of the CIA. She was no longer involved in providing Congressional oversight of the U.S. intelligence community. She was now one of its most senior players. It was, therefore, her responsibility to be in the room as the most important and sensitive mission of her career played out, especially with Marcus's life on the line.

So while Martha Dell was huddled in the White House Situation Room with the president and the National Security Council, monitoring the operation Marcus was leading at that very moment, Annie was headed to the CIA's Global Operations Center, where she, too, could track every detail of the operation in real time.

It was nearly 8 p.m. in D.C., which made it almost 6 a.m. in Karachi.

Marcus and his team should be hitting the beach at any moment.

Nodding to the armed guards standing post outside the GOC's massive steel doors, Annie swiped her security badge on a keypad, then submitted to a retinal scan. A moment later, the locks electronically disengaged, the doors slid open, and she entered the dimly lit war room with its huge flat-screen monitors and rows of staffers hunched over their computers and working the phones. On the center screen, Annie saw an encrypted feed of the warehouse in Karachi, streaming live from a Keyhole spy satellite in geosynchronous orbit ten miles above the Pakistani port city. To its left was a live feed from a Predator drone operating several miles above the beach where Marcus and his team were supposed to land. To its right was footage from another Predator providing real-time imaging of the network of roads leading to the port.

Everyone stood to attention as the deputy director entered. Annie motioned for them to take their seats and resume their work. As she took her own, the watch commander handed her a headset that allowed her to listen in on the radio traffic between Marcus and his colleagues and speak to them if need be. Another staffer brought Annie freshly brewed coffee in a CIA mug, with a splash of French vanilla creamer, just the way she liked it. She thanked him and took a sip, never taking her eyes off the images and data flowing in from Pakistan.

After all these months, and who knew how many operations, she still hadn't gotten used to seeing the man she loved taking his team into battle. There was no question that she was proud of him. But pride wasn't the driving emotion in her heart or mind. It was fear. The only thing worse than losing this man would be watching it happen in real time. Annie took a deep breath and said a silent prayer, consoling herself with the certainty that at least this was Marcus's final mission. In less than an hour, one way or another, their long nightmare would finally be over.

14

Marcus and his team reached the beach at Hawke's Bay.

For the moment, they were still operating under the cover of darkness, but only for another hour. Signaling the others to remain submerged, Marcus rose to the surface. It was too early for anyone to be on the beach or in the nearby restaurants, dive shacks, or gift shops. Nor did he see any night-shift security guards, passing police cars, or headlights on the road leading from this peninsula back to the mainland.

Marcus signaled his team to follow him and raced to the beach. Upon reaching it, he removed his helmet, turned off his oxygen supply, and began breathing the cool morning air. Pulling off his flippers, he shoved them along with his helmet into a canvas bag and sprinted to the back porch of a fish restaurant. As the others did the same, Marcus stripped off his oxygen tanks and dry suit, leaving him clad in black jeans and a black cotton T-shirt. Opening one of the gear bags, he fished out a pair of combat boots, a Kevlar vest, a balaclava, an M4 automatic rifle, and a pistol. Then he retrieved a small backpack filled with ammo, grenades, bottle of water, flashlight, tactical knife, and first aid kit, and slung it over his shoulders.

Glancing around the corner and seeing no one, Marcus led his team forward, with Jenny at his side and Pete and Navarro bringing up the rear. In the parking lot, they found the two rusty Range Rovers—one black, the other silver, each with surfboards strapped to the roofs—that had been pre-positioned by Agency operatives working under the guise of visa officers out of the nearby U.S. Consulate.

Marcus reached down and found the key in a magnetic box attached to the underbelly of the engine on the driver's side. He unlocked his vehicle, got behind the wheel, and started the engine while his team piled themselves and their gear inside. Geoff and his team did the same in the second Range Rover, and soon they were racing southeastward while Noah sent a short, encrypted signal to Langley that they were in business.

As they crossed through the heart of Karachi's commercial district, Geoff took a hard left and, as per their plan, embarked on an entirely different route to the port. Marcus stayed on his planned course, silently thanking God that they were hitting one green light after another. Still, he could see the city beginning to stir. Street cleaners. Bread trucks. Merchants opening their storefronts. Businessmen in Mercedes on their way to their sky-high office buildings to get a jump start on the day. This was not good. They were supposed to be nearly done with this operation by now. They were supposed to be heading back to the beach, not just getting started.

Sixteen minutes later, Marcus took a right on Qasim Port Road and headed for Pier 19. Pulling up to the guard booth, he saw that there was only one man on duty. Dark and gaunt and likely in his early- to midsixties, the man leaned out of the booth and asked Marcus something in Urdu. Rather than answer, Marcus tased him, dropping him to the floor with fifty thousand volts of electricity. Then Marcus leaned into the guard booth and pressed two buttons, opening the gate and lowering the steel barrier. Once the way was clear, Marcus drove into the sprawling port complex with the second Range Rover right behind him.

On cue, Noah opened the back passenger door and bolted for the guardhouse. Closing the front gate, Noah took the guard's walkie-talkie, scanned all the CCTV cameras, and determined that the coast was clear. Then he took his whisper microphone headset out of his backpack and put it on.

Just as he did, Marcus was startled to see the convoy of Pakistani government vehicles—the ones they'd seen in the satellite photos—roaring up a service road. Marcus held his breath, drew his Sig Sauer from its holster, and held it on his lap out of sight as he watched the driver of the lead vehicle salute Noah. Fortunately, Noah reacted well, standing ramrod straight, saluting in return, and then pressing the button to open the steel gate.

Jenny, meanwhile, reached into the glove compartment, drew out a small digital camera, and discreetly took pictures of each car and its license plate. Unfortunately, the windows of the BMW were tinted so they couldn't see inside. As soon as the gate was open, the motorcade exited and roared off.

Marcus knew they'd just dodged a bullet.

Maybe this was going to be easier than any of them had feared.

15

Marcus nodded his approval to Noah.

Then he flashed what appeared to be the peace sign to the young operative. In fact, he was reminding Noah that in exactly two minutes he needed to activate the device they'd brought to jam all mobile phones and radio traffic within a one-square-kilometer radius. When Noah reached down, lifted the device out of his backpack, and showed it to Marcus, both Range Rovers began moving again.

But not in the same direction.

Marcus took the service road on the right side of Pier 19. This took him and his team down the north side of a long line of office complexes, warehouses, massive LNG storage tanks, and a huge maze of crisscrossing pipes.

Geoff Stone, meanwhile, took the other service road, the one from which the Pakistani convoy had just come. That put Stone and his colleagues on the south side of the pier and thus out of view of Marcus and the others.

"Pull into that alley," Jenny—their navigator—said when they were nearly at the end of the road. Marcus slowed, took a left, and parked between two large, weathered warehouses, each badly in need of a paint job. Getting out of the driver's side door and taking his M4—locked and loaded—with him, Marcus signaled the others to follow suit. They were all dressed to look like the protective detail guarding Abu Nakba—with one exception: they now pulled black balaclava masks over their faces.

"Alpha One to Bravo Four," Marcus said over his headset.

"Bravo Four, in position," came the voice of Miguel Navarro. "And I have a tango in my sights."

"Roger that—stand by one." Marcus replied, picturing his colleague on the roof of a nearby warehouse, looking through the reticle of his sniper rifle.

Marcus sent Donny Callaghan and Pete Hwang to the left while he and Jenny Morris went right. Weapons up, they scanned windows and roofs for any signs of movement as they retraced their steps to the head of the alley. Then, in sync, Marcus ducked out of the alley and looked down the pier to the left, while Jenny looked back up the service road to the right toward the main gate. When they pulled back to protected positions, Jenny shook her head. So did Marcus. All clear.

They quickly turned left onto the service road and double-timed it past the warehouse, hugging the wall, until they reached the next alley and next warehouse. Glancing quickly around the corner, Marcus spotted one of Abu Nakba's men patrolling the alley. Fortunately, the man had his back toward Marcus and was walking slowly in the opposite direction. Dressed in black and brandishing an AK-47, he, too, wore a headset, meaning Marcus was going to have to neutralize this guy fast to prevent him from alerting the rest of the Kairos team.

"Alpha One to Bravo One," Marcus whispered.

"Bravo One, go," Stone radioed back.

"You guys in position?"

"Roger that."

"Good, so are we," Marcus said. "Bravo Four, do you have a clean shot?"

"Affirmative, Alpha One," Navarro replied. "Awaiting your order."

Jenny was right behind Marcus but facing back up the service road to guard their six. Following the radio traffic, she nudged him twice in the back, signaling she was ready. At this, Marcus lowered his M4 and let it dangle from his shoulder strap. Drawing his Sig Sauer once again from its holster, he attached a silencer to the barrel and drew a deep breath.

"Take the shot, Bravo Four," he ordered, then immediately swung around the corner and exhaled.

To his surprise, the tango had turned and was now walking back up the alley toward him. A look of shock registered in his eyes. He began to raise his Kalashnikov but Marcus double-tapped him to the forehead, dropping the man to the ground.

Just then Navarro reported, "Tango One down."

An instant later, Kailea radioed in, "Tango Two down."

Then came Geoff Stone. "Tango Three down."

Marcus was never more grateful for this team, the most professional and effective operators he had ever worked with in any branch of the federal government.

As Jenny swept the rooftops and windows looking for new enemies, Marcus moved quickly to the motionless body sprawled out in the alley, a pool of crimson growing around his head. Just to be certain, Marcus reached down and searched for the man's pulse. There was none. So, stripping the man's weapons and ammo away from him, along with his headset, Marcus put the Kalashnikov strap over his neck and threw the weapon over his shoulder. Then he turned the whisper microphone upside down and put it on his own head so that the earpiece was against his left ear. This now gave him the ability to listen in on Abu Nakba's communications in his left ear and to his own team in his right.

"Tango Four down," Marcus said into his own mic. "Perimeter secure. Phase One complete."

With the Pakistanis gone—whoever they were—and four Kairos operatives dead, they only had seventeen more terrorists to deal with, including Abu Nakba himself. Informing the rest of the group of this, Marcus now checked to see if Pete had linked up with Callaghan yet at the northwest entrance.

"Almost there, Alpha One," Pete radioed, breathing hard.

"Get the lead out, Alpha Three," Marcus ordered.

"Roger that," Pete, sounding breathless, radioed back a few seconds later. "Okay, Alpha Three in position."

"Good—Bravo Three, you ready to move?"

Callaghan confirmed that he and Pete were ready.

Next Marcus checked in with Geoff and Kailea. They, too, were in position at the loading dock on the south side of the warehouse.

"Roger that," said Marcus, checking his watch and then motioning for Jenny to move with him to the alley door on the northeast corner.

"You good?" he whispered.

Jenny nodded.

It was now or never, Marcus knew. They had to move fast.

"Stand by to execute Phase Two," Marcus said, putting on his night vision goggles as Jenny donned hers. "Three, two, one—*go—now, now, now.*"

16

The entire team stormed the massive warehouse complex from three directions.

Gunfire erupted almost immediately, and Marcus heard a cacophony of radio traffic in his left ear. Not all of it was intelligible, but the point was clear enough. The element of surprise was gone. Abu Nakba and his men knew they were here, so they'd better move fast and hard.

As they entered from the alleyway, Marcus and Jenny encountered no Kairos operatives, but they found themselves in a still, dark hallway lined with offices, all of which needed to be cleared. Jenny took the rooms on the right while he took those on the left. In each he found laptop computers, satellite phones, safes, and file cabinets that might provide invaluable intel. But bagging up the treasure would have to wait. Abu Nakba was their mission, and they could not let themselves get distracted.

Explosions suddenly rocked the cavernous warehouse. Marcus imagined the volley of grenades going back and forth and was surprised he and Jenny hadn't encountered any resistance. It didn't make sense. Where was everyone? Indeed, the longer he and Jenny moved forward without taking fire, the more tense both became. Having finished clearing each office and finding no one waiting for them, they pressed forward, perplexed, until they came to a locked door. Through the window in the door, Marcus could see it led into another hallway. Seeing no one at either end, he smashed the glass with the butt of his M4, reached his gloved hand through the shattered window, and unlocked the door from the other side.

Once again, they found more offices, more potential intel, but still no Kairos operatives. Clearing these, they came to a locked steel fireproof door painted red. In it was a small window with puncture-proof glass. As Marcus kept guard, Jenny attached a strip of Semtex and a fuse opposite the door's handle. Then they backed down the hallway, took cover, and Jenny pulled the trigger.

With a deafening explosion, the door was ripped from its hinges. The two moved quickly through the smoke and dust and darkness until they suddenly found themselves in the main warehouse. Almost instantly, someone spotted them and began firing from behind a forklift on the other side of the warehouse floor. Marcus returned fire as he moved left and took cover behind a large stack of wooden pallets. Jenny moved right until she found shelter behind another forklift.

Marcus had no intention of getting pinned down and into a prolonged firefight. He was determined to reach Abu Nakba before the old man could slip away. Taking a grenade from his belt, he pulled the pin and threw it like a fastball at the tango shooting at them. The moment the grenade detonated, the gunfire stopped, and Marcus sprinted forward. But two Kairos operatives emerged from the shadows and began running toward the far end of the warehouse. Marcus fired on one, felling him instantly. Jenny opened fire at the other, to the same effect.

Just then all the lights in the warehouse turned on. For an instant, Marcus was blinded, in the open, and highly vulnerable. Ripping off his night vision goggles and trying to regain his bearings, he suddenly heard a Kalashnikov erupt from his right. He stumbled toward the forklift Jenny had used as cover and reached it just in time. AK-47 rounds pinged off the forklift. Slowly, Marcus's eyes adjusted. But as his vision came back, he realized Jenny was not at his side. He scanned the warehouse floor but couldn't see her anywhere.

Grasping his M4, he took a deep breath, pivoted around the side of the forklift, and fired off two bursts. This suppressed the AK-47 for a moment, but Marcus wasn't taking any chances. He pulled the pin on another grenade, reared back, and threw another fastball. In the wake of the explosion, he fired off two more bursts, then turned and headed around the right side of the lift, unleashing another two bursts. Still not seeing any sign of Jenny, he sprinted toward another row of wooden pallets, all of which were stacked with steel crates of some kind.

This drew more gunfire, but not from the same direction. It was coming from a second-floor position, from a Kairos operative that Marcus hadn't noticed before. Stopping behind one of the pallet stacks, Marcus leaned right, unleashing three bursts at the second floor, then pulled back to a position of safety. He popped out a spent magazine, reloaded, leaned left, and fired again.

He couldn't tell if he'd hit his target, but he heard footsteps coming hard and fast from a narrow corridor to his right. Marcus raised his weapon and ducked into the corridor. Seeing a tango barreling toward him less than forty feet away and closing fast—eyes filled with rage—Marcus opened fire. The first rounds went wide, but the second burst found the target. The man's bullet-ridden body collapsed to the cold cement floor.

Marcus breathed a sigh of relief. But moments later, he heard gunfire erupt behind him. Before he could turn, he felt two rounds hit him squarely in the back, sending him crashing face-first to the floor. Blindsided and in searing pain, Marcus gasped for air. Fearing the worst, he checked himself for exit wounds. He found none, nor any blood, and quickly realized that his Kevlar vest had just saved his life. Rolling onto his back, Marcus suddenly saw a bear of a man racing toward him. As smoke curled from the barrel of the man's pistol, Marcus's right hand began reaching for his own pistol, but it was too late.

The Kairos operative was too fast and was now towering over him.

Mohammed Faisal burst into the office.

"Father, we need to go—*now*."

"Give me a minute, my son. I'm almost finished," Abu Nakba said, poring over the data on Faisal's desktop computer.

"No, that's impossible," Faisal replied. "We have to move you now."

"But the data, the files," the Kairos founder insisted while the gunfire intensified.

"Don't worry, Father. My men will take care of it. But you and I must go."

The Syrian eased the wheelchair through the door of his office and then—flanked by a half dozen Kairos bodyguards—he pushed the old man down a long tunnel. At the vault door, Faisal entered the passcode as explosions rocked the building. Finally, the massive steel door swung open. Pushing Abu Nakba through, Faisal waited for the rest of the men to come through. Then he entered a second and third passcode, one to shut the vault door, the other to arm the explosive booby traps attached to it. Then he raced the old man through the rest of the tunnel until they reached an exit leading into an underground parking garage, where a driver in a dark-blue Volvo sedan was waiting for them.

Marcus froze.

He had no way to defend himself. Nor time to pray. All he could think about was that his race had come to an end far too abruptly. After all that he'd been through, he wasn't going to get the chance to kill or capture Abu Nakba after all. He wasn't going to marry Annie or start a whole new life with her. Nor was he going to be able to say goodbye to his mother and sisters and their beautiful kids. This wasn't the way it was supposed to end. Still, in the next few seconds, he would exit this life and be safely in the presence of Jesus Christ, his Savior and King.

The Kairos operative's mouth curled into a twisted, sneering smile as he held a Glock 9mm pistol steady with both hands and took aim at Marcus's face. Marcus closed his eyes and relaxed his body. He couldn't believe this was how he was going to die. But he was ready. He knew where he was going. He hadn't lived a perfect life. Far from it. But he had no regrets. He was ready to meet his Maker face-to-face with a clear conscience and a grateful heart.

He heard the man pull the trigger but never heard a shot. Then he heard the man pull the trigger a second time, a third, and a fourth. But still the gun didn't fire. In shock, Marcus opened his eyes. The tango's smile had faded, replaced by confusion. Marcus couldn't imagine how, but the man's gun had just jammed. There was no other explanation. Rather than ejecting a spent mag and reloading, the man was slamming the bottom of the mag to make sure it was properly seated.

But before the guy could rack his gun and try again, Marcus's training kicked in. Instinctively, he pulled back his right foot and then drove his steel-toed boot forward, smashing it into the man's groin with all the force he could muster. The tango doubled over and began shrieking in pain. As he did, Marcus rolled back onto his stomach and sprang to his feet, then shifted his weight and delivered a roundhouse kick to the side of the man's head. That sent the tango sprawling backward. Marcus then drew his Sig Sauer to finish the man off, but as he did, he heard another burst of fire.

This time it was coming from his left. Dropping to a crouch, Marcus raised the Sig and pivoted just in time to see yet another of Abu Nakba's men charging at him, a smoking Kalashnikov in his hands. Marcus pulled the trigger five times in rapid succession. Two of the rounds went wide but the next three hit their mark, sending the man crashing to the floor.

Turning back to the first guy, Marcus found him screaming and writhing in pain, yet also groping for his pistol. Marcus didn't hesitate. He raised his own pistol and put two rounds in the man's right temple. The writhing ceased. So did the screaming. The man was gone. And Marcus rose up to find another target.

Instead, he saw Jenny racing toward him.

"What happened?" Marcus asked, aghast.

"Long story," she replied.

"You're covered in blood."

"It's not mine. Don't worry."

"You're sure?"

"Yes, of course—but we need to move fast. Callaghan just found a hidden entrance to what he fears is a secret tunnel. There's no sign of Abu Nakba, and Callaghan is afraid he's getting away."

"Then let's go," said Marcus.

Racing across the main floor toward a stack of pallets on the other side of the warehouse, Marcus saw dead bodies everywhere he looked. Fortunately, none of them were Americans. When they reached the corner, he found Pete standing guard and pointing to a stack of pallets that had been pushed aside, revealing an open metal hatch. Marcus pointed his M4 down the hole but saw no one. Just a metal ladder.

He immediately scrambled into the hole, rapidly descending roughly two stories as Jenny came down right behind him. Weapons up, Marcus led the way down a dimly lit tunnel for about thirty yards before it opened into what appeared to be a massive underground laboratory.

He stepped over another dead body and spotted several more to his right. He was startled by the fact that none of these were members of Abu Nakba's protective detail. Nor had they been shot by the Americans. All of them had been killed execution style. None were holding weapons. Nor were they dressed in black and wearing Kevlar vests and whisper microphones. Instead, they were all dressed from head to toe in the hazmat suits. A clipboard and pen lay beside one of them. A bullet-ridden iPad lay beside another. A tray of shattered test tubes rested beside a third.

18

GLOBAL OPERATIONS CENTER, LANGLEY, VIRGINIA

"Deputy Director Stewart, you should see this," said the watch commander.

"What've you got, Dave?" Annie replied, looking up from a sheaf of phone and text intercepts that NSA had just picked up in Karachi, translated, and sent over.

"Up there, on the left," the commander said, pointing her to the live Predator feed, now positioned over the headquarters of the Karachi police department.

Annie removed her reading glasses and refocused. What she saw alarmed her. Four armored vehicles, lights flashing, were parked in front of the barracks of Karachi's main police station, and what appeared to be a heavily armed SWAT team was loading into the vehicles.

"Tell me that's not connected to our operation, commander," Annie ordered.

"Wish I could, ma'am," he replied.

"How far are those barracks from the port?" Annie pressed.

"Not far," he said, "But as you can see, rush hour traffic starts early there—the roads are filling up fast. So I'd say fifteen minutes—max."

"And how much more time does the team need on-site?"

"At least twenty, but thirty would be best."

"Tell Agent Ryker he's got ten, and that's it," said Annie. "Not a minute more."

KARACHI, PAKISTAN

"Ten minutes, repeat, ten—roger that," Marcus acknowledged.

Just then, Donny Callaghan and Geoff Stone emerged from a tunnel veering off from the right side of the lab. Kailea Curtis was right behind them. They were drenched in sweat and breathing hard.

"Sorry, sir," Callaghan began. "Looks like the old man got away."

"What are you talking about? How is that possible?" Marcus demanded.

"We're counting fifteen tangos dead, sir, including the four outside," Geoff explained. "We pursued the rest down that tunnel there, sir, but by the time we reached the end, we found a huge door—like a bank vault—closed, locked, and impenetrable by anything we have with us. Probably booby-trapped as well."

Marcus fought to hold his tongue, but he was livid. To have come all this way, to have gotten this close, and yet to have failed to achieve their objective was almost more than he could take. Then Pete approached from behind.

"What is all this?" he asked. "Looks like something out of *Breaking Bad*."

Marcus had never seen the TV series about Mexican drug cartels and American drug runners operating in New Mexico, but he'd heard enough from Pete over the years to get the point. Yet this wasn't about narcotics. That was plain enough from the biohazard signs plastered everywhere and the hazmat gear all the scientists were wearing.

Marcus took the measure of the lab. Imaging scanners, freezers and cabinets, and all sorts of research equipment on workstations at the tables in the center.

"Geoff, Kai, Donny, photograph everything in here and bag up all the laptops and other intel you possibly can," Marcus ordered. "You've got five minutes—no more. Got it? *No more.*"

When they nodded and got moving, Marcus turned to Jenny and Pete.

"You two get back upstairs. Bag up everything you can from those offices. And do it fast."

"Right, we're on it," Jenny said, turning to grab Pete's arm and race back to the upper offices.

Marcus wanted to go down the tunnel and see the vault door. But he noticed Kailea standing beside three huge steel boxes.

"What are those?" asked Marcus.

Kailea didn't answer. She was white as a sheet.

As worried as he was curious, Marcus walked over to her. As he approached, he realized these were hermetically sealed isolation chambers. Each contained a window made of thick, tempered protective glass. But he stopped dead in his tracks as he saw what was inside the first chamber. Three monkeys were strapped to stainless-steel chairs bolted to the floor. They were all dead. But what was truly bizarre was that half their faces and much of their torsos appeared to have been eaten away.

Instinctively, Marcus turned away, fighting to control his gag reflex. But then, forcing himself to take deep breaths through his mouth and nose, he also forced himself to look into the window of the second chamber. Here, too, Marcus found three dead animals. But these weren't monkeys. They were, instead, a horse, a cow, and a goat. Each was covered in blood, and these, too, had been half-eaten by some monstrous disease.

Kailea, however, was not standing before either of these chambers. She was standing in front of the third—frozen, unable to speak or to move.

Marcus cautiously approached his colleague. At first, he just stared at her as she stared into the chamber. Then he turned, slowly, only to witness something more revolting than anything he had ever seen before. Worse than anything he'd experienced during his multiple combat tours in Afghanistan and Iraq. Certainly worse than anything he'd seen as a Secret Service agent.

Inside the isolation chamber were what appeared to be two Pakistani women and one man. Each was naked and gaunt. Perhaps they had been Kairos prisoners. Perhaps they had been snatched out of the slums of Karachi. Marcus had no idea. Just like the primates, they were strapped to stainless-steel chairs. The first seemed young, perhaps in her twenties. The second may have been in her forties. The only man was wrinkled and gray, putting him perhaps in his sixties or seventies. All were dead. And all had clearly bled out of their eyes and every orifice while their faces and torsos had been eaten away.

At this, Marcus lost it. He vomited all over the floor of the laboratory until there was nothing left and he was reduced to dry heaves. Kailea had finally backed away from the third chamber. She was gagging but not yet vomiting.

Marcus fought to catch his breath. As he did, Kailea pulled off her backpack, unzipped it, pulled out a bottle of water, and handed it to him. Though he couldn't speak yet, Marcus nodded his thanks, took a sip, but could not swallow, so spit it out on the floor. After doing this several times, he finally began to regain his senses.

"Can you . . . ?" he tried to say, his voice raspy and strained.

"Can I what?" Kailea asked.

"We need to document all this, and fast," he said.

"Okay, sure, I'm on it," she replied.

Pulling a digital camera from her backpack, Kailea started shooting everything. The lab. The equipment. The outside of the chambers. And then, taking a deep breath, she forced herself to photograph everything in each chamber.

By the time she finished, Geoff and Donny had bagged all the intel they could. Marcus instructed them to wire everything with explosives and set the timers. He wasn't yet certain exactly what they'd just stumbled on. But he knew it couldn't be left intact. But as the team set all the charges, a frantic message came over their headsets.

"*JENNY'S DOWN,*" they heard Pete scream into his headset, abandoning security protocols. "*JENNY'S DOWN—I REPEAT, JENNY'S DOWN.*"

19

Marcus bolted out of the lab.

As he reached the open hatch, he could hear a raging gun battle up on the main floor of the warehouse. He slung his M4 over his shoulder, drew his Sig Sauer, and climbed up the steel ladder. Back on the main floor and using several of the pallets in the corner as cover, he took a quick look to the left, then another to the right. From this vantage point, he could see neither Pete nor Jenny. But he could tell that the main source of gunfire was coming from directly above him.

Holstering the Sig, Marcus grabbed the M4 and made sure he had a full magazine. Then he began sweeping the assault rifle from side to side as he worked his way down the right side of the warehouse, past one row of pallets after another, staying close to the wall, and constantly checking his back to make sure no one could ambush him. Three-quarters of the way down the narrow corridor he was in, he spotted Pete on the other side of the warehouse, crouched behind a half stack of pallets, pinned down under withering fire from the second floor. Pete was only returning fire occasionally, and only by raising his M4 above the stack and unleashing a few bursts at a time.

Marcus quickly realized that the only hope Pete had of not getting his head blown off was if Marcus could get up to the second floor and take out this shooter. That's why, as much as he wanted to radio Pete or signal him to let him know help was on its way, he didn't dare do either, lest Pete inadvertently give away Marcus's position.

Staying low, Marcus slipped around another row of pallets, careful not to draw Pete's attention. From this vantage point, he could see a metal ladder about twenty yards ahead at the end of the corridor. But just then, out of the corner of his eye, he also spotted Jenny. She was lying on her back right behind Pete, semiprotected—for the moment, at least—by Pete and a half stack of pallets. But she was bleeding profusely. Her face had lost all its color. And her right leg was shaking wildly.

Enraged, Marcus bolted down the corridor. Reaching the ladder, he scrambled up to the second floor. But just as he did, he saw Pete stop firing, eject a spent mag, and then realize to his horror that he had used all his ammo and Jenny's as well.

Marcus was unwilling to let either of his teammates die here in Karachi. He pulled two grenades from his backpack, pulled the pin out of the first, threw it down the length of the corridor before him, and sprinted forward. The moment it detonated, he pulled the second pin—still on the run—and threw that grenade as well. By the time that one exploded, Marcus was approaching the far end of the warehouse.

Coming around the corner through a cloud of smoke and debris, he found Abu Nakba's last man on-site. Charred, mangled, and soaked in blood, the Kairos operative was nevertheless still alive somehow. What's more, he was crawling toward the AK-47 he'd dropped, away from flames now licking up a stack of pallets and about to engulf the entire section. Marcus shouted for the man to stop, but instead the man lunged for his weapon, mustering all the strength he had left. Marcus put two bullets in his heart, and that was that.

Marcus now radioed Pete and the rest of the team that the second floor was clear. He ordered Geoff Stone and his forces to rig the rest of the warehouse with explosives. Then he radioed Noah, instructing him to disable the front gates and meet the team at the Range Rovers.

"Already done, Alpha One," Noah replied. "Bravo Four and I are out front, engines running, doors open, ready to move."

Grateful that Noah was thinking ahead and that Miguel Navarro was with him, Marcus raced down the ladder and across the warehouse floor. By the time he got to Jenny's side, he found Pete putting a tourniquet on her right leg. Jenny's eyes were wide. Her pupils were dilated. She'd taken multiple rounds in her shoulder, hip, and stomach. But the worst was that her right kneecap had been almost completely blown off. What was left of her leg was still shaking terribly. Blood was everywhere.

"What can I do, Pete?" he asked, kneeling and taking Jenny's hand.

Pete, injecting her now with what was probably a heavy dose of morphine, didn't seem to hear him. If he did, he didn't reply. Jenny was trying to say something, but Marcus could barely hear her. Leaning closer and using his gloved hand to wipe blood off her mouth and face, he watched as her pale lips tried to form a coherent sentence.

"Stay with me, Jenny," Marcus pleaded. "You're going to make it. You're going to make it, Jenny. Pete's going to stop the bleeding. He's giving you something for the pain. And we're going to get you out of here. Okay? Jenny? Can you hear me? We're going to get you out of here and you're going to make it."

But she didn't respond. Her eyes were almost vacant. She was still trying to say something as Callaghan and Kailea raced up to them and asked how they could help.

"*Quiet—everybody—please,*" Marcus ordered, more harshly than he intended. "*She's trying to say something.*"

"*Did . . . did . . . ?*" she finally said, barely above a whisper.

Marcus leaned in even closer.

"*Did we what, Jenny?*"

"*Did we . . . ?*" she tried again, squeezing his hand ever so slightly.

"*What, Jenny?*" Marcus pressed. "*Did we what?*"

"*G . . . et . . . him?*"

Marcus wasn't sure what to say. He didn't want to lie to her. But nor did he dare break the news to her that . . .

But just then, Jenny's eyes rolled back in her head. Her hands went limp. Her breathing stopped, and her head dropped to the side.

"No, no—Jenny, come back—come back," Marcus ordered. *"Jenny, come on, we need you—I need you."*

He began giving her mouth-to-mouth, but Pete pulled him away.

"Stop, Marcus—she's gone," Pete replied.

"No, Pete, come on, we can save her," Marcus shot back.

"No, Marcus, we can't—she's gone, and we have to go—now. This building is about to blow."

Marcus was shaking with rage. His eyes were welling up with tears. The rest of the team was hustling bags of intel out to the Range Rovers. Noah and Navarro were gunning the engines. Then Geoff and Callaghan returned with a body bag. They said nothing, just looked at Pete, who nodded and helped them put Jenny inside.

"This isn't . . . This can't . . ." Marcus sputtered to no one in particular. *"It can't. Not Jenny. No—I don't . . ."*

Geoff and Callaghan carried her body outside, and Pete came over to Marcus.

"Hey, listen to me," Pete ordered. "Marcus, look at me."

Marcus wouldn't, so Pete grabbed his shoulders, pulled Marcus toward him, and forced his friend to look directly into his eyes.

"We can't do this here, Marcus. We've got to go—right this minute."

Marcus was still shaking. But after a moment he nodded, then let Pete take him to the vehicles and put him in the front passenger seat of the lead Range Rover. Pete jumped into the backseat and slammed the door behind him. As Noah hit the gas, Annie Stewart's voice came over the radio. It shocked them all. There was no reason for anyone from Langley to be talking to them—even on an encrypted channel—unless . . .

"Alpha One, you've got company," Annie said, explaining that four SWAT teams from the Karachi police force now were at the main entrance and about to blow the front gates with explosives. *"Get out of there now—that's an order."*

Both Noah and Geoff accelerated and got the Range Rovers to the end of the pier. Screeching to a stop, side by side, everyone jumped out and donned their scuba gear. Just then, the main warehouse erupted in a massive series of deafening explosions. They could all feel the searing heat of the fireball. But there was no time to turn and gawk. One by one, the team began jumping off the pier into the water, bringing Jenny's body bag and all the bags of intel with them.

Marcus was moving more slowly than the others, so Pete helped him suit up. Then, as per their original plan, Pete rigged both vehicles with explosives and short timers.

"*You ready?*" Pete asked over the roaring flames.

Marcus said nothing. But suddenly, one of the LNG storage tanks erupted into an even more massive explosion. The force of the blast knocked both men off the pier. They hit the water hard. Stunned but uninjured, Pete grabbed Marcus by the arm and guided him down to the two Advanced SEAL Delivery Vehicles waiting for them. The others were already on board, as was Jenny's body bag. Pete pushed Marcus in first, then climbed in behind him and closed the hatch. The instant it was sealed tight, the ASDV accelerated, beginning its long and perilous journey back to the *Maine*.

Taichung

Changhua

Nantou

Yunlin

T a i w a n
(Republic of China)

Chiayi County

Chiayi

Tainan

Kaohsiung

PART
TWO

20

A brutal winter storm was descending on the American capital.

Heavily bundled D.C. officers blocked what little traffic there was in all directions as uniformed officers of the United States Secret Service, each of them carrying automatic rifles, lined the streets and corners in a five-block radius of the White House. It was an impressive show of force but hardly necessary. After all, no pedestrian was crazy enough to be out in this horrible weather.

On the roofs of the nearby high-rise office buildings, as well as on the roof of the White House itself, teams of Secret Service sharpshooters and their spotters—also heavily bundled up and sipping hot coffee from thermoses—maintained a close vigil. Lafayette Square, just across Pennsylvania Avenue from the presidential complex, had been cleared of every homeless person, all taken to nearby shelters, though that was more for their protection than that of the First Family and their incoming guests. The gusting winds, drifting snow, and temperatures in the low single digits were making conditions not just uncomfortable but life-threatening for those poor souls who typically lived in tents in the park.

At precisely 11:45 a.m. eastern time, the steel barricades beside the Secret Service guard post closest to Blair House began to lower. A moment later, the wrought iron gates to the most exclusive residence on the planet began to swing open, and the barricades adjacent to the northwest guard station began to lower. Atop snow-covered lampposts, Chinese and American flags snapped furiously in the wind, and soon the twenty-one-vehicle motorcade roared up 17th Street. The lead police motorcycles and squad cars—sirens blaring and red and blue lights flashing—slowed down to safely make the sharp right turn onto Pennsylvania Avenue, difficult in the mounting sheets of ice. Soon they took another sharp right, pulling up the freshly plowed driveway leading to the north entrance of the White House, with two black armor-plated Cadillac limousines close behind them.

Standing at attention under the main portico—a few feet away from the Marines in their dress uniforms and heavy wool coats, several White House photographers, and a detail of plainclothes Secret Service agents—was Carlos Hernandez, the forty-seventh president of the United States. As the motorcade pulled to a complete stop and an agent entered the code to unlock the back door of the second limousine, Chen Guanzhong, the president of the People's Republic of China and general secretary of the Chinese Communist Party, stepped out. The two heads of state briefly shook hands and moved quickly inside, where they removed their coats and gloves, handed them over to aides.

Walking through the West Wing, they made small talk until they reached the Oval Office. There the two leaders took their respective seats in front of a roaring, crackling fire. When they were settled, the White House press secretary let in the pool reporters and photographers for a brief photo op. President Hernandez smiled broadly as he welcomed the Chinese leader for his first state visit since Hernandez had been sworn in some eight months earlier and expressed his hope that their two countries could "reset relations" and "dial down the friction" that had come to characterize his predecessor's relationship with Beijing.

President Guanzhong did not reciprocate. To U.S. National Security Advisor

William McDermott—sitting next to Vice President Margaret Whitney and Secretary of State Robert Dayton on the couch to the left of Hernandez's chair—the Chinese president's inscrutable expression appeared as icy as the conditions outside.

The seventy-year-old Guanzhong was a man of small stature with emotionless brown eyes, thin gray hair, a receding hairline, and round, wire-framed glasses. He wore a black pin-striped suit, a crisply starched white shirt, a bright-red power tie, and a small lapel pin bearing the flag of the People's Republic of China. Not once during the photo op did the man smile. Nor, McDermott noticed, did he even turn to look at Hernandez.

When the American president opened the floor to questions, the first came from the Associated Press's senior White House correspondent regarding how exactly the two men planned to "dial down" mounting tensions between Washington and Beijing. Neither leader said anything noteworthy. Nor did they make news when pressed with similar questions by reporters from the *Washington Post*, Fox News, and the *Wall Street Journal*. Rather, each regurgitated bland, colorless, and well-rehearsed talking points written by their aides to obfuscate rather than illuminate the strained state of U.S.–Sino relations. Hernandez spoke of "the importance of international cooperation" and "the expediency of honest dialogue over harsh rhetoric." To these, Guanzhong sat rigid but nodded slightly, suggesting to reporters that while he agreed with his American host, he did not want to appear in his thrall.

It was not until a Reuters correspondent was called upon that things got interesting.

"President Hernandez, as you are no doubt aware, last night there was a mysterious and tragic set of explosions at a liquefied natural gas facility in Karachi," the woman with a distinct British accent began. "According to Pakistani officials, whatever was being kept in the warehouse somehow caught fire and then exploded. And then—and it's still not clear how—an LNG storage tank located next to the warehouse was breached. This led to an even more disastrous set of explosions that decimated at least half the warehouses and storage facilities on that pier. The Pakistanis still haven't gotten the raging fires under control, and they're calling for international assistance. But I'm wondering, Mr. President, would you care to comment?"

"Yes, thank you for raising that," Hernandez replied. "I just got off a call with the Pakistani president moments ago. I expressed my condolences for this terrible accident and offered American assistance, for which he was quite grateful. Secretary of State Dayton will depart for Islamabad shortly, rather than attending tonight's state dinner for the Chinese president. Joining him will be Energy Secretary Clawson, along with a rapid response team from the Department of Energy. This team is highly proficient in handling these types of crises and will assist the Pakistanis in gaining control of those fires and safeguarding the rest of the LNG storage facilities. It really is a terrible, terrible accident. As I understand it, some two dozen warehouse workers and security guards were killed in the blasts, and there are a number of wounded as well. Our thoughts and prayers go out to all of them and their families. The only saving grace, I suppose, as the Pakistani president just noted to me, is that the entire accident could have been much deadlier had it happened during normal working hours, not in the wee hours of the morning, Karachi time."

McDermott nodded his approval when Hernandez glanced in his direction. The president's delivery of the statement that McDermott himself had written for him was spot-on. But privately, both he and Hernandez were furious at Ryker and his CIA team. The Agency's mission was supposed to be a surgical strike, unnoticed and certainly unreported. Instead, it had become a total disaster. Yet again, Abu Nakba had eluded capture. But this time the damage was catastrophic and very, very public. It wouldn't be long before the Pakistanis suspected—and publicly suggested—foul play. And once reporters started digging, how long would it be before fingers started pointing at Langley and then the White House?

Fortunately, the Pakistanis had their hands full just now, simply trying to contain the fires and reestablish control at the port. So far, they hadn't intimated that there was reason to suspect anything more than a series of unfortunate accidents. Nor was there any reason for the American media or international press corps to suspect as much. Thus, the official White House position was to express compassion, provide assistance, and pray that the cover story would hold.

But just then a reporter for China's state TV service asked a follow-up question.

"President Guanzhong, do you agree with President Hernandez's assessment that this event in Karachi is a 'terrible accident'?"

McDermott tensed, as did Hernandez.

"No, I cannot say that I do," Guanzhong replied. "I also spoke with the Pakistani president this morning to express my horror at this wicked development. I have also dispatched a rapid response team to assist our dear Pakistani friends in gaining control of these terrible fires and ensuring that they do not spread, take more innocent lives, and do more damage. In addition, I have also ordered my Finance Ministry to immediately provide the Pakistani government with a no-interest bridge loan of seventy-five billion yuan to help them rebuild their facilities as rapidly as possible."

The room erupted with the sound of cameras clicking away furiously. Then, after taking a brief pause to let the import of his words sink in, the Chinese leader continued.

"But no, with all due respect to my American host, I am not prepared to say this was simply an accident," Guanzhong continued. "My intelligence services have received reports that the initial warehouse explosion was caused by two truck bombs. We have also received reports that the main security gate was tampered with, hindering the ability of emergency response vehicles from getting to the scene of the disaster with all haste. Now, I cannot verify any of these reports yet. But until I know more, until all the facts are in, I am going to withhold judgment and keep asking questions."

21

The White House press secretary quickly ended the photo op.

As she herded every reporter and photographer out of the Oval Office, several stewards entered and served tea. Only when they had departed and the two leaders, their national security advisors, and their notetakers were finally alone did Guanzhong turn to Hernandez.

"Mr. President, you cannot seriously believe the Karachi explosion was an accident," he began.

"I've seen no evidence to the contrary," Hernandez replied.

"Well, I must say that strikes me as a rather naive position," Guanzhong said, holding his fine porcelain teacup.

"How so?"

"You retired from the American Navy as a three-star vice admiral, did you not? My people tell me your last position was head of your Navy's entire Indo-Pacific Command. Am I wrong?"

"You are not."

"And before that, you served as deputy chief of Naval Operations after completing several tours as head of Carrier Strike Group 5 out of Yokosuka, Japan, and commander of the USS *Ronald Reagan*, one of your country's most impressive *Nimitz*-class nuclear aircraft carriers."

"You have been well briefed," said Hernandez, taking a sip of tea.

"Then surely you cannot sit here and tell me that you don't know about the reports concerning the two truck bombs, or the supposed 'malfunction' at the main gate, or the gunfire on the pier in the minutes leading up to the explosions, can you?" Guanzhong asked.

"I am certainly aware that many rumors and conspiracy theories are swirling about, Mr. President, but I must underscore that at this hour they are all *unconfirmed*," Hernandez noted. "Why bring them up publicly when the Pakistanis have barely begun their investigation?"

"Do you honestly doubt these reports will be confirmed?" Guanzhong pressed.

"I suggest we take a deep breath, be patient, and see where the evidence leads."

"Fair enough, Mr. President, but once we have all the facts, I fear we will be dealing with a very serious case of international terrorism."

"Well, I sincerely hope that you're wrong," said Hernandez. "Who would have the motive to blow up an LNG storage facility in Karachi?"

McDermott tensed again, wishing Hernandez had not raised the question, though he was now curious to hear the Chinese leader's response.

"It could be any number of actors," Guanzhong replied.

"Such as?"

"Perhaps one of the Hindu terror groups based in India who are seeking revenge against Pakistan. Or perhaps it was that Pakistani group; you know the one . . ."

When Guanzhong could not recall the name, McDermott reminded him.

"*Lashkar-e-Tayyiba*, Your Excellency."

"Yes, that's the one," the Chinese president agreed. "Perhaps they are hoping to create a pretext for a new wave of attacks inside India."

"You're suggesting that the Sunni fanatics who run the 'Army of the Righteous' need a pretext to kill Hindus in Kashmir and throughout the Indian subcontinent?" Hernandez asked, surprised that the Chinese leader had not raised the subject of Kairos, still the most dangerous terror group on the planet so long as Abu Nakba remained alive.

"I'm not saying I know who is responsible," Guanzhong retorted. "I'm simply saying that experience is a wise teacher. Over my lifetime, I have learned not to draw hasty conclusions, particularly in the fog of war. But I can assure you that we are going to find out. And when we do, there are going to be repercussions."

"Repercussions?" asked Hernandez.

"Let's not kid ourselves," said Guanzhong. "Your country's so-called 'war on terror' has not exactly achieved the peace and tranquility in the world that your predecessors promised, has it? And now instability is creeping closer to China's borders. Just look at the incidents over the past eighteen months—in Tajikistan, Nepal, Bhutan, Burma, Laos, and the Philippines. I cannot stand idly by, Mr. President, as such dangers move eastward and northward. They threaten not only Chinese lives and commerce but the stability of our region. As you well know, sir, during the recent gathering of the National People's Congress, I pledged to make counterterrorism my number one policy priority. Therefore, might I suggest that perhaps our disputes over trade deficits, intellectual property rights, and human rights—as important as they are—should not be our main topics of discussion today. Given all that has happened overnight, perhaps it is time for your country and mine to truly de-escalate tensions between us and announce a major new initiative to cooperate on counterterrorism."

McDermott was completely caught off guard by this, and he could see that Hernandez was as well. Together with Vice President Whitney and Secretary of State Dayton, they had planned and prepared for this summit for months. After a fierce internal debate, they had finally agreed to threaten Guanzhong with massive U.S. sanctions unless Beijing stopped stealing trade secrets from American high-tech companies and released over one million Uighur Muslims from the horrific concentration camps where they were now detained. What's more, they had agreed to threaten stiff new tariffs on Chinese steel and other products unless Guanzhong agreed to significantly reduce trade barriers and open more sectors of the Chinese economy to U.S. businesses.

Yet now, in a single stroke, the Asian autocrat seemed poised to turn the tables. And to McDermott's astonishment, Hernandez seemed ready to let him.

22

Marcus had tried to rest, but sleep simply would not come.

Now, in the dead of night, with the cabin lights off, Marcus shifted in his seat, desperately awaiting word from Noah Daniels about any actionable intelligence he may have gleaned from the laptops and mobile phones they'd scooped up in Karachi. But so far, as their unmarked G5 business jet sliced across the atmosphere at forty thousand feet back to Washington, Noah had nothing for him.

As Marcus tried to be patient, he also tried to imagine what he could possibly say to Jenny Morris's parents to console them. After all, Jenny's entire family still believed she worked for the Department of Commerce. They had no idea what she really did for a living. They certainly didn't have any inkling that she worked for the Central Intelligence Agency, much less its Clandestine Service. Nor was he authorized to tell them.

What, then, *was* he supposed to say?

In the absence of answers, his thoughts drifted to other pressing matters. Like a wedding plan—or, more precisely, the lack thereof. He and Annie had promised President Hernandez that they would remain at the Agency until Abu Nakba had been captured or killed, preferably the latter, though the administration's lawyers were pressing strenuously for the former. For the first few months of the Hernandez administration, Marcus had been certain that Abu Nakba's fate would be decided quickly. That's precisely why he'd been telling Annie they should wait to get married until the job was done, the ink on their resignation letters was dry, and they could truly get serious about starting a brand-new life together, far from Washington and ideally well off the grid. But after eight exhausting and fruitless months, the Libyan was still in the wind.

All of Marcus's hopes were now pinned on Noah. If the young man could find something—anything—specific and actionable on those devices, they might have another chance. If not, what was he supposed to tell the president? What was he supposed to tell Annie? How could they keep postponing their wedding? And yet, how could they set a date and send out invitations, knowing that a new piece of intel could take him halfway around the world at a moment's notice and ruin all their elaborate and expensive plans?

This would be his second wedding, after all, and he would be content to just have family and a few of their friends present. But this was Annie's first, and hopefully her only, and she had good reasons for wanting it to be a grand affair. For one thing, she and Marcus had hundreds of friends and colleagues who cared deeply about them and would genuinely—and understandably—feel hurt if they were not invited to a ceremony. Why alienate people who had been so kind and so dear to them over so many years?

Annie had also argued that she did not think it wise to get married "in the shadows." Since human marriage, flawed though it may be, was supposed to be an earthly symbol of Christ's eternal love for the Church, was it right to treat their own day as anything other than a great celebration of God's love and mercy on them both? If they were wretchedly poor, then there would be no expectation of anything other than a modest celebration. But though they were not exactly rich, they certainly were not rubbing their pennies together. If a wedding was a celebration of the God who had made them and brought them together, then why not celebrate?

The case was compelling, Marcus had readily agreed. What's more, though he had not articulated as much to Annie, in his heart Marcus knew that he needed a "real" wedding, not a quick trip to the courthouse or a few words from their pastor in his mother's living room. Marcus sensed he needed to say to Annie—and to all his friends—that he was truly turning the page on his past life with Elena, wonderful though it had been, and making a full and wholehearted commitment to Annie. He sensed he needed to say his vows not just before the Lord but before all of their friends, and the simple truth was that involved a lot of people.

This was precisely why Marcus was hesitant to finalize their wedding plans and set a date. Not because he didn't take their nuptials seriously but because he did. Marcus didn't fear having a big wedding. He feared postponing it, possibly multiple times, and thus disappointing—or worse, embarrassing—Annie.

How could they move forward with planning the most important day of their lives when they were engulfed in the most dangerous and exhausting mission of their lives? Nothing Marcus had ever done had been this excruciating. Not his multiple combat tours in Afghanistan or even Iraq. Not his time in the Secret Service field offices or on the Presidential Protective Detail. Yes, most of the missions he'd led since joining the CIA had put him in harm's way. But nothing like this. And the pace was unsustainable. It was wreaking havoc on his body, on his relationship with Annie, and even on his soul. But with everything he now knew—especially having seen just a glimpse of the fresh horrors Abu Nakba was planning to unleash on the American people—he couldn't possibly walk away from the mission.

Marcus stared out the window into the icy darkness. The death count around him kept climbing. Jenny Morris was just the latest on a long and growing list of close friends he'd lost, and by far the most painful, at least since Nick Vinetti had been KIA in Tanchon, North Korea. And what angered him most was that Jenny had been shot in the back by a Kairos operative that none of his team knew was still in the warehouse. How was such sheer negligence even possible? It certainly wasn't forgivable. After so long in the field without a break, they were making mistakes. Costly, fatal mistakes. And now the very member of the team that Marcus trusted most—the one he was planning to turn over the reins to the moment he retired—was dead.

Suddenly Marcus felt a tap on his arm. Opening his bloodshot eyes, he found Noah Daniels standing over him with a satellite phone in his hands.

"Please, Noah," he whispered in the darkness, "tell me you have good news."

23

"I'm afraid not, sir—not yet," Noah whispered. "But Langley is on the line."

Disappointed, Marcus nodded and took the phone. Of course it was Langley, he told himself, though he had no idea what to tell them.

No doubt Martha Dell, the newly appointed director of the Central Intelligence Agency, was calling to scream at him, demanding to know what had gone wrong. The problem was, he didn't know. He had no second thoughts about blowing up the Kairos death factory or the warehouse above it. But how could he have possibly foreseen that the controlled explosions would cause the LNG storage facility to detonate as well? He and his team had spent their first hour on the plane racking their brains, trying desperately to figure out exactly what had happened and why. But they had no answers. They didn't even have a credible theory.

Marcus took the phone from Noah and glanced around the cabin. As his eyes adjusted to the darkness, he saw Pete fast asleep. And Kailea. Everyone except Noah, in fact. He envied them.

Unbuckling his seat belt, he rose and headed to the back of the plane. He passed through the galley and stepped into the medical suite at the rear of the fuselage, then shut and locked the door behind him.

"Ryker," he said finally, keeping his voice low and bracing for impact.

But it wasn't Dell on the other end of the line.

It was Annie.

"Hey," said his fiancée, her voice soft and tender.

"Hey," he said, relief flooding his system.

"You okay?" she asked.

"Honestly? No," he confessed, his voice nearly cracking under the intensity of the emotions trying once again to force their way to the surface.

"This is not your fault, Marcus."

"Then *whose*, Annie? Two dozen innocent people on that pier are dead. And so is Jenny. How am I supposed to—?"

But Annie cut him off. "Marcus, listen to me—*listen*," she insisted. "Their blood—Jenny's blood—is on Abu Nakba's hands, not yours."

"Is that what I'm supposed to say to her parents, her siblings?"

"Well, first of all, you're not going to say anything to them."

"What are you talking about? I need to tell them something."

"No, you don't. They have no idea who you are, and now is certainly not the time to introduce yourself."

"Annie, you don't understand—" Marcus protested.

But again she cut him off.

"No, Marcus, *you* don't understand. This isn't negotiable. You *weren't* in Pakistan. Neither was Jenny. She died yesterday in a five-car pileup in Switzerland on the way to a ski vacation with friends from work."

"*What?*"

"Listen to me—she died instantly. Never felt a thing. And now she's home in heaven with Jesus. Safe forever. No more pain. No more tears. No more suffering. Her friends survived, but they're badly wounded and still in the hospital near Zurich. That's the story her family was told. That's what the press release says."

"Press release?"

"Commerce just emailed and texted it to reporters less than ten minutes ago," Annie explained. "The memorial service is on Saturday in her hometown of Wilkes-Barre. Closed casket. No press. Just family and friends. The undersecretary from Commerce is heading up there tomorrow. He'll deliver remarks and pay respects to the family. A dozen or so Agency folks whose cover is also at Commerce will attend, as will the former charge d'affaires from our embassy in Moscow. But you are *not* going to be among them."

"I have to go," Marcus insisted.

"Absolutely not."

"Says who?" asked Marcus, his emotions suddenly shifting from grief to irritation and bordering dangerously close to anger.

"Says me," Annie said bluntly. "Look, I get it—I'm your fiancée. But here at Langley, I'm your boss, and I'm telling you to forget about it. If pushed, POTUS will forbid you to go. So will Dell. So don't press it, Marcus. I know you'd love to go rogue and drive up to the Keystone State so you can pay your respects to one of the most impressive clandestine officers—and kindest and most loyal friends—that you've ever had. I'd love to go with you. I loved Jenny too. But that's not going to happen. It *can't.* For the safety of Jenny's family and friends, it just can't, and you know it. So stop thinking about it, and stay focused on the mission at hand."

Marcus said nothing. He knew she was right. But it all felt wrong.

Wisely, Annie stayed silent for a bit, letting him absorb his new reality. Then, finally, she asked how his team was holding up.

"They're numb," he replied. "Most are asleep right now—I think their circuit breakers just blew."

"And you? Are you getting any rest at all?"

Marcus checked his watch. It was 5:43 a.m. in Washington. They'd be wheels down in less than half an hour.

"Not really."

"Well, try," Annie advised him. "You need to be on your A game when you land. Forget the snowstorm, Marcus; you're heading into a firestorm."

"That bad?"

"Let me put it like this: Martha wanted to call you and read you the riot act. I was able to talk her out of it, saying it might be more effective coming from me. But make no mistake. Martha's livid, and that's nothing compared to the president."

Marcus closed his eyes and took a deep breath.

"Can you meet me at Andrews?" he asked after a pause, thinking but not saying how much he wanted to hold her and be held.

"I wish I could, but no."

"Why not?"

"You're no longer coming to Langley to debrief Martha and me—that's off. Now you're briefing the president and the entire NSC."

Marcus's stomach tensed.

"When you touch down at Andrews, you'll send your team to Langley, but I've sent a car and driver to pick you up," Annie continued. "You'll be taken straight to the White House. Martha and I will meet you there. We're scheduled to meet with the NSC in the Sit Room at seven a.m. sharp. And you'd better come bearing gifts because the president is angling to tear your head off."

24

They were late.

It was now 6:29 in the morning, and their G5 had only just touched down at Andrews, slowed by the massive weather system over the National Capital Region. It certainly wasn't Marcus's fault, but he knew full well this was only going to pour gasoline onto the president's growing fire.

While the snowstorm had subsided somewhat, it was far from over. There was no way they were going to make it to the Situation Room on time. Typically, it took a mere thirty-three minutes to get to the White House from Andrews. The problem was neither the Maryland nor D.C. governments handled snow removal as efficiently as Monument, Colorado Springs, Denver, and the rest of the Front Range, where Marcus had grown up. So even though traffic wasn't going to be an issue—all nonessential government employees were going to be staying home, as would most private-sector employees—the treacherous road conditions resulting from not enough plows, salt trucks, or willpower would be.

As the G5 rolled to a complete stop and the seat belt light turned off, Marcus spotted a black government-issue Suburban waiting for him. He tensed, know-ing he'd be lucky to get to the White House complex by seven thirty—if that—and even then, he'd still have to clear security and be escorted inside.

"Tell me you found something," he said to Noah as he bolted out of his seat.

"Actually, I did," said Noah, his eyes bloodshot, his hair disheveled. He handed Marcus a thumb drive and began to explain what was on it.

"No time, Noah—call me on a secure line and walk me through it," Marcus said, shoving the thumb drive in his pocket, grabbing his leather briefcase from the overhead compartment, and heading for the door. "I'm on my way to the White House to brief POTUS. I'll meet you guys at Langley in a few hours. Pete, make sure to grab my luggage, okay?"

"Of course, but don't worry about us—*go*," Pete insisted, pushing his best friend down the aisle and out the door.

Marcus hustled down the snow-covered airstairs and raced across the tar-mac to the waiting Suburban. Climbing into the backseat and slamming the door behind him, he ordered the driver to floor it. Then he powered up his phone and began downloading his emails and text messages.

The first five texts were from his mother. She was worried about him, hav-ing not heard from him for nearly a week. Marcus winced. There was no way he could have told her about the mission in Karachi, but in his haste, he'd forgotten even to give her a cover story. He knew he should have at least asked Annie to talk to her and couldn't believe he'd been so unthoughtful as to let this drop. Marjorie Ryker, after all, was not the same since the attack in Chicago. The inju-ries she'd sustained hadn't been life-threatening, but the attack on Soldier Field had rattled her. She'd been much slower to recover physically than anyone had expected, and it was clear to everyone in the family that emotionally she was not yet back to her old self.

This was going to take more than a phone call. Marcus had to go see her. Tonight. For now, however, he was going to have to make do with a quick text message.

Mom—I'm so, so sorry for not being in touch. I had to make a sudden and unexpected trip overseas. Just landed. All safe. Don't be worried. But please forgive me! I need to go into the office for much of the day. But how about dinner tonight? Are you free?

It wasn't going to be enough. But it was all he could do just now, and he had to pray it could buy him a good eight to ten hours.

The next text that caught his eye was from Annie.

A gentle answer turns away wrath, she wrote, citing Proverbs 15:1. I've been thinking about this since we hung up. When you get here, start with an apology. Do it right up front. The president isn't going to hear anything else until you admit that things went terribly wrong. Once you've taken your lumps, they'll want to know exactly what happened and what you learned. Be honest, but whatever you do, don't be defensive. You're skating on very thin ice right now. I'm not saying it's fair. I'm just telling you it's true. Tread carefully, my love, and know that I'm your biggest fan and greatest ally in that room and I'll be praying for you nonstop.

25

MOSCOW, RUSSIA

It was nearly 2 p.m. local time when the special Air China flight touched down.

All commercial and private traffic at Vnukovo Andrei Tupolev International Airport had been halted, and security was airtight as the blue-and-white-striped Boeing 747-400 taxied to the VIP terminal. When Chinese president Chen Guanzhong stepped off the jumbo jet, he was greeted warmly by Russian president Mikhail Borisovich Petrovsky, flanked by a full Russian honor guard.

It was snowing, but rather lightly for a Moscow winter. After embracing, the two men stood at attention as a military band played the national anthems of both countries. Then they walked side by side along a freshly broomed red carpet to review the troops before stepping into Petrovsky's bulletproof limousine. As the lengthy motorcade sped into the center of Moscow on the seventeen-mile journey to the Kremlin, they made small talk and chatted amiably about their wives and children and plans for their summer vacations. It was not until they were alone, sipping piping hot chai in Petrovsky's office, that they got down to business.

"I must ask you, General Secretary, how was your summit in Washington with President Hernandez?" Petrovsky asked.

"A bit frosty at first, but eventually, you might say, we broke the ice," the Communist leader began with a meager attempt at some humor. "You know better than I do that Hernandez hasn't the charisma of his predecessor. Though I had many disagreements with President Clarke, I always found him a charming interlocutor. Carlos Hernandez could not be more different."

"Too blunt, too direct?" asked Petrovsky.

"Too American," Guanzhong replied.

"Well, the man is not exactly inclined toward nuance or subtlety," Petrovsky agreed. "My only meeting with Hernandez was a disaster."

"How so?"

"Between us, the CIA had uncovered a series of wire transfers amounting to tens of millions of dollars that my predecessor, Aleksandr Luganov, had funneled to Abu Nakba and his band of Kairos lunatics—wholly without my knowledge, of course."

"The work of Dmitri Nimkov, no doubt."

"Well, Dmitri and his minions at the FSB certainly handled all the wire transfers to Kairos, but make no mistake, the operation was all Luganov from the start."

"How can you be so sure?"

"Because Dmitri Nimkov never had an original idea in his life. Believe me, Luganov was the mastermind."

"To what end?"

"I can only assume it was to spill American blood all over the world out of revenge for years of American humiliations of our people."

"Without any of it being traced back to the Kremlin, of course."

"Of course, but it was a colossally foolish idea from the start, though hardly the only one Aleksandr Ivanovich ever had."

"You refer, I suspect, to his plan to invade the Baltics?" asked the Chinese president.

"We pleaded with Luganov not to pursue it," Petrovsky said. "One of my generals told him—at my insistence—'Mr. President, would it not be in our interest to seize Ukraine instead of the Baltics? After all, the Ukrainians are not members of NATO. Washington and Brussels will huff and puff, but in the end, they will do nothing if we take Ukraine. I have war-gamed this with my staff. I'm convinced we could be in control of Kiev in less than a month, if that.'"

"How did Luganov respond?"

"He shouted, '*I want Ukraine—all of it, and I shall have it—but we can also seize the Baltics in four days, and we must.*' I was floored. We all were. We said, 'Mr. President, with respect, how is it in Russia's interest to provoke such a confrontation with Estonia, Latvia, and Lithuania—all of whom are NATO members—when Ukraine is ours for the taking with no risk of triggering Article Five of the NATO charter?'"

"And?"

"And he started raving about 'restoring the glory of Mother Russia, no matter the cost, no matter how many Russians must suffer and die.' I tell you the truth, every general in that room came to believe—and you may think that I am exaggerating, but I assure you I am not—that the man had become certifiably crazy. Had he not been assassinated, I have no doubt he would have set into motion Armageddon."

The Chinese official raised an eyebrow.

"To be clear, I didn't lift a hand against the president," Petrovsky was quick to add. "Nor would I."

"Of course not."

"It was that boy."

"Kraskin?"

"Exactly. Oleg Kraskin. But at the time, who could have imagined that President Luganov's own son-in-law—someone married to his beloved daughter, Marina, someone the president loved and trusted more than anyone else in Moscow—could have done something so vile?"

"But Kraskin did not act alone, did he?"

"We don't think so, no."

"You think an American was involved."

"Well, we thought so, yes."

"Past tense?" Guanzhong asked, staring into his chai.

"No, no, we still think so; we just haven't been able to prove it," said Petrovsky. "Our prime suspect certainly had the skill set for it. Former Marine.

Former Secret Service agent. Now supposedly works for some State Department bureau, but we believe he really works for the CIA."

Guanzhong looked up. "You speak of Marcus Ryker, no?"

Petrovsky was stunned to hear Guanzhong say the name. "You know of this man?"

"Yes, we know him," said Guanzhong.

"How?"

"Well, we know his CV, his backstory, the murder of his wife and son. Beyond that, I'm afraid things get cloudy."

"They certainly do," Petrovsky noted.

"But you're right," said the Chinese president. "Ryker certainly fits the profile of someone who could have assisted Oleg Kraskin."

"He does," said Petrovsky. "What's more, we know Ryker was in Moscow a week or so before the assassination. He came on a Co-Del with then-Senator Dayton. They even met privately with Luganov. And we believe Ryker had the opportunity to meet privately with Kraskin later that night. But we were never able to prove Ryker's complicity. It was all circumstantial."

"And I'm sure the Americans had answers for everything," said Guanzhong.

"They certainly did," Petrovsky confirmed. "The bigger problem, though, was that when I took power, neither President Clarke nor then–Vice President Hernandez was interested in our accusations. Nor did they believe my strenuous protestations that the Red Army's plans to invade Ukraine and the Baltics were Luganov's, not mine. To the Americans, I was Russia's defense minister, so I had to be marching in lockstep with Luganov. They had no idea how profoundly I disagreed with him, that I viewed him as a madman. They believed I was preparing Russian forces to invade NATO and was more than happy to risk all-out thermonuclear war to recapture not simply territory but 'the glory of Mother Russia.' All that—combined with the Kairos attacks in Chicago and the fresh intel from the CIA that Luganov had bankrolled Kairos in its earliest days—well, it all created a highly volatile environment, especially when Hernandez emerged as president. From the moment Clarke had his stroke—if it *was* a stroke—and Hernandez took power and entered the Oval Office, he was fit to be tied. In our first phone call, Hernandez screamed at me—literally screamed—saying that if I dared raise a finger against him or the American people, he was going to single-handedly bring the Russian economy to a screeching halt, welcome Ukraine into NATO, put American nuclear missiles on Ukrainian territory—each of them aimed at Moscow—and mobilize the combined military forces of the U.S. and all of NATO for war with the Kremlin."

"Why didn't you call his bluff?" asked Guanzhong.

"*How?* At the time, I was desperately trying to solidify my authority in Moscow, not provoke a new confrontation with Washington."

"You could have turned to me," Guanzhong said. "Beijing would have stood squarely with our longtime friend and ally."

"That is most kind," said Petrovsky, looking deflated and fatigued. "But I could not take the chance. I genuinely believed Hernandez was itching to go to war."

"With you?"

"With anyone. You saw what happened in Chicago. His people had just suffered the worst terror attacks since 9/11. Clarke had just become incapacitated. There were rampant rumors in the American and European media that Clarke had been poisoned. And to me, Hernandez seemed consumed by bloodlust. His first act as commander in chief was to put all U.S. forces—including America's nuclear forces—at DEFCON Two. And don't forget, he had a smoking gun."

"Meaning?"

"Meaning he had, as I said, incontrovertible proof that Luganov had given Abu Nakba tens of millions of dollars. I'd never heard of such a thing until Hernandez leveled his accusations. Luganov certainly never consulted me about any of that. But as I looked into it, every accusation proved true. When my team and I combed through the records at the FSB, we found the bank accounts, the wire transfers. Sure enough, Luganov had sent Kairos a total of $57 million over the course of several years, all to build a private terrorist army that he could control but that couldn't be traced back to him."

"And Hernandez blindsided you with that?"

"The evidence was damning. And he could not have been clearer: if he declassified this intelligence and released it to the American public, the war drums would be deafening, and the United States and Russia would soon be at war."

"But he didn't release it," Guanzhong said.

"No, that was his one olive branch to me," Petrovsky explained. "Hernandez told me that he planned to declare war on Kairos and train all of America's attention on hunting down and destroying Abu Nakba and the entire Kairos operation. He said he would also impose 'crippling sanctions' on Russia, but he would not expose the Kremlin's involvement with Kairos—not yet, anyway. Instead, he would say that the sanctions on us were in response to all the arms and nuclear technology that Luganov was selling to the Iranians, and Luganov's refusal to get Tehran to back off its nuclear ambitions and the Supreme Leader's threats to eradicate the U.S. and Israel from the map."

"But if you crossed him, he would expose the Kremlin's involvement in Kairos?"

"Exactly, and I could not afford that."

"I must say, I did not realize that the U.S. sanctions had affected you so severely," said Guanzhong. "I thought you were weathering the storm."

"Well, I apologize for not being more forthcoming," Petrovsky replied. "We've been able to maintain this facade because we expelled almost every foreign journalist who had been operating inside Russia. And because we're feeding doctored economic reports to the few journalists who remain and to the foreign diplomatic corps. But I asked you to come see me because our position continues to worsen."

Guanzhong took another sip of tea.

"I'm glad that you did, Mikhail Borisovich, and your timing is impeccable. China would be more than happy to help our dear neighbor. But there is something I will need from you in exchange."

26

Petrovsky suggested they continue their conversation at his private dacha.

When Guanzhong agreed, Petrovsky picked up the phone on the end table next to him and spoke to his military aide. The two men then donned their winter coats, gloves, hats, and scarves, and followed their security details outside. Waiting for them amid the whipping winds and driving snow were three identical military helicopters, all spooling up their engines. Petrovsky and Guanzhong climbed into the middle chopper, while their bodyguards and aides climbed into the other two. Soon they were in the air, in a rotating flight pattern designed to make it impossible for any would-be attacker to know which helicopter the principals were actually in.

En route, the two men eschewed any talk of business or geopolitics. Instead, they reveled in their mutual love for painting, for horses, for their grandchildren. Upon landing at the Russian presidential palace known as Novo-Ogaryovo, they were rushed inside, out of the subzero temperatures to which Petrovsky was accustomed but Guanzhong was not.

As they snaked through several hallways, security was tight. Members of Petrovsky's protective detail were stationed every ten meters or so. Outside, sharpshooters in arctic combat wear were visible on the roofs of the outbuildings. Petrovsky led his esteemed guest through a thick, steel-reinforced door into a short, carpeted hallway, and then through another steel-reinforced door, until they arrived in his private study. None of their bodyguards were allowed into this inner sanctum of solace. Nor was Petrovsky's wife present, though the savory aroma of the sumptuous beef stroganoff that she had prepared greeted them even before the sight of it.

Petrovsky took his place in an overstuffed chair while Guanzhong sat down opposite him in a matching chair. Between them was a small mahogany dining table, covered in a crisp white linen tablecloth. Before them lay exquisitely painted plates and dishes dating back to the era of the czars, along with crystal goblets, gold flatware, and freshly starched white linen napkins.

As Petrovksy uncovered various dishes and served the meal, Guanzhong surveyed the room, its walls lined with books of every kind, from esteemed Russian literature to military histories and biographies of great leaders to both American and European novels, as well as works of Chinese and other Asian history. There was a roaring fire in the stone fireplace. There was also a full bottle of Stolichnaya, which Petrovsky opened posthaste, pouring them both a glass, raising his, and offering a toast.

"My great-grandfather used to say, *'I have a wish to buy a house, but I have no means; I have the means to buy a goat, but I have no wish.'* So, my friend, let us drink to having all our wishes match our means!"

The Russian erupted in laughter at his own joke as the two clinked their glasses together.

Guanzhong nodded and smiled but did not laugh. Petrovsky drank his glass empty and poured another. His guest merely took a sip and politely declined a refill. As the two men ate and talked, the Russian continued to top off his glass, and in the process loosened his tie and opened his soul.

"I must tell you, my friend, that I miss Andrew Clarke," Petrovsky said at one point. "He was a wildly successful, if colorful, businessman. An impressive CEO. And, of course, later a fair-to-middling governor. True?"

Guanzhong shrugged.

"But whatever else one might say about him," Petrovsky continued, "the man knew how to read a room and turn on the charm to get what he wanted. Carlos Hernandez, on the other hand, has never worked a day in his life in the business world. He never ran for, much less won, his own political seat at any level of the American government. He's never been a chief executive. And given his heart condition, he never even got much time serving as vice president. To the contrary, Hernandez is a total creature of the American Navy. He graduated from Annapolis and rose through the ranks to be a three-star admiral. He's used to giving orders, not building consensus, much less domestic or international coalitions—and it shows."

"It does," Guanzhong agreed. "But the more time I spent with him, the more I came to believe that we can use that to our advantage."

"How so?" asked Petrovksy, reaching for the nearly empty bottle of Stolichnaya and polishing it off.

Then he flipped open a box of Cuban cigars on his desk, picked out a Cohiba, and offered it to his guest. Guanzhong thanked him but declined. Petrovsky asked if he minded. Guanzhong said he did not. So the Russian pulled a sterling silver lighter from his jacket pocket and lit up.

"The Hernandez 'brand,' if you will, is built on two key factors, and only two," Guanzhong continued. "First, he's a military man. And second, he's a Latino."

"So?"

"So Clarke didn't choose him because he understood Washington or had any experience governing. He chose Hernandez because the admiral appealed to two critically important constituencies Clarke desperately needed to win the presidency. If Hernandez had been in good health for the past few years, he could very well have been trained as an effective understudy. The American people—not to mention world leaders—may have come to regard him as more than America's top naval commander in the Pacific. Hernandez could have genuinely helped Clarke pass his tax-cut bill and infrastructure spending bill and vet Supreme Court nominees, and so forth. Instead, all the American people know of Hernandez is that he is not healthy and—far more importantly—that he is a military man who has yet to bring Abu Nakba and Kairos to justice for those catastrophic attacks in Chicago last year."

"I'm sorry, but I'm not following you," said Petrovsky, continuing to puff away on the Cohiba. "What's your point?"

"My point is that the Americans are tired of fighting," said Guanzhong. "Not just tired. They're exhausted. They live in a bitterly divided country. They're torn apart over all kinds of red-hot issues that mean nothing to you and me but seem to matter a great deal in the U.S., everything from abortion and so-called 'transgender issues' to something called Black Lives Matter and critical race theory, and of course, rampant illegal immigration. Add to all those the real issues like soaring inflation, rising gas prices, and an economy headed into recession, and I think it's fair to say that the last thing the American people want, or think they can afford, is another war."

"With respect, comrade, I have to disagree with your analysis," Petrovsky said bluntly. "The more Kairos terrorists the CIA have captured or killed—and they have taken down an awful lot—the more we have seen Hernandez's poll numbers climb. Have you seen the latest *Washington Post*, just out this morning?"

The Chinese president shook his head.

"It puts Hernandez's approval rating at fifty-eight percent, his disapproval rating at a mere thirty-six percent, with only six percent undecided," Petrovsky explained. "From where I sit, I'd have to say that Hernandez is very well positioned to run on his own merits next year and not only win but win big."

"With respect, my most valued friend, you are reading those poll numbers all wrong," the Chinese leader insisted, leaning forward in his chair.

"How so?"

"Taking out a terror cell here or there to satisfy the people's desire for vengeance after Chicago is not the same as having the moral standing to take the U.S. into another major regional war. Think about it. After decades of fighting in Afghanistan and Iraq—and the seemingly never-ending battle with radical Islamist jihadists, up to and including those attacks in Chicago—the American people have zero appetite, *zero appetite*, for going to war with your country, or mine, or going to war again in the Middle East, even if the new Supreme Leader of Iran—our old friend, Yadollah Afshar—decided tomorrow to break out and build the Persian Bomb once and for all."

For the first time since the Chinese leader had arrived in Moscow, Petrovsky became alarmed. "I don't understand. What are you trying to say?"

"I'm saying the moment we have long been waiting for has finally arrived," said Guanzhong.

"What moment?"

"Mr. President, do you really believe that the American people want to enter a land war in Asia? Do you really think they want to risk life and limb to save a tiny, meaningless little island that most of them cannot even find on a map?"

Petrovsky could not believe what he was hearing. At first, he thought Guanzhong had to be speaking of the threat posed by North Korea against their neighbors to the south. Or perhaps the dispute between Beijing and Japan over the five uninhabited Senkaku Islands located in the East China Sea. But suddenly, in an instant of bracing clarity, Petrovsky realized—or feared that he did—what his guest was really saying. *"Taiwan?"*

"What else?" Guanzhong asked. "Yes, Taiwan."

"You're going to take it?"

At this Guanzhong turned and looked the Russian president in the eye.

"I am," he said softly. "And I want your help, and your blessing."

"I'm not sure what to say," Petrovsky replied. "You said earlier that you weren't aware how hard the American sanctions have hit our economy. By the same token, I must say my people haven't seen you make any obvious preparations for war."

"That's because they have not been obvious," Guanzhong conceded. "During COVID, with almost no foreigners in our country and the world focused on their own internal affairs, we retooled many of our factories. We began stockpiling large quantities of medicines and other emergency supplies, including oil, gasoline, basic food staples, and of course, potable water. We accelerated production of precision-guided missiles, UAVs for intelligence gathering as armed drones, and other needed munitions. And we built massive underground storehouses for all these supplies, as well as subterranean transportations systems to shield movement of our most advanced weapons systems from the prying eyes of the Americans, the Taiwanese, and everyone else who might be watching. At the same time, we hardened and modernized many of our electrical power plants and the grid itself. What's more, under the guise of a national mobilization of our reserve military units to help with COVID matters, we have secretly ramped up our military manpower without drawing any significant attention."

"But when COVID ended, you demobilized all or most of those units," Petrovsky protested.

"We put out announcements to that effect and did demobilize some units, but most of that was a ruse to lull our enemies into complacency. I am happy to see it worked, though don't get me wrong—you are by no means an enemy, comrade."

"I must say you are right," Petrovsky admitted. "We've been so consumed by events here at home, we have not detected anything in the eastern sphere that suggested to us that you were preparing for war. I mean, we've certainly seen the PLA engage in various large-scale drills and exercises in and around the South China Sea, but you have done those for so long and on such a regular timetable that we have not thought them unusual, much less preparatory."

"Good," said Guanzhong. "But this is why I have come—to let you know that the invasion is coming, and soon."

"How soon?" Petrovsky asked.

"Very soon," the Chinese president assured him.

"Well, then," Petrovsky said, his mind reeling. "How can Russia help its greatest friend and ally?"

27

"*Where the hell is Ryker?*" Hernandez barked as he entered the Situation Room.

"En route, sir," said CIA director Martha Dell.

Dell started to explain that the severe weather had delayed Ryker's plane into Andrews, but Hernandez waved her off, taking his seat at the head of the large conference table and demanding that Dell and Annie Stewart—seated behind Dell, next to the White House chief of staff—walk him through the latest classified summary of all the top intelligence reporting overnight.

Joining the National Security Council meeting in person that morning were Vice President Whitney, Defense Secretary Cal Foster, Chairman of the Joint Chiefs of Staff James Meyers, and National Security Advisor Bill McDermott. Joining via secure videoconference from the U.S. consulate in Karachi were Secretary of State Robert Dayton and Energy Secretary Mickey Clawson, both of whom had just arrived in Pakistan a few hours earlier. The attorney general and the secretaries of Treasury and Homeland Security were traveling and unavailable to join the meeting.

Given the previous day's tense and complicated summit—and the state dinner with the Chinese president that followed—this was Dell's first opportunity to formally brief the council on the catastrophic events in Karachi. As everyone opened the black leather binders before them—each bearing the executive seal of the president and the words *President's Daily Brief* embossed in gold leaf—she walked her colleagues through what was known and unknown.

"Let me begin by stating unequivocally that all the headlines you're reading about 219 innocent civilians being killed in the explosions are fake news," Dell began.

"What's the real number?" asked Hernandez.

"At this point, sir, we can confirm that Ryker and his team killed twenty-three Kairos operatives," Dell replied. "In the back of the PDB, you'll see photos of each one, which were taken by Ryker's team, along with brief bios compiled by our analysts at Langley. As you know, tragically, we also lost a great case officer, Jennifer Marie Morris, one of the best operatives the Agency has ever recruited, trained, and deployed. So that's twenty-four. Beyond this, yes, unfortunately there was collateral damage. As best we can tell, another seven people—maintenance crew and night-shift security guards who were working in nearby buildings—were killed as well."

"So thirty-one people dead in total?" McDermott asked.

"That's our best assessment at this hour," Dell confirmed. "In addition, we know that another nine people were injured, two of them seriously. All are being treated at local hospitals."

"Then where are they getting this number, 219?" pressed Defense Secretary Foster, whose irritation was obvious both from his countenance and his body language. "It's being reported everywhere."

"That number is coming from an Islamic aid organization based in Islamabad," said Dell. "They put out a press release overnight, and the international media is just running with it without verification. It's a completely made-up number designed to inflame the situation—and help raise them a boatload of money."

"Well, it's certainly not helping that the Pakistani Ministry of Information and Broadcasting hasn't pushed back on the number," said the vice president.

Hernandez was visibly angry but for the moment said nothing.

Dell nodded to Annie, who lowered the lights and pointed a remote at the large monitors mounted on the walls around them. As the screens flickered to life, Annie hit Play, displaying aerial footage from CNN, the BBC, and various Pakistani news outlets showing raging fires, monstrous plumes of thick black smoke, and hazy but unmistakable images of the utter devastation on what was left of the pier. As Dell provided play-by-play coverage of what the group was watching, Annie also ran video imagery taken from the Keyhole satellite and the two surveillance drones that had been monitoring the operation from the beginning.

"Martha, I still don't understand how in the world any of this could have happened," Hernandez said when the footage ended and Annie brought the lights back up. "You assured me that this operation would be a surgical strike. This is anything but."

"That's what Ryker assured me, and I apologize for that," Dell replied, shifting in her seat. "At the moment, I can't tell you why Ryker ordered the warehouse to be blown up. That was never part of the plan. Nor can I tell you why Ryker and his team used so many explosives. I'm sure we'll find out in a moment. But something else was being stored in the warehouse that, when detonated, exponentially magnified the effect of the initial explosions, and did so with such force that it ruptured one or more of the LNG fuel lines, causing the whole pier to be wiped out."

"For crying out loud, it looks like Hiroshima or Nagasaki," Hernandez fumed.

That was a bit of hyperbole, but Dell held her tongue.

"And there I am yesterday, lying through my teeth to the head of Communist China that I haven't got the foggiest clue who could be responsible for any of this," Hernandez continued. "Do you get how wildly all this has thrown off our game plan with Beijing? I was supposed to lower the boom on their massive trade violations and rampant and brazen theft of American intellectual property. Instead, I found myself signing a joint MOU on how we're going to work together to combat terrorism."

Annie cringed as the commander in chief pounded the table and declared the Agency's mission "a disaster on every conceivable level." But she was even more upset that Dell seemed to be distancing herself from Marcus. And it got worse from there.

Secretary of State Dayton—previously Annie's boss on the Senate Intelligence Committee before coming to work for the Hernandez administration—weighed in from the U.S. consulate in Karachi on the heated meeting he'd just finished with his Pakistani counterpart. The foreign minister, Dayton said, was demanding that Washington triple their financial assistance or get out of the country.

"What are you saying, Robert?" asked Hernandez. "Do you think they suspect we're behind all this?"

"No, Mr. President," Dayton responded. "They don't *suspect* it. The foreign minister all but *accused* us of it."

"What did you tell him?"

"That Pakistan is an important ally and friend of the United States and there is no conceivable reason that we would blow up a port facility so vital to their economy and national sovereignty."

"Did he buy it?"

"I don't think so."

"Did you press him on why he thinks it's us?"

"Of course."

"And?"

"He wouldn't answer directly," said Dayton. "But it was clear they're fully expecting to be able to extract a great deal of money out of us as compensation."

This last point generated intense debate around the table for the next several minutes about just how much to give Pakistan in order to—as Vice President Whitney put it—"appear more helpful and compassionate than the Chinese to a world that's watching this very closely," and frankly, "to keep Islamabad's mouth shut."

"Or they could be bluffing," Annie said, almost under her breath.

Suddenly, President Hernandez's head whipped around.

"Miss Stewart?"

"Yes, sir."

"Did you just say something?"

28

Annie swallowed hard.

It was not her place to speak in a principals' meeting. She was experienced enough to know that she was only a deputy. Then again, she hadn't meant to say anything aloud, much less for her comment to be overheard. But she'd been caught, and with every eye on her—including Dell's—the president asked again.

"Miss Stewart, would you care to repeat yourself?"

A massive influx of adrenaline shot through her system. Annie's heart was racing. Her mouth was dry. But she didn't dare ask for a drink of water.

"My apologies, Mr. President," Annie said, leaning forward in her chair. "I'm just wondering if this discussion about how much to give Pakistan is premature."

"*Because . . . ?*" Hernandez pressed, his voice thick with sarcasm.

"Because they don't have any hard evidence that we were involved," Annie replied, trying to keep her voice calm and firm.

Even Dell was staring daggers at her. But there was no point backing off now, so Annie continued.

"Sir, with respect, I'm just saying that we know for certain that there is no

CCTV footage of anything that happened on the pier," Annie explained. "One of our operatives disabled the security system the moment he took over the guard station at the front gate. Given the intensity of the explosions, we also know that there is no way for the Pakistanis to have recovered any DNA evidence from our fallen officer. Nor could they have recovered, much less been able to analyze, any spent rounds from our teams. And our people were using the most advanced encryption technology on the planet in their on-the-ground radio transmissions. We can be certain the Pakistanis didn't intercept any of it. So what's left? What kind of hard, real, conclusive evidence could they possibly have?"

The room was quiet.

"Isn't it possible that Islamabad is making a series of assumptions and hoping we'll incriminate ourselves?" Annie asked.

"Deputy Director Stewart, I know you're rather new to the Agency and the NSC, but aren't you forgetting a key piece of the story?" asked the president. "If the Pakistanis knew that Abu Nakba was there, then we're the most likely suspects to come after him, right? And we know for certain that a high-ranking Pakistani official was visiting the warehouse just minutes before the team arrived, correct?"

Hernandez turned to Dell, who confirmed that was true but quickly added that the CIA still had not identified the official.

"Nevertheless," said Hernandez, "don't we have to assume that whoever that official was, he informed his superiors in Islamabad that Abu Nakba was not only on their sovereign soil but in that specific warehouse?"

"Perhaps, but this is exactly my point, Mr. President," Annie explained. "Neither you nor Secretary Dayton should be on the defensive. To the contrary, you should be going on offense."

"Meaning what?"

"Meaning we have the moral high ground here, not them. We're not harboring the world's most wanted and deadly terrorist. They are. Secretary Dayton should be asking the Pakistani leadership, '*Why would terrorist groups from India or the Middle East or North Africa or anywhere else have been interested in that warehouse? Who or what was in that building? And what exactly was being stored there to cause such a massive explosion? And even if there were two small truck bombs, how could these have wrought such extensive damage?*' My point, sir, is that we shouldn't offer a dime in additional aid or assistance until we get answers. I say we press them—hard and in private, but really hard. They're hiding something. That much is certain. So let's make them tell us what they know."

"But again, Miss Stewart, if Islamabad knew that Abu Nakba was in that warehouse, then aren't we the most likely suspects?"

"If they knew Abu Nakba was in that warehouse, then they're the ones who need to explain themselves, not us. And let's remember, Mr. President, we're not the only ones hunting down the Libyan. So is the Mossad. So is MI6. So are the Emiratis and the Saudis. But more to the point, sir, if the Pakistanis at the highest levels of their government knew that Abu Nakba was hiding out in their country, then why didn't they arrest him? Why aren't they handing him over to us at this very minute? Are they our ally in the war on terror or not?"

Suddenly, a phone rang.

McDermott answered it.

"Hold one," the national security advisor said, then turned to Hernandez. "Mr. President, he's here."

"About time." The president sniffed. "Send him in."

McDermott relayed the message and hung up the phone. Annie could see the tension in his eyes. As she scanned the faces of the VP, the SecDef, the chairman of the Joint Chiefs, and the others around the table—POTUS included—there certainly didn't appear to be a single ally of Marcus in the room, though she hoped Secretary Dayton still had a soft spot in his heart for the man who had saved his life and hers back in Afghanistan a million years ago.

A Marine guard opened the heavy steel door, and Marcus entered.

Only Annie was glad to see him. On the outside, she kept her composure. But inside, her heart was suddenly racing.

Though she'd never told anyone but him, and only since they'd become engaged, Annie had had a crush on Marcus since the moment she'd first met him. Ever since she'd looked into those eyes on that tarmac in Kabul, back in the days when he was still single, back before Marcus had married Elena, before he'd become a father, before he'd suffered so much loss. It still astonished her that they'd been friends for so long. It astonished her even more that the very man she had deeply admired and respected for years had ever asked her out on a date. Much less asked her to marry him.

Still, being engaged to Marcus Ryker had proven the most difficult and painful thing Annie had ever experienced. She couldn't love him any more than she did. But with his every new brush with death, fear spiked within her again that they would never get married. No matter how glad she was that he was alive and safely home, the sight of him now was completely jarring and brought all those tightly held fears surging right back to the fore.

After all, Marcus wasn't wearing a suit and tie. Nor was he wearing utilities or even casual clothes. Rather, he was still dressed in what he'd worn into combat.

And he was covered in blood.

29

It suddenly hit Annie—Marcus was covered in Jenny's blood.

He hadn't showered before coming to the White House. Nor had he shaved. And he looked as drained as he was disheveled.

Annie's first instinct was to worry that the members of the NSC would see all this as a sign of disrespect. But as she watched the room react to her fiancé's appearance, Annie realized Marcus had intentionally come to the Situation Room like this. It was a huge risk, and yet he seemed to know what he was doing, for as she scanned the stunned expressions of the principals around the table, she sensed his appearance was already having its desired effect.

Marcus stopped before the president, stood ramrod straight, and saluted.

Hernandez was aghast. Looking Marcus up and down, the president finally said, "At ease," then motioned Marcus to take a seat at the far end of the table, next to Bill McDermott.

Marcus complied, walking down to his old Marine commander and nodding but saying nothing. As he took his seat, Annie caught his eye. He nodded at her as well. He couldn't really do more in this situation. Nor did Annie expect more.

But his attention—particularly in this room and with so much at stake—meant more to her than she could possibly let on just then.

"We couldn't be more devastated about the death of Miss Morris," President Hernandez began as he called the NSC meeting to order. "She was a fine officer."

"The best I've ever worked with, sir," Marcus replied as he poured himself some water, drank down the entire glass, and then refilled it.

"At the appropriate time we will honor her with a star on the wall of fallen officers at Langley," Hernandez continued.

Marcus nodded but did not comment.

"But I have to say, Ryker, I am—to be perfectly frank—disappointed."

Annie glanced back at Marcus. She silently prayed that he would hold his tongue, though she feared this was not one of his strong suits.

"Let me be crystal clear: after all the savagery that Kairos wrought in Chicago—the attacks on Willis Tower, on Soldier Field, on the pope, on me, the slaughter of so many Americans, and so many more injured—the American people want justice. They want Kairos wiped off the face of the earth. They want Abu Nakba to pay for what he's done. They want his head on a platter, as do I. And you'll recall, Agent Ryker, that in the midst of our bitter national grief and mourning, I addressed the American people from the Oval Office the very evening of the attacks and promised the living and the dead that I would not rest until we had our vengeance. Then, behind closed doors, I put you in charge of making that happen. There were some who wanted *your* head on a platter. But I didn't fire you, Mr. Ryker. Nor did I demote you. To the contrary, I promoted you. In fact, I gave you carte blanche to destroy Kairos once and for all. I promised you'd have whatever you needed to get the job done. Manpower. Money. Materiel. The full resources of the U.S. government. The active assistance of America's allies. You name it. It was all yours."

The president paused for a moment, as if to let the gravity of his words sink in.

"But for all the trust I placed in you, what do I have to show for it?" he finally continued, fiddling with the presidential cuff links adorning his freshly starched blue and white dress shirt and its French cuffs. "True, Kairos has been somewhat denuded over the past eight months. But let's face it, Ryker, you're no closer to capturing or killing Abu Nakba today than when I put you in charge of this unit.

In fact, with this latest debacle, you've very likely driven the Libyan to ground for good. It's unlikely we'll ever pick up his trail again. And if that weren't bad enough, I now have the governments of Pakistan and China breathing down my neck. There are whispers that the U.N. Security Council is going to launch an investigation. We already have multiple ongoing investigations by the House *and* the Senate Intelligence Committees into how the disaster in Chicago happened. And now this. Are you getting the picture here, Ryker? Do you even begin to see the magnitude of the disaster you've caused by failing to accomplish the mission I gave you?"

30

Every eye shifted and was now riveted on Marcus.

Annie again silently prayed he would guard his tongue, choose his words carefully, and begin with an apology. But she got only two of the three.

"I serve at your pleasure, Mr. President," Marcus began. "Say the word and I'm fully prepared to resign immediately and quietly slip away. You'll never hear from me again. I won't be writing my memoirs. I won't be talking to *60 Minutes*. Or sitting down with the *New York Times* or the *Washington Post* for a front-page interview. I won't be selling my story to the tabloids or taking potshots at you and the administration on talk radio or prime time cable shows. That's not how I operate, Mr. President. I have always lived in the shadows, and I prefer it that way, as I believe everyone in this room—and those participating by videoconference—can attest."

As Marcus took another sip of water, Annie exhaled—that is, until Marcus cleared his throat and continued speaking.

"That said . . ." he began.

Annie braced herself for what was coming next.

Marcus set down his glass and placed his hands on the conference table, palms down.

"With respect, Mr. President, over the past eight months, my team and I have hunted down and destroyed nine previously unknown Kairos cells. We've captured or killed 104 operatives. In six different countries. On three continents. We've found and destroyed more than three and a half tons of weapons and explosives. As a result, there hasn't been a single terrorist attack on U.S. soil since Chicago. My team and I haven't taken any time off. Nor have you offered us any. We've worked seven days a week. Often sixteen to eighteen hours a day. We've given you much to report to the country. And you haven't hesitated to do so, and as a result, your poll numbers have rebounded. The majority of Americans now approve of the job that you're doing to keep the country safe. You're in a strong position to win your own first full term. And though I'm not a registered member of either political party—and have adamantly steered clear of partisan politics during my time in the Marines, through my time in the Secret Service, and right up to the present—I certainly wish you and your family much success. I pray for you every single day. If I have lost your confidence, then so be it. I wish I could tell you that we were successful in killing or capturing Abu Nakba, but I will not apologize for—nor do I regret for one minute—the Herculean efforts that my team and I have expended in the hunt."

Boom.

There it was, thought Annie.

Marcus had been measured and respectful, but he had no intention of surrendering. Nor was he finished.

"What I do deeply regret, and will forever, is the loss of such fine women and men along the way, my dear friend and colleague Jenny Morris most of all. But Jenny would be the first to tell you, Mr. President, that she had no greater honor than to lay her life down to protect the country she loves. And she would also tell you and the entire NSC without hesitation that every single member of our team is ready and more than willing to lay down our lives for our country as well. If those sacrifices and those results are not enough for you—if you believe that it's time for me to step down so that you can appoint someone else to lead this mission—you will get no resistance from me. But I categorically reject your assessment of our efforts as a *'failure,'* much less a *'disaster.'*"

The room was quiet.

While the rest of the room's attention shifted to the president, awaiting his response, Annie fixed her gaze on the man she loved and admired more than anyone she had ever met or known. True, he had not apologized like she had counseled him. But she had never been prouder of him than she was at that moment. He had kept his cool and maintained his honor. There was no question in her mind that the commander in chief was about to relieve Marcus of his post. But clearly Marcus had no regrets, and the more she thought about it, neither did she. To the contrary, she agreed with Marcus 100 percent. He *had* acquitted himself with courage and conviction. And when the president let Marcus go, she would finally breathe a huge sigh of relief. She, too, would be able to resign. Abu Nakba would be someone else's problem. They had not exactly finished their mission, but no one could accuse them of not having given it their all or having nothing to show for all their sacrifices.

"There is one more thing, Mr. President," Marcus said, handing McDermott a thumb drive. "Before you relieve me, it is my responsibility to inform you that the situation is exponentially more dangerous than any of us had feared."

31

"How so?" asked a startled president.

"Sir, we may not have captured or killed its leader, but we did gather critical intelligence of what Kairos is planning next," Marcus replied.

"Go on."

"Well, sir, it would seem they have developed a new biological weapon and are preparing to deploy it inside in the American homeland."

"What kind of weapon?"

"It's an extremely lethal virus, Mr. President, that they're calling Cerberus. It's named after the 'death demon of the dark,' the three-headed hound of Hades found in Greek mythology who was responsible for guarding the gates of the underworld and stopping tormented souls from ever escaping."

Marcus turned to McDermott, who begrudgingly uploaded the thumb drive and began to put up on the plasma screens various digital photos taken by Marcus's team.

"As best we can ascertain, sir, Cerberus is a new and extreme variant of the Ebola virus," Marcus explained. "Unfortunately, it acts much faster than Ebola.

Once a person is infected, his or her organs disintegrate—literally melt, rot, decompose, break apart—within minutes, not hours or days. The victim then begins bleeding profusely from every orifice. They die the most excruciating death imaginable."

"Is there a cure?" asked Hernandez.

"Not that I'm aware of, sir, though I haven't had time to talk to USAMRIID," Marcus replied, referring to the U.S. Army Medical Research Institute of Infectious Diseases, based at Fort Detrick in Maryland.

"And how do you know any of this?" Hernandez pressed.

"Sir, we discovered a top-secret Kairos lab several floors underneath the warehouse in Karachi," Marcus replied. "We can't be certain that's where the virus was created. But we do know that's where Abu Nakba's people were testing it."

"On animals?"

"Yes, but also on humans. If I may, I'd like to show you a video we recovered off one of the laptops in the lab. But I must warn you, this is not for the faint of heart."

The president nodded his assent. Annie intended to look away but could not. Rather, like everyone else in the room, she found herself as spellbound as she was repulsed while she watched various Pakistani migrant workers—men, women, and children, drawn and gaunt, hands and ankles bound—forced into a testing chamber by armed workers wearing hazmat suits. An aerosol mist of some sort was then released from a nozzle in the ceiling of the chamber. Soon, the eyes of the poor souls were bleeding out. The shrieking was inhuman. The people writhed in sheer agony as they began to bleed from every part of their bodies and their bowels erupted.

"All right, all right, I've seen enough," said Hernandez, ordering McDermott to stop the video and bring the lights back up. "You're absolutely certain, Ryker, that this is Kairos's next move?"

"That's what the evidence indicates, Mr. President," Marcus replied. "According to the memos, emails, text messages, and videos that my team has been able to review so far, Abu Nakba has for the last six months been directing what's left of his Kairos operation not only to develop the highly lethal Cerberus virus but to experiment with a range of methods to weaponize it. It's not clear to us yet that they have settled on the method. But from what we've been able to glean so far, it would appear they hope to use the virus to unleash a massive and devastating strike inside the United States soon."

"How soon?" Hernandez demanded.

"Their target date seems to be July fourth," said Marcus. "But now that we've raided their facility and discovered what they're planning, we have to consider the possibility that Abu Nakba will move up that date and order the strike much sooner."

Annie found herself scanning the room and trying to assess what each principal was thinking. One thing was clear: everyone on the NSC was coming to grips with the magnitude of the threat and the stakes of not getting out in front of this and neutralizing the threat before Kairos could act. Annie was also struck by the fact that all color had drained from the president's face. He was no longer seething mad. Now he was scared. They all were, herself included.

"Does the intel indicate that Kairos has other labs where they are producing or testing this virus?" Vice President Whitney asked.

"We have to assume so, Madame Vice President, but at the moment I don't know where," said Marcus. "Hopefully as we review the vast number of files on the laptops that we scooped up in Karachi we'll learn more. But the lethality of Cerberus is why I had no choice but to order my team to blow up the lab and the warehouse. I simply couldn't afford to allow any of this virus to survive. And I didn't dare take any samples with us."

"What else was being stored in that warehouse that caused such a massive series of explosions?" asked General James Meyers, chairman of the Joint Chiefs.

"That I can't say, sir," Marcus conceded. "We simply don't know."

Cal Foster, the secretary of defense, spoke next. "Have you identified the Pakistani official who came to visit the warehouse—or the lab—just prior to your arrival?"

"No, sir—nor can I say for certain that the official was Pakistani."

"The cars were all decked out with Pakistani flags," Foster noted.

"True, but it could have been a foreign official under Pakistani protection," Marcus replied. "Or posing as a Pakistani."

"Do you have any leads on where other Kairos cells or operatives are located?" asked McDermott.

"Not yet, but again, we've only just begun to go through the files we've gathered."

"Any leads on where Abu Nakba is now?" asked Whitney.

"No, ma'am."

"Has the NSA picked up any useful chatter in the aftermath of the Karachi operation?" the VP pressed.

"I'm afraid not," said Marcus.

At this, President Hernandez leaned forward in his seat, looked down the table, and asked one final question. "So, just to be clear—at this point, Ryker, do you have any leads at all that could lead us to Abu Nakba or any of his people?"

"I'm afraid not, sir," Marcus conceded. "The trail has run cold."

32

"Then we'll take it from here, Agent Ryker," Hernandez said. "You're dismissed."

And that was that.

Marcus stood, retrieved the thumb drive from McDermott, saluted the president, and walked out of the Situation Room without saying a word. Putting his coat back on and gathering his phone from the bank of lockboxes in the vestibule, he exited the White House and stepped out onto West Executive Avenue. There he found his driver waiting and the black Suburban running and asked to be taken to Langley.

It was slow going as they pulled through the northwest gate, took a left onto Pennsylvania Avenue, and then another left onto 17th street. Despite the best efforts of the D.C. municipal department to keep the streets plowed, it was still snowing hard and accumulating quickly. Marcus had always loved Washington winters, but as he peered out the ice-encrusted window, he could feel his heart pounding in his chest and the adrenaline coursing through his veins. For all the differences he'd had with President Clarke—and there had been many—they were nothing like this. Marcus felt betrayed by Hernandez. For months, the president had ignored all the progress they were, in fact, making at ripping up the global Kairos terror network.

And now this.

Of course Marcus was terribly disappointed that Abu Nakba had slipped from their grasp yet again—probably more than Hernandez. But where was the commander in chief's sense of perspective? Where was his gratitude for all that Marcus and his team were accomplishing for the country and the toll it was taking on all of them?

Arlington Memorial Bridge was almost deserted as they crossed the icy Potomac, exited the District of Columbia, and entered Virginia. As they passed Arlington National Cemetery, it became clear to Marcus why he was so angry. Andrew Clarke had been a complete and utter novice when it came to intelligence and national security affairs. The man had never served in the military. Nor did he have any understanding of what it truly meant to serve in harm's way, deep behind enemy lines. That's why Marcus had cut him so much slack. But Carlos Hernandez? *Seriously?* The man had spent almost his entire adult life in the American military. He had served in combat. He had led special-operations forces. He had lost comrades in battle. He had buried close friends. He knew the immense personal toll such losses took and how hard it was to shake them off. Hernandez, in short, was no novice. He knew better. He had no excuses. And if he was going to cut Marcus loose, Marcus had no intention of cutting him any slack at all.

As the Suburban made its way north up the George Washington Memorial Parkway, Marcus told himself he couldn't afford to become consumed by anger or some ridiculous victim mentality. Yes, Hernandez was probably firing him at that very moment and ordering Dell to replace him. Fine. He would not apologize for doing his job and protecting his country. If a man of Hernandez's immense experience didn't want him around, Marcus was not going to fight for his job. The president had every right to can him. Marcus couldn't afford the luxury of taking it personally. But the truth was, he did—and more than ever he feared for the security of the country with a genocidal maniac like Abu Nakba, armed with Cerberus, on the loose.

Then again, it probably was best to get fresh eyes on the problem. At least he and Annie could shake off the dust of this sick town and go off and finally get married. Hopefully, Annie would agree to a private ceremony, maybe up in the mountains of Colorado, after all. Once the news of his firing broke, as it surely would momentarily, there was no way that he could imagine a big wedding. Three-quarters of the people he had been planning to put on the guest list, maybe more, were people he would be happy never to see again. He certainly wouldn't want a wedding that drew media coverage or told Kairos and Iranian operatives exactly where he and his family would be on a specific date at a specific time. Given that Annie was likely now a target of Abu Nakba and the mullahs in Tehran as well, he suspected she would suddenly be fine with a small wedding.

Besides, with the money they saved they could afford to take more than a measly one-week honeymoon. Now they probably could jet off to some remote island in the Caribbean or the South Pacific for a full month, maybe even two—drop off the grid entirely, enjoy a real honeymoon far from the Beltway, and start dreaming of and planning for a whole new life. Marcus had no idea what either of them would do for a living. Nor did he care. They both had some savings socked away. They both had homes they could sell. And they could always live on the Outer Banks at the lovely home Annie's uncle had left her. What more did they need?

Arriving at CIA headquarters, the driver brought the Suburban into the garage reserved for senior officers. Marcus thanked him and took the private elevator reserved for the director and the DDI. Reaching the seventh floor, Marcus checked in at the guard station, clipped his ID to his belt, and walked the halls until he found Pete Hwang.

"So how was the president this fine morning?" Pete, all spruced up and wearing a clean suit, inquired.

"Don't ask," Marcus replied. "Tell me Noah has found something more, something specific we can use to shut down Kairos for good."

"Not yet, but give the kid some time."

"We don't have time, Pete. These attacks could be coming at any minute."

"Nevertheless, a shower couldn't hurt, right?"

"In a minute—first I want to see Noah."

"No," said Pete, stopping in his tracks in the middle of the hallway. "You need to clean up first. Doctor's orders."

Marcus stopped, shook his head, and realized Pete had stopped in front of the men's room.

"I stopped by the house and picked up some of your things," Pete said, handing him a key. "They're in my locker. Let's talk when you're done."

Marcus smiled, grateful for his friendship with Pete over all these years. Then he slapped the good doctor on the back, took the key, checked its number, and headed inside. Going over to the bank of lockers, he found Pete's, opened it, and found a fresh pair of blue jeans, a black turtleneck sweater, underwear, socks, and a beat-up pair of casual leather shoes. Ever since the attacks in Chicago and the growing chatter the NSA was picking up of death threats against him, Marcus had moved out of the apartment where he, Elena, and Lars had lived in the southeast section of D.C., in a neighborhood called Eastern Market, walking distance from the Capitol and the Library of Congress. He'd moved into Pete's town house in Old Town Alexandria, just across the Potomac River in northern Virginia. Over the past eight months or so, they hadn't spent much time there, but it had been fun to be roommates again for the first time since their days in the Corps.

Grabbing a fresh towel off the rack, Marcus stripped down, stepped into one of the shower stalls, and turned on the water. For the next few minutes, Marcus just stood there in the billowing steam. He tried to slow down his swirling thoughts, but it wasn't going well. He hated the idea of leaving the mission unfinished, especially knowing that the Kairos threat was suddenly far more dangerous than he'd previously imagined. He would also miss his team. In many ways, they'd become closer to him than his own family. He could hardly imagine not seeing them every day, much less imagine them going into battle without him. Once again, he found himself furious at the president, not so much for disparaging his own commitment to the cause but for dismissing the hard work and success of this extraordinary team.

The only consolation was that Annie would soon be back from the White House. So would Dell. The director would call him into her office and formally deliver the news. It wouldn't be a long-drawn-out affair. Nor would it be personal and vindictive. She would thank him for his service. Probably tell him that she agreed that he and his team had been far more effective than the president had given him credit for. Then she would tell him that his service to his country in the CIA was at an end.

She would likely ask him to recommend his replacement. With Jenny gone, either Kailea Curtis or Geoff Stone would fit the bill. Donny Callaghan could also do the job, if called upon. But Marcus had no second thoughts. He would recommend Kailea Curtis. She didn't just have the grit and the guts—not to mention the skills—to lead the team. She had something extra, an X factor that Jenny had also had, something that gave her the ability to inspire and motivate the rest of the team better than the guys.

Annie, of course, would resign simultaneously. Dell would protest but ultimately relent. Then he and Annie would amble down to Human Resources, fill out the necessary paperwork, turn in their badges and other gear, and that would be that. Pete already had one foot out the door. Maybe they could all go grab lunch together. Maybe at some fun seafood restaurant in Annapolis.

Saying goodbye to Kai, Geoff, Donny, Miguel, and Noah would be the tough part. There was no getting around that. They were just as exhausted as he was. They desperately needed a break, but there was no way they were going to get one. Not for the foreseeable future, anyway. Still, after a couple of good meals and a few good nights' rest, he was certain they'd bounce back. They always did. What's more, they'd be highly motivated and reenergized by the extreme threat of the Cerberus virus entering the United States, the fear that Abu Nakba would wreak vengeance on a completely unsuspecting populace, and a ticking clock that was rapidly counting down to zero hour.

Suddenly, Marcus heard the door of the men's room burst open.

"Marcus, Annie's trying to reach you," Pete shouted over the whoosh of the shower. "She and Dell are ten minutes out. Dell wants to see you the minute they arrive. But come see me first."

And so it began.

33

Marcus turned off the water and stepped out of the shower.

After toweling off, he dressed and shaved, then headed to Pete's office, only to find Noah Daniels there as well. Both men looked as grim as Marcus could remember.

"We have a new problem," Pete said immediately.

"Only one?" Marcus quipped, trying to lighten the mood.

Neither man laughed. Noah, pacing the floor, looked positively ashen.

"What is it?" asked Marcus.

"The hard drives," Noah replied.

"What about them?"

"They're empty," Noah said. "Gone—everything."

"I don't understand. Just a few hours ago you were pulling all kinds of things off them."

"Right, but now they're all wiped clean."

"How? By whom?"

"I don't know—the moment we got here from Andrews, we took all the laptops and phones directly to my guys down at DST," Noah explained, referring to the Agency's Directorate of Science and Technology. "I told them to clear their schedule, that these were now their top priority, and we needed to be able to report to you, Dr. Dell, and the president by the close of business."

"And?"

"I went to take a shower, change, and get a quick bite to eat," Noah continued. "By the time I came back, the shift supervisor at DST informed me that the SIM cards on the phones still contained data on calls made and received, but they'd found nothing on the laptops. No files. No data. No email traffic. Nothing."

"How is that possible?" Marcus pressed. "The files on those hard drives are all we have."

"I know, but it's vanished—all of it," Noah said. "The only thing we can come up with is that the Kairos guys had installed some sort of virus or device on each laptop that was programmed to completely eradicate the system's files and memory if, perhaps, a certain passcode wasn't entered every day at a certain time, or something along those lines. We can't say for certain. We're as baffled as you are. But the bottom line is that the files are gone, all of them, wiped clean and irrecoverable."

Marcus was still trying to process the magnitude of this development when there was a knock on the conference room door behind him. Too stunned by the news Noah had just delivered, neither Pete nor Marcus opened the door. Instead, Kailea Curtis poked her head in and informed them that Director Dell was back and needed to speak with Marcus immediately.

Marcus took a deep breath and shook his head. Then he followed Kailea to the other end of the hallway. Two members of Dell's protective detail were standing post by the elevators. Three more were positioned outside her office door. Each knew Marcus well, given how much time he spent on the seventh floor.

"The director will see you now," said Dell's assistant.

Before Marcus could turn the handle, however, Annie opened the door. Stoic and silent, she gave him a nod as she stepped back and motioned for him to step inside the director's spacious corner office. As he did so, he was surprised to find the room empty. Dell was nowhere to be seen, though he heard water running in her private bathroom.

Live feeds from Fox News, CNN, MSNBC, BBC, and Al Arabiya were playing on a bank of video monitors on the far wall, all muted. None of the coverage caught Marcus's attention as particularly noteworthy, much less worrisome, except perhaps for the BBC's coverage of the Chinese president's visit to Moscow. What he wouldn't give to know exactly what Presidents Petrovsky and Guanzhong were saying to each other, particularly in the immediate aftermath of the U.S.–Sino summit in Washington and the devastating explosions in Karachi. Were they chalking up the latter to terrorism, or pointing their fingers at the Hernandez administration? If so, how were they plotting to exploit the situation? Marcus made a mental note to ask Annie about it later. Then again, he reminded himself, it wouldn't be their problem later.

As he waited for Dell, Marcus began to reconsider his assessment of what she was about to say to him and how. He thought of her as a friend, or at least an ally, but was that true? Didn't the evidence suggest she was a far more loyal ally of the president's than of his? Hernandez had promoted her to director, after all, making her the first African American ever to hold the post, and certainly one of the Agency's most qualified—and most imposing—leaders.

Almost sixty, Dell had grown up in the projects outside of Atlanta, and in her case the cliché was true: what hadn't killed her had definitely made her stronger. She was street-smart and not easily intimidated. She'd proven herself an impressive field agent, and later an even more impressive intelligence analyst. In her time as the Agency's DDI—the deputy director for intelligence, the position Annie now held—Dell had been responsible for both stealing and analyzing secrets from all manner of foreign governments, but particularly from the enemies of the United States. She had also been responsible for keeping the commander in chief and all senior policy makers in Congress and throughout the U.S. government briefed on the most up-to-date and accurate interpretation of those secrets as possible. She'd been elevated to director after her predecessor had been summarily fired by Hernandez, and neither Marcus nor Annie had any doubt she was born for the job.

Graduating first in her class from Georgetown University in national security studies, Dell had earned her master's degree from Oxford in Russo–Sino relations. What's more, she'd earned not one but two PhDs from Stanford, both dealing with aspects of Chinese foreign and military policy. Fluent in Russian and Mandarin—as well as Arabic, which she'd picked up *after* finishing her postgraduate work—she'd been recruited to the CIA in her late twenties and spent six years in the field, running agents and training future spooks. Over the past two and a half decades, she'd served in a range of highly trusted Agency positions. If that weren't enough, Marcus had been on the gun range with Dell and knew firsthand that she was a wonder to behold with a Glock 9mm.

Marcus heard the water stop, and the door to the director's private restroom opened. Dell switched off the light, stepped back into her office, and closed the door behind her. She walked over to her desk and took her seat without acknowledging the presence of either Marcus or Annie. Putting on her reading glasses, she picked up a file marked *EYES ONLY*, and began perusing its contents. She did not ask Marcus to take a seat, so he remained standing.

"Tell me you have a new lead," Dell said without looking up.

"Nothing yet," Marcus replied.

"Then tell me that Noah and his pals in DST are poring over every file on every computer and phone you guys brought back."

Marcus hesitated. Was she toying with him? Were the hard drive problems in the file she was now reading? Was she testing him? Or did she genuinely not know?

Apparently surprised not to get an immediate response, Dell now looked up at him over the top of her glasses.

"Mr. Ryker, I asked you a question."

Marcus exhaled and gave as succinct an explanation as he possibly could. In his peripheral vision, he saw Annie wince. She didn't know. Maybe neither of them did.

"Please tell you're messing with me, Mr. Ryker," Dell said.

"No, ma'am, not today."

Now it was Dell who exhaled slowly. Taking off her glasses, she looked over at Annie, then back to Marcus.

"But the files can be recovered, right?" she asked.

"It would not appear so, ma'am."

Dell sat silently. Then, she swiveled in her chair and made herself some coffee in an Agency mug from a Keurig machine on the credenza behind her. Only after she'd taken her first sip did she turn back and face Marcus.

"Do you think Abu Nakba is still in Karachi?"

"I have no idea, ma'am."

"Best guess."

"Probably."

"Probably still in Karachi?"

"Where else is he going to go?" asked Marcus. "We've got people watching all the airports. Train and bus stations. Ports and military bases."

"But he could drive out, right?" Dell pressed. "Or rather, he could have someone drive him to another city, and fly out of the country from there. True?"

"Yes, but not commercial. We'd pick him up immediately, even if he were flying under an assumed name and a fake passport."

"Isn't it more likely he'd fly private?"

"Sure, and thus be tougher to track."

"How far is it to Islamabad?" Dell asked.

Marcus shrugged.

"From Karachi, almost a thousand miles," said Annie.

"What about to Lahore?"

Annie took that one too. "Almost eight hundred miles."

Suddenly, the phone rang.

Dell took the call. "Not now—I'll call him back," she said, then hung up the phone and turned back to Marcus. "If you were Abu Nakba, would you stay in Pakistan or slip away and find a new base camp?"

Marcus was confused—not by the question but by the whole conversation. Why was Dell stringing him along? Why wasn't she lowering the boom? It wasn't like her, and it didn't make sense.

"Look, ma'am, I have no idea," he replied. "But really, what does it matter? That's a question you ought to ask Officer Curtis."

"Why her?"

"Because I'm recommending that you put her in charge of this unit. True, Jenny had more field experience and years with the Agency. But I have no doubt Officer Curtis will do an outstanding job."

"What are you talking about, Ryker?"

Marcus glanced over at Annie, then back at Dell.

"What are *you* talking about, ma'am?" he replied. "After I left the Situation

Room, didn't the president ask for my resignation? I'm ready to give it, effective immediately. And again, I'm recommending Officer Curtis as my replacement."

Marcus swiped a notepad and pen off Dell's desk and scribbled a one-sentence resignation letter. Then he signed it, dated it, and slid it across to her.

"Forget it," Dell said, picking up the notepad, tearing off the top sheet, and feeding it into the shredder under her desk.

"I don't understand."

"Look, you gave POTUS your word that you'd stay until you brought Abu Nakba to justice. He's none too happy with your performance in Karachi. That's for sure. But he has no intention of letting you go. There's too much at stake, and it's certainly no time to change horses now."

Marcus didn't know what to say.

"You're not going anywhere," Dell continued. "Now, look, we have a literal ticking time bomb out there. The president and I will alert DHS and come up with a game plan to keep this Cerberus stuff out of the country. But you, Annie, and your team need to come up with a game plan to get us back on offense. And you need to make certain that Abu Nakba pays dearly for Chicago and everything else he's done to us and our allies. That's it. That's the mission. And make no mistake: POTUS has no patience for another screwup. Are we clear?"

34

It wasn't often Marcus found himself completely stunned.

But Dell had managed to do it.

"Yes, we're clear, ma'am," he replied.

"Good, now get out of here, and happy hunting," Dell added.

Taking her cue, Annie exited through a side door—a soundproof, bulletproof door—that led to her adjacent office. Marcus followed suit.

The moment he closed the door behind him, Annie pressed him against that very same door and kissed him hard on the lips. For the second time in less than a minute, Marcus again found himself completely stunned. But he wasn't complaining. To the contrary, he wrapped his arms around Annie and kissed her back until they could barely breathe.

"Welcome home," Annie finally gasped.

But Marcus wasn't ready to stop. Her held her tighter and they continued to make out like two high school kids under the bleachers. The only reason they were finally forced to stop was that the phone on Annie's desk began ringing.

Wiping her mouth and running her hand through her hair, Annie caught her breath and picked up.

"Yes?" she asked into the receiver as Marcus walked over to her windows to find the snow coming down harder now.

"How soon can it be refueled? . . . And the weather? . . . You're sure? . . . Okay, then tell the pilots to warm up the engines and run through their preflight checklist."

"Going somewhere?" Marcus asked after hearing Annie hang up, still looking out the bulletproof windows and absorbing the view of acre upon acre of snow-covered pines on the Langley campus.

"Actually, you are," Annie said as she came up behind him and put her arms around his chest. "You and Pete."

Marcus actually laughed out loud, something he hadn't done in some time.

"I don't think so, young lady," he said, turning to her. "I finally come home, and you're already shipping me off? We don't even have any leads."

"That's the point."

"What's the point?"

"That's why I'm sending you to Colorado."

"To do what?"

"Meet with the Raven."

"The Raven?" Marcus asked. "What for?"

Annie kissed him on the forehead, then walked back over to her desk and picked up a folder.

"We're completely out of leads, out of options, and rapidly running out of time. The only hope I see at this point is for you and the Raven to knock your heads together and figure out if the Russians have something—*anything*—that can lead us to Abu Nakba."

"His last report said he'd hit a brick wall," said Marcus.

"Maybe he's missing something."

"I doubt it—he's pretty good at this; but I can call him."

"No, Marcus, you need to go out there," Annie insisted. "You need to reestablish contact, reestablish your friendship, and impress upon the Raven in no uncertain terms that the only way—and I mean the *only* way—that he stays safe from the Russians is if he keeps delivering actionable intel for us. And further impressing on him that there's literally nothing we need more right now than the location of Abu Nakba. So take this file, give me a kiss for the road, grab Pete, hightail it back to Andrews, and read this on the flight."

"What's in there?"

"An itemized rundown of everything the Raven has been doing for the last eight months."

Bewildered, Marcus walked over to the desk and took the file.

"Uh, I think you're forgetting one thing, Deputy Director Stewart."

"Oh yeah, and what's that?"

"Dr. Hwang isn't cleared to meet the Raven."

"He won't. You won't even tell him why you guys are heading to Aspen," Annie assured him. "We've rented you an SUV and reserved two adjacent rooms at the Ritz-Carlton. Once you touch down, drop Pete at the hotel and then proceed to the Raven's place alone."

"Then why send Pete at all?" asked Marcus. "I can certainly go out there by myself."

"I don't want you traveling alone right now," Annie replied. "I want Pete out there with you to watch your back and, you know, provide a little moral support."

"You mean you want me to convince him to stay on the team."

"That, too," she replied with a wink.

"Come on, Annie, you know full well the Kremlin has been upgrading their network security and closing every hole the Raven had been exploiting."

"Then we just have to pray he can find something that gets us closer to our target."

"That's highly unlikely, and you know it. The moment Hernandez hit Moscow with all those sanctions, they completely backed away from Kairos."

"Did they?"

"Do you have any proof to the contrary?"

"Just because we don't have proof that Moscow is continuing to fund and supply Abu Nakba doesn't mean they're not."

"You can't be serious," Marcus pushed back. "When Hernandez met with Petrovsky in Helsinki, he read him the riot act and imposed crippling sanctions on Russian oil and gas companies. He simultaneously tipped Interpol to arrest dozens of members of the European Parliament whom the Raven had discovered were secretly on the Kremlin's payroll. Petrovsky was humiliated, but that wasn't enough. POTUS gave Petrovsky one year to convince us that the Kremlin had not only completely severed ties with Kairos but with Iran as well or he was going to bring Ukraine into NATO and base American missiles in Ukraine. And by all appearances, it's working."

"Look," Annie replied, "I get it that Petrovsky looks like he's backed away from Kairos and is dialing down Moscow's ties with the terror masters in Tehran. But what if we're wrong? What if it's all for show? What if he's found another way to funnel money to Abu Nakba to plot his revenge? Can we really afford to take any chances? And what other options do we have? You just told the director and me that everything you guys brought back from Karachi is now completely useless. So as far as I can tell, the Raven is our only play."

Marcus looked into those gorgeous green eyes, sighed, and nodded. "Fine. For you, I'll go," he said softly. "But not without another kiss."

Then he walked around the desk, pressed her against the wall, and kissed her like he was never going to let her go.

35

At 3:19 a.m., the Boeing 747-400 finally touched down.

As Chen Guanzhong stepped off the jumbo jet, flanked by his security detail, he moved quickly into his bulletproof limousine. Soon the president of China was speeding across the capital toward Zhongnanhai, the presidential palace and residence, located adjacent to the grounds of the historic Forbidden City.

At 4 a.m. the weary leader entered his palatial office and was greeted by the sole advisor he had summoned, Dai Wangshu, China's minister of state security. The two men, both in their seventies, were longtime and trusted friends. They had first met more than a half century earlier while serving as young officers in the PLA. Though the two had taken separate journeys, they had never lost contact with one another and now were close allies once again.

Following in the footsteps of his prominent and powerful father and aided by his vast network of connections and tremendous clout, Guanzhong had pursued his post-army life in politics. He had joined the Communist Party, worked at his father's side, and risen to become the man's chief of staff. In due time, he was selected to serve in the Politburo himself. There he had garnered glowing accolades from his colleagues as a hardworking and loyal party member, a savvy geopolitical analyst, an ideological hard-liner, and a brilliant economic strategist.

Dai Wangshu, by contrast, chose to pursue a career in the military, following the path of his father and grandfather, both of whom had been high-ranking generals. However, whereas his father had risen to become the head of the nuclear-armed ballistic missile force, the son was better suited for espionage. When Guanzhong emerged as the party's general secretary and the country's president, he immediately named Wangshu head of China's intelligence services. While that had been only three years ago, the two men had accomplished a great deal in such a short period.

"How did it go in Moscow?" the spymaster asked. "Will Petrovsky back us?"

"I believe so," Guanzhong replied.

"But . . . ?"

"The American sanctions have hit Russia much harder than either of us realized," replied the president. "Petrovsky wasn't quite so blunt, but I believe his economy is teetering on the verge of collapse."

"That's not what any of our sources are telling us."

"Exactly," Guanzhong said. "Now, add to that the fact that the Israelis are selling natural gas to Europe—and that NATO countries are scaling down their purchases of Russian gas—and the Kremlin is approaching panic mode. Petrovsky confided in me that his government is hemorrhaging cash."

"And?"

"He was quite candid that the last thing he could afford right now is to back us financially in a new war in the Pacific."

"But, Your Excellency, if we're going to keep to our timetable, you're going to need his assurances soon," insisted Wangshu.

"Remember the ancient proverb, Dai," the president reassured him. "'*Only when the year grows cold do we see that the pine and cypress are the last to fade; only when we get into trouble do we know who our genuine friends are.*'"

"Meaning what, exactly?"

"Meaning that we must help our Russian friend now, when he is in dire need," replied Guanzhong. "And when we strike Taiwan, I have no doubt he will be with us."

"What do you have in mind?" said Wangshu.

"I offered Petrovsky to start buying large quantities of Russian gas, effective immediately. We will certainly need all that fuel when the war starts. And our purchases can offset much of what Europe has stopped buying from him. Plus, I reminded him that those sales will be insulated from the American sanctions that are punishing our Russian friends so terribly."

"Very shrewd," said Wangshu. "You might also offer to buy a minority share in Russia's biggest oil and gas companies and pay with cash."

"I already did," said Guanzhong. "What's more, I offered to provide Moscow with low-interest loans, and prepay for five years of grain shipments."

"My friend, you are very generous. And yet he still refused you?"

"No, no—I didn't say he refused," Guanzhong clarified. "Petrovsky did not say no. He simply said he needs a few days to think it over."

"What is there to think about?"

"Be patient, my friend," Guanzhong insisted. "I did not press him because I did not want to humiliate him. But I am confident that he will call me soon and tell me he's on board. What other options does he have?"

The spymaster said nothing as Guanzhong stood and walked over to one of the large, bulletproof windows in the corner of the room, allowing him to stare out over the twinkling lights of the Chinese capital.

"Now, I think it's time to call your friend," the president said softly, still gazing out the window. "He survived, did he not?"

"It was close—too close—but yes, he survived," said Wangshu.

"Then meet with him—discreetly, of course, not here in Beijing, but soon," said the president. "It's the last piece of the puzzle, and I want to be sure it's ready."

36

A severe winter storm warning was now in effect for the entire D.C. region.

All public and private schools were closed, including universities and community colleges. All churches, synagogues, and mosques in the area had canceled their weekend services. All stores and malls were closed, as were restaurants, movie theaters, and other entertainment venues. The governors of Virginia and Maryland had shut down all state offices in and around the District of Columbia, where the storm was hitting hardest. The mayor of D.C. ordered all city employees to stay at home except for those involved in snow removal and emergency services. The federal government was essentially shut down, as was the Metro. No buses or trains were running. National, Dulles Airport, and BWI had grounded all incoming and outgoing flights.

Annie's plan, therefore, had to be put on hold. Marcus and Pete had intended on flying to Aspen that night on an unmarked Agency plane. But when Joint Base Andrews also grounded all flights, the men slept on the floor of the seventh-floor conference room, along with the rest of their team, none of whom could get home given the raging snowpocalypse.

Marcus hoped the situation would improve overnight, but it was not to be, as the snow kept coming fast and furious all of Friday. So as tired and discouraged as they all were, they just kept working.

Or going through the motions, anyway. Noah pressed the DST folks to see if there was any possible way to recover even some digital scraps of the files that had disappeared off the laptops and phones they'd brought back from Karachi. Pete monitored the health of the team, made sure they were drinking enough water, taking breaks to get meals from the mess, and even taking occasional catnaps. The doctor insisted they had to let their bodies deal with jet lag and the general exhaustion they were battling but also truly let themselves mourn Jenny's death. If not, they were going to crash when they least expected it, and crash hard.

Kailea, Geoff, Donny, and Miguel spent several hours at the Agency's indoor gun range, which they pretty much had to themselves since so few employees in Clandestine Services were able to make it into the office. They spent time working out at the gym and doing laps in the pool. They also made dozens of phone calls to their counterparts in foreign intelligence services and sifted through hundreds of NSA transcripts, State Department cables, and field reports from CIA officers and sources all over planet, desperately searching for the needle in the proverbial haystack—that one small, seemingly insignificant clue that just might lead them to Abu Nakba. But though none of them admitted as much to their colleagues, their hearts were not in it. They all knew the stakes. They knew the clock was ticking. That more attacks were coming. That many more lives were in danger. But the mixture of fatigue and grief had pushed each to the breaking point.

Marcus worked on his after-action report, not just because Dell had insisted but as an excuse to avoid seeing his teammates. While he also went to the gun range and swam laps, he made sure to do so only after his colleagues had left. He longed to spend time with Annie. But given that she and Dell were holed up in Dell's office dealing with multiple crises, he barely got to see her at all.

As he ran laps around Langley's indoor track, Marcus resisted all thoughts of Jenny, her death, or their friendship, fearing he might slip into a depression from which he could not quickly recover.

Finishing his fourth mile and starting on his fifth, Marcus's thoughts inevitably turned to the Raven. Maybe Annie was right. Every other effort to track down the Libyan had failed. Every other road they'd traveled down had been a dead end. Nothing they were doing was working. Abu Nakba was outfoxing them at every turn. Maybe the Raven really was their only hope.

37

It had certainly happened before.

Time and again, Oleg Kraskin—aka, the Raven, the highest-ranking Russian mole ever to work for the Agency—had provided astonishing actionable intelligence that no one else could have. He was almost single-handedly responsible for stopping a full-scale Russian invasion of the Baltic states a few years earlier. After that, he'd helped uncover North Korea's plot to sell nuclear warheads to Iran. What's more, he'd helped thwart the Kairos plot to blow up the Dome of the Rock and the U.S.–Israeli–Saudi peace summit in Jerusalem.

Almost no one inside the Agency knew how long the list of intelligence successes attributable to the Raven really was. But Marcus knew. So why had he spent so little time with Oleg of late? Why hadn't he stayed in closer contact? After all, the man was all alone in the world. Hunted by the Kremlin. Estranged from his wife, Marina. Unable to ever see his beloved son, Vasily, again. And living under a false identity on the outskirts of Aspen with no family or friends to lean on. True, Oleg had not been so helpful lately. But was that his fault? The more Marcus contemplated it, the more he concluded that Annie was, in fact, onto something. It was far too soon to write off Oleg, much less to assume that his most valuable days as an intelligence operative were behind him.

By the time he'd finished running his laps and headed to the locker room for a quick shower, Marcus couldn't wait to fly to Aspen and sit down with the Raven face-to-face. Annie was right. Oleg was their last and best hope.

But just that conclusion led him right back to thinking about Annie.

When they'd first met on that tarmac in Kabul two decades earlier, Marcus couldn't possibly have imagined the sweet and encouraging friendship that he and Annie would develop. For two decades, it had been platonic, without a hint of impropriety during his entire marriage to Elena. But how much had changed since then. Now Annie was the deputy director of the Central Intelligence Agency. And his boss. And the love of his life, the only woman he could conceivably imagine who could give him a second half of his life that was truly worth living.

To be sure, Annie could never replace Elena, Marcus's high school sweetheart, his first true love. But nor did she need to. Elena would always hold a cherished place in his heart. But Marcus was now at peace with the notion that marrying Annie didn't mean he had to forget about Elena, or their son, Lars, or all the amazing memories they'd made together. Marrying Annie didn't mean disrespecting Elena's family or their shared and wonderful history. Elena had been God's precious gift to him in the first half of his life, but then for reasons of his own, the Lord had taken her home. Though their courtship and marriage had not been perfect, it had proven magical, if far too brief.

Now, in his sovereignty, God clearly had another season for Marcus. He hadn't expected it. Hadn't wanted it. But nor had he ultimately been in control.

"The Lord gave, and the Lord hath taken away; blessed be the name of the Lord."

His mother had made him memorize that verse at the age of ten after the death of his father. And now, the Lord who loved him and promised to be his Good Shepherd was reminding him of it again. Annie was God's perfect gift to him, living proof that the God of all mercies was offering him a second chance at love, at happiness, at joy, at the intimacy he had feared he might never know or experience again.

Stepping out of the shower and drying off, Marcus dressed in faded blue jeans, a white T-shirt, and a black crew-neck sweater. Thinking about Annie pushed back every other thought. It calmed him. And encouraged him. And he was grateful. But just then, Marcus got a text message from his mom.

Can you call? she asked.

Marcus had a better idea. He headed back up to the seventh floor and found Pete in the conference room with the rest of the team. Empty pizza boxes were littered across the table, as were half-empty cans of soda, crumpled-up napkins, and stacks of files, all marked *TOP SECRET* and *EYES ONLY*. Hunched over a laptop, Pete was at the far end of the conference table, poring over the latest batch of NSA intercepts while simultaneously on a conference call with analysts at Fort Meade.

"Pete, I need your Jeep," Marcus whispered. *"Is it still in the garage?"*

Pete waved him off and turned away, but Marcus wasn't deterred.

"Hey, doofus, really, I need to borrow your Jeep," he said again.

Again, Pete turned away from him, pressing the receiver closer to his ear as he scribbled down notes on a legal pad. Marcus was about to take a third swipe when he saw, nestled under the stack of manila folders piled around Pete, the man's wallet, ID, Sig Sauer, a spare mag, and the keys to his Jeep. Marcus scooped up the keys, jangled them over his shoulder, and bolted out the door before Pete could say a word.

Next Marcus headed to the other end of the hall to find Annie but was intercepted by Eileen, Dell's executive assistant.

"She's in with the director," the stern-looking older woman told him.

"Can I just pop my head in?" Marcus asked.

"No, they just started a videoconference with Dai Wangshu."

"The Beijing spymaster?"

"That's the one."

"How long will they be?"

"The director told me to hold all calls for at least the next few hours."

"Can you just walk in a message to Annie?"

"I'm sorry, Mr. Ryker. The director was adamant. No interruptions."

Marcus glanced at his watch. It was already 5:54 in the evening. The sun had gone down. It was pitch-black outside. The good news was that the snow had finally stopped falling. The Weather Channel was reporting the storm was moving out to sea. If all went well, he and Pete could fly to Aspen the next day.

"Okay, just let her know I went out," Marcus told the woman. "She can reach me on my satphone if she needs me. I should be back by midnight, Lord willing."

"You sure you want to go out in this mess?"

"Believe me, Eileen. I've been through worse."

"Oh, I have no doubt, young man."

It took him more than an hour, but Marcus finally reached the Washington Navy Yard at just after seven o'clock. Grateful for Pete's four-wheel drive, he cleared security at the main gate, then parked on a freshly plowed street around the corner from the base housing to which his mother had been assigned. Inside, the lights were all on, and he could smell the smoke pouring out of his mother's chimney.

Marcus trudged up the snow-packed walkway and was about to ring the doorbell when he spotted a shovel leaning against the front of the house. Putting his gloves back on, he decided to first clear the walkway and the sidewalk in front of his mother's home before returning the shovel to its place. Then he rang the doorbell.

When Marjorie Ryker opened the door, she was floored to see her son and all the work he'd just done. "The Prodigal Son has returned," she laughed, welcoming him inside with a bear hug and a kiss on both cold and rosy cheeks.

"I know. I'm so sorry I haven't called in a bit," he said as she shut the door behind him.

"Oh, don't mind me, I'm just playing with you. Here, let me take your coat. Annie said you were traveling. How long are you home for now?"

"I was supposed to fly back out today. But obviously that wasn't possible. Maybe tomorrow."

"Well, thank God for this storm, then. The Lord certainly has his ways, doesn't he?" She laughed as she hung up his coat and scarf and tossed his gloves onto the register to dry. "Isn't Annie with you?"

"Unfortunately, no; she's working late, so it's just me tonight."

"Well, come into the kitchen and get warm. The guys signed up to cook dinner at the chapel for families whose husbands and fathers are deployed. Marta's hosting a slumber party for all the cousins at her place. And Nicole is home, soaking in a bubble bath, getting a well-deserved night off. But wow, I never expected to see you tonight. Sit down. Take a load off. Let me warm you up a bowl of beef stew and dumplings. Just made it last night."

"That sounds heavenly."

"Something to drink?"

"Sure, what do you have?"

"I might have a beer or two your brothers-in-law haven't polished off," she said, opening the refrigerator and poking around. "Okay, well, no beer. How about a glass of wine?"

"Maybe a good strong cup of coffee instead, and I mean really strong," Marcus replied. "I still have to drive back to Langley tonight."

"Of course, dear; coming right up."

"Good. Now, tell me how you're holding up, Mom."

"No, no, sweetheart, there's nothing interesting happening around here. You first. Skip all the boring classified stuff and just tell me when the wedding is going to be and how I can help."

38

The storm had passed.

The airports had reopened.

But now there was a new challenge. At Andrews, there were no private jets available, given the high number of other senior U.S. officials whose flights had been canceled or postponed in recent days, officials whose rank and plans trumped theirs.

In the end Marcus and Pete were forced to fly commercial. To their relief, United flight 1493 took off on time from Washington Dulles Airport at 5:14 that afternoon. Unfortunately, the flight was packed, they weren't together, and they both were relegated to middle seats. The only consolation was that the plane had a Wi-Fi plan for purchase. So Marcus bought the package on his United app, plugged in a pair of earbuds, and watched a replay of Jenny's memorial service on the YouTube channel of the church she'd grown up in—the Presbyterian church that her ninety-two-year-old grandmother still attended faithfully, the one that had led her to Christ and taught her the Scriptures. It was a lovely, moving service. Marcus still felt terrible for not attending.

Alone with his thoughts for the rest of the flight, a deep sense of sadness and remorse pervaded Marcus's soul. He was so grateful that Jenny was a believer. He knew beyond a shadow of a doubt where she now was. And he was grateful that one day he would see her again in heaven. But nothing could make her death any less cruel, or his guilt any less excruciating. One of his closest friends and confidantes was gone.

Three hours and fifty-seven minutes later, the Embraer jet touched down at Denver International Airport. Though the blizzard along the Front Range had also passed and DIA crews were working around the clock to clear the runways and tarmacs, the skies weren't exactly friendly. It was still snowing, though not nearly so hard. The temperature was hovering around twenty degrees Fahrenheit, and it wasn't until nearly 9 p.m. mountain time when they were finally able to pick up the Jeep Grand Cherokee that the Agency had reserved.

Ahead of them lay a two-hundred-mile trek into the mountains. In decent weather, the journey had taken Marcus a good four and a half hours. Who knew how long it would take in the snow. As Marcus got behind the wheel and Pete turned on the radio, they immediately began hearing reports of numerous accidents along I-70. What's more, ski fanatics from all over the country were streaming into Denver and heading in the same direction, though not all to Aspen. The resorts of Vail and Breckenridge were among the desired destinations, and there were others. At least they were going to have plenty of time to catch up along the way.

Marcus began by thanking Pete for being willing to go with him. "I know you'd love to be done with all this," he said as he cranked up the heater and the windshield wipers to full power. "But we're still nowhere close to accomplishing our mission."

"Actually, I'd like to talk to you about that," Pete replied as he pushed back his seat as far as it would go, tilted it back, kicked off his boots, and put his feet on the dashboard. "I've resigned."

"What? Resigned? When?"

"Thursday—the moment we got back to Langley."

"While I was at the White House?"

"Yeah—I'd already typed the letter before we left for Karachi. I told myself that if I made it back to the States alive, the first thing I'd do would be to sign it and head over to Personnel and hand the sucker in. The twenty-eighth is my last day."

Marcus was blindsided. "Couldn't we have talked about it first?"

"You're kidding, right?"

"No, I'm not."

"Come on, man, how many times have I told you I'm done?"

"Yeah, but you never are."

"That's because you keep convincing me I'm needed for one more mission, and like a moron, I keep believing you."

"I do need you, Pete, and you're not a moron, no matter what I say about you behind your back," Marcus said, glancing over at his friend but then right back at the road. "With this Cerberus threat, I need you now more than ever."

"Nevertheless, I'm done."

"Why?"

"Because I don't have any more to give—and frankly, neither do you."

"Poppycock, Pete. Yeah, I'm tired, but I'll be fine."

"No, you won't," Pete pushed back. "You're exhibiting all the classic signs of burnout, Marcus. We all are. We're losing our edge. We're making mistakes. It cost Jenny her life. I don't want to be next, and I sure as hell don't want you to be either."

"Pete, the mission isn't done," Marcus insisted.

"It is for me."

"*Now? Really?* When the stakes are higher than ever? We are duty-bound to find Abu Nakba and take him out once and for all. Him and the rest of his Kairos crew. And when we do, we'll have earned our right to retire and sail off into the sunset. But if we don't, and thousands or, God forbid, millions of Americans wind up dead, are you really going to be able to live with the knowledge that you threw in the towel?"

"Marcus, do you hear yourself? How many times have you made that case to me? It's not going to work anymore. Let's be honest. We're not spring chickens. In the world of special-ops forces, or even CIA clandestine operatives, we're way past our prime, my friend. It's time to pass the baton, while we still can."

"*Past our prime?* Speak for yourself."

"I am. Look, I've made my decision. Now it's time for you to make yours. If you were smart, you'd resign too—you and Annie both."

"You know we can't do that."

"Of course you can. You just don't want to."

"I do want to. But Annie and I gave our word to the president that we'd see this thing all the way to the end."

At this, Pete sat up and readjusted his seat.

"Marcus, you realize, don't you, that there is a very high likelihood that if you go back out there into battle, you're coming home in a box, right?"

Marcus was silent.

"Every casino has house rules, Marcus, and you seem to have forgotten them. So let me remind you. The house always wins. Always. Eventually, every gambler loses. Every single one. And I'm telling you, man, you've been playing this game way too long, and frankly I'm terrified that your luck is about to run out."

39

Mohammed Faisal was awakened by the incessant ringing of his satellite phone.

Groping in the darkness, he switched on the light on the nightstand next to his bed and stared at his watch. It was only 4:48 in the morning. He couldn't imagine who in the world could be calling at such an early hour. He pulled the phone out of its charger on the floor and finally answered on the ninth ring.

"Hello?"

"Tell me you're all safe," said the voice at the other end.

A jolt of adrenaline was suddenly injected into his system. He jumped out of bed and stood ramrod straight in nothing but his boxers.

"We are, Colonel. Thank you for checking in. That is most kind."

"Any chance you've been spotted?"

"None—we haven't moved, haven't spoken to anyone, haven't seen anyone since it happened."

"You're certain?"

"Positive."

"Because there's no room for error."

"Colonel, we're clean."

"Fine—then how close are you to the tarmac?"

Faisal walked over to the window and pulled back a corner of one of the drapes.

"I can see it from here."

"Do you see anyone out there?"

"Just a small flight crew. They're servicing a Dassault Falcon 8X. There's nothing else out there."

"Good. That's the plane I sent for you. Wake the old man up and get moving. I want you in the air in fifteen minutes. The crew will give you more details once you're airborne. Clear?"

"Yes, sir," Faisal confirmed.

The call went dead, and Faisal sprang into action. First he entered the adjoining dorm room and found Abu Nakba finishing his morning prayers.

"It's time, Father," Faisal explained. "We need to move quickly. Don't worry about your bag. I'll take care of everything."

The old man nodded, grabbed his cane, and with Faisal's assistance rose to his feet and headed to the door. Grabbing their bags, Faisal briefed the two bodyguards standing post in the hallway. They radioed the rest of the security team, and within minutes everyone was exiting the main residence hall of the Pakistan Air Force's Air War College, where they had been holed up for the past several days, avoiding any contact whatsoever with the cadets, their commanders, or anyone else on campus.

Soon the French business jet was streaking down the runway, gaining altitude, and banking north. Two and a half hours later, they touched down in Tashkent, the capital of Uzbekistan. A light dusting of snow lay on the ground. The temperature was hovering in the midtwenties. Faisal could see his breath. He worried the old man could catch a cold or, worse, pneumonia. Then again, they weren't staying long, not even overnight. Just then, Faisal's satphone rang.

"Was that your plane that just landed?" asked the man on the other end.

"Yes," said Faisal, instantly recognizing the voice.

"You're taxiing right toward us—do you see the ARJ21 off to your left?"

Faisal unbuckled his seat belt, crossed to the left side of the plane, and looked out a window. He spotted several business jets but only one that had been manufactured in Shanghai. It was painted white, with no other visible markings on the fuselage, but the tail number matched the one the voice on the other end of the line now gave him. Minutes later, Faisal helped the old man off the first jet and onto the second.

Waiting for them was Li Bai Xiang.

Clocking in at five foot ten inches tall and about 175 pounds, Xiang was in his midfifties with a thick shock of jet-black hair, dark narrow eyes, and an inscrutable expression that suggested an odd fusion of annoyance and amusement. The only distinctive feature Faisal observed was the tattoo of a ferocious red dragon on the back of the man's left hand.

"Abu Nakba, it's an honor to finally meet you face-to-face," Xiang said, bowing slightly to the old man.

"The honor is mine, Colonel," the old man replied.

"Come, please, sit across from me," Xiang insisted. "We have a long flight and much to discuss."

Mohammed Faisal helped the Kairos leader follow the colonel to a private compartment located at the back of the plane and settle into a cream-colored leather swivel chair across from the Chinese official while their mutual security details took their seats toward the front of the cabin.

Faisal was about to sit, but Abu Nakba held up his hand.

"Do not be offended, my son, but there are matters that I must discuss with the colonel in confidence," he said.

"As you wish, Father," Faisal replied, ever deferential.

Alone, Li Bai Xiang shut the door, took his seat, and fastened his seat belt. Moments later, they were hurtling down the runway.

"Where are you taking me?" Abu Nakba asked directly.

"All in due time," Xiang replied. "The real question is: Where are you taking us?"

40

Few states plow and salt their roads faster or more effectively than Colorado.

Having grown up in a small town outside of Colorado Springs, Marcus knew why. The ski industry drew more than fourteen million visitors every year to the state, generated some $5 billion in annual economic output, supported nearly fifty thousand jobs for Coloradans, and was critical to the state's brand. But none of it was possible unless skiers could make it to the mountains and onto the slopes.

Still, it was almost 5 a.m. when they finally reached Aspen. Pete had been driving the last shift, allowing Marcus to sleep. When they arrived at the Ritz-Carlton, Pete headed inside to check in while Marcus drove to a nearby service station to fuel up. As the gas pumped, Marcus opened the trunk, unzipped his suitcase, retrieved a locked steel case, and closed the trunk again. Getting back into the Jeep, Marcus opened the case and removed his Sig Sauer. He inserted a fresh magazine, then put the pistol in the shoulder holster under his leather jacket and stuffed several spare mags in his pockets. Then he got back out of the vehicle, removed the nozzle from the gas tank, saved his receipt, and got back on the road.

Given the weather, it was nearly 6 a.m. when he pulled into the driveway of the snow-covered A-frame house. Marcus texted Annie and Pete, letting both know he'd arrived safely. Annie was all business. She texted back confirming that the Raven was definitely home based on live video from surveillance cameras on the property that the Agency had discreetly installed in several locations to keep an eye on one of their most valuable assets.

Trudging up the unplowed walkway to the front door, Marcus rang the doorbell twice. When there was no sight nor sound of movement inside the house, he pounded on the front door. Eventually, the porch light flicked on, and the door opened slowly.

Oleg Kraskin was stunned.

"Marcus?" said the Russian, unshaven and dressed only in a T-shirt and boxers. *"What in the world are you doing here?"*

"I just flew in for a few days of skiing and figured I needed a buddy."

Oleg wasn't amused. "I've never been skiing in my life, and I certainly have no intention of taking it up now. But please, come in. I'll make a fire and put on a pot of chai."

Every other time Marcus had come, he'd gotten an immediate bear hug, but there was none this time. Oleg, already tall and lanky, had clearly lost weight. His eyes and face looked weary, and he moved like an old man. Surveying the small house—something that seemed built out of a child's Lincoln Logs—Marcus saw that the place was a mess. There was a stack of dirty cups and bowls next to a ratty old La-Z-Boy recliner facing a large-screen TV mounted on the wall. Old newspapers littered the floor. Glancing through the bathroom door, which was slightly ajar, he saw that the tub and shower stall clearly hadn't been scrubbed in quite some time.

Oleg, however, showed no signs of embarrassment. Nor did he hasten to straighten things up. Rather, shoulders drooped, hair askew, he padded to the kitchen and filled up a pot with water. Turning on the gas on the front burner of his stove, he rifled through a drawer, found a box of matches, and lit the burner. Before putting out the match, he also lit up a cigarette, took a drag, and tossed the match into the sink, piled high with dishes.

Marcus picked up an old pair of blue jeans and several dirty pairs of socks off the only other chair in the living room. He wadded them up and heaved them into the loft. He did the same with the clothes draped over the ladder. Then he scooped up the newspapers off the floor, ripped off one sheet after another, crumpled them into balls, and tossed them into the fireplace, alongside a fresh stack of logs and kindling.

By the time the Russian began pouring chai in the kitchen, Marcus had built a roaring fire and was sitting in the overstuffed chair reserved for Oleg's nonexistent guests. His leather jacket lay on the floor next to him, covering his shoulder holster and pistol. He'd taken off his Timberland boots and had propped his feet on a coffee table Oleg had made from the pine trees in the backyard.

There were still no photographs on the walls, just a small framed one on the desk in the corner, upon which sat three large computer monitors. The photo was faded, but the image was unmistakable. Oleg had his arm around his wife, who was holding their infant son at his baptism.

"Honey?" Oleg said.

"No, plain," Marcus replied.

A moment later, Oleg returned to the living room, handed Marcus a steaming mug, and set his own on the coffee table, from which Marcus removed his feet. Then Oleg slumped into his own recliner as Marcus took a sip, noticing that Oleg, in turn, did not even touch his.

41

"Okay, spit it out, my friend," Marcus began. "What's wrong?"

"What are you talking about?" asked Oleg, his accent as thick as ever.

"Why the long face and a house that looks like it was trashed during a pity party?"

"Seriously?" Oleg shot back, immediately offended. "After all that I've done for you? A pity party? That's what you call it? You've come to mock me?"

"No, but—"

Oleg cut him off. *"I will never see my wife and son again,"* he bellowed.

"Neither will I," Marcus retorted.

"The Kremlin wants to put me before a firing squad."

"With me right next to you, or did you forget?" asked Marcus.

"I'm effectively a prisoner in this house," Oleg continued. "I don't have a passport. I don't have a car. I can't do my own grocery shopping. Supplies are dropped off at my front door once a week. I have almost no contact with any human beings except for an occasional call from some flunky at Langley, and fewer and fewer of those. You never come to see me. Miss Jenny never comes to see me. You guys barely write, much less call. You promised me a good, new, safe life. But you've both left me here to rot. The only time I ever hear from either of you is when you need something. Now, let's see, have I forgotten anything?"

"Are you done?" Marcus asked after a long pause.

"Hardly," said Oleg. "I'm just warming up."

"Well, spare me," Marcus replied. "Look, Oleg, you made the decision to betray your country. We didn't ask you to do it. You came to us. You knew what you were doing. You knew the risks. You knew the cost. But you did it anyway. And by the way, you were right to do it. You stopped a war. Probably saved millions of lives. And Jenny and I risked our lives to save yours. We never promised you paradise. We promised to keep you alive and far from a government for whom a firing squad would hardly suffice. They don't just want to execute you, Oleg—they want to torture you mercilessly and then butcher you like an animal. So maybe it's time you man up, take responsibility for your own choices, and start showing a smidgeon of gratitude for the sacrifices we've made to protect you."

"*Gratitude?*" Oleg yelled, his pale face suddenly bright red with rage. "*You cannot be serious. Vasily is growing up without me. Barely even remembers me. Marina just got remarried last weekend. That's right, remarried—to one of the guys I went to law school with. And where am I? Alone—in solitary confinement—in your infernal, hypocritical country. It's you and Miss Jenny who should be grateful to me. How dare you—*"

But this time Marcus cut Oleg off. "Jenny's dead," he said without emotion.

That stopped Oleg cold. "What?"

"I'm sorry to be the one to tell you."

"How? When?"

But Marcus ignored the questions. "I'm sorry about Marina, Oleg. I hadn't heard. And I'm sorry about Vasily. I know you love them—both of them—dearly. But you cannot hold any of this against me, and certainly not against Jenny, God rest her soul. You made your choices. Don't complain about them now. You could've demanded that we get Marina and Vasily out of the country along with you as the price of turning over your father-in-law's war plans. But you didn't. And it wasn't an oversight. It wasn't a mistake. You knew full well that if you brought Marina and Vasily with you into exile, eventually Marina would get homesick. She'd reach out to her mother, or to one of her friends, tipping off the FSB and leading them right to your doorstep. Bringing Marina and Vasily meant merely postponing your execution, not canceling it. So you cut them loose. Why? Because you wanted to live."

"You call this living?" Oleg demanded.

"Living in squalor is your choice, not mine, and not the American government's. Grow up. Your quality of life is up to you. Not us. You asked us to get you out of Russia and we did. You asked us to keep you alive and we have. You're not in a casket. You're not rotting in a prison cell. You're alive and safe and free. The rest is up to you. But none of that is why I've come here today."

"Oh, no? You didn't come here to lecture me, to tell me what a failure and disappointment I am?"

"I'd say you're doing a fine enough job of that yourself," Marcus countered. "I came because I need your help again."

"Forget it," Oleg growled.

"You don't have a choice and you know it," said Marcus. "Your agreement with the Agency is that you help us in any way we ask, or we hand you over to Moscow."

"Fine, then hand me back. The FSB just found and shut the last back door I had into the Kremlin's computer network. There's nothing more I can do for you."

"When?"

"Four or five days ago—what does it matter?"

"Why didn't you text me?"

"I did text you," Oleg insisted. "You never wrote back."

This caught Marcus off guard. He said nothing at first, just stared into the crackling fire. It was possible—even probable, he now realized—that Oleg was telling the truth. The last few months had been a blur. What's more, when Annie had asked him to head out to Aspen, it hadn't even occurred to him to check the secure text messaging account that Noah had set up for him to communicate with the Raven, an oversight Marcus now regretted. Still, he had to get Oleg focused and back on mission. After all, at this point, he really was the Agency's only hope of finding Abu Nakba.

Taichung

Changhua

Nantou

Yunlin

T a i w a n
(Republic of China)

Chiayi County
Chiayi

Tainan

'Kaohsiung

INTERLUDE—
30 JULY, 1997

42

"*The van is ready—are the bombs? Both of them? Khaled needs to know. Now.*"

Not yet thirty, the young man—full of swagger and bravado—had just burst into the squalid, humid, back-alley metal shop in Nablus, in the heart of the West Bank, like he owned the place.

Walid Abdel-Shafi paused from his painstaking work but refused to look up. He was nearly twice this kid's age, and it took all the restraint he could muster not to slap him hard across the cheek. But the clock was ticking, and the highly volatile but not-yet-completed explosive device lay on the wooden table before him. Sweat dripped down his back, matting his long and increasingly gray hair, all pulled back in a ponytail.

What in the world was wrong with this new generation? Walid asked himself. Whatever happened to respecting one's elders? Was there no deference toward those who'd been blowing up the Zionist occupiers since long before any of these cocksure neophytes were even conceived? And even if not, did this moron have no fear of interrupting a man in the final stages of assembling a device that could vaporize both of them in a fraction of a second?

"That one, yes," Walid grunted, nodding at the large leather attaché case resting on the concrete floor beside him. "I need a bit more time on the second."

"Khaled says there is no more time," the young man snapped, a satellite phone pressed to his ear.

"Watch your tone, *habibi*," Walid replied through gritted teeth.

The kid muttered something into the phone, then turned on his heel and headed back to the van. Alone once again, Walid wiped his brow on his sleeve and double-checked his work. Satisfied he hadn't missed anything, he reached down, picked up the two large cylinders bound together by duct tape and a tangle of wires, and tucked them into the second attaché case with great care.

Inside each was six pounds of acetone peroxide, a combination Walid dubbed "APEX," but had been nicknamed by his fellow bomb makers as the "mother of Satan." Given the lack of access that Hamas operatives in the Gaza Strip had to C4, Semtex, and other forms of plastic explosives, APEX was a formula Walid had come up with on his own using hair bleach and nail polish. It was a uniquely lethal concoction of ingredients available even in a refugee camp on the outskirts of Gaza City, where Walid had spent his formative years. Combining acetone and hydrogen peroxide, Walid had created a secret sauce of triacetone triperoxide, or TATP.

One upside: it contained no nitrogen and thus could elude even the most sophisticated explosive detection equipment.

Another upside: it could truly pack a punch.

The downside was that even the slightest wrong move could trigger an accidental detonation. That's where the "mother of Satan" moniker had come from after several of Walid's colleagues had lost fingers, hands, and even their lives.

Taking a deep breath, Walid wiped his hands dry with a dirty rag, then walked over to a bin of scrap metal. With a small garden trowel, he scooped up a bunch of razor-sharp pieces, walked back to the table, and slowly poured them around the device. Then he took a scoop from another bin filled with rusty nails and carefully poured them around the bomb as well. He repeated this procedure several more times until the leather case was full.

Only then did he connect the timing fuse and the trigger, drape the trigger over the top edge of the case, and zip the case nearly shut. He carefully lifted the case off the table by its handles with his left hand, while picking up the first case with his right hand. Walking across the oil-stained floor of the metal shop, he opened the back door with his foot, then made eye contact with the blowhard on the satphone and nodded.

It was time.

The white Chevy van—bearing the distinctive yellow Israeli license plates that one of his men had stolen just that morning—was already running. The two would-be *shahids*—martyrs—were already sitting in the backseat. One was from Nablus, the other from Ramallah. Neither were dressed in classic Muslim garb. They certainly didn't look like they had just come from praying in the mosque. Both were in their midthirties, dressed in business suits—one dark gray, the other navy blue—and crisply starched white shirts. As such, they were unlikely to draw attention. Most likely, Walid hoped, they would simply blend into the crowd with hundreds of similarly clad Israeli businessmen grabbing something to eat and drink on their lunch break.

Walid approached the already-open side door of the van, leaned forward, and handed one case to the *shahid* on the left, then the other case to the *shahid* on the right. Both knew what to do and what not to do. He had personally trained them, and there was nothing more to say to them now. Closing the side door, he motioned for the kid with the satphone to get into the front passenger seat. Walid, meanwhile, walked around the front of the van and climbed into the driver's seat.

Glancing at his watch, he saw that it was already noon. The kid wasn't wrong. They were running late. They had to move.

Forty-five nerve-racking minutes later, they were working their way through thick traffic in the center of Jerusalem. By this point, the satphone had been dismantled and shoved into the glove compartment. None of the rest of them had been allowed to bring mobile phones. There was no turning back now, and no way for Khaled Meshaal, the leader of Hamas, to contact them from Amman for any reason, much less to call off the mission.

As they inched their way up Agripas Street, they soon reached the Clal Building and approached the edge of the Mahane Yehuda market, Jerusalem's biggest and most famous *shuk*, dating back to the nineteenth century during the time of the Ottomans.

"Allah be with you," Walid said softly as he came to a stop at a traffic light.

"And with you," the *shahids* said as they exited the van and headed into the open-air market.

When the light changed, Walid turned the corner and entered a nearby parking lot, took a ticket from the attendant, pulled into an empty spot, and turned off the engine. Immediately the young aide to Meshaal got out and began walking away from the market and toward the central bus station without looking back. Walid waited for him to disappear, then also got out of the van, taking with him an opaque plastic water bottle he'd brought from Nablus.

But rather than following Khaled's orders, he began walking toward the market.

43

The sky was a brilliant blue that Wednesday afternoon.

Not a cloud to be seen.

Even now, Walid could feel the sun beating down on his face and neck, and yet again he was grateful. He was not the only person in the crowd who was sweating profusely.

He ducked down an alleyway and bought himself a cup of coffee and a pastry, hoping to blend in. Then he continued ambling through the market until he reached the same green door that he'd found several days earlier on a scouting trip.

Turning the handle, he was relieved to find it was still unlocked. He closed the door behind him and found himself in a small garden courtyard. There was no one in sight. By his watch, it was already nine minutes after 1 p.m. He scrambled up the stairs, reaching the roof. It, too, was empty of people, though the presence of fresh laundry swaying in the modest breeze indicated that someone had been there recently.

From the west side of the roof, Walid had the perfect vantage point. He had chosen the location himself, both for its name—*Mahane Yehuda* was Hebrew for *Camp of the Jews*—and for its foot traffic. He could see the throngs of mid-day shoppers. They were almost entirely Jews, though he did spot a few Arabs here and there. He also spotted a few soldiers grabbing a shawarma. Children kicking soccer balls. Fathers drinking Turkish coffee, reading newspapers, and laughing with colleagues over stupid jokes or arguing over stupid government policies. Mothers pushing baby carriages and haggling over the price of oranges and pistachios and a pair of new shoes.

When he looked at his watch again, it was 1:14 p.m. Scanning the crowd, Walid soon spotted the first *shahid* nearly one hundred yards away. He could see the man holding the leather attaché case in his left hand and glancing at his watch on his right hand. Then he watched the man stop, look up to the sky, shout, *"Allahu Akbar,"* and evaporate in a huge blast of fire and smoke.

The boom was deafening, even from this distance. But Walid never closed his eyes. Amid all the smoke and soot and ash, he could see body parts flying in every direction and severed torsos littering the pavement.

Then, on cue, he saw the wave of terrified Israelis who had not yet been murdered or mangled fleeing the epicenter of the blast. That meant they were running toward him. Taking several steps backward, away from the edge of the roof, this time he closed his eyes and turned his face toward the blazing sun. He waited several beats. Then finally he heard the second *shahid* yell, *"Allahu Akbar,"* and felt the blast wave of the second detonation. For him, Walid had built an even more powerful bomb, and the massive explosion nearly knocked the Libyan off his feet.

Engulfed in smoke and covered in soot and ash, Walid kept his eyes closed as he unscrewed the top of the opaque plastic water bottle that was not filled with water. Rather, it was filled with blood—his own blood—and now he poured it over his head and onto his hands, slathering it all over his face and neck. Then he splashed what was left against his sweat-drenched white shirt and on his black slacks, tossed the bottle and satchel aside, wiped his eyes, and headed toward the stairway as smoke and dust continued raining down upon him.

Making his way down to the main level, Walid Abdel-Shafi exited the green door and stumbled down the alleyway. All around him were mangled, panicked, screaming people. In the distance, above the cacophony, Walid could hear the sirens of police cars and ambulances and army vehicles approaching from all directions. But they were not on scene yet. Drenched in blood like everyone else, he drew minimal attention as he staggered back to the parking lot, acting dazed and confused.

When he reached the van, he fumbled for his keys, then got in, turned the ignition, and pulled away. Because the van had yellow Israeli plates, not white plates from the Palestinian Authority, no one stopped him. Nor was there any traffic to fight any longer. No one else was leaving the scene of the blasts. On the contrary, everyone was racing toward it.

Walid did not return to Nablus, of course. He didn't live there. Hadn't grown up there. Nor had he spent much time there. Rather, as he finally reached Highway 1, he was soon heading west. When he reached the exit for the Arab Israeli town of Abu Ghosh, he pulled off, found the gas station he was looking for, and drove around back. Grabbing his backpack from the trunk, he slipped into the men's room and locked the door behind him. He quickly stripped off his clothes and shoved them into a garbage bag he'd brought with him. Then he washed all the blood off his face, hands, and arms and splashed water through his hair until he'd gotten all the blood out of it, as well.

Pulling a towel out of the backpack, he dried himself off and shoved the towel into the garbage bag. Finally, he got himself dressed in a clean black T-shirt and ratty old blue jeans. Then he stuffed the garbage bag into the backpack, zipped it up, and exited the men's room.

He'd already scouted out this location and knew there were no CCTV cameras nearby. There was, of course, always the risk that someone could have spotted him covered in blood arriving at the station or entering the restroom. But that risk, he'd calculated, was minimal.

He considered it a far greater risk that Israeli security forces were going to put up roadblocks all over the country. He had an expertly forged Israeli ID in his wallet, along with a credit card from Bank Leumi, and plenty of Israeli shekels and receipts in Hebrew. His forged driver's license indicated that he was an Israeli Arab who lived in Ashdod. That, plus his mastery of colloquial Hebrew, ought to get him through all the roadblocks and checkpoints, he figured. But having a bag of bloody clothes would raise a host of questions he had no desire to answer. So he quickly tossed the backpack into the dumpster behind the gas station, got back in the van, and was soon continuing west.

Walid listened on the radio to the latest reports from Jerusalem.

Sure enough, dozens of roadblocks had been set up on the capital's periph-ery. No one was allowed in or out. The entire city was being hermetically sealed.

He silently thanked Allah for helping him slip away just in time.

The casualty figures kept climbing, and he rejoiced at every update. Just as good, Israeli politicians were already going on the air to curse Yasser Arafat and the leadership of the Palestinian Authority, denouncing them for abandoning both the letter and the spirit of the Oslo Accords. Soon Walid learned that the White House was sending its special envoy for Middle East peacemaking to the region the following day. Then he heard reports that the IDF were conducting raids in Nablus, Ramallah, Jenin, and Hebron, and just as he had anticipated, they were rounding up hundreds of suspects.

As he passed Highway 6, Walid learned that only sixteen Israelis had died, though another 178 had been wounded. He was grateful for the two *shahids* who had given their lives to strike such a blow at the Zionist occupiers. But inwardly he was stunned that the Jewish death toll was so low. How was that possible in a crowd so big? His bombs should have killed several hundred. It didn't make sense.

He told himself the authorities must be deliberately hiding the real numbers to blunt his victory. But secretly he feared that Khaled Meshaal and the rest of the Hamas leadership was going to be angry with him. Furious, actually. They had planned this operation for months. Invested a good deal of money into making it happen. And were eager to boast both publicly and privately of pulling off the biggest single massacre of Israelis in decades. Now what? Surely the number of deaths would climb. But Walid had promised up to 250 deaths. What if they did not even top two hundred?

For the first time in his life, Walid began to consider the possibility of breaking away from Hamas and starting his own resistance group.

He certainly would never join Fatah. The Palestinian Authority and its cronies were riddled with corruption. Yet Hamas, he knew far too well, was also led by incompetents. No matter how much Walid did for the cause, Khaled Meshaal was constantly second-guessing him and rejecting his strategic recommendations with pathetic, half-hearted measures of his own. Islamic Jihad was no good either. The Palestinian cause deserved better. Not lackeys hiding in Amman or Doha or Tunis. Not doddering old men railing against the Zionists yet secretly looking to the West for funding and legitimacy. The farther he drove, the more inflamed he became by the prospect of abandoning Hamas and founding a jihadi group truly worthy of its name.

When Walid finally reached the Israeli city of Ashdod, not far from the Gaza Strip, he parked the van in the garage of a sketchy hotel by the beach, took the elevator to the fifth floor, and returned to the room he had previously rented for the week. Showering, he took special care to shampoo and rinse his long, flowing mane. Then, wearing only a bathrobe, he cranked up the air conditioning, flipped on the television, and flopped down on the bed. He set the alarm on his watch and soon fell asleep to live coverage of the ongoing emergency rescue operations in Jerusalem and the IDF's military operations in the West Bank, tearing the PA apart house by house.

At precisely 3 a.m., the alarm on his watch went off. Silencing it quickly, Walid promptly got dressed, left his room, and headed down the back stairwell. When he exited through the rear of the hotel, he saw a pair of headlights turn on across the parking lot. He walked over to the Volvo, noting that the engine was already running. He nodded to the driver and got into the passenger's seat. Ten minutes later, Walid was dropped off on a deserted section of road within walking distance of the beach. Seeing no one in any direction, he removed his sandals, rolled up his pant legs, and made his way to the water's edge.

He peered into the darkness in one direction, and then the other. He saw no one at first. Had the mission been compromised? Had the exfil team been caught by the Zionists? These and a dozen other fears raced through his mind, but a few minutes later, he heard the engine of a small craft, and then the engine noise cut out.

He spotted a single flash of light. He could see nothing else, but he estimated the flash had come from no more than twenty or thirty meters offshore. Wading into the chilly Med, Walid began swimming against the current in the direction of the light. Sure enough, he quickly reached a small rubber raft. Hamas operatives wearing scuba gear and carrying automatic weapons grabbed him and pulled him aboard.

Walid said nothing. Nor did the three men who had come for him. Instead, they restarted the engine, turned the vessel around, and headed out to the open sea before turning toward Gaza.

A few hours later, Walid and his handlers reached the safe house. Walid went straight to his room, collapsed onto a cot, and stared up at the ceiling fan above him.

45

How strange it felt to be back in Gaza.

Walid's father was a Libyan oil worker and a disgrace to Islam. A cruel and selfish man, a drunkard and an apostate, he had abandoned his family when Walid was only three. That's when Walid and his mother had departed Tripoli on a putrid steamship and traveled back to Gaza, where she had been born and raised.

With immense pain, he could still recall glimpses of those early years growing up in Khan Yunis, the teeming refugee camp on the southern end of the Strip, just a few miles from the glistening Mediterranean. He could still hear the sobbing, not only of his mother but of the widows who had lost their husbands and sons to the war with the Zionists just a few years before their arrival, as tears streaked down hollow, dusty faces. He could still see rage in the eyes of the packs of teenage boys who roamed the alleyways of the camp, vowing their revenge against the Jews and longing to be old enough to be welcomed into the Muslim Brotherhood's embrace. What's more, he could still smell the back rooms filled with stale cigarette smoke and see the bitterness in the eyes of weary old men as they sipped steaming cups of Turkish coffee and huddled around the wireless, listening to Gamal Abdel Nasser—the savior of Egypt—describing the '48 war as "Al Nakba," the catastrophe that had seared the Arab soul, and vowing to "throw the Jews into the sea."

As Walid stared into the ceiling fan, he remembered reaching his own teenage years, joining one of those packs of wild, embittered youths, and then—after the humiliation of the Zionists' victory in 1967—starting his own pack, dragging his young followers to the mosque every Friday and insisting they read his dogeared copies of the works of Hassan al-Banna and Sayyid Qutb, the Egyptian-born founders of the Muslim Brotherhood.

"Nasser is a fraud," he had told his troop. "And the Baathists of Iraq and Syria are cowards. Pan-Arab nationalism is a secular movement and provides no answers to our humiliation. It rejects the notion that only devotion to Allah can save us. That is why its followers are not just losing but losing badly, and not just to the Christians but to the Jews."

"Reject Allah, and Allah will reject you—but there is another way," he would whisper in the alleyways, taking a drag on his own cigarette while rewarding his loyal and growing band of street thugs with cigarettes of their own. *"The Qur'an must be our constitution, the Prophet must be our leader, jihad must be our path, and death in the name of Allah must be our only goal."*

He could still hear himself saying it, the boys repeating it, quietly at first and then in a murderous mantra.

And to such sweet memories, Walid finally fell asleep.

He woke at dawn. He was in the basement of a dilapidated old warehouse in Khan Yunis, just a few kilometers from the Egyptian border. It was a safe house he'd never been to before, but at least he recognized the men guarding him. They offered to make him breakfast, but Walid was not hungry for food, only for information. Accepting only a cup of piping hot Turkish coffee, he ordered one of his young aides to turn on the television. He couldn't imagine why they weren't already glued to the news and gathering every scrap of information they possibly could about the impact of the bombings and the extent of the IDF raids.

To his shock, however, the first thing he saw when the screen finally flickered to life was grainy images of him—and his van.

How was that possible?

Where had the CCTV cameras been?

And how had the Zionist criminals so quickly zeroed in on him and his vehicle?

Had the young Meshaal aide been caught?

Had he talked?

That was the only explanation Walid could think of. Dumbstruck themselves, his men turned to him for answers, but he had none. He needed a moment to himself to think, to plot his next moves. He asked where the toilets were and was directed to a ramshackle outhouse twenty steps away behind the warehouse. It was a crude wooden structure with a corrugated tin roof. But it would have to suffice. As he stood over the putrid hole in the ground, Walid forced himself to stop looking backward. It was pointless to figure out how the Zionists had found him. The only option now was to devise a way of escape. He could not afford to be furious at himself for being so sloppy with his tradecraft, or at others for betraying him, which, surely, they had done.

And yet the longer he stood there, the clearer the picture became. His photo was suddenly being broadcast all over Israel and the world. This wasn't a curse. This was a blessing, albeit in disguise. The Israeli announcers were calling him the mastermind of the suicide attacks in Jerusalem. He was the chief architect and engineer. Not Khaled Meshaal. Not Sheikh Ahmed Yassin. Not any other senior Hamas leader. The eyes of the world were riveted on *him*. The Zionists were hunting *him*. What better way to build his global brand? What more effective way was there to lay the groundwork for his departure from Hamas and the establishment of his own resistance movement? Before today, no one in the Muslim world had ever heard of him. But now . . .

Just then he heard two helicopters. They were faint at first but approaching rapidly from the north. Walid zipped up and began to run when he heard the whoosh of the first inbound missile. An instant later, the warehouse was obliterated in a massive fireball, killing a dozen of Hamas's most elite operators. Only moments later came the second Hellfire missile, and a blast sent him hurtling through the air.

He had no idea how long he had blacked out. When he finally awoke, Walid Abdel-Shafi had third-degree burns over most of his body. He could barely see. He could barely hear. Someone was tying a tourniquet around his left arm, just above the elbow, desperately trying to stanch the bleeding. Someone else was trying to pull a long, jagged piece of the corrugated roof out of his right leg.

And all the while a third man was shouting at the top of his lungs, *"Abu Nakba, stay with us. Abu Nakba, please, stay with us—we will save you."*

Taichung

Changhua

Yunlin

Taiwan
(Republic of China)

Nantou

Chiayi County
Tainan

Tainan

Kaohsiung

Taitung

PART
THREE

46

Annie Stewart awoke long before her alarm went off.

It was far too cold to go outside for a run, so she rolled out of bed, splashed some water on her face, pulled her hair back into a ponytail, and stepped onto her treadmill. After running the equivalent of five miles, she took a long, hot shower.

She dressed, brewed a pot of tea and made herself a small bowl of yogurt, berries, and granola. After breakfast, she brushed her teeth and put on a little more makeup than usual to cover the dark circles under her eyes. Then she took her Glock 9mm pistol out of the drawer by her bed and put it in her handbag along with several additional magazines. She grabbed her CIA credentials and mobile phone, then stepped into the kitchen one more time. There, she filled two Thermos bottles with fresh Brazilian brew and headed out the front door. Waiting was her security detail and her bulletproof black Suburban SUV, its engine already running.

"Morning, Mike," she said to her lead agent.

"Morning, Miss Stewart—sleep okay?" he inquired as he helped her into the backseat and shut the door before getting into the front passenger seat.

"Can't complain," she said, careful not to lie but certainly not prepared to tell these three men that she'd barely slept a wink.

She handed one Thermos bottle to the lead agent and the second to the agent beside her. As they poured cups for themselves and one for the driver, she chatted with them about the day's forecast and a bit about the latest college basketball scores and rankings. Anything to take her mind off the pressures that were building all around her.

Most of the city's streets had been plowed overnight, and the distance from her town house to Lincoln Park Baptist Church was only a few blocks, so the drive didn't take long. As the car pulled around back, she spotted the ever-present D.C. Metro police car—lights always flashing—maintaining its high-profile presence as per the order of the mayor. When they entered the parking lot, Annie could see two more members of her detail waiting for her by the church's back door.

They were good men—strong, kind, capable—as were the other six standing post at other entrances to the historic church building. Yet it was sad that they were necessary. Annie longed for the days when no one cared who she was. But those days seemed long gone. Not only was she the second-highest-ranking official at the CIA; she was also engaged to a man with a $20 million bounty on his head courtesy of the terror masters in Tehran. What's more, this very church had been the scene of a major terrorist attack just a few years earlier, one that had taken the lives of several of their closest friends, including Pastor Carter Emerson, the African American army veteran who'd survived Vietnam and become a beloved shepherd of lost souls, only to be gunned down by Kairos terrorists in his own pulpit. Neither the Agency nor the D.C. police were taking any chances of a sequel.

The morning service was already underway, the congregation was already standing, and the organ was already playing "Battle Hymn of the Republic" as Annie slipped into the last pew and gave a hug to Maya Emerson, Carter's widow. Now well into her seventies, and one of the most beautiful and godly women Annie had ever had the honor to know, Maya hadn't given up on life. She certainly missed her late husband terribly. They had, after all, been married for more than fifty years. But Maya remained a pillar of the church community. Shaking every hand every Sunday morning. Visiting the sick and those in the hospital. Leading Bible studies at her home and the church prayer meeting every Tuesday evening.

It went against every instinct in Annie's body and all the Southern manners by which her parents had raised her to come to church late and duck out early. She hated missing the "coffee and conversation" hour between services. She hated missing all the fellowship time with friends and the opportunity to meet and welcome strangers. These had always been elements she'd loved about Sundays, ever since she was a little girl. But security protocols, combined with the ever-pressing demands of her new job, made it impossible to be a normal church member. What's more, Annie knew that her presence, and that of her security detail, was a distraction to others, making it difficult for the rest of the congregation to focus on each other, much less on Christ and his Word.

47

"I don't understand," Marcus said. "You're saying they've plugged *every* hole?"

"*Da,*" Oleg replied.

"*All* of them?"

"*Da.*"

"I don't believe it."

"It's true."

"There are no back doors, no Trojan horses?" Marcus pressed. "There's no way to hack back into their system?"

"I told you it would happen. Now it has."

"That's not possible, Oleg. We've got to know what Petrovsky said to President Guanzhong and whether the Kremlin is still funneling money to Kairos."

"I've tried everything. What do you think I've been doing every day of every week while you completely ignore me?"

Marcus, increasingly desperate, tried to stay focused. "What about all the gigabytes of data that you've already downloaded from Petrovsky's and

Kropatkin's computers?" Nikolay Vladimirovich Kropatkin had served as the head of the FSB and had recently been appointed to oversee all of Russia's myriad intelligence services.

"What about them?" asked Oleg. "Langley has all of it."

"Isn't there anything in those files—?"

"Marcus, you're not listening to me. There's nothing there, nothing that could lead you to Abu Nakba. I didn't miss it. I didn't overlook it. I'm not blind. I'm telling you—there's nothing there."

"Isn't it possible the Russians are still working with Kairos—and really do know where the Libyan is—but are keeping that information on a separate system? Or on paper files? Something that you're not aware of yet?"

Oleg leaned back in his chair and stared up at the ceiling. All the venom was gone, and he now spoke very softly. "You really don't get it, do you, Marcus? I've done everything that I possibly can. This is what I do. This is what I've done all day every day since you brought me out here and set me to work. Nonstop. Without a break. But I've reached the end of the river. There's no more gold to pan for. There are no more tricks up my sleeve. So I'm done. There's literally nothing more I can do. I'm spent. I'm trapped in this house all by myself. Alone. Night after night. Day after day. Week after bloody week. And you think I should be grateful. Well, I'm not. And if you don't understand why, I have no more interest in trying to explain it."

Marcus looked down at the threadbare carpet.

This isn't happening, he told himself.

And yet it was.

This man was America's last hope of finding any morsel of intelligence that might lead to Abu Nakba. Yet Oleg had nothing. Worse, he appeared on the verge of a nervous breakdown. Marcus couldn't bear the thought of having to break this news to Annie, much less Dell, much less the president. But nor could he keep them in the dark.

Exhaling, Marcus rubbed the stubble on his unshaven face and turned to the windows facing east. The sun was beginning to rise over a nearby mountain ridge. It wasn't snowing any longer. The morning skies were still cloudy, but through the smudged windows, Marcus could still see a few patches of blue.

"Would you excuse me for a moment, Oleg?" he said, rising to his feet. "I need to make a call."

Oleg, glassy-eyed and in serious need of a shower, made no response.

Marcus headed out the front door without jacket or gloves and trudged back through the snow to the Jeep. He unlocked it, climbed into the driver's seat, and turned on the engine. Then, cranking up the heat, he speed-dialed his fiancée.

48

Annie's phone began to buzz in her handbag.

Normally, she would ignore her phone during church. When else could she pull herself away from the tyranny of the urgent? If Dell or the Global Ops Center really needed her, Agent Mike would be sure to get her attention. And that morning she was especially looking forward to the pastor's message.

Barry Jackson, the young Chicago-born pastor—barely in his forties—was a U.S. Army veteran who had served in the second Gulf War. Like Carter, his predecessor, Barry was a brilliant theologian and an exceptional speaker. Yet what Annie appreciated most about him was that he had the true heart of a shepherd and a deep inner strength that came through in his teaching and his character. He was a warrior without bravado.

The man had just begun this week's sermon when he heard the buzzing of Annie's phone. He raised an eyebrow at her, albeit with a smile, and Annie was tempted to let it go. But knowing it could be Marcus, she fished her phone out of her bag and checked the caller ID. Sure enough, she had to take this call. Elbowing Mike, she discreetly slipped out of the pew as the phone continued buzzing. She quickly headed down a back hallway and stepped into the ladies' room while Agent Mike guarded the door.

"You just pulled me out of some powerful gospel preaching, Marcus, so tell me some good news," she whispered without preamble.

"I'm afraid I can't—our mutual friend has nothing."

"That's impossible."

"That's what I thought too, but it's true."

"Do you believe him?" Annie asked.

"Unfortunately, yes," Marcus replied as he recounted the substance of the conversation he and Oleg had just finished.

"So now what?" Annie asked.

"I have no idea," Marcus admitted. "But I'm worried about him. He's severely depressed."

"Maybe he just needs a little motivation," Annie suggested.

"Meaning what?"

"Meaning maybe you need to light a fire under him."

"How so?"

"Tell him we'll snatch Vasily, spirit him out of the country, and reunite the two of them—but only if he finds a way to hack back into the Kremlin's network," Annie said. "And make it clear that if he doesn't play ball, we'll have to hand him over to Petrovsky and Kropatkin."

"I don't know," Marcus said. "I don't think motivation is the problem. I think we're beyond that. And what if he calls our bluff?"

"Do we have a choice? Listen—we don't have time to put the man into counseling. Right now, we need results—and fast."

"I hear you, but—"

"Marcus, tell me you have another plan and I'll consider it."

"I don't."

"Then do it," Annie ordered. "And give him a deadline."

"How long?"

"Well, today's Sunday. Give him 'til Friday, close of business. If he can't get into the system by then, tell him we're putting him on the first plane back to Moscow."

"You sure the president will go for that?" Marcus asked.

"Leave that to me," Annie insisted. "But honestly, I doubt it will get that far. Based on everything you and Martha have told me, this guy is a true genius. We just need to get him refocused and back in the game. We'll get him the help he needs after he gets us what we need."

"All right, I'll give it a try and call you back."

"Good—and hey, I love you, and I'm praying for you."

"Thanks," said Marcus. "Love you, too. Sorry to interrupt you at church."

"Yeah, you'd better be. Barry gave me the look when I ducked out of his message."

"I'll bet he did."

"Oh, and Marcus?" Annie said. "Happy Valentine's Day."

Marcus hung up the phone and winced. He missed Annie so much it hurt. He desperately wanted all this to be over and for the two of them to get married and live happily ever after. But for now, he had a job to do, and as distasteful as this new assignment was, it had to be done. So he'd better get on with it.

Turning off the engine, Marcus stepped out of the Jeep, then shut and locked the door behind him. But just as he walked back toward the cabin, he heard a single gunshot echo through the canyon.

49

Marcus froze.

All his senses heightened, listening for unnatural movement in the rustling trees around him, he slowly turned and scanned every square inch in every direction. Yet he saw no one. Heard no one. There were no cars on the road. No snowplows. No signs of people. Nor was there a second gunshot.

There were only two options.

Either the Russians had found Oleg Kraskin and sent a sniper to take him out. Or . . .

Moving cautiously toward the front door, Marcus slowly turned the knob, then tapped the door open with his boot.

It was instantly clear this wasn't the work of the Russian intelligence services. Every window was still intact. No holes. No broken glass.

Nevertheless, the Raven was sprawled out on the living room floor. Lying face up. Eyes still open. Lifeless and hollow. Staring up at the ceiling. Half of his jaw was blown off. A pool of crimson spreading around his head, soaking into the carpet. And Marcus's Sig Sauer lay in his right hand, smoke still curling out of its barrel, the acrid stench of sawdust, graphite, and nitroglycerin hanging in the air.

A shiver ran down Marcus's spine. But it wasn't fear that rippled through him. It was guilt. How could he have been so reckless as to leave his weapon in the house? It was a cardinal rule of any handgun owner. It was the law of the land in the Secret Service, the DSS, and the Central Intelligence Agency. You never left your weapon unattended. Especially if it was loaded. You always kept it with you. It didn't matter that he'd only intended to step out of the A-frame for a few minutes. It just wasn't done. And now the Agency's most valuable foreign asset—and very possibly their last chance of finding Abu Nakba—was dead. Not at the hands of an assassin but by suicide. And Marcus could have prevented it.

Forcing himself to take several deep breaths, Marcus pulled out his phone to call Pete and then Annie. As much as it galled him, he wasn't going to be able to take care of this disaster on his own. He was going to need help and quickly. Yet just before he dialed, he caught himself. Taking a few more moments to consider the situation, Marcus concluded it was too soon to call it in. He needed time to think. What's more, he needed time to find and neutralize the surveillance cameras providing security officers back at Langley with 24-7 monitoring of the house.

Putting on his gloves, Marcus climbed up the ladder and scanned the loft. In addition to Oleg's unmade bed, filthy sheets, and dirty clothes strewn all about, he found a small desk, a chest of drawers, and some bookshelves filled with works of Russian literature. On the nightstand beside the bed was a lamp, another photo of Marina and Vasily, a pair of binoculars, a dog-eared book about bird-watching, and at least a dozen bottles of various prescription pain relievers, along with an empty bottle marked *divalproex sodium*. Marcus tensed. It was a mood-stabilizing drug typically used by people suffering from bipolar disorder. Pulling out his phone, he quickly took pictures of everything, including each bottle of pills. Then he shoved his phone in his back pocket and picked up the binoculars.

Peering through the upstairs window into the backyard, he scrutinized the bird feeder hanging from the branch of a snow-covered pine. Then he examined every tree with a direct sight line to the house. He spotted an old gasoline-powered generator out back. Finally, on a telephone pole off to the right side of the property, about thirty feet up, he found it—a tiny camera no larger than a silver dollar. It was ingeniously positioned, easily mistaken for a natural knot in the wood. And it provided perfect coverage of the entire back of the house. It did not, however, provide coverage of the front or the driveway. That was good, Marcus concluded. He could leave it be.

At the same time, he felt reasonably confident that the Agency didn't have any video cameras or listening devices inside the house. The Raven wasn't considered a security threat. Up to that moment, he'd been fully cooperating with Langley. The surveillance was designed to keep the CIA's asset safe, keeping an eye out for strange people or vehicles that might approach the house, and making sure Oleg never left the property.

So where were the cameras that covered the front and sides of the house?

Marcus scrambled down the ladder and started toward the door, careful to step around the body and ever-widening pool of blood. That's when he decided to fill up a pan of water and douse the flames in the fireplace. It was getting too warm. If anything, he needed the temperature to drop significantly to keep the body cold.

Most of Oleg's pots and pans were crusted in filth and stacked in and around the kitchen sink. He'd use one of them if he had to, but he preferred to find something clean. He didn't need the house smelling like smoke *and* leftover spaghetti. He rooted through the cupboards but found most of them bare. Then he opened the pantry. A few boxes of pasta. Some jars of tomato sauce. A few cans of corn. And a half-empty jar of peanut butter. *Slim pickings*, thought Marcus, suddenly realizing that a delivery of groceries could be coming that day. That was a complication he didn't need. But nor could he worry about it. There simply wasn't time.

He was just about to close the door to the pantry when something caught his eye. Toward the back of the main shelf, just off to the left, he spotted a wooden knob. Curious, he reached in and pulled. It didn't open. He wriggled it a bit more and found that it slid to the right. Behind the sliding door he found a digital control panel resembling a touch-tone telephone keypad and a flat-screen monitor divided up into six black-and-white live images.

It turned out there were two cameras covering the back, not just one.

Two more cameras covered the approaches to the right and left sides of the house. Of the two remaining cameras, Marcus could see that one must be located on a telephone pole across the street. It provided a clear, wide-angle view of the front of the house and the driveway, including his Jeep. The second camera had to be located under one of the gables on the front of the house, providing coverage of the driveway and road and the dense forest beyond.

This wasn't good. There was no way Marcus was going to be able to reach these two cameras, much less mask or disable them, without being seen on video in the process, and thus caught. Worse, he'd just be wasting valuable time.

A plan was forming in his head. Still not ready to call Annie, he called Pete instead.

50

"Pete, I need you—*right now*," Marcus said when his friend picked up.

"Sure," said Pete, "but you've got our wheels."

"Rent a car through the concierge," Marcus instructed. "Have them pull it up to the front of the Ritz and call you the minute it arrives. Once you're in it and you're alone, call me back."

"Why? What's going on?"

"Just do it and I'll tell you more soon," Marcus insisted.

It seemed like an eternity, but Pete finally did call back. Apologizing for taking so long, he explained that nearly every rental agency was out of vehicles. However, he'd finally persuaded the concierge to let him use one of the Ritz-Carlton's vehicles. It had cost him a pretty penny, but he was now sitting in a midnight blue Mercedes SUV. Marcus gave him the address and waited for Pete to plug it into the GPS.

"How long 'til you get here?" Marcus asked.

"Twenty-three minutes," Pete replied.

"That'll have to do. Don't stop anywhere. Don't talk to anyone. And don't try to go faster to make up time. The roads are slick, and I don't need you winding up in a ditch."

"Want to tell me what this is all about?"

"Not yet," Marcus said. "Call me when you're five minutes out."

Hanging up the phone and shoving it in the pocket of his jacket, Marcus peeked through the blinds. The snow had started falling steadily again, which would only help keep any potential onlookers off the streets. There were still no signs of people. No cars. No trucks or plows—yet. And—thank goodness— no one delivering groceries. Nor did he see anything that suggested a threat. Moving cautiously to the windows on the north side of the house and seeing nothing out of the ordinary, he lowered the blinds to prevent anyone who might emerge later from being able to see into the house. From there he checked the windows in the bathroom and the kitchen and lowered those blinds as well. Then he double-checked the back door to make sure it was locked and returned to the front door to await Pete, occasionally looking out the peephole just to reassure himself that all was okay.

What he did not do was look back at Oleg. Marcus certainly wasn't a stranger to death. But this was different. Oleg Kraskin was the second friend whose death he'd been forced to face over the past few days, and it shook him. Strangely, he had met both Jenny Morris and Oleg on the very same day back in Moscow. In fact, it was unlikely he would ever have met Jenny—or been recruited into the Agency—if it hadn't been for Oleg.

Marcus remembered that first encounter like it was yesterday. He'd been in Moscow on an advance mission, preparing for a state visit. He'd stayed in the Hotel National, just across the street from the Kremlin. He could still hear that strange knock on the door between his room and what turned out to be Oleg's. He recalled the Russian explaining to him, in no more than a whisper, that his father-in-law—the president of the Russian Federation—was planning to order the Red Army to invade Estonia, Latvia, and Lithuania. Even all these years later, Marcus could feel Oleg's phone in his hands and see those images of highly classified war plans in the phone's photo gallery. And he would never forget the cab ride, racing through the crowded streets of Moscow, arriving at the American embassy, and demanding the Marine guards let him in so he could bring the evidence to his friend Nick Vinetti, the embassy's deputy chief of mission.

So much had happened since then. Yet all of it was so fresh, so vivid in his mind. One minute, he was fixing the roof of the Lincoln Park Baptist Church in Washington, D.C., grieving the loss of his wife and son, trying to figure out where God was in the midst of his pain. The next minute he was HALO jumping into enemy territory and helping Oleg plot the assassination of Russian president Aleksandr Luganov.

That would have been crazy enough. But it had only gotten more intense and more painful from there.

Jenny had been shot and almost died helping Marcus get Oleg out of Russia.

Nick had been killed on an operation in North Korea.

Pete had nearly been killed on the same mission.

Carter Emerson had been murdered by terrorists in Lincoln Park Baptist.

Annie had nearly been murdered in Jerusalem.

Marcus and Kailea had nearly been tortured to death in Lebanon.

President Andrew Clarke had suffered a massive stroke at the White House.

And now Jenny and Oleg were both dead.

Marcus found himself struggling to breathe. His face was perspiring. His heart was pounding. His mouth was suddenly dry, and he was feeling light-headed. Staggering to the kitchen, he could find no clean glasses. So he ripped off his right glove, turned on the faucet, gulped down several handfuls of water, and splashed water on his face and the back of his neck.

Just then his phone rang.

Turning off the faucet and drying his hand on his blue jeans, he answered the call. It was Pete. He was inbound.

Marcus stumbled to the bathroom and opened a metal panel behind the door. Before him were the circuit breakers to Oleg's house. Staring at his watch, he waited three more minutes, then threw those breakers, knocking out all power to the house. He quickly moved back to the kitchen, praying his experiment worked. There was no way he could have tested it sooner. He had one shot, and this was it.

Fortunately, when he opened the pantry door, he found the video surveillance system dead. It was connected to the same power grid as the rest of the house. The problem was that the generator located out back would, no doubt, kick in momentarily.

They had to move fast.

51

The unmarked business jet landed on runway 35R.

It did not taxi to the main terminal at Daxing International Airport, nick-named "the starfish" because of its unique design with multiple "tentacles." Nor was it headed for the private aviation terminal. Rather, the jet pulled into a rarely used hangar on the east side of the airport. Only after the enormous bay doors shut and the plane was shielded from prying eyes did the three men and their bodyguards step off the jet and into a convoy of three unmarked white SUVs.

Exiting the airport grounds, they drove into the heart of Beijing, inching their way through bumper-to-bumper traffic until they pulled into a massive parking garage. There, lest anyone was following them, they all changed ve-hicles. Different makes. Different models. Different colors. They exited the garage at different times. No longer did they appear to be a convoy. But they were all still heading north, beyond the capital district, up into the mountains, as if they were tourists heading to China's famed Great Wall.

As the lead vehicle crossed the Huaijiu River—a good fifteen or twenty minutes ahead of the others—it exited off the main highway onto a paved but unmarked road that cut through an immense forest. Several kilometers in, the vehicle reached a fifteen-foot steel gate topped by barbed wire and flanked by guard towers, searchlights, and heavily armed PLA soldiers. The driver slowed to a halt, rolled down his window, handed over his government ID, and spoke briefly in Mandarin. The moment he received his ID back, the steel gate opened.

Soon the SUV was heading up a winding mountain road for several more kilometers until it reached a sprawling retreat complex nestled under hundreds of soaring pines. Rather than pulling up to the official welcome center, however, the vehicle turned onto a side road. Twenty minutes later, it finally reached another armed checkpoint, and then a group of three large cabins overlooking a frozen mountain lake.

Li Bai Xiang, a senior officer with China's State Security Ministry, exited the car first. Mohammed Faisal was next. Then both turned and helped the Libyan into a wheelchair and into the main lodge. Expecting his boss to be spent by jet lag and nauseated by the drive, Faisal discreetly offered him the opportunity to go to his room and lie down for a while. But the old man wouldn't hear of it.

"You're certain, Father?" Faisal asked. "There is no shame in taking some time—"

But Abu Nakba cut him off. "I've been summoned for a reason," he insisted. "It would be most rude to delay."

"As you wish, Father," Faisal replied.

With Xiang leading the way, Faisal wheeled the old man into the great hall, where they found a roaring fire in a huge stone hearth and immense bay windows giving them a beautiful view of the icy lake. They also found waiting for them Dai Wangshu, China's minister of state security, who immediately rose from his overstuffed leather chair beside the fireplace and bowed to his guest.

"Your Excellency, the most revered Abu Nakba, what an honor to welcome you to the People's Republic of China," Wangshu began.

"You are most kind," the Libyan replied, bowing his head but not standing from the wheelchair. "It is my honor to accept your most gracious invitation."

"I believe this is your first time to our country, is it not?"

"It is, and I only wish it was under better circumstances."

"Soon enough, my friend, soon enough you will be done with your work and are welcome to retire in the very home whose design you gave us. I am pleased to report that it is almost finished, to your exact specifications."

"You are most kind, Minister—most kind, indeed."

"China takes care of our faithful allies and warriors, and no one has been more faithful—or more successful—than you, Your Excellency."

The old man looked away from his host, into the crackling fire. At this, China's intelligence chief asked Li Bai Xiang and Mohammed Faisal to retire to a separate room, where they could have their own consultations. He needed some time alone now with the Kairos founder and chief strategist.

Once they were served tea, Dai Wangshu pulled his chair over to Abu Nakba.

"It's hard to believe, my friend, that this is the first time we have actually met face-to-face," the spymaster said when they were finally alone.

Abu Nakba, still staring at the roaring fire, said nothing.

"Forgive me, but I must ask you, Father: is something wrong?" Wangshu asked. "Should you not be filled with great joy and hope for the future?"

"*Joy?*" asked the Libyan, his face growing red, his fists clenched. "How could I possibly be filled with joy? How could I possibly have hope for the future? All my life's work is in ruins. Every operation I have designed and tried to execute has been a disaster, thwarted time after time by the Americans—sometimes by the criminal Zionist entity—but especially by the *jinn* at Langley."

"A disaster?" asked the spymaster. "This is how you see it?"

"Do you not agree that the recent destruction in Karachi was a wretched debacle?"

"Certainly a disappointment," Xiang admitted, "but not fatally so. The Americans have not connected China to the enterprise. When we visited the site posing as a Pakistani convoy, the simple ruse seems to have derailed their best intelligence."

"Do not dissemble, not to me, Minister," Abu Nakba shot back. "You and I both know that my work has been an unmitigated disaster. We both know this is why you summoned me. Your generous investment in Kairos has been utterly wasted. We have failed to achieve any of the objectives for which you recruited me. I have not come to defend myself. I have come to confess my failures, to apologize profusely for disappointing you and your superiors so profoundly, and to accept full responsibility. I alone am to blame. My men have made their own share of mistakes, but I assure you, each of them is brave and selfless and more honorable than I. But they were poorly led. They did everything I asked of them. But whatever their failures, they are not responsible. I am, and I alone."

"You think that is why you're here," Wangshu asked. "You genuinely believe that my superiors and I are angry at you?"

"And why not? You have every reason to be," Abu Nakba said, still staring into the fire, unable to look his primary benefactor in the eye.

The spymaster smiled wryly. "My friend, for all your years of wisdom and hard-earned experience, you could not be more wrong."

52

Abu Nakba turned his head and looked back at Wangshu.

"What did you say?" the old man asked.

"You heard me," Wangshu replied. "My colleagues and I could not be happier with your successes."

"How can you say that?"

"First and foremost, no one on the planet knows that I recruited you, bank-rolled you, armed you, and provided you weapons and critical intelligence every step of the way," Wangshu said softly. "No one knows the role China has played in attacking the United States and the British and the Israelis, all under the cover of Kairos. And that's entirely due to you. You have covered your tracks masterfully. The Iranian Supreme Leader and the IRGC think they bankrolled you. They're convinced that you and Kairos work for them and them alone. At the same time, you obviously convinced the Turkish president that he was your only sponsor and that you work directly for him. Perhaps most impres-sively, look how you manipulated the Russians. Luganov and Nimkov may not have given you as much money as Tehran, Ankara, or us, but they never even considered the possibility that you were not wholly and completely a Russian subsidiary, loyal to them and unconnected to anyone else. I cannot tell you how many times I worried that you could not pull off such duplicity. I was convinced our involvement would be revealed. But in the end, you have kept your word, and though very few in Beijing know of our role, I can personally guarantee you that all of them are deeply impressed by you and very, very grateful."

"I'm . . . I really can't . . . I honestly don't know what to say," the old man replied. "But keeping China's involvement in Kairos secret means nothing in light of our failures."

Wangshu shook his head. "You honestly see your operations as *failures*? That's like saying Osama bin Laden was a failure because if those planes had hit the Twin Towers one hour later, he would have killed fifty thousand people and not just three thousand since more workers would have been in the offices. True, but so what? Mr. bin Laden wasn't a failure. He achieved something never done before in all of human history. He didn't just kill three thousand people. He dragged the imperialists into two wars. He cost their economy trillions of dollars. He changed their entire way of life. And he evaded them—and humiliated them—for nearly a decade."

"That means nothing," the old man protested. "Despite all your money, all your logistical and intelligence support, Kairos hasn't achieved a fraction of what al Qaeda did."

"But Kairos has killed hundreds of people and inflicted tens of billions of dollars of damage on multiple continents and in multiple cities over multiple years."

"That's not enough."

"You assassinated the U.S. national security advisor and the American ambassador to Russia. You kidnapped the CIA's top operative and started a war between Hezbollah and Israel. You pulled off that spectacular attack in Chicago last year, setting the Sears Tower—or whatever they now call it—ablaze, hitting the Americans with dirty bombs, and very nearly killing the pope and the American president in the process. And what about that peace summit in Jerusalem? You very nearly blew the whole thing up on live worldwide television. Imagine if you'd really pulled it off? You would have killed not only the

American president and secretary of state but the Israeli prime minister and the crown prince of Saudi Arabia."

"But that's just it, Minister; we didn't kill any of them—we failed."

"You didn't fail. You sparked panic and confusion throughout the United States. You consumed enormous and valuable American time, effort, energy, and focus. What's more, you may very well have been the cause of President Clarke's stroke. And you accomplished all of this without exposing Chinese involvement. This is more than we ever imagined was possible."

"But I promised you so much more."

"We never believed you."

"I beg your pardon."

"You heard me."

"I heard you," Abu Nakba agreed. "But I cannot understand your meaning."

"Then listen more closely," the spymaster replied. "None of us—not President Guanzhong, not me, not my team—none of us ever believed that you could really pull off these elaborate plans, despite your promises. Don't get me wrong. We were grateful that you were thinking so big. But we never needed you to succeed completely. We just needed you to keep the Americans absorbed in their so-called 'War on Terror.' To be consumed by it. To spend so lavishly on it."

"Why?"

"So that we could finalize preparations to make our next moves unnoticed."

"Your next moves?"

"Yes, and I can assure you we are finally ready."

"To do what?" Abu Nakba asked.

"What else?" replied Dai Wangshu. "Invade Taiwan."

It wasn't often that Abu Nakba was speechless.

But he was now. He stared at the Beijing spymaster, unable to formulate a response.

"Surely, this cannot surprise you," said Wangshu. "You certainly know what our president has declared in no uncertain terms—that reunification of the motherland must be fulfilled. This is part of China's core strategic doctrine. But most people, including the U.S.—and including you, apparently—have never believed that we would really use military force to accomplish our objectives. Believe me, if we could have brought Taiwan back into the fold through diplomacy, economic coercion, political manipulation, or any other method, we would certainly have preferred this. But after decades of trying all other methods, our president and politburo have concluded that there is no other way."

He paused, but Abu Nakba said nothing.

So Wangshu continued. "As you no doubt know, a quarter of a century ago, our military was painfully inferior to the Americans—antiquated, backward, obsolete. It was a humiliating, shameful reality, I must confess. But this is no longer the case. After enormous investments, tremendous discipline, and relentless focus, we now—finally—have the military capacity to seize Taiwan once and for all with a massive lightning strike. We have a vastly larger navy now, with 340 ships, including aircraft carriers. We have fast-attack speedboats. Submarines. Hypersonic missiles. And far better trained and disciplined warriors. At the same time, the Americans have grown old, fat, slow, and distracted. Yes, they still have the world's biggest economy—for now. But they have cut their Navy from 600 ships in the 1980s to a mere 285 ships today. Why? Because we have lulled them into a false sense of security. And because through you—and others like you—we've been distracting them, bleeding them dry, persuading them to throw most of their resources into their never-ending 'War on Terror' rather than preparing to stop us from seizing Taiwan, controlling the Pacific, and eventually dominating the world."

The spymaster paused for a moment and poured himself another cup of tea.

"Will it be easy to grab the island? Honestly, no, it will not. Will it be costly? Yes. But we are now certain there is no other way. President Guanzhong has concluded that China cannot save Taiwan unless we first destroy it."

"But . . . I don't . . . Why . . . ?" Abu Nakba stammered.

"Why what?"

"Why *now*?" the old man clarified, forcing himself to regain his composure and capacity to speak. "I mean, you have every right, of course. And Kairos will support you completely. But President Guanzhong was just in Washington. He just held a summit with President Hernandez. They were so amiable together. They weren't confrontational. They forged a new counterterrorism agreement. I thought . . ."

"What? That Sino–American relations were improving?"

"Yes, exactly."

"Good. That's exactly what you were supposed to think," said Wangshu. "You, and the Americans, and the Taiwanese, and everyone in the Pacific Rim and around the world. Why give your enemies a reason to mobilize? To prepare for war? Is it not better to cause them to relax, to lower their guard, to breathe easy while you prepare to deliver the death blow?"

"Of course," said the old man. "But again, I must insist, why right now?"

"Because we finally can," said Dai Wangshu. "That said, I have summoned you here to solicit your help."

"Whatever you need, I am your servant," said Abu Nakba.

"That is most kind, and I will get to your role in a moment. But to answer your question more precisely, we perceive an urgent threat—and a rare opportunity."

"I don't understand," the old man admitted.

"The threat is posed by the emerging political situation in Taipei."

"You cannot possibly be intimidated by Yani Lee," said the Kairos leader. "Yes, she was Taiwan's first woman president and its most popular leader in years, but isn't she on her way out of office?"

"Yes, she is term-limited. But Yani Lee is not the problem."

"Then who is?"

"Ben We-Ming."

"Who is he?"

"Taiwan's vice president and now the head of the Democratic Progressive Party."

"The ruling party."

"Precisely."

"Okay, and?"

"You don't follow the politics of Taipei very closely, do you?"

"Perhaps my hands have been filled with other matters."

"Perhaps," said Wangshu. "Nevertheless, the rise of Ben We-Ming—as the head of the DPP and an increasingly popular politician on the island—poses an urgent threat to Chinese national interests."

"Why?"

"Because he's a separatist who openly calls for Taiwan's independence."

"Doesn't every Taiwanese want to be independent?" asked Abu Nakba.

Wangshu suddenly turned icy. "Not at all—and how dare you say such a thing?"

"I apologize," said the old man. "I meant no disrespect. I simply meant that—"

"If you really believe this, you are woefully mistaken," Wangshu insisted, leaning forward in his seat. "All the people of China—on the mainland and the island—want one China, not two. But there indeed are criminals who seek to incite the people of Taiwan against the motherland."

"And Ben We-Ming is one of them?"

"Ben We-Ming is their leader. No one has spoken more about Taiwan becoming totally separate from Beijing than he. And the fact that he is rising fast in the polls and may soon be elected president means we must act now to stop this threat."

"I see," said the Kairos leader, realizing for the first time just how out of step he was with his benefactors in Beijing. "What then is the 'rare opportunity' of which you speak?"

"Hernandez," Wangshu replied.

"What about him?" asked Abu Nakba. "He was the commander of all U.S. naval forces in the Pacific. If there is anyone in Washington who knows how to wage war with China to prevent you from taking Taiwan, it has to be Carlos Hernandez."

"Ah, but here you are wrong."

"How so?"

"First of all, Mr. Hernandez is distracted by all the wonderful mischief you've been making," said Wangshu, leaning back in his chair. "And second, he will soon be distracted by all the more mischief you're about to make."

The Libyan raised his eyebrows.

"We understand you and your team have perfected Cerberus?"

"Yes, this is true; all we need is a place to mass-produce it," the old man replied. "And then we can smuggle it into the United States and unleash its magic."

"That is just what I wanted to hear," Wangshu said, an ever-so-slight smile emerging. "For I believe we will be coming into possession of just such a facility very, very soon."

54

Marcus heard a car pull into the driveway.

He heard a door open and shut. Then came the knock on the front door.

Peering through the blinds, Marcus was relieved to see Pete. He opened the door but at first shielded his friend from what was behind him. Only after explaining the situation and his plan did he let Pete in and ask for his help. Pete gasped at the sight of Oleg's corpse and took a step back. But Marcus reminded him how little time they had and how much needed to be done.

"Quick, take my phone and snap some pictures," Marcus ordered.

Pete complied, taking pictures of the macabre scene.

Next, Marcus used a pen to carefully take his Sig Sauer out of Oleg's hand and set it gently on the guest chair. Then the two men rolled up Oleg's body in the carpet, carried it outside, and put it in the Jeep, whose windows were already covered by ice and snow. Back inside, Marcus found a box of black garbage bags in the kitchen cupboard. Picking up his own pistol with a pen again, he placed it inside one of the bags, tied it off, and put it in the glove compartment of the

Jeep. It would have to be tested at the Agency's lab to prove that Oleg's fingerprints were all over it. The technicians at the lab would also have to test Oleg's right hand and find gunpowder residue. That, plus all the photos Pete had taken of the scene, ought to prove to Dell and anyone else that the Raven really had committed suicide and not been killed by an enemy—or by Marcus.

"Okay, that's everything," Marcus said. "Drive to the hotel, drop off the car, and then take a cab straight to the airport. I'll meet you there."

"Can't you just follow me and give me a ride?"

"No, I've got to clean up here," Marcus replied, glancing at his watch. "But go now, before the generator kicks in."

Once Marcus was alone again, he headed back into the house. Finding Oleg's mobile phone on the living room desk, he removed the SIM card and put both in his jacket pocket. Then he grabbed both of Oleg's laptop computers—the one on his desk and the other up in the loft—put them in a garbage bag, and tossed them into the Jeep. Stepping inside one last time, he realized the generator still hadn't started. So he walked over to the circuit breakers, flipped all the switches, waited a moment, and exhaled when all the lights and the heat finally came back on.

He went into the kitchen and was even more relieved that the surveillance system had rebooted and was functioning properly. If anyone back at Langley was monitoring the feeds closely, then a flurry of phone calls had been made over the last five or six minutes, and police were on the way. But Marcus was counting on the notion that no one was watching things quite so carefully on a bitterly cold Sunday morning in northern Virginia.

Taking one last look around the place, he took a few deep breaths, then decided that he'd done all he could. He stepped back outside, got into the Jeep, and drove down the mountainside toward the Aspen airport.

Only then did he call Annie.

55

Annie had just arrived home from church when her phone buzzed.

"I hope you're calling with good news on the most romantic day of the year," she said with a smile.

"So, listen," Marcus began, sounding somewhat breathless. "We've got a problem."

Annie's smile faded. "What is it?" she asked, immediately going to the window and checking that her security detail was outside.

"I don't know how to tell you."

"Then just spit it out, Marcus."

"I'm afraid things out here have gone from bad to worse."

"How so?" Annie pressed.

"I promise I'll explain everything in a moment," he replied. "But first I need to know where Robert is?"

"Robert who?"

"Robert Dayton—the secretary of state."

"I have no idea—why?"

"I need to know where the secretary is, right now."

"Is he in danger?"

"Annie, please, just find out where he is."

"Hold on a second." Annie hit the mute button on her phone, scrolled through her secure email app, and checked Dayton's confidential schedule. When she found the information she needed, she took herself off mute. "London," she said.

"Where in London?"

"At Number 10, meeting with the PM."

"For how long?" Marcus insisted.

"I think he leaves tonight."

"And where's he going next?"

"What's happening, Marcus?"

"Just tell me his next location, and I'll tell you everything."

"Okay, hold on," she said, her suspicions growing.

She again checked her email app, then said, "Mexico City."

"Good," said Marcus. "Okay, listen, I need you to dispatch an Agency plane to Aspen immediately. Tell them Pete and I need to get to Mexico City ahead of the secretary. Then put our names on the log sheet as if we're serving on the secretary's advance team."

"Why?" Annie insisted. "What in the world is going on?"

Marcus took a deep breath, then quickly told her what had happened and walked her through his plan.

When he was done, Annie was aghast. "Are you insane?" she asked, louder than she'd intended.

"If you've got something better, I'm listening," Marcus replied.

Annie's mind was reeling. "No," she finally said. "I'm afraid I don't."

"Then you'll take my plan to Dell and then to the president, right? And I don't have to tell you, time is of the essence."

56

It was just after 3 a.m. when their Learjet touched down.

Marcus and Pete were immediately greeted by a security detail sent by the Agency's chief of station, whisked into the back of an armored black Chevy Suburban, and driven at high speeds to the heavily guarded American embassy compound on the western side of the capital.

Once secure in the underground parking garage, they were taken by elevator to the top floor, where they were introduced to the ambassador and DCM, spending several minutes with both. Then they met in the ambassador's conference room with the special agent in charge of Secretary of State Robert Dayton's advance team. After being briefed on the key elements of the secretary's itinerary and routes of travel, they were briefed on the latest intelligence regarding potential threats. They downed multiple cups of coffee, asked lots of questions, and then thanked the SAIC for his time, knowing it was as valuable as it was limited, given that Dayton was expected to land in just a few hours.

Taking their leave, they headed to the parking garage, linked back up with their own security detail, and handed their driver an address scrawled on a piece of embassy stationery. In return, as per Marcus's request upon landing, the driver handed him a steel box containing a new Sig Sauer pistol and a half dozen fully loaded magazines.

Nearly an hour later, they pulled up to an abandoned warehouse in Ciudad Neza, a seedy and crime-infested municipality just east of the city. Marcus scanned the environment. In the trash-strewn streets, boys played soccer. On the steps of dilapidated apartment buildings, old men smoked cigarettes and stared at them warily. There were no women to be seen.

"Pull around back," Marcus ordered.

As the driver complied, Marcus and Pete noticed their security detail drawing M4 submachine guns out of black canvas bags.

"Gentlemen, we're trying to keep a low profile," Marcus told them.

"Then you came to the wrong neighborhood, sir," said their driver.

When the vehicle came to a stop, everyone got out of the Suburban except the driver, who turned the vehicle around, backed it up to the rear door of the building, and locked the doors but kept the engine running. Marcus and Pete headed inside and immediately found more Americans brandishing M4s.

Then Annie emerged from the shadows.

"You're late," she told them.

"You're early," Marcus replied.

"Ticktock," said Pete. "We've got work to do."

The first thing Marcus and Pete did was pull the pin on several grenades and toss them into the corner. The explosions not only kicked up a great deal of dust and smoke; they also could be heard throughout the neighborhood. Annie then nodded to the members of her detail. They opened sporadic bursts of fire against the far wall. It was all designed to simulate a firefight inside the warehouse, and Marcus prayed everyone in the neighborhood would buy it and steer clear. Just then, two members of Marcus's detail entered the dusty warehouse through the back door, carrying Oleg's body still rolled up in the carpet.

"Over there," Marcus directed. "In the corner. Prop him up in the chair behind the desk."

The men complied, setting down and unrolling the bloodstained carpet, then positioning the Raven's body as directed.

"Hand me your M4," Marcus said to one of his bodyguards, "and everyone stand behind me."

The group, including Annie and Pete, walked over to the far wall, close to the desk, then turned to face the open space of the warehouse. At the same time, Marcus took the weapon, walked over to Oleg, and likewise turned around. Then, on the count of three, he unleashed two bursts at the back door from which they'd entered. That done—and with spent brass lying all around Oleg and the desk—Marcus directed the group to reverse course and stand near the back door. Laying the M4 on the desk, he joined the group, borrowed a second M4, again counted to three, and unleashed two more bursts, this time at Oleg and the desk. Then he handed the M4 back to its rightful owner, walked over broken bits of glass, shards of wood, and the remains of the desk and laptop that had sat upon it. He picked up the first M4, returned it to its owner, and told Annie it was time.

The CIA's deputy director walked across the room, pulled a digital camera out of her bag, and took a dozen photos.

"Now you, Ryker," she ordered, giving the group no hint that she and Marcus were engaged to be married.

Marcus stood next to the corpse, withdrew his Sig Sauer, and pointed it toward the ceiling. Annie took more photos, and that was that. Marcus's detail rolled out a body bag, carefully put Oleg's bullet-ridden corpse in it, and quickly carried it back to the Suburban.

"Okay, everyone, let's move," Annie said, ordering her team out of the building.

She, too, headed for the exit, then turned back to Marcus. "You too, Ryker. Get moving—just don't die, and don't get arrested," she said.

"Yes, ma'am," Marcus said.

When Annie and her team were gone, Marcus and Pete hustled out the back door and into their vehicle as the driver revved the engine. Already hearing sirens in the distance, they had no time to spare. Once every door slammed shut, the tires squealed, Marcus found himself jerked back in his seat, and they were on the move, heading straight for the airport.

As they did, Marcus leaned his head back and closed his eyes. He could barely believe the director of the CIA and the president of the United States had signed off on his crazy plan, but they had. Now they had to wait and see whether it would work.

57

PRESIDENTIAL PALACE, BEIJING, CHINA—16 FEBRUARY

"Your Excellency, President Petrovsky is on the line for you."

Chen Guanzhong looked up from the maps he was poring over, removed his reading glasses, and thanked the young military aide who had just stepped into the room and bowed. Then the Chinese president turned to the generals huddled around his conference room table and asked for their forgiveness.

"Comrades, could I have the room?" he asked. "This shouldn't take long."

Each man bowed, then stepped out into the hallway. Guanzhong instructed his aide to bring him his laptop while he took his seat at the end of the table and pushed aside the topographical maps of Taiwan and binders filled with the most recently updated plans for invasion. Soon the secure video call was patched through, and he was looking at a crisp, clear image of Mikhail Borisovich Petrovsky.

"Mr. President, to what do I owe this great honor?" Guanzhong began with a broad smile.

"Your Excellency, thank you for taking my call," said Petrovsky, his voice clear and sharp over the encrypted satellite feed, though his countenance was far from cheery. "I have given your proposal a great deal of thought and discussed it only with my closest and most trusted counselors, as you requested."

"And are you calling with good news, or bad?"

"Good—very good, in fact. I am calling to say that the Russian Federation appreciates the exceedingly generous offer you made the other day. I would like to say yes to all of it—the purchase and gracious prepayment for a five-year supply of Russian oil and natural gas; the purchase and prepayment of Russian grain; and, yes, we would be willing to send you our most elite units from the Red Army to conduct joint war games with you as early as March first."

"That is wonderful news, Mikhail."

"We are most happy to work with you, Chen. However, there is one area to which we cannot fully agree."

"Ah, and what might that be?"

"We are not prepared at this time to be quite as generous as you would like in terms of selling such large minority shares of our biggest oil and gas companies," said Petrovsky.

"I see," said Guanzhong. "But I take it that you are open to selling some portion of those exemplary companies?"

"We are, but not 49 percent."

"What are you thinking of instead?"

"We would like to offer you 20 percent for now, and after two years, we would be open to discussing this further."

"I must be candid with you, Mikhail; given how precarious your current financial situation is, I have to say I am surprised and somewhat disappointed."

"Please understand, Chen, you are not asking for a typical financial transaction," Petrovsky explained. "You are asking us to join you in a major war in Asia, one that will fundamentally disrupt the world order in ways that we have not seen since the Second World War."

"You object to the cause?"

"Not at all. Russia has always maintained that Beijing owns the island of Taiwan and that China must be united."

"Then you object to the timing?"

"No, I would not say that," Petrovsky replied, measuring his words carefully. "To be sure, this was not a timing of our choosing but yours. Still, we do not object. To the contrary, I fully support your aims and timetable. Some of our generals are a bit more reluctant, particularly given how NATO continues to expand on our western flank. Still, we have discussed these matters at length, and I can assure you I have persuaded them that we have no greater friends than the People's Republic of China and that strengthening our alliance—particularly now—will be as beneficial for Moscow as it will be for Beijing."

"I am glad to hear that," said Guanzhong. "And I am making—as you say— an 'exceedingly generous offer' to the people of Russia. Yet for all this, you are offering less than half of what the people of China want in return."

"Only for now. As you well know, Russia has never allowed a foreign government to purchase so large a stake in any of our most vital and strategic national assets. This would be a first. And for there to be full national acceptance, we believe it would be wise to move one step at a time."

Guanzhong went silent for several moments, letting his disappointment show and wondering whether Petrovsky might be tempted to increase the offer to 25 percent. But the Russian president said nothing further, so Guanzhong spoke again. "Maybe there is a compromise to be had," he said.

"What do you have in mind?" asked the Russian.

"Do you recall our conversation after dinner?"

"About the ski resorts?"

"No, no, about the pharmaceutical plants you are building in Cuba, Venezuela, India, and . . . where was the other?"

"Ethiopia."

"Ah yes, Ethiopia."

"What about them?"

"It is an ingenious strategy—stealing trade secrets from the Americans and British and then creating low-cost, generic drugs that you can sell cheaply in the developing world. That is truly brilliant. I thought about it all the way back here to Beijing, and I must tell you, I am quite jealous."

"That is very kind, but I can't take any credit. It was an idea that President Luganov set into motion before his untimely demise."

"And are these plants finished?"

"Nearly so—well, the one in India is complete; the others will be finished shortly. Why do you ask? Would you like to buy a share in our expanding pharmaceutical industry as well?"

"Not exactly," said the Chinese premier.

"Then, if I may, what is your interest in a Russian drug-making plant?"

"As it happens, there is a certain project I'm working on," Guanzhong continued. "One that actually requires a massive pharmaceutical production plant."

"Go on," Petrovsky now said with trepidation.

"And I'm thinking that perhaps, in lieu of 49 percent control of those oil and gas companies that are so impressive and so lucrative, you might be willing to simply give China that facility in India. As a way of expediting our agreement."

"For free?" asked Petrovsky, aghast.

Chen remained silent.

"Did I just hear you correctly?" Petrovsky pressed. "Are you asking me to simply hand over to you a brand-new state-of-the-art pharmaceutical production facility that has not even opened and from which we have not earned a single ruble?"

"No, no, no—of course not," said Chen, smiling again. "You wouldn't be handing it over for free. You'd be getting all the other financial benefits that we just discussed, and you'd be our most important partner in the most important military operation of the twenty-first century, an operation that will fundamentally transform the balance of power in the Pacific and change the course of human history. But I need your answer right now, Mikhail. Our entire offer hinges on this and expires the moment we end this call."

It was obvious Petrovsky could not believe what he was hearing. Yet Guanzhong thought he should not have been caught so off guard. This was the way Chen played the game. Not just with Russia, but all over the globe. Month after month, he was gobbling up foreign national assets while making beggar nations feel like they were getting a bargain. Aleksandr Luganov would never have agreed to such an offer, Guanzhong knew. Then again, Guanzhong would never have made Petrovsky's predecessor an offer he could so easily refuse. And that was precisely the problem. Luganov had been operating from a position of tremendous power and vitality. Yet the former president's lunacy had put Petrovsky in an unenviable position, one of terrible weakness, one of near servitude to Russia's friends to the east.

"Comrade, I am a very busy man; please don't make me wait much longer," Guanzhong pressed. "Do we have a deal?"

Petrovsky was cornered, and Guanzhong knew it. There was no other choice.

"We do, my friend," Petrovsky conceded. "Send me the paperwork, and I will sign immediately."

"That is very kind, Mikhail Borisovich," Guanzhong replied, elated. "Your friendship will not be forgotten."

The moment he hung up with Moscow, Guanzhong called his spy chief. "Call your friend and tell him we're in business," the premier said, referring to the Libyan.

"Petrovsky said yes?" Wangshu asked.

"He wasn't happy about it, but yes, he gave me what I wanted," Guanzhong replied. "Now, call Nikolay Kropatkin immediately. I want the paperwork on my desk in an hour, signed and countersigned. Then get your friend on a plane to India by the end of the day. Send him an elite security team, the best you have. And send with him a team of scientists and production engineers from Wuhan, experts who can run the plant with precision and speed. Beyond that, tell no one else. This will only work if it does not leak."

58

Martha Dell landed at Václav Havel Airport at 1:26 a.m.

Her unmarked Gulfstream 5 business jet taxied to a secure hangar where she was greeted by the Agency's Prague station chief. A moment later, she and her protective detail piled into a motorcade of three armored Suburbans and were taken to the heart of the historic Czech capital, where more American agents were waiting at a former baroque palace known now as the Grand Mark Hotel.

Waiting on the porch of the hotel's rooftop restaurant, all covered in snow, was another detail—that of Nikolay Kropatkin, the Russian spymaster.

"Nikolay, it's been too long," said the CIA director, dressed casually in blue jeans and a black North Face jacket, as she smiled and stretched out her hand.

"I'm sure life has been very busy for you, Dr. Dell," Kropatkin replied, bundled up in a thick navy-blue wool coat and fur hat, shaking his counterpart's hand but unwilling to return the smile.

"And for you," she said.

"You said it was urgent, Martha," the Russian said as he lit up a cigarette. "Let's not stand on formalities. I'm needed back in Moscow by noon."

"Very well, then, Nikolay," Dell said. "I have a gift for you."

"A gift?"

"A birthday present, in fact. After all, next Monday is your sixty-third, is it not?"

"I've lost track," said the Russian, taking another drag on his cigarette.

"Well, I have not."

"You're most kind, but how much will this little 'gift' cost me?"

"Oh, it's not a little gift," Dell said, shoving her hands back into the pockets of her jacket to keep them warm. "It's something you've been wanting for quite some time. But you're right; I would like to trade it for something *we've* been wanting for quite some time."

"I'm not interested in making trades with a country that is strangling my economy and driving millions of Russians into poverty."

"Don't be so sure," Dell replied, pulling three black-and-white photographs out of her left pocket and handing the first one to the spymaster.

"Is this who I think it is?" he asked, genuinely in shock. "Oleg Stefanovich Kraskin?"

"You told us you wanted him, and you told us why," Dell explained.

"I assumed you'd forgotten."

"We didn't."

She handed her colleague another photo of Oleg's broken and bloodied body.

"Where did you find him?" Kropatkin asked.

"Ever since he assassinated your president, we've been keenly interested in tracking him down," Dell lied. "Unfortunately, as you know, he has proven rather elusive for someone not trained in the art of spycraft like you and me. But several weeks ago, we received a tip from a source that we've used in the past, though not often because she's sometimes steered us in the wrong direction. Anyway, the source caught our attention when she said she knew where Oleg Kraskin was and had conclusive evidence that he was plotting to emerge from hiding to assassinate our secretary of state."

"Dayton?"

"Yes."

"That's not possible."

"That's what we thought at first," Dell replied, following the exact playbook—and parroting the exact script—that Marcus had written for her. "But this time the source proved to be worth the trouble."

"And the money, I suppose."

"Correct. The intel wasn't cheap, but nor was it wrong."

"Where was Mr. Kraskin, our most despicable traitor, hiding all this time?"

"Cuba."

"Impossible," said the Russian. "Nothing happens in Cuba without us knowing."

"Nevertheless, we found your man holed up in a little hacienda east of Havana. I wanted to send in a team to grab him, but President Hernandez denied my request."

"Why?"

"He said you guys would be furious if we renditioned Russia's most wanted man out of one of your most important allies. He said it would make relations with you worse, even if we did end up handing Kraskin over to you."

"So you were just going to grab President Luganov's murderer and keep him?"

"No, no, we planned to interrogate him at length, and then offer him to you—if the price was right."

"But your president said no."

"True, but not just because it would upset you and President Petrovsky."

"Why else?"

"He wanted to see if the source was telling the whole truth."

"You mean he wasn't certain Kraskin was really plotting to assassinate Secretary Dayton?"

"Exactly."

"And?"

"We tracked Kraskin as he boarded a yacht headed west across the gulf, ultimately bound for the port of Tampico. From there, we followed him as he made his way to a warehouse in Mexico City. We watched him buy gear from a member of a Colombian drug cartel—a sniper rifle, ammo, and so forth. Where he got all the money for that, we still don't know. But we learned that Mr. Kraskin was planning to link up with several surviving members of Kairos, and then confirmed that they were, sure enough, engaged in a highly advanced plot to take out the secretary."

"And so you killed him?" The Russian was livid. "Why in the world would you do that when you knew we wanted him alive?"

"We didn't plan to kill him, just grab him," Dell explained, sticking to Ryker's script. "But what can I say? The man pulled a gun, and one thing led to another."

Kropatkin couldn't help himself. He pulled out a fresh pack of cigarettes and lit one up. "I cannot tell you how disappointed I am," he said after taking several drags. "I'd very much have liked some time alone with Mr. Kraskin."

"I'm sure you would have," said Dell. "But there's more."

"What do you mean, *more*? What more could there be? You just showed me the bullet-ridden body of the man we wanted to put on trial after extracting every scrap of intel he had."

"There's more, Nikolay."

"Fine—what else?"

"Well, given all the accusations you guys have made against us, this next photo might strike you as ironic. But I thought it only fair to show it to you."

"I cannot wait," Kropatkin replied.

Dell ignored the sarcasm and handed over a photo of Marcus Ryker standing over the body, gun drawn. Kropatkin was genuinely speechless, so Dell continued.

"As you know, Agent Marcus Ryker works for the DSS and was part of the secretary's advance team," she explained. "As it happened, Ryker was the man assigned to track Kraskin. He's the one who found him and, in the end, took him out."

The confusion on Kropatkin's face was priceless.

"So this is a big story. President Hernandez wants to give it to the media ASAP and, of course, take all the credit as part of his ongoing war on terrorism," Dell continued.

"But . . . ?"

"But he's willing to make a deal with your president, if the price is right."

"That's why you've come? To play one of your stupid game shows?"

"No, I've come to tell you we're willing to give you the body," Dell replied.

"And photos of the crime scene—without Ryker in them. President Petrovsky can go on television and show the photos and take all the credit for hunting down the man who killed President Luganov, and your prime minister, and your predecessor at the FSB. What's more, your president can say that it was Russian intelligence who prevented the assassination of an American secretary of state. And when he's done, my president—and Secretary Dayton—will publicly praise your government for a job very well done."

"In return for what?" Kropatkin asked, clearly waiting for the other shoe to drop.

"Actionable intelligence on the whereabouts of Abu Nakba."

"The Libyan? You must be joking," Kropatkin scoffed. "We have no idea where he is. Your president told us to stay away from him, and we have. You know that."

"I don't believe you, Nikolay."

"And I couldn't care less what you believe. We told you everything we knew about him when you discovered his men had entered the U.S. through Mexico, bringing dirty nukes with them. We told you the old man had been in Iran, then went to Afghanistan, then vanished into thin air, and all that was true. We admitted that Luganov and Nimkov had bankrolled Kairos in its startup phase to the tune of 100 million rubles. We gave you all the paperwork on how it was done through various shell corporations in the Caribbean. We also gave you all the details on those six Russian satphones that Nimkov gave Kairos. And we've given you tips on the identities and locations of three other Kairos assassins. Does any of that ring a bell?"

"It does, and yet—"

But Kropatkin cut her off. "No, that's that. We don't know where he is. And frankly, we don't care. He's not our man. So he's not our problem."

"Don't play games with me, Nikolay," Dell warned, suddenly becoming icy. "Oleg Kraskin wasn't our man. So he wasn't our problem. Yet we're the ones who found him. We're the ones who took him off the board. And now we're offering him to you on a silver platter."

"But therein lies the difference, Madame Director," Kropatkin replied after taking another drag on his cigarette. "You tracked Kraskin down. But we have no idea where Abu Nakba is. I cannot give you what I do not have."

"Nikolay, there's no need to get angry."

"There is, actually—you're putting me in an impossible position."

"To the contrary, I'm offering you the deal of the century."

"How? By asking me for something I cannot possibly give you?"

"Look—let's just say for the sake of discussion that you're telling me the truth. I don't believe you for one minute. But let's just say I'm wrong. Fine. You're the chief of the Russian intelligence services. You have assets all over the planet. You have close ties with Beijing. And Pyongyang. And Tehran. And Beirut. And Damascus. And most of the terrorist organizations in the world. You have friends in dark places. Chits to call in. If you really don't know where the old man is, go find him, just like we found the man your president wants so badly."

The Russian took a final drag on his cigarette, then dropped the butt to the floor and stamped it out in the snow with the sole of his wing tips. "Drop the sanctions," he said as he exhaled a lungful of smoke.

"Pardon?" Dell asked, not sure she'd heard him right.

"You heard me, Madame Director. Drop the sanctions."

"You can't be serious."

"I've never been more serious. If we really could track down the precise location of Abu Nakba—and that's a very big *if*—but if we did, then your president should drop the sanctions. In fact, he should do it anyway."

"That's not how the game is played, Nikolay, and you know it. We're proposing a simple trade—one bad guy for another. Nothing more. Nothing less."

"Your sanctions are humiliating, Martha. President Hernandez has made his point. Now enough is enough."

"I'm sorry. The deal on the table is Abu Nakba for Oleg Kraskin. That's it. I understand you want the sanctions lifted, and I'm sympathetic."

"Are you?"

"I am."

"Is your president?"

"I believe he is. But you're going to have to give us something far bigger than Abu Nakba if you want President Hernandez to lift all—or even some—of those sanctions."

The two of them just stood there in the falling snow and the bitter cold. Dell waited but Kropatkin said nothing.

"Very well, Nikolay," she concluded, putting the photos back in her pocket. "President Hernandez will release the story and photos on Oleg Kraskin himself and take the credit. Sorry to have wasted your time."

With that, she turned and walked toward the door to the rooftop restaurant, her security detail closing ranks around her. But just as she put her hand on the door handle, she heard the Russian spymaster say, *"Wait."*

Dell paused. Careful to keep a straight face, she turned and looked back over her shoulder.

"Give me a few hours," said Kropatkin. "I will take this to President Petrovsky. Perhaps I am wrong. Perhaps I spoke too hastily. Maybe he will want to make you a counteroffer. I doubt it, but that's his call, not mine."

"You've got twenty-four hours, Nikolay—not a minute more," Dell replied. "Then we go public."

59

Marcus began to breathe again.

Along with Annie and the president, vice president, secretary of state, and national security advisor, Marcus had just watched the entire conversation. The video feed had come from a special pair of glasses with a tiny built-in camera worn by a member of Dell's security detail. The audio had come from a tiny microphone in one of the buttons on Dell's wool coat. Neither had been perfect. There had been occasional glitches in the transmission. But everyone in the Situation Room had certainly gotten the gist of the conversation.

Hernandez turned to Marcus. "So what's your take?" the president asked. "Did that go the way you had hoped?"

"Better, Mr. President—much better," Marcus replied.

"How so?"

"First, with the exception of that last piece about the sanctions, Dr. Dell followed my script to the letter."

"And?"

"And it seems rather clear that Kropatkin desperately wants Oleg's body back and for Petrovsky to be able to take the credit for the kill."

"Is that how the rest of you read it, as well?" Hernandez asked.

Whitney nodded. So did McDermott. And Secretary Dayton. But Marcus was surprised to see that Annie hesitated.

The president noticed it as well. "Deputy Director Stewart, are you reading things differently?" Hernandez asked.

"Yes—well, maybe slightly, sir."

"How so?"

"I'm not sure it's accurate to say that Kropatkin *desperately* wants Oleg's body back," Annie explained. "I don't think *desperate* is the right word."

"What is?"

"Sir, I think what Kropatkin really said is that he's quite angry that Oleg Kraskin is dead. Why? Because he wanted to interrogate the worst betrayer of the Kremlin in a generation."

"And by *interrogate* I assume you mean *torture mercilessly*?" Hernandez pressed.

"Absolutely," Annie confirmed. "And then execute what's left of him."

"Go on," said the president.

"Sir, I think it's *President Petrovsky* who is desperate to get Oleg back, and he doesn't really care if Oleg is dead or alive," Annie continued. "That's why when Dr. Dell began walking away, Kropatkin realized that he'd overreached. That he'd demanded too much. That's when he recalibrated and told Dell he would take our offer back to Petrovsky and let him make the decision for himself whether to accept this deal or not."

"Perhaps," said Hernandez. "But do you believe Kropatkin doesn't know where Abu Nakba is?"

"I'm honestly not sure," said Annie. "At first I thought he was bluffing. I mean, he's a professional liar, after all. But the more he protested, the more I began to wonder if he really doesn't know where the old man is."

"Methinks he doth protest too much," said the president.

"Perhaps," said Annie. "But in this case, I think I believe him."

"What about you, Ryker?"

"Annie might be right, sir. I'm honestly not sure. But I thought Dr. Dell handled it perfectly, just like we had gamed it out. If they don't know where Abu Nakba is, then they certainly have plenty of ways to find him, if they want to."

"Do you think Petrovsky will accept our offer?"

"Well, as I explained from the beginning, it's a gamble, Mr. President," Marcus replied. "But let's just say I think the odds are in our favor."

Hernandez polled the others, and that proved to be the consensus.

Vice President Whitney, however, was not satisfied. "Mr. President, I'm wondering, could we discuss the sanctions for a moment?"

"Meg, please tell me you're not about to agree with Nikolay Kropatkin."

"No, sir, not exactly."

"Good, because otherwise I might need to dump you from the ticket."

It was meant as a joke, but under the circumstances, the president's quip didn't get a laugh.

"I serve at your pleasure, Mr. President," Whitney said, gracing Hernandez's quip with a smile, then continued her point. "But what I'm suggesting here, sir, is that getting Abu Nakba is your top foreign-policy priority right now. And if you could really swap Oleg Kraskin's dead body for Abu Nakba—dead or alive—it's a huge, huge win for you personally, for the American people, for our national security, and for our standing in the world. Right?"

"Exactly," Hernandez confirmed. "It would be huge."

"*Huge* is an understatement, Mr. President," Secretary Dayton chimed in. "Such a move could very well secure your election and strengthen your hand on the world stage as well."

"I agree," said the VP. "But I'm just saying that if you could secure all that in one transaction—if it was handled deftly, sensitively, just right—it might be worth taking a serious look at recalibrating our relations with Russia at the same time."

Marcus was intrigued with this line of thinking, but then McDermott spoke up.

"Mr. President, with all due respect, I hardly think that a 'recalibration' would be called for as Moscow grows ever closer to Beijing," the national security advisor argued.

"Aren't we trying to grow closer to Beijing as well, Bill?" Hernandez asked. "Isn't that what this summit was all about—defusing tensions with the Chinese, working together on counterterrorism, and trying not to derail our economic cooperation?"

"No, sir, not at all," McDermott replied. "Until the debacle in Karachi, you were about to threaten Beijing with a massive round of economic sanctions, plus huge new arms sales to Japan, South Korea, Taiwan, Singapore, and Australia, plus efforts to deepen our ties with the Philippines, Vietnam, and other regional states. Let's be clear, sir. China is not our friend. You've said it countless times. And because they're fixing to emerge as our most serious threat in the Pacific, we need to do everything in our power—while we still have time—to strengthen our existing alliances in the Pacific, and to try to separate Moscow from Beijing."

"But maybe we have an opportunity here to defuse tensions with both the Russians and Chinese all at once."

"Sir, the Communist Chinese are hell-bent on invading Taiwan in the next few years, dominating the Pacific, and emerging as the most important economic power on the planet. That's what your most recent National Intelligence Estimate concluded. And that's why we worked so hard in this room to map out a very tough line against Beijing going into the summit. But—again with respect, Mr. President—you let the incident in Karachi throw you off your game plan, sir. I urge you not to go further."

"What are you saying, Bill? That you *don't* want to get Abu Nakba back?"

"No, sir. I want him as much as you do. I'm just saying that the deal Agent Ryker gamed out is a good one. Brilliant, actually. Oleg Kraskin for Abu Nakba. Nothing more. Nothing less. And Deputy Director Stewart is right. Petrovsky is desperate to get Oleg back and get credit for taking him down. There is absolutely no reason to sweeten the deal, certainly not with talk of lifting sanctions on Moscow."

Vice President Whitney adamantly disagreed. "I think you're wrong, Bill. Cutting Ryker's deal *and* lifting the sanctions on Moscow just might prove the thing that could entice Moscow out of Beijing's camp altogether."

60

"Ryker?" Petrovsky almost shouted.

It was not yet five in the morning. The Russian intelligence chief had just landed by helicopter inside the walls of the Kremlin and had requested to see the president urgently.

"Yes, Mr. President—that's what she said," Kropatkin replied.

"Then walk me through it again."

"Dell says that Ryker is working for the DSS and that he's the one who was tracking Oleg Kraskin from Cuba to Mexico."

"And she's saying that Ryker is the one who killed Oleg Kraskin?"

"Yes, sir."

"Do you believe her?" Petrovsky pressed, pacing about his office and trying to imagine Marcus Ryker—Sig Sauer in hand—standing over the bullet-ridden body of Oleg Stefanovich Kraskin.

"Does it matter?" asked Kropatkin.

"It does to me," said Petrovsky.

"I understand, Mr. President, but with respect, at this point I'd say who killed Kraskin is immaterial. Whether it was Marcus Ryker or someone else, the Americans have killed Russia's most wanted criminal. They have his body. They have the photos. And they are willing to turn them over to us immediately—and let you take all the credit for the kill—but you must decide quickly."

"What's there to decide?" Petrovsky asked, looking out the window over a fresh blanket of snow falling on his beloved city. "The Americans want something I cannot give. You told Dell we have no idea where the old man is, correct?"

"Of course."

"And?"

"She didn't believe me."

"But in this case, you were actually telling the truth."

"Perhaps she's having a hard time distinguishing the difference," Kropatkin conceded.

Petrovsky turned back toward his spy chief. "So what are we supposed to do? I can't have the Americans taking credit for killing Oleg Stefanovich. I have to be able to do that myself. It would be a masterstroke of publicity. Unexpected. Shocking. Decisive. Think about it. There's no question that such news would single-handedly solidify my political standing in the country. My polls could easily shoot up by thirty or forty points overnight. Especially if I can follow it up in the coming days by announcing these huge new deals with Beijing that will dramatically boost our economy, create jobs, and mitigate the suffering our people are enduring because of the American sanctions. But if the Americans make the announcement? If Hernandez does? Then he becomes the hero. He looks strong. Decisive. A true global statesman. And I look weak. Unable to hunt down the man who killed my predecessor. Potentially giving rise to a new round of rumors that I was complicit in Luganov's death."

"No one thinks that, Mr. President."

"*Like hell they don't, Nikolay!*" Petrovsky shouted. "If I can't bring his killer to justice, if I can't turn the economy around, if I can't bring glory to Mother Russia, then how long do you think it will be until someone tries to put a bullet in my face?"

Kropatkin knew better than to reply.

Petrovsky continued pacing the room for several moments, then stopped abruptly and turned back to his spy chief. "Let me ask you a question, Nikolay."

"Yes, sir?"

"If I were to authorize you to do so, do you think you could actually hunt down Abu Nakba and give me a precise location that I could give the Americans?"

"With only twenty-one hours and nine minutes remaining?"

"Exactly."

"I honestly don't know, sir."

"You must have a satellite phone number for the Libyan, or an email address, or something, right?"

"I've never had direct contact with him, sir."

"Not you, but Luganov and Dmitri Nimkov did."

"Well, they clearly wired money to Kairos. But as best as my team and I have been able to determine, the point of contact was a man named Hamdi Yaşar."

"Who is he?"

"He was a senior producer for the Al-Sawt television network in Qatar. But sometime last year the Americans figured out he was Abu Nakba's consigliere. So the CIA grabbed him out of his apartment in Doha, with his wife and kids right there in the house."

"And where is he now?"

"Rotting in Gitmo, I believe."

"And the Americans couldn't get him to talk?"

"I'm sure they did, which is how they're rolling up so many Kairos operatives," Kropatkin replied. "But Abu Nakba is craftier than all his Kairos thugs put together. There's no way he's going to allow Hamdi Yaşar to bring him down."

Petrovsky kept pacing. "And you're sure we haven't sent the old man any more money?"

"Positive."

"Out of some black-box slush fund, perhaps?"

"Definitely not, sir. We stopped the moment you put me in power and we realized what Luganov and Nimkov were up to."

"So where's the old man been getting his money from since then?"

"I don't know."

"You haven't tried to find out?"

"The Americans told us to stay away from Abu Nakba. You told me to cut him off. So no, I haven't tried to find out."

"If you were Abu Nakba, where would you turn for money after us?"

"Good question."

"For which you have no answer?"

"Unfortunately, I don't."

"Well, then give me an educated guess."

"Sir?"

"Could it be the Qataris, given that Hamdi Yaşar was living in Doha?"

"I highly doubt it, sir."

"Why not? They've welcomed Hamas and Hezbollah leaders, among others."

"True, but it would be too obvious for Abu Nakba to be living in Doha and to be bankrolled by the Qataris. Wouldn't the Americans have already thoroughly examined all that?"

Petrovsky kept pacing.

"Where's Yaşar from originally?" he finally asked.

"Turkey, I believe," Kropatkin said. "But I highly doubt the Turks would have been involved. I mean, they're members of NATO, after all."

"Yes, but they keep gravitating toward us and the Iranians, do they not? For that matter, what about Tehran?"

"They're Shias," said Petrovsky. "Abu Nakba is a Sunni."

"So what? The Iranians are bankrolling Hamas, and they're Sunnis. They've been harboring senior al Qaeda leaders, letting them live in Tehran, and they're Sunnis too."

"All true," said Kropatkin.

"Call your friend at the IRGC."

"Entezam?"

"Yes, Entezam."

"And tell him what?" asked the Russian spy chief.

At this, Petrovsky stopped pacing. He turned and looked Kropatkin in the eye. "Whatever you have to."

61

The first call Nikolay Kropatkin made was not to the IRGC chief.

It was to Yadollah Afshar. It had been rather common for the Russian spymaster to communicate directly with Afshar when he served as president of the Islamic Republic of Iran. But after a monthslong and rather heated internal debate in Tehran, Afshar had just the week before been elevated by the Assembly of Experts to serve as the country's new Supreme Leader. Kropatkin had never spoken to the man's predecessor, or to any previous Supreme Leader. But now was the time.

"Your Excellency, thank you for taking my call," Kropatkin began.

"It is my pleasure, Nikolay," Afshar replied.

"Let me begin by personally congratulating you on this greatest—and most deserved—honor, and by extending the heartfelt congratulations of President Petrovsky, as well. Indeed, I am calling on his behalf to set up a call between you two, and to see if you would be open to accepting his invitation to come to Moscow next month for your first foreign trip."

"Thank you, Nikolay, thank you very much. You are most kind. We have been through much together over the years. Some good. Some bad. But I have always been grateful for your friendship and your counsel and that of your esteemed president. Please tell Mikhail Borisovich that I would be delighted to receive his call."

"That's wonderful news; I will inform him," said Kropatkin. "And the visit? Can he count on you to come to Moscow on your first trip abroad?"

"I would be delighted to come. It's been too long since I was in the Kremlin. But just to be clear, it will have to be my second trip. President Guanzhong has already invited me to come to Beijing, and I gave him my word."

That fact should not have caught Kropatkin off guard, nor should it have stung so much, but it did. Nevertheless, the Russian spy chief was careful not to let his voice betray his emotions. "Well, that's wonderful. You'll be in very good hands. As you know, President Petrovsky just hosted President Guanzhong here in Moscow, and their talks went exceptionally well."

"I am very glad to hear that, Nikolay—very glad, indeed."

"Again, it is my honor, Your Excellency," Kropatkin replied. "So, may I have my president call you at nine a.m. your time tomorrow?"

"Of course, and please tell my friend I am very much looking forward to the call."

With that, Kropatkin hung up the secure line, jotted down some notes, and then asked his executive assistant to place the call that was, in fact, far more important to him. It took several moments to track down the head of the Iranian Revolutionary Guard Corps, but soon Mahmoud Entezam was on the line.

"Comrade, what a great surprise—how wonderful to hear your voice," said the IRGC chief.

"And yours, Mahmoud. Do you have a few minutes?"

"Of course, of course; for you I have all the time in the world."

"Well, I doubt that, but it has been a while. We need to catch up. How are you? How is your family?"

"We are all well, by the mercies of Allah. And you?"

"Busy, but good, my friend."

"And Svetlana?"

"Pregnant."

"Again—really?"

"Would I lie to you?"

"That will be number three, will it not?"

"Number four, actually—you're getting sloppy, Mahmoud."

"Oh, my goodness, I apologize. Clearly, we need to speak more often. But I commend you; step by step you're catching up."

Kropatkin laughed. "Svetlana and I will never catch up, my friend. We have no intention of having nine children. What's more, we cannot even imagine it. How do you ever get any peace and quiet?"

Now Entezam laughed. "Why do you think I love intelligence work, my friend? It's quieter than home."

The two spent the next fifteen minutes catching up on each other's wives and children in more detail, and only then did Kropatkin brief the IRGC chief on the conversation he had just had with the Supreme Leader and the call that Petrovsky was going to place the following morning. Entezam expressed his gratitude for the information and apologized that Moscow couldn't be Afshar's first foreign trip, particularly given how deeply Tehran appreciated its alliance with Moscow and all the arms and nuclear technology Iran had received from Russia over the past several decades, not to mention all the trade deals the two countries had successfully negotiated with each other and the intelligence cooperation that remained second to none. To that end, Entezam asked his colleague for a briefing on Petrovsky's meeting with President Guanzhong.

"It went well," said Kropatkin. "It's been encouraging for me to see how the two men have really developed a great deal of respect for each other. We've come a long way from the days of the Cold War when the Americans were playing us and Beijing against each other."

"Maybe, maybe not, but never let your guard down, not even for a moment," Entezam replied. "President Petrovsky is right. The arrogance of the Americans is toxic, and the only chance we have to stand against their unipolar world with Washington as chief among equals is to coalesce together in an anti-American alliance. Anything you and the Chinese can do to significantly advance that objective, you must."

"As must you, Mahmoud," said Kropatkin, still searching for the right moment to ask the question that was the real reason for this call. "But may I be candid with you?"

"Of course."

"I have to say that for all the progress we have made with Beijing in recent years, I found myself uncomfortable with their decision to negotiate a counter-terrorism agreement with the Americans. Did that not strike you as, well, odd?"

"It did, actually," said Entezam. "The Supreme Leader felt particularly blind-sided. Between us, this is precisely why he's going to Beijing first—to find out what in the world is going on and ask President Guanzhong why he would do such a thing."

"Well then, the Supreme Leader is probably right to do so, but he should come to Moscow immediately following and compare notes with President Petrovsky."

"That's a good idea."

"Because the truth is, the Americans are the biggest terrorists in the world," Kropatkin said, lowering his voice slightly as if to take Entezam into his confidence. "I mean, just look at the destruction they wrought in Afghanistan, Iraq, and Libya, and that's just for starters."

"Exactly," said the IRGC chief. "Over the last century, the Americans have killed more people than any other government on the planet, including dropping two atomic bombs on Hiroshima and Nagasaki. Yet they strut around like they are morally superior to us all. It makes me want to vomit."

"I couldn't agree more," replied the Russian. "Which is why I've been thinking that you and I need to meet. Will you be traveling to Beijing and Moscow with the Supreme Leader next month?"

"I don't think the optics of that would look quite right."

"Then how quickly can you come to Moscow and meet with me quietly, in the shadows, without attracting the attention of the CIA?"

Entezam laughed. "You tell me. No one is watching my airports or yours more closely than Langley. I think we'd need to meet someplace else to avoid being noticed."

"Where do you suggest?"

"How about Tashkent, or perhaps Almaty?"

"Tashkent would be best. How does tomorrow sound?"

"*Tomorrow?*" Entezam asked. "Why so quickly?"

"Can you do it?" Kropatkin pressed.

"Impossible. I'm sorry. It would have to be next week at the earliest. But why do you want to meet?"

There was a long pause.

"Nikolay, are you still there?"

"Yes, I'm here," the Russian spy chief said at last. "The truth is, I have some money I need to move."

"How much money?"

"A great deal."

"To whom?"

"To a mutual acquaintance of ours," Kropatkin said. "Someone who is accomplishing more than either of us, combined. I want to tell him thank you and to keep up the fine work but without Moscow's fingerprints. And between you and me, without my boss knowing anything about it. Maybe not even yours."

There was another long pause.

"I understand," Entezam said finally. "How can I help?"

"Well, for reasons I'm sure you can appreciate, I haven't been in direct contact with this acquaintance since President Luganov and Dmitri Nimkov were . . . well, you know. Too many eyes watching and ears listening. I just couldn't take the risk or put our acquaintance in danger. But as I recall, the last time you and I discussed the matter, he'd just been to visit you, and then he was headed to Afghanistan, to the Hindu Kush region, I believe."

"Yes, that's true, but that was some time ago."

"Well, I believe it's time to reengage. As I said, I'd like to send him a sizable gift to say thank you. And I'm wondering if . . ."

"If I could help you two reconnect?"

"Yes, if it wouldn't be too much trouble."

"*Trouble* is right. I mean, that 'acquaintance' is, shall we say, radioactive."

"Interesting choice of words."

"Nevertheless, since the winds shifted in the Windy City, we have not had any direct contact with him either."

"None?"

"If it was too dangerous for you, Nikolay, it was certainly too dangerous for us."

"But you know where he is, right?"

"I did know, as of a few days ago, but not right now. But I can find out and tell you in the next few days."

"No, no, let me be clear," said Kropatkin. "I don't want to know where he is. I don't want to see him. I don't want to meet with him. I don't want to talk with him. I don't want to have any direct contact with him or his people. None at all. It's still too risky for us. All I want is to get him a message and some money. A lot of money, actually. And I'm wondering if you could help facilitate that for us."

"And what do I get for taking such a huge risk?" Entezam asked.

"What do you want?"

"How much is this worth to you?"

"Look, Mahmoud, I don't want to negotiate with you—not over this," said Kropatkin. "In fact, I don't even want credit for the gift. Honestly, what I'd prefer is to send the money to you and then you get the money to him. Don't even tell him it's from me. Take credit for it yourself, or for the Supreme Leader. Tell him that you've been watching all that he's been doing over the past few years, and you want to see him do more."

"How much more?"

"Eight billion rubles more."

"Eight *billion*?" asked Entezam, the shock in his voice audible. "That's like—what—a hundred million dollars?"

"Give or take."

"You want to send him that much?"

"I do—and the IRGC takes all the credit, to the extent that you want it. But again, none of my fingerprints or those of my country can be on it. Can you do that? Can you make that happen?"

"Honestly, I don't know," Entezam conceded. "But let me get to work on it and call you back."

62

"Come on—we should've had a hit by now. Talk to me, people."

Unshaven, unshowered, and on the verge of becoming undone, Marcus paced the floor of the Global Operations Center, his suit coat off, his tie askew. He was slugging down one mug of coffee after another, pestering one communications specialist after another for updates, and driving everyone a bit crazy, his fiancée included.

"How long has he been like this?" asked Dell, fresh back from Prague.

"Two days," Annie said to her boss from her vigil in the director's conference room one floor up, overlooking the CIA's state-of-the-art war room through a long rectangular one-way window.

"You're saying he hasn't been home in two days?" Dell asked.

"Three, actually," Annie replied. "But the first was spent harassing Noah and his team to work harder to recover the files that disappeared off all those phones and laptops they scooped up in Karachi."

"Where's he sleeping?"

"On the couch in my office," Annie said. "But only for a few hours at a time."

"He's a wreck."

"You're telling me. But every time I broach the subject of him going home, getting some rest, and—you know . . ."

"Defumigating."

"Right. Then he tells me, 'Sleep is for suckers.'"

"The man's going to have a nervous breakdown."

"That's what I told him," said Annie. "That's what Pete told him. Kai, too. But he's convinced we're going to get a hit at any moment."

Dell sighed. "Ask him to come up and see me," she said, pouring herself a fresh cup of coffee.

"I can ask, but I honestly don't know if I can pull him off the floor."

"Then tell him it's not a request," said Dell. "It's an order."

A few minutes later, they heard a sharp rap on the conference room door. Annie walked over, opened it, and there stood Marcus, as disheveled and bleary-eyed as she'd ever seen him.

"Hey," she said with a bemused smile.

"Hey," he replied. "You rang?"

Annie stepped aside, revealing Dell sitting at the head of the conference table.

"Come in, Agent Ryker. Have a seat."

"Yes, ma'am," he replied, brushing past Annie and sitting down several chairs away from the director. "How can I help?"

"Well, you could start by going home and taking a shower."

"We have plenty of showers here in the building, ma'am," Marcus noted.

"Then I suggest you avail yourself of one."

"I'm fine, ma'am."

"Actually, you're not," Dell said, her voice calm but firm. "You need to take a deep breath, go home, take care of yourself, and let Annie and me and the rest of our staff do our jobs."

"I can't leave, Martha," Marcus insisted. "Not when we're this close."

"Mr. Ryker, there are still six more hours before the deadline expires. When Nikolay calls with news—*if* he calls with news—trust me, you'll be the first person I call. But you're not doing yourself or anyone else any good by pacing the floor of the Ops Center and demanding updates from the watch officers every few minutes."

"I don't mean to be a pest, ma'am, but if it's all the same to you—"

But Dell cut him off. "It's not all the same to me, Marcus. Not anymore. You're no good to the Agency if you don't take care of yourself. So here's what's going to happen. Pete and Annie are going to drive you back to Pete's apartment right now. Annie's going to get you to your room, tuck you into your own bed, and give you a kiss goodnight. Then she's going to close the door and stand guard with Pete in the living room with their satphones sitting on the coffee table right beside them. The moment there's news, I'll call them, they'll wake you up, make sure you shower and shave and put on a clean suit. And then they'll drive you back here, and we'll game out our next steps. Are we clear?"

"Yes, ma'am."

"Good. Now get out of my sight—and for heaven's sake, put some deodorant on before I see you again."

63

Twenty minutes later, Pete parked in front of the three-story town house he and Marcus shared.

Annie had expected an earful from Marcus on the drive over about how unfair Dell was being. Instead, Marcus had fallen sound asleep from almost the moment he and Annie had curled into the backseat and Pete had started the engine. Now, with Marcus still half-asleep and barely coherent, the two of them managed to get him out of the car, up the front stairs, and into his room. Once there, Marcus collapsed onto his bed without changing or washing up.

Careful to maintain a pure reputation, Annie had never actually been in Marcus's room before. There wasn't much to see. Marcus rarely spent time there and had done nothing to decorate. Aside from two framed photos on the dresser—one of him, Pete, Nick, Bill, and Annie on the tarmac in Kabul the day they'd first met so long before; and another next to it of Marcus, Elena, and Lars posing with President Clarke in the Oval Office—there was nothing else to see but a pair of running shorts draped over a chair, and a T-shirt and several pairs of socks littered on the floor. Annie put Marcus's Sig Sauer, badge, and keys on the nightstand next to the bed. Then she clicked off the lamp, left the room, and closed the door behind her.

"Coffee?" Pete asked from the kitchen, already brewing a pot.

"I think if I see another cup of coffee, I'm gonna take hostages."

"Well, we don't want that," Pete laughed as he opened the refrigerator. "I'm not sure what else I have to offer you. We haven't exactly been in town much lately."

"No, you certainly haven't," Annie replied. "What about a glass of wine?"

"Really?"

"Really."

"Sure," said Pete. "Merlot or a cabernet?"

"Merlot sounds perfect," said Annie, kicking her shoes off, taking a seat on the couch, and covering a yawn.

Pete soon handed her a half-full glass and a can of mixed nuts.

"Sorry, best I can do on short notice," he said.

"Oh, that's great—you really are Saint Pete," she said, and they both laughed as Pete switched on the gas fireplace and slumped down into his favorite recliner.

"What shall we drink to?" Pete asked.

"How about the Raven?" she said, the smile fading from her eyes and lips.

"Ouch," said Pete.

"No, I mean it," Annie replied. "To Oleg Kraskin—he stopped World War III with Russia, stopped Iran from getting the Bomb, and as sad as it is, his death may very well help us hunt down Abu Nakba."

"To Oleg Kraskin," Pete replied. "And imminent retirement."

The two leaned toward each other and clinked glasses, and Pete took a sip. Annie closed her eyes and said a silent prayer. Even then, however, she did not take a drink but rather stared into the crimson liquid, swirled it around in the goblet, and let the aroma fill her senses.

"I'm worried, Pete," she finally said.

"About Marcus?"

"Yeah."

"Me, too," said Pete. "I told him—when we were in Aspen, and again in Mexico—he should retire, marry you, and hand this mission over to younger guys. But no matter what I say, he's determined to see it through."

"He's a patriot," Annie said.

"He's a fool," said Pete. "Someday, we'll get the old man. I have no doubt about it. But it's already cost us a lot of friends. And I'm worried it's going to cost us more."

There was a long, awkward silence.

"It's okay, Pete, you can say it," said Annie. "You're worried Marcus isn't going to make it through the next firefight."

"Aren't you?"

Annie said nothing.

"Look, if I knew you'd marry me—you know, as a runner-up—then I wouldn't be so worried," Pete joked. "I mean, hey, let him roll the dice and see what happens."

Annie didn't laugh, but she did smile. "You're a sweet guy, Pete; you always have been."

"Oh yeah, I'm a peach. That's why my wife left me. And my kids barely talk to me. And my parents won't forgive me. And why I have trouble forgiving myself."

"You're too hard on yourself."

"Maybe, maybe not. I'm a workaholic. I know it. Always have been. But it's cost me too much, and I don't want to do that anymore. I don't want to be that guy anymore. Marcus is furious with me. Says I'm abandoning him and abandoning the cause just when he needs me the most."

"You're not abandoning him. You've given more than most, and you've been a great friend to Marcus in the process. But you're not wrong. Enough is enough."

"He doesn't see it that way."

Annie nodded and stared into the fire. "Well, for what it's worth, I do," she said, finally taking a sip of merlot and savoring every drop.

64

An unexpected knock on his office door startled Petrovsky.

"Come," he bellowed, then finished his call and hung up the phone.

The door opened, and his executive assistant popped her head in. "Mr. President, Minister Kropatkin needs a moment," she explained.

"Send him in."

The intelligence czar entered a moment later, buttoning up his suit jacket and straightening his tie but still looking unusually disheveled.

"You look terrible, Nikolay," said the president. "I assume you have bad news."

"Nothing one way or the other, actually, not yet."

"But you've spoken to the Iranians."

"I have."

"And?"

"General Entezam says he's had absolutely no contact with Abu Nakba since the attacks in Chicago and that his staff has had minimal contact with anyone in Kairos during the same time frame. But he assured me that at our request he will personally reengage and let me know if and when he connects."

"Did you make him aware that the clock is ticking?"

"He knows it's urgent, but I couldn't say more without arousing suspicion."

"Who else have you been talking to?"

"I've also reached out to my counterparts in Pakistan, Cuba, and Venezuela. I had to be coy, hedge a bit. It didn't seem wise to come right out and say I need to know where Abu Nakba is and I need to know immediately. After all, if the Americans do find the old man and take him out—with or without our help—we don't want our allies thinking that we handed him to Washington on a silver platter."

"I'm not sure that's our main concern right now."

"With respect, sir, it is. Let's not forget that the Americans could just be setting us up, hoping to drive a wedge between us and our most trusted allies."

"Perhaps, but right now Carlos Hernandez has something I need more than anything else in the world, and you know as well as I do that I have nothing to offer in exchange."

"Well, that's not exactly true, sir," Kropatkin replied.

"What do you mean?"

"I mean we're sitting on extremely valuable intelligence right now, the kind that the Americans would give almost anything to know."

At first, Petrovsky just stared at his spy chief, trying to understand his meaning. But when he realized what Kropatkin was implying, his demeanor grew instantly dark. "Don't go there, Nikolay. I cannot believe you could even contemplate such a betrayal."

"Mikhail Borisovich, I'm just saying, if you really want the Americans to hand over the body of Oleg Kraskin and all those damning photos, then you need to give them something in return."

"You can't possibly be suggesting I should tell the Americans that Beijing is preparing to invade Taiwan."

"I'm not suggesting you should. That's not my place, sir. I'm simply saying that this information has to be far more valuable to the Americans—and to President Hernandez in particular—than the location of Abu Nakba."

"Nikolay, have you gone insane?" Petrovsky shot back. "I mean, seriously, have you completely lost your senses? Recommending that I sabotage our alliance with China in order to help the Americans?"

"No, of course not," Kropatkin countered. "The objective wouldn't be to help the Americans. Not at all. It would be to help Mother Russia. To save our economy. To save your presidency."

"But the risks, Nikolay—how can you not see them?"

"I do see them, sir. But think about it. I've just learned that Martha Dell is en route back to Prague, ready to receive our answer. If I take off in the next half hour, I can still get to her ahead of the deadline."

"And say what? That we still have no idea where Abu Nakba is—something they are never going to believe—but that if they'll give us Oleg Kraskin's body and the photos and let us make the announcement, then we'll tip them off to the threat to Taiwan?"

"Yes, but only in return for Washington dropping the sanctions on us."

Petrovsky was now on his feet, pacing his office and trying to understand how his intelligence minister had just gone mad in such a short period of time. "Nikolay, think of what you're proposing. I mean, let's say for the sake of argument that I'm stupid enough to take your advice and that Carlos Hernandez is crazy enough to agree. The moment he starts sending his entire Pacific fleet toward the Strait of Taiwan *and* announces that he is dropping all economic sanctions against us, everyone in Beijing—indeed, everyone in the world—will know that I cut a deal to save my neck and sell out the Chinese."

"No, sir—not if we insist that Hernandez doesn't drop the sanctions for another six to eight months. You and he can hold a summit at Camp David in which he refuses to drop or even ease the sanctions, but then have a second summit—in, let's say Prague—where he finally relents and we sign a new trade and nonbelligerency pact, or whatever. By that point, you'll be soaring in the polls because you successfully hunted down Oleg Kraskin and brought him to justice. Taiwan will be safe. We won't be dragged into some crazy war in Asia. Hernandez will be running for reelection on the basis that he stared down the Chinese. And President Guanzhong—knowing nothing about any of this—will start working overtime to draw you ever closer, back into his orbit, to keep you from becoming too close to the Americans."

At this, Petrovsky stopped pacing. For several minutes, he stared out the windows at another fresh blanket of snow covering not just the Kremlin but his entire precious capital. Finally, he turned back and looked his spymaster square in the eye. "You're asking me to take one hell of a risk. You know that, don't you?"

"Honestly, sir, I believe the far bigger risk is forfeiting a chance to trumpet to the nation and the world that you successfully found and killed the biggest traitor in the history of the Russian people. And forfeiting the chance to rescue Russia's economy from crippling American sanctions."

There was another long silence.

Then President Petrovsky made up his mind. "Very well, Nikolay. I'm sending you to Prague. But you had better make this work, or I'm holding you personally responsible."

Taichung

Changhua

Nantou

Yuelin

**T a i w a n
(Republic of China)**

Chiayi County
Chiayi

Tainan

Kaohsiung

PART
FOUR

65

The hazy orange sun was beginning to set over the glistening Arabian Sea.

Day was slowly turning to dusk, and the runway lights began flickering to life as the beacon light from the makeshift tower methodically swept in circles through the darkening winter skies. On final approach to the small private airfield—situated some sixty miles or so east of the provincial capital—the pilots of the Dassault Falcon business jet lowered the landing gear and instructed everyone on board to buckle their seat belts and prepare for landing.

Abu Nakba was startled awake by the announcement and by the presence of Mohammed Faisal hovering over him. The aide silently removed the dishes from the old man's late lunch, then returned from the galley to put up his boss's tray table and help him fasten his seat belt.

Soon enough, all was quiet and calm again. Faisal took his seat across the aisle and prepared himself for the descent. The rest of their Kairos colleagues had already done the same. The cabin lights were dimmed, and Abu Nakba felt the jet banking a bit northward. He turned and stared out his window at the lush

255

carpet of palm and banana trees below him and the miles of canals, lagoons, and sparkling lakes stretched out beneath them. For all his years and all his travels, Abu Nakba had never been to India, never wanted to, never even imagined having a reason to. Just forty-eight hours earlier, he had never heard of the province of Kerala, much less of its famous backwater region. Yet here he now was.

The journey from China had taken longer than he'd expected—requiring layovers in Burma, Bangladesh, and Sri Lanka, all designed to throw foreign intelligence agencies off their trail—but for the old man, it was worth the extra effort. He couldn't afford to be sloppy. Not at this stage of his life. Not at this stage in their most important operation. Too much had yet to be done. Too much was at stake to cut corners now.

His back ached, as did his legs. He was drowsy and eager to sleep in a real bed again. But at long last, they were almost to their new base of operations, and he was still marveling at the generosity of his benefactors in Beijing.

When they had landed, Faisal helped Abu Nakba down the steps of the plane and onto the tarmac while his men found the three Range Rovers exactly where they'd been told they would be and pulled them up to the plane. Once the Libyan was settled and reasonably comfortable in the backseat of the middle vehicle, the men off-loaded their bags and gear and strapped them to the luggage racks on the tops of the vehicles. Then they began the long journey into the jungle, their headlights cutting through a heavy blanket of fog that was quickly engulfing them.

The impaired visibility made the drive more treacherous than they had anticipated. Indeed, it took them nearly ninety minutes—twice as long as they had planned—before they reached the sprawling new pharmaceutical plant that had been built by the Russians, forked over to the Chinese, and now bequeathed to Kairos. Located in the middle of nowhere—surrounded by lagoons and canals—there was only one bridge from the mainland leading to the facility, and that was blocked by a steel barricade and flanked by two guard stations, one on each side of the road.

Abu Nakba was pleased to see that heavily armed Kairos commandos were already on-site and providing perimeter security. The guards required each person in each vehicle—including the movement's founder—to show photo IDs and be subjected to retinal scans. All of this data was then run against a computerized database. Only when 100 percent matches were established was each person given a laminated photo ID to wear at all times. This, too, pleased the old man. Though he had no intention of personally complying with the directive, he drew comfort from the lengths to which his team was making the physical security of the complex their top priority. As the steel barricades lowered, and their convoy proceeded across the bridge, Abu Nakba made mental notes of the fencing, the barbed wire, the CCTV cameras, and the infrared sensors that ringed the perimeter.

Li Bai Xiang was waiting for them at the main administrative building. The chief of operations for China's Ministry of State Security had first met them in Tashkent and accompanied them to Beijing, but then he had disappeared. Now they knew why.

"General Xiang, what a pleasant surprise to see you again," said Abu Nakba as Faisal helped him out of the Range Rover.

"Minister Wangshu sent me ahead to make sure all was ready for your arrival," Xiang replied, bowing to the old man and then directing a half dozen young, fit-looking Indian nationals at his side to take the suitcases, trunks of weapons, and other gear off the luggage racks and show Abu Nakba's security detail to their quarters. "Please allow me to apologize for the lengthy and circuitous journey. It was only done for your safety and for the safety of this state-of-the-art facility."

"No need for apologies," the old man replied. "I deeply appreciate all that you and the minister are doing. Would it be possible to have a tour of the complex?"

Xiang looked surprised. "Surely that can wait, Your Excellency. We have prepared a lovely meal for you, and then I'm sure you'll want to retire to your quarters."

"I'm not here to eat or to rest, General," the old man insisted. "I'm here to prepare for battle."

"Well, then, yes—of course—let me show you around."

Abu Nakba dismissed all but one of his bodyguards, asking only Omar Nazim—the head of his detail—to stay behind. They were now, the Libyan explained, in a highly secure complex, and his men needed food and showers and sleep far more than he did. At first they protested, but when he insisted, they finally obeyed and followed the Indian servants to the mess hall and their rooms.

Faisal helped the old man slide back into the Range Rover, and Li Bai Xiang got in the backseat beside him. Nazim, armed with an AK-47 and an automatic pistol, got into the front passenger seat. Faisal drove.

"Prepare yourself, Your Excellency," said Xiang as they proceeded down a service road. "Things here are moving faster than you might have expected."

"That is good to hear. How quickly can we begin mass production?"

"If all goes well, we hope by the end of next week."

66

They pulled up to a massive rectangular, windowless building.

Kairos and Chinese commandos wearing headsets and carrying Kalashnikovs guarded every entrance. They patrolled the roof, the parking lot, and the service roads around the facility. Faisal and Xiang helped the old man out of the Range Rover while Nazim watched their backs. They all showed their freshly minted ID badges to the supervisor of the security personnel working on the night shift. When he was satisfied, he radioed for his colleague inside to unlock and open the door.

Inside, Abu Nakba was astonished by what he saw. Dozens of Chinese and Indian nationals were hard at work, methodically dismantling, shrink-wrapping, boxing up, and carting away huge pieces of equipment on the main production line. All of it was being wheeled to a loading dock on the other side of the football field–size plant and put on trucks. Meanwhile, dozens of other workers were wheeling in massive crates of equipment from a separate loading dock at the far end of the plant.

"By Monday—or Tuesday at the latest—the entire facility should be retrofitted, Your Excellency," Xiang explained over the cacophony. "Once all the equipment has been swapped out, hooked up, and tested, then we're planning several days of system tests. By next Friday or Saturday, we're hoping to commence full-scale production of the Cerberus virus, and as you recommended to the minister, the aerosolized virus will be loaded into cans of hair spray, deodorant, air freshener, and furniture polish, all of which are precise knockoffs of famous American brands."

"How soon until they arrive in the States?" asked Abu Nakba, mesmerized by the scale of the operation.

"We expect to start moving the first shipments to the U.S. on or around March fifth or sixth, give or take," said Xiang. "It'll take seven to ten days for the cargo ships to reach various American ports. Then another three to five days for trucks to transport everything to actual stores. And then another two to three weeks for our versions to start being purchased and used by consumers."

"So you're looking for the outbreak to commence in early April?"

"Exactly," said Xiang. "And once the outbreak begins, our projections put the death toll near two million Americans in week one, ten to twelve million in week two, and upwards of thirty-five million in week three. That's when we will launch our missile attack on Taiwan, to be followed up shortly thereafter with a full-on ground invasion."

"The Americans will never know what hit them," Abu Nakba marveled.

"And even if they can quickly trace the source of the epidemic to these various products—which is highly unlikely because they'll be in such confusion, such panic, such mass hysteria," Xiang noted, "even if they can quickly determine which aerosol products have been used to release weaponized biowarfare agents into the country, they'll be confused by the fact that the products are coming from India, one of America's most trusted allies."

"But won't the products be stamped with codes indicating the exact factory, country, date, and time of manufacture?" asked the Kairos founder.

"Normally, yes, but we're falsifying all of that to further throw the Americans off the trail," Xiang replied.

"But in the end," the old man pressed, "even if it takes some time, won't the FBI and CIA be able to determine the precise location the products were shipped from?"

"In theory, yes, but it will be too late by then," Xiang insisted. "We're only going to run this plant for two weeks, three at most, and then we're going to shut it all down and disappear into thin air. By the time anyone shows up here, tens of millions of Americans will be dead, thus crippling the United States as a superpower once and for all. Meanwhile, China will seize Taiwan and then decimate the Philippines and Singapore with massive missile attacks. Once this happens, Beijing will emerge as the dominant power in the Pacific, and we'll be well on our way to becoming the world's only true superpower."

Abu Nakba was caught off guard by the last statement. "Forgive me, General, but did you just say you're attacking Singapore and the Philippines, as well?"

"Didn't Minister Wangshu tell you this?"

"He most certainly did not."

"Well, then, please forgive me," said Xiang. "I have gone beyond my brief. Please share this information with no one and forget I shared it with you."

Mohammed Faisal's satellite phone rang.

Startled by both the conversation and the sudden interruption, Faisal excused himself and stepped outside the plant to take the call in the cool and quiet night air. But the voice at the other end startled him again, as he hadn't heard it in months.

"As-salaam alaikum, my friend."

"Wa 'alaykumu s-salam," Faisal replied. "Is that really you, General?"

"It is, and I must say that it is good to hear your voice," replied IRGC Chief Mahmoud Entezam. "Forgive me for having to go dark for so long. This was an operational necessity. And there are still risks. But I simply couldn't wait any longer. So how are you? How is our friend? Are you both safe and well?"

"You are so kind to ask. Yes, we are safe—and well—by the mercies of Allah."

"I'm so glad to hear it," said Entezam. "Now listen, I have news for you—good news—but I don't have long. Are you free to talk for a moment?"

"Yes, yes, of course. What is it?"

"I have just come from a meeting with the Supreme Leader. He sends his most precious blessings upon you and upon our mutual friend. He has been overjoyed by the successes that you both have achieved, and he has authorized me to send you a tangible expression of his gratitude."

"That is most kind but not necessary, General," Faisal replied. "Father is keenly aware of your love and friendship and that of the Supreme Leader. Indeed, he cherishes you both and will for all of eternity."

"Nevertheless, the war is not over," said Entezam. "Indeed, it has only just begun. Therefore, His Holiness has personally asked me to inform you that we are prepared to wire you the equivalent of one hundred million dollars as a token of his esteem, and to, let us say, advance the cause."

"My goodness, that is exceedingly generous," Faisal said, genuinely shocked by the words of affection and the offer. "But Father could not possibly accept. You have already done so much—too much."

"Nonsense. It is our duty before Allah to invest in this work, and it has been our honor from its earliest inception," Entezam insisted. "Please, Mohammed, don't insult me or the Supreme Leader by rejecting this gift. You and I have been friends for too long. I know your children. You know mine. We have watched them grow up into mighty warriors for Allah. We have both sacrificed so much for this cause. I know you to be a pure and faithful soul. And I hope you regard me the same."

"Of course—you are one of my dearest friends and allies."

"Then please, accept this modest gift as a symbol of our friendship and gratitude."

"I . . . I really . . . I just don't know what to say," Faisal stammered. "It is hardly a modest gift. It is the most generous gift we have ever been offered. But I genuinely cannot accept. Father would be mortified if he even thought that I had considered doing so. Please don't put me in such a position."

"Mohammed, let me be clear—I cannot take no for an answer," said Entezam. "I wholeheartedly endorse this gift. But it was not my idea. And it is not my money. I am acting upon a direct order from the Supreme Leader, with whom I am meeting in less than fifteen minutes. He expects me to inform him that all the funds have been successfully transferred. Don't make me tell him they have been spurned."

There was a long silence.

"Mohammed? Are you still there?" asked Entezam.

"I'm still here," said Faisal.

"Then shall I wire the money now?" the IRGC chief asked.

"General, may I discuss this with Father and call you tomorrow?"

"Absolutely not," said Entezam, his tone suddenly shifting. "Must I really tell the Supreme Leader of the Islamic Republic that you *may or may not* welcome his gift?"

"No, no, of course not," Faisal replied, quickly trying to do damage control. "Please forgive me, General. My hesitation merely comes from being overwhelmed by the Supreme Leader's generosity and not ever wanting to presume upon his kindness, much less his assistance. It is not meant to insult His Holiness, nor does it reflect the views of my superior. It is my fault, and mine alone. Please tell the Supreme Leader that Father would be immensely honored to receive his most generous and gracious gift and that we are humbled beyond words that he would even contemplate such kindness, much less actually extend it."

"Very well," said Entezam. "Thank you for clarifying. Now, to what account shall I wire the funds, and where can you and I meet to talk about where we go from here?"

68

Marcus awoke to the sound of a satphone ringing.

But it wasn't his.

Come to think of it, he had no idea where his phone was. Nor did he have any idea of the time. Bleary-eyed and trying to remember exactly where he was, he groped around in the dark to find a light switch but ended up knocking over a lamp and shattering the bulb. At least the ringing stopped. Marcus could now hear someone talking in another room, though he couldn't identify the voice.

Suddenly, a door swung open and light flooded the room. Marcus winced and turned away, then saw his Sig Sauer, badge, and keys on his nightstand. And his lamp on the floor. Regaining his bearings, he realized this was his room. He was fully clothed and lying on his own bed. He didn't remember how he got there. The last thing he remembered was being in the Global Operations Center.

But now Annie was standing in the doorway.

"Get up, Marcus," she ordered. "That was McDermott. POTUS wants us in the Oval immediately. Get in the shower. I'll pack your bag. You're wheels up in ninety minutes."

"The Russians came through?" Marcus said, on his feet now, a shot of adrenaline coursing through his systems.

"He didn't say," she said, rummaging through his dresser drawers for clean clothes. "Just get into the shower—*now*. We're leaving in ten."

"I only need five," said Marcus, going to his closet and grabbing an already-packed duffel bag he used in emergencies.

Then he headed into the shower and turned it on to get it warm.

"Tell Pete to get the car started and brushed off, and I'll be right down," he shouted over the sound of the water.

"Pete's not coming," Annie shouted back.

"What do you mean *Pete's not coming*?" Marcus asked as he ducked his head out of the bathroom and pulled off his shirt.

"Just what I said."

"He *has* to come."

"He's done, Marcus."

"Not until the end of the month."

"He told me last night. He's done."

"We'll see. Just get the car started. I'll grab Pete and we'll be right there."

Annie shrugged and started toward the door, then hesitated, turned around, and came back to kiss him hard on the lips.

"Whoa, thanks, good morning to you, too," Marcus said, smiling and fully awake now, as he came up for oxygen. "To what do I owe the pleasure?"

"To the fact that this next kiss just might be our last," she said, then kissed him one more time before exiting the room.

As Marcus hopped into the shower, he realized she wasn't kidding, and his smile quickly faded.

Two minutes later, he shut the water off, toweled down, brushed his teeth, and shaved. Then he dressed, scooped up his duffel bag, gun, badge, and keys, went straight to Pete's room, and pounded on the door. When Pete finally opened it, he was wearing nothing but boxer shorts, and his hair was askew. "I know," he said. "I just got off the phone with Mac."

"Then grab your stuff and let's go."

"No, Marcus, I'm done."

"Pete, come on, we don't have time for this. We're being deployed."

"No, *you're* being deployed. I've retired."

"You told me you were mustering out at the end of the month. That's nine more days."

"Technically, it's only five more days," Pete replied.

"How do you figure?"

"This is a weekend. I'll go into the office every day next week, fill out all my retirement paperwork, go through my final debrief and exit interviews, turn in my badge and weapon, then kick back and relax on that final weekend. The twenty-eighth is a Sunday."

"Come on, Pete; I need you," Marcus said as he heard Annie honk the horn on the street below. "How are we going to find another medic in ninety minutes?"

"You've got Kailea. You've got Geoff. They've got plenty of medical training."

"But they're not doctors—and they're not you."

"You'll be fine. Now go. POTUS is waiting."

"Pete, don't do this to me."

"I'm spent, Marcus, and so are you. Let Kailea lead this one. You know she's ready. You trained her yourself. But I can't. And you shouldn't. You're engaged now, Marcus, to an extraordinary woman. Don't risk everything you've ever wanted when there is a team that's perfectly ready to deploy, a team that's younger and stronger than you and me and still has a fire in their bellies."

"Pete, please, one more time and that's it. I promise," Marcus insisted.

"Forget it, Marcus. I've got a really bad feeling about this one, man. I'm not going. And honestly, I'm terrified that if you do, you're never coming back."

At 3:52 a.m., Marcus and Annie entered the West Wing alone.

Pete was not at their side. Nor was he heading to Joint Base Andrews to link up with the rest of the team and load their gear onto the G5 that was already on the tarmac and revving up its engines.

After clearing security, they expected to be directed to the Oval Office but were escorted instead by a Marine in full-dress uniform to the Situation Room. Bill McDermott was waiting for them in a rumpled suit and wrinkled shirt, evidence that he'd been there all night. Defense Secretary Cal Foster was also there in blue jeans, a polo shirt, and cowboy boots. But that was it. The rest of the chairs around the conference table were empty. Soon the screens mounted on the wall at the far end of the Sit Room flickered to life, and CIA director Martha Dell was patched in via a secure video link from the U.S. embassy in Prague. Moments later, Secretary of State Robert Dayton was patched in from the American embassy in Mexico City.

Just then, President Hernandez entered the room, followed by Vice President Whitney. Both were dressed casually, and both looked about as stern as Marcus had ever seen them.

"Take your seats," said Hernandez, taking his own. "Martha, I understand you have news."

"Yes, sir, on multiple fronts," Dell began. "Let me begin with the biggest development. Just minutes before your deadline, Mr. President, I met with Nikolay Kropatkin. He was apologetic but said they've not yet found Abu Nakba. However, he insisted that his team is scouring the planet for him."

"Well, it was worth a shot," said Hernandez. "I guess we'll go ahead and request time from the networks for me to give a prime-time address announcing that we have hunted down President Luganov's assassin and brought him to justice."

"Actually, sir, the Russians still want Oleg's body, and Petrovsky wants to take credit for that kill."

"No way," said the president. "Time's up."

"I realize that, sir, but Nikolay made an intriguing counteroffer."

"I'm not interested in the Russians jerking us around."

"You may be interested in this, sir," Dell insisted. "And that's why I requested this emergency meeting."

"Go on."

"Nikolay gave me a bombshell—he says Beijing is preparing to invade Taiwan in the next month or so, and possibly sooner."

"That's impossible," said Hernandez, turning to his national security advisor. "Bill, we're not picking up any unusual Chinese troop or ship movements, are we?"

"No, sir, none," said McDermott.

"Nor will we, Mr. President," Dell explained. "Apparently, the Chinese have developed an entirely new war plan. It involves a sneak attack of between two thousand and three thousand ballistic missiles aimed not only at the Taiwanese but at our ships, troops, and bases in Okinawa, Guam, and throughout the Pacific Rim. What's more, Nikolay says President Guanzhong is planning a nuclear strike on Taipei and on Taiwan's national command center in the mountains south of the capital."

"A decapitation strike."

"Yes, sir, and one that also so severely shocks and disorients us and our allies that we're too slow to mount a counteroffensive and tempted to decide it's not worth defending the island after all."

The commander in chief and his war council were completely blindsided by the report and unsure whether to take it seriously.

"Dr. Dell, I must say, I find it hard to believe Guanzhong would do such a thing, especially after how well our recent summit went," said Vice President Whitney. "Besides, even if all this were true, why in the world would the Kremlin betray their closest ally by telling us?"

"That's just it, Madame Vice President," Dell replied. "Nikolay says President Petrovsky is sickened by the prospect of nuclear war in the Pacific, a war that could quickly escalate into a full-blown nuclear exchange between us and the Chinese and might drag Moscow in too. That's why Petrovsky sent Nikolay back to Prague. First to apologize that they haven't found Abu Nakba yet. But second to offer this intel in exchange for three things."

"And what's that?" asked the president.

"Petrovsky wants you to immediately strengthen our defense of Taiwan and in the western Pacific under the pretext of a long-planned military exercise."

"That's an interesting request coming from Moscow. What else?"

"And he wants Oleg Kraskin's body and all the photos we promised so that he can make a big prime-time announcement Sunday evening, Moscow time."

"That goes without saying—and?"

"And Petrovsky wants your assurance that in exchange for ironclad proof that this is precisely what Beijing is planning, in six to eight months—after what will appear to the world and especially to the Chinese as protracted and bitterly contested negotiations between Moscow and Washington—you and Petrovsky will announce that you're phasing out all economic sanctions of the Russian Federation and signing a new trade deal with Moscow as well."

"That's asking an awful lot," said Hernandez. "What kind of proof are they offering? Because it would have to be pretty good."

"It is, sir," Dell replied. "Nikolay played a recording for me."

"What kind of recording?"

"The actual conversation inside Petrovsky's office of Guanzhong laying out for Petrovsky his entire plan and timetable."

"You're not serious."

"I am, sir."

"The whole conversation?"

"Ninety-six minutes."

"In Russian?"

"No, they were speaking in English."

"And you believe it's authentic, Martha?"

"I'm certain of it, Mr. President, but there's more."

"Like what?"

"Well, sir, as I mentioned, Nikolay was quite apologetic that he doesn't know where Abu Nakba is," Dell explained.

"Yeah, I bet."

"Believe me, I understand your skepticism. Nevertheless, just as Marcus had hoped for and predicted, immediately after briefing Petrovsky, Nikolay called Mahmoud Entezam in Tehran."

"Remind me who that is?" said Hernandez.

"Mr. President, General Entezam is the commander of the Iranian Revolutionary Guard Corps and the strategic mastermind of all of Iran's terrorist recruiting, training, funding, and operational deployments. NSA confirms that a thirty-seven-minute call was placed from Nikolay Kropatkin to the IRGC chief."

"Saying what?" asked the president.

"Unfortunately, the NSA was not able to crack the encryption or record or translate the call. But we have the exact time and the exact phone numbers that were used, and a number of other details have led the analysts at Fort Meade to say with very high confidence that it was, in fact, Kropatkin talking to Entezam."

"What else?"

"Well, sir, immediately following that call, we have learned that Entezam called one of the six satellite phones that the Russians gave Abu Nakba several years ago."

Marcus's heart started racing.

"That call was brief, no more than five minutes," Dell continued. "But immediately following that call, Entezam had a private meeting with the Supreme Leader at his residence in Tehran. And after that meeting ended, Entezam called the same satphone. This time the call lasted for eighteen minutes."

Marcus shot a glance at Annie. Though her expression betrayed nothing, Marcus could see from the look in her eyes that she shared his sense of cautious optimism.

"As you'll recall, sir," Dell continued, "we know that three of those satellite phones were destroyed in the bombing you ordered on the Kairos compound in Ghat, Libya, based on the intel that Agent Ryker and his team developed. Another one of those satphones was used in the Willis Tower last year—just briefly, of course, but long enough for the NSA to pick up the signal, alert us that Kairos operatives were in the tower's Skydeck, and allow Agents Ryker, Morris, and Hwang to reach those operatives, neutralize them, and substantially foil their attack on the Mass that the Pope was holding and that you and the First Lady were attending at Soldier Field."

Defense Secretary Cal Foster now spoke up. "Martha, isn't it true that until today, the NSA had never picked up any evidence that either of the other two satphones had ever been used since the attacks in Chicago?"

"That's correct, Mr. Secretary," Dell replied. "Indeed, sir, DDI Stewart, Agent Ryker, and my senior analysts had reluctantly come to the working assumption that Kairos discarded those phones or that they had been damaged or destroyed somehow and that Abu Nakba and his men must have acquired new ways to communicate amongst themselves."

"Until today?" Foster asked.

"Correct, sir," Dell confirmed. "Entezam—or someone using Entezam's private office phone line—has now called one of those satphones twice. Again, both calls were encrypted, so we don't know what was said. But NSA can confirm that both calls were made from the IRGC headquarters in Tehran and answered by someone in a remote jungle region in southern India."

"India?" asked Hernandez.

"Yes, sir."

"That's odd, isn't it?"

"It is, Mr. President. So odd that I retasked one of our Keyhole spy satellites operating over Karachi to move into position over this location in southern India, in the province of Kerala, so we could get some real-time imagery of that section of the jungle and hopefully some solid answers."

"And what did you find?"

"A treasure trove, Mr. President," Dell replied. "The site where both calls were received is a pharmaceutical factory."

"What?"

"Brand-new. State-of-the-art. And guess who it was built by."

"Who?"

"The Russians."

"Those lying bastards."

70

"Not necessarily," said Dell.

"What's that supposed to mean?" the president asked.

"Sir, the deed of ownership for the plant was recently transferred from a Russian state-owned pharmaceutical company to a Chinese one."

"Kropatkin told you this?"

"No, sir, I didn't dare bring this up with him," said Dell. "I called my station chief in New Delhi. She told me that her people just stumbled across the transaction. They'd even sent word of the transfer in a confidential cable to Langley last week. But no one paid attention to it because it didn't seem significant."

Now the SecDef spoke up again. "Why would the Communist Chinese want to own a pharmaceutical factory in some jungle in southern India?"

"That's what I wanted to know," Dell said. "I just got back the first wave of photos from our Keyhole satellite. I'm putting them up on the screen."

Everyone in the Situation Room, Marcus included, was floored. They were looking at images of Chinese- and Middle Eastern–looking commandos—all heavily armed—manning guard towers and doing patrols as if they were guarding nuclear secrets, not an aspirin factory.

"Am I seeing this right, Martha?" Secretary of State Robert Dayton asked. "The Chinese are now in bed with Kairos?"

"That's impossible," said McDermott. "No one in the U.S. intelligence community has picked up any evidence of Chinese collusion with Abu Nakba."

Vice President Whitney was equally baffled. "Could this just be another diversion, another ruse by Abu Nakba to get us off his scent and on some wild goose chase?"

"It certainly feels that way," said McDermott. "This just doesn't add up."

The president then turned to the head of his Kairos hunting unit. "Agent Ryker, you've been unusually quiet. What do you make of it?"

"Well, sir, I think our little gamble has hit the jackpot," Marcus began. "Offering the Raven to the Russians was a huge risk. But it's working far better than any of us had hoped. It turns out that Petrovsky is, in fact, so desperate to take credit for killing Oleg Kraskin—and so desperate to get out from under U.S. sanctions—that he's decided to betray Beijing, Kairos, and the mullahs in Tehran all in one day."

"You don't think this is a diversion?" Hernandez pressed.

"No, sir, I don't," Marcus replied.

"Did you ever suspect the Chinese were bankrolling Kairos?"

"No, Mr. President, I have to admit that such a possibility never even crossed my mind. But it makes total sense. The Chinese are hell-bent on retaking Taiwan en route to dominating the Pacific. But the only way to do that, Guanzhong realizes, is a massive, Pearl Harbor–style surprise attack that catches us completely off guard. That's why he agreed to the summit with you and hammered out a joint counterterrorism strategy with you."

"To lower our guard."

"Exactly, and it's working."

"But bankrolling Abu Nakba?"

"It's brilliant," said Marcus. "Beijing wants to bleed us, right? They want us spending hundreds of billions of dollars to fight a war on terror so we don't spend enough money building ships and bombers and fighter jets and missile-defense systems. They want us fixated on the Middle East and North Africa so we're not adequately defending our allies in Asia. And who better for President Guanzhong to use as his proxy than Abu Nakba? Kairos does all the dirty work without any Chinese fingerprints, and Beijing gets ready to clean our clock in Taiwan."

"Maybe," said the president. "But what does any of this have to do with a pharmaceutical plant in some remote jungle in India?"

No one spoke, not even Marcus.

So Annie took that one. "There can only be one reason, Mr. President," she said. "The Chinese are working with Abu Nakba and Kairos to mass-produce the Cerberus virus and are planning to release it into the United States ahead of the invasion of Taiwan."

71

"Annie's right, Mr. President," Marcus suddenly exclaimed.

Every head turned toward Ryker.

"Look, sir, I realize that we don't have all the facts yet, but I don't think we can wait. We can keep gathering intelligence and do it aggressively now that we know what we're looking for. But if I may, sir, I recommend that you direct Secretary Foster to order the entire Pacific fleet to steam toward Taiwan, Japan, South Korea, Guam, and the Philippines, and to start moving as many squadrons of bombers and fighter jets into the theater as you possibly can, and antimissile batteries as well.

"At the same time, sir, I'd like my team in the air, headed for India. Annie should get her team at Langley gathering more details about this pharmaceutical plant and a plan for us to get inside it, take down Abu Nakba—assuming he's there—and destroy the plant and whatever active Cerberus strains are on-site. In the meantime, I'd recommend that you send Dr. Dell to Taipei and Secretary Dayton to Tokyo."

It really wasn't Marcus's place to be giving such recommendations to the president of the United States. But given that the room seemed to be still trying to grasp the magnitude of Beijing's threat—and duplicity—and seemed unable to yet think through a strategy of denying the communists their objectives, Marcus took it upon himself to accelerate the conversation.

"Let's be clear, sir," he continued. "There are only two ways we can stop Beijing from this act of madness. The first is to flood the South and East China Seas and the Strait of Taiwan with so much American and allied firepower—to create such a tsunami of deterrence—that President Guanzhong cannot help but come to the realization that you're willing to go toe to toe and that there is absolutely no way he can win this thing without suffering losses far worse than his war games have projected.

"Second, we've got to take Abu Nakba and this Cerberus threat to the homeland off the table immediately. Do both of these, sir, and you keep this apocalyptic genie in the bottle, safeguard the lives of millions of Americans, and convince our allies once again that we're the only true superpower on the planet. But fail to do either or both, and . . . well—honestly, sir—I think we're looking at the end of the American empire as we've known it. The stakes are that high, and I don't believe we have a moment to spare."

Marcus knew he was completely overstepping his authority and acting as if he were the national security advisor, not the head of the CIA's Kairos task force. He knew he was skating on very thin ice with the commander in chief. If he hadn't been so tired and so rattled by Dell's presentation, he would have known better and probably kept his mouth shut. But there was no taking back any of it now.

Hernandez said nothing.

For a moment, he glared at Marcus, then looked down at the notes he'd been taking on the legal pad before him. Seconds ticked by. No one else said a word. Marcus looked at his own notes but could feel every eye staring at him. What he'd just done was beyond chutzpah. It was dangerously close to insubordination. He was an agency staffer, not an elected official, not a cabinet officer, not a principal of any U.S. government entity.

Marcus's stomach tensed. He desperately wanted to look over to Annie for reassurance yet feared finding a look of horror on her face. So he kept his head down, continuing to stare at his notes and pray silently—and fervently—that the Lord would sovereignly make this all work out for the best. Maybe Pete was right. Maybe it was time to step down and hand this unit over to someone like Kailea, a proven warrior who also had the good sense to know when she should hold her tongue.

Just then, he felt Annie's hand under the conference table reaching for his. He took it and squeezed. Marcus didn't want to look at the expression on her face. He couldn't bear to see her disapproval. Still, he was grateful for this simple act of mercy. The president might be about to fire him. And he had every right to do so. But at least Annie still loved him, and for the moment, he clung to her love like a life preserver in a storm.

Finally, the president spoke. "In the future, Agent Ryker—*if* you have a future with this administration—I'd be grateful if you'd refrain from usurping the role of everyone else in this room, including mine," he began, his voice low and measured. "Let's be honest. Karachi was a disaster, and I'm still furious at you about that. But there isn't time to rehash that now. And I will concede that your gambit with the Russians has paid off better than any of us had hoped. As for the rest of this . . ." Hernandez paused as if searching for the right words.

Marcus held his breath.

"Well, you're not wrong. You're out of line, Ryker, but you're not wrong. So I'm going with your recommendations."

Marcus began breathing again.

"Cal, get back to the Pentagon and activate Oplan 5077 immediately," Hernandez ordered the secretary. "Martha, head to the airport and have your pilots take you to Taipei as rapidly as possible. Bill, call your counterpart over there and let them know she's coming. Robert, I want you to head to Tokyo. I'll call the prime minister and ask him to clear his schedule for you. Annie, get back to Langley and put together a plan to take down the Libyan and destroy that plant. And, Marcus, get yourself and your team to Andrews, and don't bother coming back to the White House unless you have Abu Nakba's scalp with you."

Marcus finally looked up and met Hernandez's eyes. "You have my word, Mr. President."

Marcus bolted out the side door onto West Executive Avenue.

Annie was right behind him and tossed him her keys.

They could have—and probably should have—asked for a CIA or White House driver to get them to Joint Base Andrews in a bulletproof four-wheel-drive rather than Annie's pale blue Fiat 500L, a vehicle so small that Marcus had dubbed it her "clown car." But the truth was they just wanted a few minutes alone together before Marcus went once more unto the breach.

Marcus fastened his seat belt, then revved the engine and pulled out onto Pennsylvania Avenue. He'd run this route countless times. Normally, it should take about thirty minutes. Yet even on a Saturday, and even without any traffic to contend with aside from snowplows and salt trucks, the treacherous road conditions were forcing him to drive well under the speed limit

"Would you let Kai know our ETA?" Marcus asked as they exited the White House grounds and worked their way out of D.C. "Waze is saying it's going to take us fifty-one minutes."

"That long?" asked Annie.

"And tell her Pete's not coming."

"You got it," Annie said as she began texting Kailea Curtis. "But don't you think Pete would have already informed everyone on the team?"

"I have no idea. But just in case he hasn't, the team needs to know he's bailed on us, and we've got no time to get another qualified medic."

"Okay, I'm on it," Annie said, dashing off another short text as Marcus cranked up the windshield wipers and blasted the heat.

When Annie was finished, she turned back to Marcus.

"What?" he asked, feeling her gaze. "What's wrong?"

"I'm just wondering."

"About what?"

"Are we going to talk about what happened back there?"

"I'd rather not."

"We probably should," said Annie. "I mean, as the president said, you're not wrong. But—"

"I know. I know. And I'm sorry. I just—"

"You don't have to apologize to me," Annie replied. "Look, I know what kind of pressure you're under. Pete's feeling it too, and that's why he decided to step off the field before he makes reckless mistakes. We talked about it well into the night. Pete's worried about you. And he's worried about himself. And I told him I thought he was doing the right thing."

"You mean quitting the game when we're on the two-yard line?"

"I mean knowing when you've pushed yourself too far and it's time to stop."

"Look, Annie, I know you love Pete. But I love him too, and I've known him a lot longer than you. And I'm telling you that I've never known anyone like him, never had a better friend than him, never known anyone with more courage or more stamina or deeper reserves. I've been on combat missions with Saint Pete in Kandahar where we were under constant mortar fire and didn't sleep for four days straight. I was a wreck, but Pete barely batted an eye. I remember when we were in Iraq one time—in the Green Zone in Baghdad—and there was this brutal firefight. Lasted for nearly a week. And he and I set up a makeshift MASH unit in one of Saddam's palaces that we'd captured. He was the only doctor there, and we couldn't get any replacements because the fighting was so intense that no one else could get to us. And Pete was like a machine. I mean, he treated burn victims, and extracted shrapnel from I don't know how many of our guys, and amputated limbs, and did blood infusions, and on and on and on, and he just kept going. I was whipped. So were Mac and Nick and most of the guys in our unit. But Pete just never stopped. We started calling him the Energizer Bunny. And when we got back to civilian life, I remember back before we had Lars that Elena and I went to visit him and his then-wife in Manhattan. And we'd all just gotten to their place after watching a movie and it was like midnight or one a.m., or whatever, and suddenly, he gets a call from the hospital. They needed to do an emergency triple bypass surgery on some guy, and the surgeon who was on call couldn't get there. So Pete agreed to do it. He asked me to drive him to the hospital. So I did. And I watched him scrub in and go into surgery. He didn't come out for nineteen hours. I was asleep on a gurney in the hallway. When he finally came out, he changed his clothes and asked me if I wanted to go with him to his club and play some tennis before we went back and reconnected with the girls."

"What are you saying?" Annie asked as they finally crossed the frozen Potomac and got on 295, heading south.

"I'm saying I know Pete, and I know what he's capable of, and I'm telling you this has nothing to do with being in the 'red zone' or 'burnt out' or 'on the edge,' or whatever."

"Maybe he just doesn't want to die," Annie replied.

"Who does?"

"But there's a difference between you and him, Marcus, and you know it. You're a follower of Christ. You know exactly where you're going when you die, and that's why death doesn't scare you. But Pete isn't a 'saint,' and he knows it. He's drifted away from the Church. He's alone. And he's trying to figure out what to do with the rest of his life. That's not wrong. And yet you're putting enormous pressure on him to live the same life as you, and you shouldn't. Because if you die out there on this mission, then I'm the one who mourns—single and alone. I'm the one who suffers. Well, me and your mom and sisters and their families and all your friends. But you? You won't be suffering. You'll be in heaven. You'll finally be with Elena and Lars. And with your dad and your grandparents. And with Jenny. And best of all with Jesus, the God who loved you and gave himself for you. Safe and whole and secure and happy and free forever and ever and ever. That's what gives you the courage to give your all out there, and I love that about you. But you know full well that if Pete went on this mission and didn't make it back—if he died out there, as spiritually lost and confused as he is right now—that's it for him. I can't say he's really a true believer. Can you? And if he isn't, he doesn't go to heaven, right? He doesn't spend eternity with Christ. You know what happens, and it's terrifying to imagine. I wish it wasn't true. I wish Christ hadn't been so clear, so definitive, so precise about the eternal penalty for rejecting him. But you know as well as I do that Jesus talked more about the dangers of hell than the joys of heaven."

Marcus was silent as he kept driving along 295 south.

The snow was coming down even harder now and Marcus turned up the windshield wipers to their highest setting. He was beginning to worry whether their flight was even going to be cleared for takeoff.

Annie spoke again as they exited onto 495 east and crossed through Oxen Hill. "I know how close you've become with Pete, and I know you want him out there with you. Because he's the best at what he does. Because you need him. You trust him. And he's always been at your side. But that's exactly why you need to let this go, why you need to be grateful that Pete isn't putting himself into mortal danger again. Let's keep praying for him, that the Lord will open his eyes and draw Pete close to his heart. But until then, let's respect his decision. I need you to be focused over there, not distracted by anything or anyone. Because I'm really worried about you. Not your soul. I know you love Christ more than anything, more than me, and I'm so grateful for that. But I have to be honest with you, Marcus—I'm genuinely afraid that I'm going to lose you on this mission. And even though I'm doing my best to keep it together, the truth is I honestly don't know how I'm going to survive if you don't come back."

Marcus said nothing. Instead, he checked the rearview mirror, then both side mirrors, then turned on his turn signal and pulled off the highway into the freshly plowed parking lot of a Home Depot. It was empty but for a few cars out front, probably belonging to the night crew. Pulling the Fiat into a space far from the others, Marcus came to a complete stop and turned off the engine.

"What are you doing, Marcus?" Annie asked. "We're already late."

"It's okay," he said, staring deep into Annie's gorgeous green eyes. "They're not going to leave without me. But I just wanted to say, you're right about Pete. I'm sorry I didn't see it sooner. I should have, but I didn't."

"It's okay," she said, her voice thick with emotion.

"No, it's not, but I'll make it right," Marcus told her. "Before we take off, I promise I'll call him and apologize and tell him he's doing the right thing."

"Thank you."

"But look, I'm also going to tell him that if I don't come back, I absolutely forbid him from asking you out, unless, of course, he gives his life to Christ."

Annie tried to suppress a laugh but couldn't. And now the tears really started flowing. Marcus reached into her glove compartment, found some napkins, and gave her one to dab her eyes and another to wipe her nose.

"But seriously, Annie, I wouldn't go on this mission—I really wouldn't—if I didn't believe this is what God wanted me to do."

"I know."

"But this is it—really; this is the last one. If we get Abu Nakba, great. But if we don't, I'm done. I'm out. And you, too. When you get into the office, write up our resignation letters. Sign yours. And then sign mine."

"Marcus, it's okay, don't—"

"No, I'm serious. I want you to sign my name—you're the deputy director of the CIA; I'm sure you can forge my signature beautifully—and then put both letters in separate envelopes and set them on Martha's desk. It'll be a few days until she gets back to D.C., but I want them waiting for her upon her return. I don't want there to be any doubt or ambiguity in her mind or ours. We've done our service, and now we're done."

"You're serious?"

"Dead serious," said Marcus.

"Not sure that's the right expression for this particular moment."

"Probably not," he conceded. "But that's not all."

"Okay, I'm listening."

"We're not just going to leave the government, Annie. We're going to get married. Now, I know you're a modest person and frugal and discreet, and I love you for that. But we're not going to elope. And we're not going to have a quiet little backyard wedding. For me, you know that would be fine. But this is your first wedding, and—"

"Uh, it's going to be my *only* wedding, Mr. Ryker," she corrected. "It's you or nobody. I've waited this long to marry the man of my dreams. There is no one else for me, and there never will be. I'm serious, Marcus. If God wants me to be single for the rest of my life, then so be it. But I'm not marrying anybody but you."

"Not even Pete, if he gets saved?"

Annie shook her head and laughed again. "Definitely not."

"Well, don't tell him that until after he gives his life to Christ."

"Fair enough."

"But look, Annie, I'm serious. We're going to do this right. I have some money stashed away—not much; don't get too excited—but we're going to use it to have a real wedding, and a lovely reception, and we're not going on some simple, traditional one-week honeymoon."

"No?"

"Absolutely not. We're going to send out our invitations the moment I get back. We're going to get married on the first Saturday in May. That should be just enough time to get everything ready and for all our family and friends to set aside time. And the moment the reception is over, you and I are going to disappear for three months."

"*Three?*"

"Unless you want it to be longer."

"No, no, three sounds good."

"We're going to go to the Caribbean or Greece or the Maldives or wherever you want. And we're going to walk on white sandy beaches. And swim in azure waters. And go sailing and parasailing and scuba diving. And we're going to drink fun drinks with those little umbrellas."

"And cherries—I know you love cherries."

"Absolutely—lots of cherries—and we're going to relax and decompress and play and swim and talk and laugh, and no one is going to know where we are, or how to get in touch with us, and we're going to dream about our futures and where we're going to live and how many children we're going to have and it's going to be paradise. I know it's long overdue—and I'm sorry about that—but I'm going to make it up to you. By the grace of God, I'm going to make it all up to you and spend the rest of my life loving you and serving you and savoring every precious second that I have on earth with the most beautiful and godly and wonderful girl in the whole wide world."

Marcus didn't give her a moment to reply. Instead, he unbuckled both their seat belts, took Annie in his arms, pulled her toward him, and began kissing her like he hadn't another care in the world.

Until his phone started ringing and wouldn't stop.

At first, Marcus ignored it and just kept kissing her. But finally, she insisted he take it. As much as they wanted to be free, they weren't yet. So Marcus took a breath and answered. And then his mouth dropped open.

"What's wrong? Who was that?" Annie asked when he hung up.

"It was Pete," Marcus said.

"Pete? Why? What does he want?"

"He said he's with the team."

"At Andrews?"

"Yeah—he just got there."

"What for?"

"He says he's coming with us, after all," said Marcus.

"What?"

"He says he's on the plane, that everyone's on the plane, and the pilots are ready to take off, and they're wondering when I'm going to bother showing up."

73

Martha Dell's plane landed at a Taiwanese military base at 4:56 a.m.

Langley's Taipei station chief met her and her security detail on the tarmac and drove them up into the mountains to the national military command center being targeted by Beijing for nuclear destruction. Upon being cleared into the cavernous complex, Dell was ushered into a windowless conference room, where she was greeted by the three most powerful leaders on the island.

Mrs. Yani Lee was Taiwan's esteemed but outgoing president.

Ben We-Ming was the country's highly controversial VP and current presidential candidate who was leading by sixteen points in the latest poll published by the *Taipei Times*.

Henry Wang was the sixty-two-year-old former chief of staff of the Taiwanese armed forces who was now serving as defense minister.

"Thank you, President Lee, for seeing me on such short notice," Dell said, bowing and shaking the president's hand.

"It is an honor to welcome both a good friend and a senior representative of our most trusted ally," Lee replied as they all took their seats. "President Hernandez said it was urgent. As you know, I'm supposed to leave for Tokyo in a few hours on a long-planned state visit. Should I cancel? What's going on? Your president didn't want to say, even on a secure line."

"No, I wouldn't cancel," said Dell. "For the moment, we need you all to be going about business as usual, as though nothing is out of the ordinary. But the truth is that everything has just changed."

"How so?" Lee asked with alarm.

"With respect, the issue is you, Mr. Vice President," Dell said, turning her attention to Ben We-Ming. "We have credible and disturbing intelligence, sir, that your record of very public and vehement support for Taiwan's independence, combined with your soaring poll numbers, has convinced the powers that be in Beijing that they can no longer pursue a peaceful approach to reunification."

"Meaning what?" We-Ming asked. "More bullying? More incursions into our airspace and territorial waters? More missile tests over our heads?"

"I'm afraid not," said Dell. "The Chinese are preparing for a massive surprise attack. We expect it could happen anytime after March 1, but sooner rather than later."

"That's not possible," said the defense minister. "We've detected no major troop movements. No cancelation of military leaves. Yes, we're seeing more ships in port, fueling up and so forth. But nothing to indicate an imminent invasion."

"That's because the invasion will only come after a massive missile barrage, followed by nuclear strikes against this facility and very likely against Taipei itself."

"Nuclear? That's ludicrous," said President Lee. "Who's your source? Where are you getting this from?"

"Chen Guanzhong," said Dell.

The very name seemed to suck all the air out of the room. The three leaders were in shock, and it took a moment for President Lee to seek a clarification.

"I . . . I'm afraid I . . . don't understand," she stammered. "Are you . . . are you saying that President Guanzhong told your president that he's going to launch a nuclear attack on Taiwan in the next few days or weeks?"

"No, Guanzhong didn't tell us directly," Dell replied. "He was speaking to—well, let's just say a colleague—and we intercepted the call."

It wasn't exactly true, of course. Neither the NSA nor the CIA had intercepted a phone call. But Dell couldn't possibly say that the Russian president was her source and that a surreptitious taping system inside Petrovsky's office in the Kremlin was the method. Too much was at stake to intimate—much less to come right out and admit—that Moscow was in any way involved. But it didn't matter. The three Taiwanese leaders were not asking about sources and methods. They were simply asking if Dell was speculating or had actual proof of an imminent attack.

Dell was grateful that no photographer was present to capture the haunting combination of confusion and outright fear on all three faces. But when none of them asked her any more questions, she pulled a digital recorder out of her jacket pocket and played for them excerpts of the conversation.

74

Bill McDermott entered the Oval Office from a side door.

"You called, Mr. President?"

"Bill, take a seat," said Hernandez as he signed the latest stack of orders sent over from the Pentagon to deploy the 82nd Airborne Division and an additional fifty thousand American combat soldiers and Marines to the East Pacific in the next six hours.

The national security advisor, a clipboard in his hand, closed the door behind him, took his seat across from the *Resolute* desk, and waited quietly for the commander in chief to finish. Finally, Hernandez set his pen down, flexed his aching fingers, and took off his reading glasses.

"Any hue and cry from Beijing yet?" he asked.

"Not yet, but it's early," said McDermott. "They see we're coming. But they don't see the magnitude of it yet."

"So they're keeping their powder dry."

"For now, yes, but you do realize, Mr. President, that if they misinterpret what we're doing—if they see this as an offensive move rather than just an exercise, Guanzhong could simply scrap his game plan and order the missile attacks to start tonight or tomorrow or the next day. And that's not the only scenario I worry about."

"What else?"

"What if Vice President We-Ming decides he has to sound tough and spouts off something about Taiwan's right to self-determination and never-flagging commitment to democracy and independence?"

"It would hardly be the first time," said Hernandez.

"But it would be the worst possible timing, sir. The gun is already in Guanzhong's hand. It's cocked, and it's ready to fire. If We-Ming or literally anyone else in the Taiwanese government says the wrong thing right now—combined with our air, ground, and naval forces moving at high speed across the Pacific—I can almost guarantee you Guanzhong is going to pull the trigger."

"Before his scheme to release Cerberus into the U.S. is ready to activate?"

"If he has to, yes."

"That's why Martha is in Taipei right now, holding their hands and making sure they don't do something suicidal."

"I hope that's enough."

"What do you recommend?"

"That's what I've been mulling for the past few hours, sir," McDermott explained, looking down at his notes.

"And what have you come up with?"

"Well, sir, first, I think you need to step into the pressroom, take a few questions, and I'll make sure you get asked about RIMPAC," McDermott began, referring to the Rim of the Pacific Exercise, the world's largest series of naval exercises involving forces from the U.S. and twenty-five other countries.

"And say what?"

"You know, 'Nothing to worry about. Business as usual. We do this every year. Just working with our closest friends and allies in the Pacific Rim to make sure we're always ready for every contingency, real or imagined.' Calm. Confident. Not quite casual. But clear enough for Guanzhong to know you know the Pacific as well as he does and you're not going to be pushed around."

"Okay—anything else?"

"Yes, sir. Call him."

"Who, Guanzhong?"

"Yes. Let him howl, but make sure he hears you loud and clear. *'The U.S. hasn't changed our tune. We still hold to our One China policy. We seek a peaceful resolution to the tensions in the Strait of Taiwan. But we will not tolerate under any circumstances an act of aggression in the Pacific theater. Period.'* That sort of thing."

"Okay, fine, scratch out a few lines for me to use and I'll head over to the pressroom in a few minutes."

"Already done, sir," McDermott replied, handing over a three-by-five card he had attached to his clipboard. "And there's one more thing."

"What's that?"

"Ryker."

"You're worried about him," said the president.

"Aren't you, sir?"

"Of course. You know I was about to fire him."

"Then why didn't you, sir? He's exhausted. Burnt out. And putting the lives of his team in real danger."

"You're talking about Jenny Morris?"

"Her death is a huge loss for the Agency."

"It certainly is, but that's not all on Ryker."

"He was leading the team. The buck stops with him. Plus the LNG explosion, the Raven's suicide. He's making mistakes, Mr. President. Big ones. And it's not just fatigue. He's engaged. He keeps delaying his wedding for one more mission, one more mission, one more mission. But everyone around him is telling him to hang it up. Annie. Pete. His mother. Everyone sees he's in trouble. Except him. You see it too. But for some reason you've sent him back out there again."

"Isn't that Martha's call, not mine?" Hernandez asked.

"Technically, but she's swamped, sir. And she's half a world away."

"Well, it's too late now, Bill. What's done is done."

"Not necessarily, sir."

"Meaning what?"

"You're the commander in chief. Martha doesn't have the last word. You do, sir. So bench him."

"Bench Ryker? Now? He's already in motion."

"The moment he lands in Manama, have me call him."

"And you'll say what?"

"There's a new development. You're putting the mission on pause until you can see him and talk to him personally."

"He'll say, *'Fine, let's do a videoconference.'*"

"And I'll say, *'No, the president needs to see you in his office immediately. It's urgent and it's personal.'*"

"What about his team? What about the SEALs?"

"I believe it's time to put Kailea Curtis in charge, sir. She's the fastest-rising star in the Agency. The team has the highest respect for her. She won't miss a beat. In the meantime, I'll talk to Martha and Annie and make sure we're on the same page with all this. Believe me, sir. I've known Annie since she first came to Washington. She loves Marcus. She wants to marry him tomorrow. And she's terrified he's going to die out there on the battlefield all because Ryker is too stubborn to know when enough is enough."

75

MANAMA, BAHRAIN

The unmarked Gulfstream 5 business jet landed in the wee hours of the morning.

With little intelligence on the pharmaceutical plant and no plan yet on how to infiltrate it, find Abu Nakba, take him out, and destroy any capacity for Kairos or the Chinese to produce the Cerberus virus there, the team had spent most of the sixteen-and-a-half-hour flight considering their options and developing various contingency plans. They did make time to mock Pete mercilessly for considering not joining them on what they all hoped was their final mission. Fortunately, Pete had taken it all in good cheer, joking that if Marcus didn't make it home alive, he was going to elope with Annie and didn't want anyone to think he hadn't truly earned the right to be next in line. Even Marcus laughed. But though he didn't say it, Marcus's fear now was not that he wouldn't make it home safely but that Pete wouldn't.

Upon landing at Bahrain International Airport, the team was met by the CIA's Manama station chief and driven to the regional headquarters of the U.S. Navy. Located on the northeast corner of the island, the facility served as the home port of the American Fifth Fleet and the operational hub of U.S. Central Command. Waiting for them was the head of the Joint Special Operations Command (JSOC), who had just flown in from Fort Bragg in North Carolina, the head of DEVGRU—the Naval Special Warfare Development Group, better known as SEAL Team Six—and a squadron of highly trained operators, all fresh in from Virginia Beach.

Until daybreak, they met secretly on the bleachers of the base's basketball court so as not to attract any attention from the nearly nine thousand U.S. personnel living and working on-site. After introductory remarks by the JSOC commander and a prayer by the head of the SEALs, Marcus briefed the SEAL operators on the history and habits of Abu Nakba and what they had learned about Kairos's modus operandi during their dozens of raids on Kairos strongholds over the past eight months, including the most recent operation in Karachi. Marcus also walked them through the nature of the Cerberus virus, exactly how deadly it was, and how Kairos was likely planning to use it to kill millions of Americans. Then he gave them a quick overview of the rapidly rising threat against Taiwan and how the two plots were intertwined.

When he was finished, you could hear a pin drop. This was the first time the SEALs had heard any of this, and the magnitude of the threat against the American homeland—and America's allies in Asia—was suddenly brutally clear, as were the stakes if they failed to stop Abu Nakba and his forces.

Kailea Curtis went over the satellite imagery they had of the pharmaceutical facility and its environs.

Finally, Donny Callaghan—the longtime SEAL Team Six commander on loan to the CIA—walked everyone through a draft plan of attack that he, Marcus, and Kailea had sketched out on the flight. Admittedly, it was very rough. They were still waiting for the latest round of more detailed satellite photos from Washington and whatever intercepts and other tidbits the NSA and Langley had been gathering. But at least it was a start.

When they were done, the commander of JSOC fired off a series of questions, which Marcus fielded as best he could. Then the commander opened the floor to his operators. They didn't hold back. They were calm, professional, and unflappable. But it was clear they weren't convinced that what lay ahead of them had been carefully thought through and properly vetted.

Marcus agreed. "Look, I wish I could tell you we know exactly what we're walking into," he told the group as Noah signaled to him that it was time to roll. "The truth is, we don't. Not yet. Not completely. By the time we get to the *Maine*, we will. You have my word. But for now, get some rest. Agent Curtis and I will be back to get you in a few hours."

Marcus asked Geoff Stone, Callaghan, Noah Daniels, and Miguel Navarro to stay with the others and do their best to get some rest. Then he turned to Kailea and Pete and asked them to follow him. He led them off the court over to the head coach's office, which Marcus was using as his own.

"Kai, would you wait out here for a moment while I talk to Pete?" Marcus asked. "Then I'll be right with you."

76

Pete closed the door.

"What's up, boss?" he asked when they were seated.

"First of all, I can't thank you enough for changing your mind and coming with us."

"Marcus, please, you already said way too much on the plane. I'm here. I love you. I'd rather not die. But if I do, then I won't blame you. Now, can we just leave it at that?"

"Fair enough, but the 'not dying' part is what I want to talk about."

"Marcus, I've heard your sermon way too many times. You want me to 'get saved' and have 'fire insurance,' or whatever, and I appreciate it. I get it. Really. You don't need to say anything more. It's my decision and mine alone. But can't we just focus on the task at hand?"

"Pete, I didn't call you in for a sermon."

"You sure?"

"Yeah, I'm sure."

"Okay, then why? I barely slept a wink on that flight, and I could really use a few good hours."

"I know, and it'll only take a moment," Marcus assured him.

"Great—what've you got?"

"When we get inside the compound, I'm not taking you in with the rest of the team," Marcus began.

"What do you mean?"

"Kai and I and the others will take the dormitory, aided by the SEALs. I know you're normally at my side, but not this time."

"Then where will I be?"

"You'll have two objectives. Before we take the dorm, I want you and Noah to enter the dining hall. You'll go through the back and make sure it's clear. At that hour, it should be. Then you'll set up all your gear and supplies to create a makeshift MASH unit. If we have casualties, we'll bring them to you."

"But I don't need to—"

"Hold on; I'm not done," Marcus said, cutting him off. "Once you're finished with that—and it should only take a few minutes—I want you up on the roof doing overwatch."

"As a sniper?"

"Exactly."

"But that's Miguel's job."

"Not anymore. It's going to be you this time. You'll take out the guards at the entrance of the dorm as we begin the operation. Anyone that gets past us, you need to take them out. Anyone approaches the dorm, you take them out. Everyone on that compound knows they are making a bioweapon to kill millions of Americans. So the president has given us shoot-to-kill authority. Got it?"

"Marcus, I appreciate that you're trying to protect me, but if, God forbid, one of you is hit inside that dorm building, I need to be right there to treat them immediately. Every second counts. You know that."

"I do, Pete, but this isn't negotiable. I need you on that roof. And I need Navarro in the building with us. Are we clear?"

Pete was silent for a bit, then nodded his head.

"Good, because there's something else," Marcus said.

"Should I be worried?"

Marcus ignored the question. "Look, Pete, you're my best friend. That's why

I want you with me when we go into India. But it's also why when we get back, I'm wondering, would you be my best man?"

Pete hadn't seen that coming. "Are you serious?"

"A hundred percent."

"Really?"

"Really," Marcus assured him. "Look, you've been right all along. I've been stupid not to do this sooner. But it's not because I'm getting cold feet; it's just that—"

But Pete cut him off. "I know, I know, you're a man who likes to finish one task before starting another. But this isn't a task, Marcus. This is the rest of your life. And when you find a woman as amazing as Annie, you should start the rest of your life immediately."

"Well, I may not be the sharpest knife in the drawer," Marcus conceded. "But you're right. And I'm ready. As soon as we get home, we're going to set the date and make this thing happen. So will you do it?"

Pete laughed. "Are you kidding? I thought you'd never ask."

"Good. Now get out of here, and send Kai in."

When Kailea shrugged and stepped into the office. Marcus asked her to shut the door and have a seat. She did, looking like she was bracing herself for bad news.

Marcus began by explaining that he was switching Pete for Navarro and briefly explained why.

"Good idea," she replied. "No sense sending Pete into harm's way if he's going to need to take care of the rest of us."

"Exactly," said Marcus. "But listen, there's something else I need you to do, as well."

"Please don't make me stay up on the roof with those two," Kailea joked. "I mean, you know I love them both, but . . ."

"Don't worry," he said. "I need you in that building with me."

"Then what?"

"I'm making you my number two on this mission," Marcus said.

"Are you sure?"

"Of course I'm sure—and when we get home, you're going to be the new head of the Agency's counterterrorism division," he added. "Congratulations."

She was in shock. "*Sir?*"

"You heard me. This is it for me, Kai, my last time in the field. Whatever happens out there, I'm out. I've already submitted my resignation. So has Annie. Come what may, we're done. We're marrying and we're moving as far away from the Beltway as humanly possible."

"Whoa . . . I just didn't see that coming right now. I don't know what to say."

"You don't have to say anything. Annie and I have already cleared it all with Dell. And she cleared it with the president. I told them both that you're my only choice for the job. It wasn't even close. You've earned it, hands down, and if you want it, it's yours."

"Wow, really, that's . . . Thank you, sir. I accept. I just . . . Thank you."

"You're welcome. I wasn't sure what to make of you when you dropped into that booth at Manny's Diner that Sunday morning all those years ago and announced that you were my new partner. But I couldn't be more grateful for your hard work, your courage under fire, and your loyalty."

"Thank you, old man—right back at you."

Marcus laughed at the inside joke and the memory of meeting this woman for the first time.

"I have just one piece of parting advice for you, Curtis."

"I can only imagine, sir," she said, smiling. "*Don't die, and don't get arrested,* right?"

"You got it," Marcus said, smiling back. "Oh, and one more thing—I almost forgot. It's actually a personal request, from Annie."

"Whatever she needs."

"Good, because she'd wanted to ask you herself, but she's been a bit busy the last few days, and she just wants everything to be in place when we get back to D.C."

"I'm sorry, sir, I'm not following you."

"Annie would like you to be her maid of honor."

Kailea hadn't seen that coming either. "Are you serious?"

"It's not me asking, Curtis—this is all Annie. She's loved getting to know you over these past few years. And as you know, she doesn't have any family anymore. So this is a big ask. She's going to really want you helping her with everything. Will you do it?"

"Absolutely, sir. Please tell her I'd love nothing more."

77

"Gentlemen, we're about to be outmanned and outgunned," Marcus began.

"We'll be far from home. With no air support. In a friendly country that doesn't know we're there. Facing the most fearsome and experienced operatives Kairos has ever put on the battlefield. Each one a killer. Each one a survivor. Each one ready to lay down his life—eager to become a *shahid,* a martyr—to protect his master. And they're not alone. They're supported by hundreds of highly skilled veterans of the Chinese PLA. Elite. The best of the best. Chosen from a country with 1.4 billion people. By a leader who is now hell-bent on unleashing full-scale genocide with this new Cerberus virus—that is, if you and I don't stop them.

"Yes, they have home-court advantage," Marcus continued. "Yes, they're well-fed and well-rested. And true, they won't be cooped up in a sardine can for the next few days. You and I will be hundreds of feet under the ocean. Unable to move about at will. Unable to breathe fresh air. But I'll take our odds any day of the week and twice on Sunday. When I look into your eyes, gentlemen, I don't see weary, jet-lagged, faces. I don't see men wishing for a few more hours of sleep. No, I see hunters champing at the bit to be released into the wild to do what you do best. I don't know most of you. Not personally. And you don't know me. We've only had a few hours together. But I know you represent the elite. The best of the best of a country of 330 million people. And I want you to know that you were hand-chosen for this mission. And you said yes back in the States even though your commanders couldn't tell you a single word about what you were saying yes to—and I want you to know how grateful I am. Not just that you're SEALs. Not just that you're about to go with me into battle with sheer evil. Far more importantly, I'm grateful that you guys aren't coming for me."

That line got a laugh.

"Now, I wish we could hang out in this beautiful country while the folks at CIA and DIA and NSA keep gathering data and clarifying the picture of what we're up against. But there simply isn't time. To get ourselves all the way to India before that plant goes live and actually starts producing the virus—which we believe is just a few days from now—we have to move."

Then he turned the briefing over to Kailea Curtis.

She explained that they were taking three different unmarked business jets. Their destination: Colombo, Sri Lanka. Given their need for stealth, they couldn't fly military planes to the tiny island nation off the southern coast of India for fear of drawing unwanted attention. Instead, Marcus and his team from CIA would take off first. Ninety minutes later, half the SEALs would take off in the next plane. Two hours after that, the other half would lift off. When they landed in the country's capital and most populous city, they would be transported to an undisclosed location before traveling by boat into the backwaters of Kerala, India.

Nearly ten hours later, all three planes had covered the 2,350-mile journey, and the teams converged at a hotel not far from the airport under the cover of darkness. There they had about an hour to rest and shower before they were driven to a private marina north of the capital. Loading onto two vessels that Annie and her team back at Langley had rented for them, they headed out to sea.

Forty-five minutes from shore, Marcus and Kailea cut the engines and turned over control of both boats to the JSOC commander. Then they all donned the scuba gear they'd brought from the States, tested their radios, and plunged into the inky-black sea. Waiting just below them, right where it was supposed to be, was the USS *Maine*, the Ohio-class nuclear submarine that just twelve days before had taken Marcus and his team to and from Karachi. One by one, they entered the submarine through a special hatch, removed their scuba gear, took hot—but brief—showers to warm up, dressed, and gathered in the mess hall for their last hot meal for some time.

78

Annie Stewart was running two massive intelligence operations simultaneously.

Half of her team in the Ops Center was watching for any reaction by Chinese missile and naval forces to the Pentagon's announcement that RIMPAC was being held early this year. They were simultaneously tracking the movement of more than one hundred U.S. Navy vessels out of Pearl Harbor and Guam, steaming at high speed across the Pacific toward Taiwan, Japan, and the Philippines. At the same time, they were tracking the movement of hundreds of U.S. bombers, fighter jets, and transport planes carrying Army and Marine combat forces to bases in Guam, Japan, and South Korea.

The DoD press release had caught everyone off guard. So far, none of the two dozen Asian, European, and other allies that usually participated had begun to submerge their submarines or muster their surface ships. Annie was reporting to the NSC that her team hadn't detected any change in Beijing's military posture. But that was confusing. Not only was Beijing's military not yet reacting to a massive mobilization of American forces into the Pacific, Annie and her team were hearing crickets from the Chinese Foreign Ministry, which they had expected would be shrieking at the top of their lungs.

The other half of Annie's staff in the Global Ops Center was furiously trying to gather whatever additional details they possibly could find on the pharmaceutical plant in India and forwarding relevant data to Marcus via encrypted servers as the *Maine* sped across the Indian Ocean. The most troubling development was that the plant was now fully operational. As far as Langley knew, Kairos and the Chinese could already be mass-producing the Cerberus virus. And Marcus and his teams were still eighteen hours away.

THE KREMLIN, MOSCOW, RUSSIA

At 9:03 p.m. local time, Mikhail Borisovich Petrovsky addressed his nation.

"Citizens of Russia, this presidential address comes at a watershed period for our country," he began. "We live in a time of radical and perhaps irreversible change in our world, a time of crucial historical events that will determine the future of our country and our people, a time when each one of us bears a colossal responsibility.

"I know it has been difficult—the cruel and unwarranted American sanctions have taken their toll on our otherwise vibrant and heroic economy, slowing our mighty economic engine, destroying jobs, creating shortages across the country, and triggering rampant inflation. The price of fuel has soared. So has the price of meat. And fruit. And vegetables. Even bread.

"Yet none of this is your fault, dear citizens of the motherland. Nor is it mine. Together, you and I inherited a painful legacy. When President Luganov was assassinated in cold blood—in his own home; indeed, in his own private study—along with the head of the FSB and, shortly afterward, our esteemed prime minister, these wicked acts set into motion a season of instability that the American imperialists seized and took advantage of.

"But you, the brave and selfless citizens of the Russian Federation, you have not cowered in the face of such aggression. You have not wavered in your love of Mother Russia. No, you have held your heads high and shown great courage that would make your parents and grandparents—who endured far worse in their day—very proud.

"Tonight, after so much bad news, I am honored to bring you good news. Tonight, you need to know that Russia has achieved a tremendous victory in our war against the criminals who seek to undermine and destabilize our country and its government. Tonight, I can report to you that due to the brilliant and tireless work of our intelligence and security forces, we have finally hunted down the traitor responsible for all three assassinations—Oleg Kraskin—and brought him to justice once and for all."

As Petrovsky said this—and spun a dazzling tale of tracking the traitor to Mexico City, cornering him in the lair of Colombian drug lords, and killing him in a ferocious firefight—he held up glossy and gruesome color photos, mounted on pieces of foam board, of Kraskin's bullet-ridden body.

And beamed.

79

The sun was not yet up, but Abu Nakba had not slept at all.

The pain shooting through his right leg—the one crippled in an Israeli air strike in Gaza so many decades earlier—had intensified through the night and was now almost unbearable. Nevertheless, when the expected knock at the door sounded, he was ready.

"Come in, Mohammed," the old man said.

The door opened, light from the hallway flooded the room, and Mohammed Faisal entered. "The call to prayer is about to begin," the younger man said.

Faisal helped the Libyan go through his ritual washing as he, too, went through his own ablutions. Soon, all over the compound, the recorded voice of a Saudi muezzin was heard calling the faithful to humble themselves before Allah. Faisal and Abu Nakba knelt on the prayer carpet they had brought from their compound in Ghat, Libya, the very carpet that the old man's mother had bequeathed to him after her death, a carpet fashioned in the Old Shuq in Gaza

City back in the early 1920s. Together, the two men—some forty years apart—faced Mecca and recited their morning prayers.

When another knock came, Faisal—pistol at his side—rose to answer it.

Omar Nazim, the head of Abu Nakba's security detail, stood in the hallway of the unimpressive, unpainted, and unadorned barracks where they and the rest of the plant managers, workers, and security staff slept each night. Nazim had brought them both a tray of light breakfast, some freshly baked pita and a small bowl of yogurt and dried fruit, but the old man waved them away. He had no appetite for food or drink. All he wanted was to see the new shipment that had just arrived from Beijing.

Minutes later, Abu Nakba was limping down the hall, Faisal and Omar Nazim at his side.

They helped him through a side door, down several steps, and into the back of a golf cart. Glancing at his watch, the Libyan urged the men to pick up their pace. Faisal obliged, taking the wheel while Nazim, brandishing an AK-47, kept a watchful eye on every guard and worker they passed.

Much to Abu Nakba's relief, as they toured the grounds, he saw that two Chinese-built antiaircraft missile batteries were finally in place. One was positioned on the south end of the compound, near the pharmaceutical plant. The other was located on the north end, near the main administrative building. Both were well camouflaged.

Convinced that the compound was now nearly impregnable from the air, Abu Nakba rested in his sense that it was also impregnable from the land. After all, the Chinese had clearly spent a small fortune erecting miles of electrified fencing, manning guard towers 24-7, and setting up scores of CCTV cameras. What's more, Nazim had established regular patrols and even rigged the bridge to the mainland with explosive charges, just in case.

Rather than returning to the dormitory or going to the mess hall for breakfast, the old man now asked Faisal to take him to the main plant. Faisal dutifully complied. Upon parking, he helped the Kairos founder limp up to the guard station while Nazim watched their backs. They flashed their badges, entered, and were given hazmat suits by the shift supervisor, who wore one himself. Faisal helped Abu Nakba into his, then donned his own, after which they passed through the newly installed air lock.

When they were inside the plant, Abu Nakba marveled at the high-tech and high-speed operation underway. Hundreds of empty deodorant spray cans were spinning by on a conveyor belt. They entered some sort of chamber, where they were filled with an aerosolized version of the Cerberus virus. Computerized machines then capped the cans, inserted them into cardboard packaging bearing some American brand name, and fed them down a conveyor belt, where Indian workers loaded them onto pallets, shrink-wrapped them, and used forklifts to stack them inside shipping containers for delivery to the United States.

Over his many decades, the Libyan had used countless types of technology to bring death to his enemies. But he had never imagined a setup quite like this. It was all the doing of Li Bai Xiang and his superiors, for whom Abu Nakba would forever be grateful. Beijing was paying him a fortune for one simple reason: Kairos was now days away from sending the virus to American soil to deliver the final death blow.

80

Another day had passed.

Meaning Kairos and the Chinese were one day closer to sending their genocidal virus into battle against the American people. Yet only in the past hour had the *Maine* reached the mouth of the famed Kerala backwaters.

"Any more questions?" Marcus asked his forces as they finished their final briefing.

There were none.

"You sure?" Marcus pressed as he glanced at the clock on the wall. "Last call."

It was 1:23 on Thursday morning. They'd been discussing the final battle plan since midnight, and it was time to wrap things up and put it into motion. One of the SEALs in the back of the mess hall raised his hand.

"Sir, I get why President Hernandez wants American forces to take down Abu Nakba, given all the devastation that Kairos has wrought and what they're obviously planning next. But you haven't mentioned the Indian government. Do they know we're coming? And are they providing any support at all?"

"Good question, and I'm sorry I didn't think to cover it," Marcus replied. "No, we have not informed anyone in New Delhi. There are several reasons for that. The first, of course, is basic operational security. To maintain the element of surprise, we've worked hard to keep the number of people aware of our mission to the bare minimum."

Seeing heads nod, Marcus continued.

"The second is that the folks at Langley are in the process of reevaluating India's trustworthiness as an ally. Let me be clear: I'm not saying there's evidence that the Indians are colluding with Kairos or are even aware of the group's presence on their soil. Given the history of tensions between India and China, it strains credulity to believe New Delhi is assisting Beijing in preparing an attack on the United States. But if some rogue element of the Indian intelligence or security services is providing Kairos and/or the Chinese a safe haven, we can't afford the possibility that our operation would be compromised and the folks at the compound would be tipped off that we're coming.

"Third, and finally," Marcus continued, "if the Indian government proves to be innocent in all this—which I for one certainly hope to be the case—we want to be able to give them two options when it's over: either plausible deniability, or the ability to say they were involved in a joint operation, allowing them to take partial credit and not look like we humiliated them by violating their sovereignty."

The answer seemed to satisfy the operator who had asked it.

"Anything else?" Marcus asked.

But they were done.

Marcus thanked them for being the tip of the spear in their country's defense. Then he asked them all to bow their heads, if they so chose, as he led them in prayer for God to show them mercy, give them great success, and bring them all safely home to their family and friends. Then he said amen and led them out of the mess.

Donning their scuba gear and filling waterproof bags with weapons, plenty of ammunition, communications gear, and other essentials, Marcus, Kailea, Pete, Geoff Stone, Donny Callaghan, Miguel Navarro, and Noah Daniels squeezed into the very same Advanced SEAL Delivery Vehicle they'd used in Karachi. Then Donny—their designated driver this time around—closed and locked the hatch behind them, turned on the computerized navigation system, and positioned himself at the controls. They could all feel the shudder as the ASDV separated from the *Maine*.

This was it.

They were moving.

Radio silent.

And there was no turning back.

In the utter darkness, Marcus closed his eyes and counted to fifty as he tried to slow his breathing. Feeling his heart racing, he knew he needed to calm himself down. The exercise worked but not as well as it had in the past. So Marcus did it again. And a third time. Eventually, both his pulse and breathing slowed considerably.

In his mind's eye, he pictured the SEALs loading into the other ASDVs behind them. He then mentally reviewed every square inch of the latest satellite images. The three canals that led to the pharmaceutical plant from three different directions. The electrified fencing. The guard towers. The exact locations of the CCTV cameras. The electrical substation and backup generators, providing everyone and everything on-site with continual power. The main production facility, now working at full tilt. The loading docks. And the rows of tractor trailers being filled with pallets of the deadliest biotoxin ever produced.

Next Marcus mentally focused on the buildings they'd be assaulting, recalling the satellite photographs in the minutest detail. The dining hall was a squat, one-story structure with windows and entrances on the east and west sides. Attached to it was an annex that appeared to be a workout facility. Outside was an Olympic-size pool, though not yet filled with water.

The main administrative building was a two-story structure with entrances on the north and south sides. The CIA was fairly certain this was the headquarters for the security personnel, given the armored SUVs that were typically parked out front, together with a small fleet of patrol cars and golf carts. The compound's communications facilities were also housed there, as evidenced by the multiple antennas and three satellite dishes on the roof. The rest of the building comprised offices that appeared unoccupied.

Across the street from the dining hall was a six-story dormitory building. This is where they believed the Libyan and his bodyguards slept, though where exactly they had no idea. They were going in blind—and shorthanded. And this was what worried Marcus most.

Initially, Marcus had wanted to come in fast and hard by helicopter, firing rockets to take out the guard towers and using fifty-caliber machine guns to take out most of the guards themselves. But when Annie and her team had spotted the arrival of two antiaircraft batteries, Marcus had nixed that scenario, deciding instead to penetrate the compound's perimeter underwater, using the canals to slip under the electrified fencing undetected. Marcus had requested a full squadron of fifty SEAL operators to accompany him and his team of six from Langley. But the head of the SEALs and the commander of JSOC said this was impossible. The Navy only had three ASDVs in the theater. Even packing them like sardines, that would only allow seventeen SEALs to join Marcus and his six colleagues, giving them a total of only twenty-four fighters.

The problem was that Langley's reconnaissance indicated almost two hundred workers operating inside the compound. As many as 150 of them were Chinese nationals who were running the production facility in what appeared to be three eight-hour shifts of fifty people each. Marcus believed the Chinese workers were likely to be unarmed, but some could be trained and capable members of the Chinese army or security services. The main threat was that most of the other fifty people on-site appeared to be ethnic Arabs and Iranians. These were the last of the Kairos terror network, and Marcus had to assume they were highly experienced and hardened killers. These were the ones manning the front gate and the guard towers and conducting the hourly patrols.

Would some of them be asleep at this hour? Sure. But how many? Marcus had no idea. This was the main reason Annie was so worried, and Marcus knew she wasn't wrong. The Americans would have the element of surprise. But they were badly outmanned and had no air support to back them up until they could disable the antiaircraft batteries, and he saw no way of doing that until all fifty Kairos terrorists were neutralized.

Soon, Marcus felt their ASDV slowing down. Then he felt Callaghan tap him on the arm. They had arrived. Marcus tapped Kailea's arm. She, in turn, tapped Pete, and soon everyone was notified. Pete unlocked and opened the hatch and headed to the surface with his gear. Then Marcus grabbed his waterproof satchel of weapons, ammo, grenades, and other gear, and followed suit.

81

When Marcus broke the surface of the water, his heart almost stopped.

They were not where they had planned to be and were thus dangerously exposed.

The canal they had navigated through ran parallel to the main service road. But they had planned to surface behind the dining hall, because that would give them maximum cover to remove their scuba gear, get their weapons and comms gear ready, and watch for any sign of patrols. The good news was that all the interior lights of the dining hall were off. As expected, no one was there. The problem was that all the lampposts lining the street were on, and Marcus and his team had just surfaced about fifty yards shy of the hall itself. This gave them a direct view of the dormitory at their ten o'clock and the main administrative facility at their two o'clock. But if anyone was looking out of either building, or if a patrol was coming by foot or by vehicle, they were well illuminated and at serious risk of being spotted.

Marcus signaled for everyone to resubmerge. Diving deep to stay well under the waterline, he swam the additional fifty yards before resurfacing again. This time he found himself directly behind the dining hall. Scrambling onto the grassy bank of the canal, Marcus removed his helmet and his regulator and turned off his oxygen tank. Scanning for any signs of life and immediate danger but seeing none, he opened his waterproof satchel, pulled out a few dry towels, and spread them out on the grass. He quickly withdrew his M4 assault rifle, attached the suppressor, inserted a magazine, and chambered a round. Only then did he pull off his fins, tank, and wet suit and lay those out on the grass beside his helmet and regulator.

One by one, his colleagues did the same.

Now wearing only a black cotton T-shirt and black tactical pants, Marcus pulled on a clean pair of black cotton socks and black combat boots. Then he pulled out a Kevlar vest, a small backpack, and a tactical belt with holster and put them all on. Drawing out two Sig Sauer pistols, he inserted magazines, chambered a round in each, and shoved one in the holster on his waist and the other in a separate Velcro holster he wrapped around his right thigh. In short order, he loaded up with his grenades, canteen, power bars, a small first aid kit, an encrypted satphone, and a combat knife. Finally, he powered up his night vision goggles, whisper microphone, and radio, making sure they were all working. He looked around at his team—designated Red Team for this mission—and saw that they were all ready to go as well.

The Blue Team commander radioed in and gave the prearranged code word. This confirmed that they were now on the bank of the canal located on the far side of the compound, within striking distance of the electrical substation and one of the antiaircraft missile batteries.

Marcus told him to hold tight while he radioed Gold Team, whose commander said they needed two or three more minutes. They had just surfaced in the canal under the bridge near the main gate, and two of his SEALs were rigging it with remote-controlled explosives that could blow the bridge to kingdom come, if and when it became necessary.

Just then Marcus heard a vehicle approaching. Pressing himself against the back wall of the dining hall, he gripped his M4 and radioed all three teams to stay down and avoid contact. Thirty seconds later, a sedan marked *SECURITY* drove past. A minute later, the Gold Team commander reported the vehicle was crossing the bridge.

Marcus's stomach tightened as he glanced at his watch. It was now 2:46 a.m. Based on Annie's last dispatch, there wasn't supposed to be a shift change of workers in the production facility until 7 a.m. But the patrols, she said, occurred at random times. Langley had determined no predictable pattern. What's more, while some security officers moved in vehicles, others were foot patrols the Americans were less likely to hear coming.

Marcus ordered everyone to hold their positions, scan for any sign of additional patrols, and report back. They could not afford to be spotted, much less fired upon. Their plan was premised entirely on the element of surprise. Yet the clock was ticking.

Two minutes passed.

Then three.

Then four.

Finally, after nearly five minutes, his team leaders reported back that all was clear. Marcus relayed the news to the Global Operations Center at Langley.

"Blowtorch, this is Arrowhead, requesting authorization. Repeat, this is Arrowhead; we are in place and ready to strike. Requesting immediate authorization to commence."

After a hiss of static, Annie's voice came over his headset. Her signal was clear, and her voice was strong.

"Affirmative, Arrowhead, this is Blowtorch. You are green to commence Operation Windy City. I repeat, you are green to commence Operation Windy City. We'll send up a flare for you all—Godspeed."

"Roger that, Blowtorch. Much obliged."

As Marcus's heart started racing afresh, he ordered both other teams to activate Phase One. When the team leaders confirmed, Marcus turned to Pete and Noah and nodded. Both men instantly jumped to their feet and moved to the back door of the dining hall. Using a crowbar, Pete broke in as quietly as he could. He flipped on his night vision goggles before heading into the darkened kitchen, his M4 at the ready, a large backpack, sniper rifle, and tripod strapped to his back. Noah slung a large duffel bag and his M-32 grenade launcher over his shoulder and followed Pete inside, his M4 up and all his faculties on high alert.

Methodically checking every corner of the dining hall, they were soon satisfied that the place was empty. Pete then removed his backpack, unzipped it, and unpacked all manner of medical supplies, sterilized surgical tools, and various bottles of pharmaceuticals and laid them out on one of the large tables. Noah, meanwhile, found a wooden ladder leading to a hatch and headed up to the roof. Pete finished his preparations, then scrambled up the ladder to join Noah.

Staying low so as not to attract attention, they moved to the edge of the roof closest to the road. This gave them clear views of both the dormitory and the production plant. While Pete set up his tripod and sniper rifle and attached a suppressor, Noah unzipped his duffel and removed two small drones, each fitted with night vision cameras. He powered them up, then removed two remote-control units from his bag along with two small monitors and set these and himself up behind one of the air-conditioning ducts where he would be least visible. Then he pulled a satellite phone out of the duffel bag, turned it on, and set it down on the roof to his left. Finally, he withdrew a device about the size of an Xbox console, set it to his right, powered it up, and raised its four antennae. As he did, Pete settled into position and took aim at one of the two guards outside the main entrance to the dormitory.

Simultaneously, on the far side of the compound, the Blue Team's sniper was scrambling to the roof of the pharmaceutical plant, getting himself set up, also attaching a suppressor, and taking aim at the second guard. Two other SEALs were crawling toward the electrical substation about thirty yards to their left, armed with a set of bolt cutters and a kit of plastic explosives and charges.

Near the front of the compound, two SEALs were climbing up the banks of the canal and positioning themselves on each side of the bridge. Both hid themselves in tufts of tall grass, attached silencers to the barrels of their sniper rifles, adjusted their reticles, and took aim at two Kairos terrorists manning the main guard station, both of whom were drinking coffee and chatting calmly, oblivious to the storm that was about to break.

Once everyone confirmed they were in position, Marcus commenced the countdown.

82

"*Five, four, three, two, one—execute,*" Marcus ordered.

Pete immediately squeezed the trigger.

He was not an expert sniper. He certainly didn't have the skills of a Nick Vinetti or Miguel Navarro. But taking out a lone stationary figure at this range was not difficult, and sure enough, the bullet hit the man at the base of his skull. Pete saw a puff of pink mist, and the man dropped to the ground. A fraction of a second later, the guard beside him fell as well, taken out by the SEAL on the roof of the production plant. Both snipers then pivoted and took out the Kairos operatives guarding the missile battery. Simultaneously, the two SEALs at the bridge fired their weapons, dropping the two guards at the front gate. Two Gold Team SEALs fired at the two guards manning the missile battery to their right.

This done, the Gold Team now sprinted for the main administrative building. Bursting through the front and back doors, half the team raced for the security command center and opened fire on everyone inside while the other half took out the rest of the guards who were smoking and drinking in the break room across the hall.

On the roof, Noah released the two drones, both of which were nearly silent. He sent one to the left side of the dorm and the other to the right, then directed them to hover at an altitude of four hundred feet for the moment to keep them from drawing any unwanted attention.

Several hundred yards away, the two SEALs hiding in the bushes next to the substation leapt from cover, each brandishing a set of bolt cutters. They quickly snapped the lock and chains off the gate in the barbed wire fence surrounding the facility, then entered and proceeded to cut the power to the entire compound.

All the lampposts went dark. So did the fluorescent lights inside the plant. And Marcus could hear the hum of the assembly line grind to a halt. That was it. That was their cue. Marcus gave a hand signal to Kailea and the rest of his team. Everyone jumped to their feet and raced across the now-darkened street. Marcus checked the pulse of the two guards and confirmed they were dead. As Marcus covered their six, Kailea and Geoff stripped them of their weapons, ammo, and radios, while Callaghan and Navarro quietly opened the east-side door to the dormitory and crept inside, neutralizing two more guards they found in the vestibule.

The moment Kailea and Geoff were finished, they followed Callaghan and Navarro inside. At that point, Marcus radioed Noah, ordering him to "make the call." Then he, too, entered the dorm and shut the door behind him.

Noah brought both drones down from their hovering altitude to about sixty-five feet off the ground and trained their night vision cameras at the windows on the dorm's sixth floor. Then he picked up the satphone and dialed the phone number that Annie had provided them.

Mohammed Faisal was startled awake by his satphone ringing.

General Entezam and his team were not scheduled to land for another few hours. Had the plans changed? Was the trip off? Bleary-eyed, Faisal jumped out of bed and raced for the phone, which was plugged into a base charger on the other side of the room.

"Hello? Hello, General, is that you? Hello? Hello?"

Confused, Faisal asked several more times but heard nothing.

Was it a bad connection? Was it a mistake? Wide-awake now, adrenaline coursing through his system, Faisal double-checked to make certain the phone really was charged. It was. So what was the problem? he wondered. It would be humiliating to have the head of the IRGC trying to call him—or, more likely, trying to call Abu Nakba—and unable to get through. Yet the phone was working fine.

Pacing about the darkened room, he decided to wait for Entezam to call back. No one else he could think of had the number. Parched, he set the phone down on the nightstand next to him, then sat down on the edge of the bed, picked up a half-finished bottle of water, and took a swig.

"Sixth floor, south side, three doors down," Noah said over his whisper mic.

When he heard Marcus acknowledge, he set the drone controllers down, leaned forward, and turned on the Xbox-sized device next to him. This immediately sent out a jamming signal, rendering all mobile phones and satellite phones within a thousand yards in any direction completely useless—as well as the portable radios the Kairos and PLA operatives were using—without affecting any of the frequencies the Americans were using.

Marcus radioed the Blue Team sniper and asked if he had a shot.

"Negative, Arrowhead," he replied.

"Did you see movement?" Marcus asked.

"Roger that, but only briefly. I also saw a few flashes of dim light, likely from the phone. But now the room is pitch-black. I'm getting a bit of glare off the window from the moonlight. And my angle is terrible."

"Keep trying," Marcus replied, then ducked into the stairwell and began bounding up six flights of stairs with Kailea close behind. Geoff Stone and Donny Callaghan followed suit, as did Miguel Navarro.

When he reached the fourth floor, Navarro stopped, opened the door, and pointed his M4 down the hallway, scanning for signs of movement but seeing none.

At the fifth floor, Callaghan did the same.

As per their plan, only Geoff came all the way up to the sixth floor, confident that the two floors below them were covered, as was the stairwell. When he reached the landing, he silently tapped both Marcus and Kailea, indicating he was in place and ready to move.

Simultaneously, SEAL operators from Blue Team worked their way up the south lawn until they reached the opposite side of the dorm. The lead operator double-checked the pulse of the felled guard and confirmed he was dead. Then he stripped the man of his weapons, ammo, and radio and cautiously entered the first floor of the dorm through the west door, taking up his position there.

Two other members of Blue Team moved up the west stairwell in order to cover the second and third floors. Still two more headed up to the sixth floor, though they stayed away from the door and its window, lest they get caught in crossfire.

83

Mohammed Faisal polished off the bottle of water.

He was about to crawl into bed and get a few hours' more sleep when he thought he saw movement out on the south lawn. It couldn't be someone from the plant. He glanced at his watch and confirmed that the shift change wasn't for several more hours. Instead, the movement seemed to come from the bushes near the bank of the canal. It could be a security patrol, but why would they be operating so close to the fence line? Had they seen something? Had there been a breach?

Faisal walked closer to the window, leaned forward, and peered out, hoping the moonlight would illuminate whatever was out there. He saw no more movement and assumed it was probably just an animal of some kind. But as he was about to go back to bed, something else caught his eye.

Movement. But not on the ground. This was in the air. About forty yards out. Hovering at his eye level. It couldn't be a bird or a bat. Neither would just hover there. Leaning closer to the window once again, Faisal strained to get a better view. That's when he thought he spotted a small red light on whatever was out there. It was no bigger than a pinprick. But it was flashing. How was that possible? he asked himself. None of it made any sense. *Unless...*

Mohammed Faisal's heart almost stopped. But all the questions evaporated. It was a drone. They were being watched. The Americans had come. Or maybe the Israelis. Or both. Suddenly the mysterious phone call moments earlier made perfect sense. Fearing for Abu Nakba's life, he grabbed his AK-47 and raced for the door to the hallway. But the moment he pulled it open, he ran directly into Marcus Ryker, who smashed him in the face with the stock of his M4.

Marcus had been just as startled as the man he'd blindsided.

The problem was that the blow didn't knock the man unconscious. Rather, it broke his nose and sent him reeling backward, causing him to smash against his nightstand. This, in turn, sent his lamp—and the Kalashnikov—crashing to the floor. And then the man started screaming as he covered his nose with his hands and writhed in agony. The noise was going to wake everyone on the floor.

Marcus was in no position to take a prisoner. This clearly wasn't Abu Nakba, though it had to be an operative senior enough to be responsible for the Libyan's phone. But the shrieking was blowing everything, so Marcus drew his silenced Sig Sauer pistol and double-tapped him to the head. Spotting the Russian-made satphone on the floor, Marcus moved to grab it. But just then, a Kairos operative opened his bedroom door and stepped into the hallway to find out what all the ruckus was about. Kailea, still positioned in the stairwell, instantly double-tapped him. She, too, was using a silencer, so her weapon made little sound. But the man's body and gun hitting the ground did. Soon, Noah reported he could see motion in most of the rooms on the sixth floor.

Marcus scooped up the satphone, removed a plastic evidence bag from one of his pockets, slipped the phone inside, sealed it, and stashed it in his backpack. He was wearing leather tactical gloves, so he wasn't worried about getting his own prints on it.

All the men on this floor were senior members of Kairos and very likely Abu Nakba's most trusted bodyguards. That thought made the hair on the back of Marcus's neck stand erect. A tremor—like a shock of electricity—rippled through his body. The Libyan was close. Very close. He radioed that to the others, announced that he was coming back into the hallway, and asked Kailea to hold her fire.

To his shock, however, a Russian-made AK-47 automatic rifle suddenly opened fire in the room immediately to his left. Whoever was in there was trying to shoot through the cement block walls at him. The rounds weren't going to make it through. The walls were too thick. But chunks of concrete began flying through the air, filling the room with dust.

Dropping to the ground, Marcus was struck with the horrifying realization that everyone in the building—and likely everyone on the grounds—now knew that the compound had been infiltrated, and a firefight was underway.

84

Callaghan reported that Kairos operatives were bursting out of their rooms and opening fire.

Geoff Stone reported the same thing on his floor.

The SEALs covering the other floors did as well.

The Americans were returning fire but were concerned they could quickly be overrun.

Marcus ordered everyone to stop talking unless they'd been hit or possessed critical intelligence. There was too much chatter, and most of it was unnecessary.

Next he ordered everyone to remove their suppressors and start throwing grenades down the hallways. The more noise, the more chaos, the better. They had lost the element of surprise, but they couldn't afford to lose the initiative. Marcus also directed the SEAL on the roof of the production plant to open fire on the room beside him. Yes, the angle was terrible. There was little chance of taking out the shooter. But they had to start pushing back. And once he was finished strafing that room, he should start taking out the windows of every room on the sixth floor, then rinse and repeat for every room in the building.

That done, Marcus radioed the SEALs who had taken control of the main administrative building. Anything they could do to open fire on their side of the dormitory would be helpful, he told them. Seconds later, he heard them engage the battle in force.

Marcus knew they also had to keep the PLA operatives in the plant from arming themselves and storming out into the street and rushing their positions. So Marcus ordered Pete to start shooting out the windows of the plant and firing at the main and side doors, as well. Then he told Noah it was time to use his M-32 grenade launcher to fire at the plant. With all the power having been cut, those inside were operating in darkness. And their phones and radios had been jammed, so they were unable to communicate with their colleagues in other buildings. Therefore, there was no way they could know just how many attackers were positioned outside the plant. It was Pete and Noah's job to add to the confusion and keep them pinned down and unwilling to come outside for as long as possible.

"Hold your fire; I'm coming out," Marcus radioed Kailea and Geoff.

The lunatic in the room next to him had stopped firing. He was probably reloading, giving Marcus his only opportunity. First, however, Marcus pulled the pins on two grenades and rolled them to his right, one close, the other a bit farther down the hall. Marcus ducked back into his room and covered his head until the explosions were over. He pulled two more pins and rolled two grenades to his left. The first rolled all the way down the hall. The second stopped right in front of the shooter's door. Marcus again took cover. But the moment the grenades detonated, he grabbed his M4 carbine, sprinted into the hallway, and kicked in what was left of the shredded wooden door. Through the smoke and dust, he found himself staring into the eyes of a man he recognized—Omar Nazim, the head of Abu Nakba's security detail. Marcus unleashed a burst of automatic weapon fire until Nazim's riddled, smoking body crashed to the floor.

Then Marcus ordered Kailea and Geoff to join him in going door-to-door in search of the Libyan while the SEALs in the stairwell at the far end of the hall covered them. The hallway erupted with gunfire. In most cases, Kailea and Geoff found it best to throw a grenade through what was left of the doors before going in and making sure the Kairos terrorists were neutralized.

Marcus, however, had no interest in killing Abu Nakba with a grenade. He wanted to look this monster in the eye. What's more, he needed a body he could photograph, fingerprint, and take DNA samples from. The American people had to know they'd truly rid themselves of this mass murderer.

Approaching the next room, Marcus's heart was pounding. It wasn't the cacophony or the acrid stench of gunpowder. It was that with every step, he could now sense the sheer evil. Grenades detonated in room after room. Bullets whizzed by his head. Marcus felt chunks of sheetrock raining down on him. But he pressed forward through the smoke and dust, swung the strap of his M4 over his back, drew his two Sig Sauer pistols, and kicked in the next door.

85

"We have a KIA—I repeat we have a KIA," someone shouted over the radio.

Pete Hwang froze.

An American had just been killed in action. It wasn't one of his own team-mates. It was the voice of a SEAL he did not recognize. Still, the very sentence knocked the wind out of him because he knew there would be more.

Suddenly, two SUVs filled with Kairos operatives came roaring in from the service road that led past the plant. Pete heard them coming, then watched them screech to a halt in front of the dormitory's main entrance. As he ordered Noah to warn the team inside, he opened fire. He didn't trust himself to go after each terrorist as they exited the vehicle and raced for the door. He didn't have the skills to make that work. So he trained his attention on the door itself and shot every man trying to get in.

His counterpart—the SEAL on the roof of the plant—immediately joined the fight, picking off as many terrorists as he could. But suddenly he began shouting over the radio that a third vehicle was approaching from the direction of the main administrative building. Rather than stopping in front of the dorm, however, this one was heading for the dining hall.

Hearing that, Noah reloaded the grenade launcher and fired off his first shot. It went wide, exploding just behind the car as four Kairos commandos leapt out and raced into the hall. Pete told him to drop the launcher and cover their backs. Switching out the M-32 for his M4, Noah took up a position on the other side of the air-conditioning unit, giving him a bit of cover and a clear shot at the hatch that he and Pete had used to get to the roof.

Pete, meanwhile, kept firing until he was out of ammo. As he reloaded, he radioed the SEAL to cover the door. But it was too late. Two Kairos team members rushed inside. And then a third. Pete screamed over the radio to warn his colleagues, but no sooner had he done so than he heard gunfire erupt inside those very hallways and the very stairwell where his friends were positioned.

Both the front lawn and the steps to the dormitory were littered with the dead and wounded. For the moment, he could identify no more targets. But as Pete finished reloading, Noah shouted to him to move immediately. If any of the Kairos operatives made it to the roof, Pete would be a sitting duck. Grabbing his gear—including his own M4—Pete scrambled over to Noah's position. And just in time.

The hatch suddenly flung open, and someone thrust a Kalashnikov toward them and began spraying the roof with bullets in every direction. Both Pete and Noah ducked for cover as one round after another pinged off the metal AC unit. And then Pete heard the distinctive sound of a ball of serrated cast iron rolling toward them.

"*Grenade*," he shouted, shoving Noah to the ground and throwing his body over the young man as the force of the explosion almost drove both men off the roof and nearly deafened them.

Concrete, plaster, and shards of metal rained down all around them, and they were engulfed in a cloud of dust and smoke. Coughing and wheezing, his ears ringing, Pete grabbed his weapon and got to his knees, then to his feet. He knew he'd never hear movement on the other side of the roof and would thus have no warning that Kairos operatives were on top of them. So he staggered forward—not to his right to retrace his steps but to his left, around what was left of the mangled AC unit. Just then he saw someone coming through the hatch.

Raising his M4, he unleashed one burst, but it went wide. As the man turned toward him and began to raise his own weapon, Pete unleashed another burst, and these rounds hit their mark. The man dropped his weapon and slumped forward, blocking the hatch with his lifeless body and buying Pete and Noah a few minutes to regather themselves.

Looking over at the production facility, Pete saw a series of explosions on the roof. He looked down and realized that two terrorists had burst through a side door and were throwing grenades at the sniper above them. Pete was still unable to hear anything, so the screams of the SEAL never reached him. Pete stared helplessly as the man—just a bloody torso now—tried in vain to crawl to safety. But one of the Kairos operatives was heading for a metal ladder that ran up the side of the plant. Pete fired off two bursts from his automatic weapon but was out of range. Staggering back to Noah, he rummaged through the rubble, found his sniper rifle, took aim, and fired two rounds. Both of them missed, allowing the Kairos operative to reach the roof, reach the SEAL, and murder him execution style.

Enraged, Pete took aim again. He tried to steady his breathing. He wasn't having much luck, but he squeezed the trigger anyway, firing another shot. Finally, one round hit the operative squarely in the chest. The man was wearing body armor, so the bullet didn't kill him. But the fall did. The force of the round threw him off the roof, and he landed flat on his back and never moved again.

86

"*I'm almost out,*" Navarro yelled up the stairwell, dangerously low on ammo.

"*Hold on,*" Callaghan yelled back. "*I've got a few mags left.*"

Both men were feverishly fighting back a wave of Kairos operatives determined to take them out and get to the sixth floor. So far, the two Americans were holding their own. But without help, they weren't going to last much longer.

Callaghan threw his last grenade down the fifth-floor hallway to buy himself a few seconds of cover, then ran down to the fourth floor, intending to give Navarro three of his last four magazines. Callaghan had only one more spare, plus the half-used one in his weapon. But he knew Navarro needed them more. The SEALs on the other side of the building were picking off the fighters on floors one, two, and three. But they, too, were running low on ammo. Now they had a KIA—and apparently three others wounded, one critically—as three more Kairos operatives entered the building.

When Callaghan reached Navarro, he tapped him on the back, then briefly took over his position, firing back at the terrorists trying to make it up the stairwell. Navarro gratefully took the three mags and loaded one into his M4. Just then a Kairos operative burst into the stairwell on the fifth floor, came around the corner, and unleashed a burst of AK-47 fire. Riddled with bullets, Navarro collapsed to the floor. Callaghan was hit too, but Navarro had taken most of the rounds. Fortunately, Callaghan was able to wheel around and fire back, dropping the terrorist instantly. The man was severely wounded but not yet dead. Instead, he was twitching furiously and trying to reload. Callaghan didn't want to use another round on him, so he pulled out his tactical knife and slit the man's throat.

Then he turned and checked Navarro's pulse but found nothing.

"Red Leader, I have a KIA on the fourth floor. I repeat, I have a KIA on the fourth floor. Navarro is gone and I cannot hold this position much longer."

The words pierced Annie's heart.

The Kairos counteroffensive against Marcus and his team was in full swing, and the tide was turning against them. They had already lost three warriors, and four more were wounded. That meant that nearly a third of their force was out of commission.

Annie had no idea precisely how many Kairos operatives were still in that dormitory or what kind of weapons and stores of ammunition they had with them. But she hated the odds. On any given night, her analysts had estimated that upwards of half to two-thirds of the roughly two hundred total personnel on the compound were asleep or hanging out in the dormitory. The rest were working in the plant. But all of them were ready to lay down their lives to foil this assault.

Marcus's men simply didn't have the firepower to kill them all. The entire operation had been built on stealth and speed. Both were now gone, and the longer this thing took, the greater the odds of total failure grew.

"Ma'am, Director Dell is on the line," said the watch officer, startling Annie as her eyes shifted from screen to screen, watching the live images streaming in from the Keyhole satellite nearly two hundred miles above the battlefield and the two drones hovering just sixty-five feet above it.

Annie picked up the receiver from the console she was standing behind as she calculated her next move.

"Annie, we've got a problem," Martha began without pleasantries. "The Chinese dragon has finally awakened. Guanzhong just ordered a full mobilization of its ground and naval forces and canceled all leaves. He's expected to address the nation soon."

"Yes, we're following it, Martha, but I've got bigger problems at the moment."

"India?"

"Yeah." Annie gave her boss a quick update.

"What do you want to do?" Dell asked.

"I don't think we have any choice," Annie replied. "I need you to ask the president to authorize the launch of four F-35s off the *Ronald Reagan*, which is already in the Indian Ocean, not far from the Gulf of Oman."

"No, that's impossible. The president said no air support, not with the Chinese missile batteries in place, and Marcus accepted that."

"The situation has changed," Annie insisted, trying to keep her voice calm. "The SEALs took out the missile controllers in the early minutes of the battle and destroyed all of their equipment."

"It doesn't matter. You know as well as I do that the Chinese system can operate independently and fire the moment it picks up an incoming threat."

"Martha, for God's sake, they're F-35s—they're the most sophisticated weapons we have in our arsenal, and they're designed to take out enemy targets in far more dangerous conditions than this."

"It's really that bad?" Dell asked.

"I'm afraid so," Annie replied. "Look, our guys are performing valiantly out there. But if we don't do something fast to change the dynamic, there's a very real chance that they're all going to be killed and the plant will still be operational."

"Didn't Marcus's guys knock out the power and jam all the phones?"

"Yes, but I can't say how long that will last," Annie admitted. "The Kairos counteroffensive is gaining momentum. Most of the PLA forces are inside the plant. Our guys have kept them pinned down until now, but that's starting to change. Two PLA operatives just bolted out the side door of the plant. One of them got to the roof and killed another of our SEALs. Once they realize how few men we have on the ground, they're going to go on a rampage."

"Just tell me one thing, Annie," Dell insisted.

"What's that?"

"Have we gotten Abu Nakba?"

"No, ma'am, we have not."

87

Kailea was hit in the leg.

Marcus saw her go down. He tried to reach her but was pinned down by the roar of AK-47 fire all around him. Pulling the pin on each of his last two grenades, he rolled them down the hallway and pressed himself to the floor, as did his colleagues. The moment the grenades detonated, Marcus ejected the spent mags from both Sig Sauers and reloaded. Then he scrambled back to his feet as he motioned to Geoff to take care of Kailea and the SEALs to provide covering fire.

He was going after Abu Nakba.

Smashing through what was left of the door beside him, Marcus found shattered glass and blood everywhere.

He also found the Libyan.

Wounded and hunched over, the old man was positioned behind the bed frame in the far corner of the bedroom.

It was bizarre to finally—suddenly—be in the same room with him. After all this time. All these missions. All these miles. Yet there he was. Wearing a blood-spattered robe. Bloody sandals. His normally white beard was also covered in blood dripping from his mouth.

But it was the old man's eyes that drew Marcus's attention. They weren't filled with fear or cowardice. Not in the slightest. Rather, Marcus saw in them pure rage. A lust for vengeance. And a determination to be a *shahid* and take Marcus with him.

In Abu Nakba's right hand was a Russian-made F-1 hand grenade. His left hand held the safety pin, which was wrapped around the old man's left thumb.

"Well, well, Marcus Ryker, it's really you," he said, his voice low, raspy, and difficult to hear over the roar of the automatic weapons fire in the hallway. "I never actually imagined we would meet face-to-face, but I have to tell you that—"

But Abu Nakba never finished the thought.

Marcus had no interest in what this murderer had to say. Nor did he have any intention of giving the man the time to distract him with some long-winded monologue and then blow them both to kingdom come. Marcus squeezed the triggers of both Sig Sauers. Two rounds exploded from the barrels, streaked across the tiny room, bored right through the old man's eye sockets, and blew out the back of his head, spattering blood and brain matter all over the cinder block wall behind him.

As Abu Nakba's body slumped to the ground, however, the grenade fell from his hands. As it rolled toward him, Marcus dropped both pistols, scooped up the grenade, and heaved it out the blown-out window. It exploded before it even hit the lawn.

And that was it. At long last, the hunt for the "Father of Catastrophe" was finally over. The monster was no longer free to roam the countryside, robbing, killing, and destroying everyone and everything in its path.

"*Geronimo,*" Marcus shouted into his microphone, using the same code word the SEALs had used when they'd killed Osama bin Laden years earlier, then repeating it.

The Libyan was no more.

Annie heard the code word but did not react immediately.

She could hardly believe it was true. She wanted it to be, of course. But she could barely process the magnitude of what Marcus had just said. The rest of the Global Operations Center, however, had no such problem. At the sound of Marcus's voice, every member of the staff erupted in applause and wild cheering. Nothing else was going right that day. But one thing now had. Operation Windy City had just scored a stunning success.

Most of the officials in the White House Situation Room erupted in applause as well.

But not everyone.

President Hernandez was pleased, to be sure. But while Vice President Whitney and the rest of the NSC staff celebrated, even popping corks on some chilled Dom Perignon they had brought in just for this moment, Hernandez remained sobered by all the dangers that still lay ahead.

Picking up the phone on the console before him, however, he speed-dialed Annie Stewart.

"Now get them home, Annie," he said. "Get them all home."

88

Marcus's team killed off the Kairos men on the sixth floor.

When Geoff had finished putting a tourniquet on Kailea's leg, he helped her hobble into Abu Nakba's room as Marcus removed his backpack and fished out a small digital camera.

"It's really him," Kai said, staring at the corpse. "And you literally blew his brains out."

"Better him than me, right?" Marcus replied.

"No argument here," she said.

Geoff helped her sit down on the bed while Marcus snapped dozens of photos of Abu Nakba, pulled out a tape measure to get his height, and took hair and blood samples for DNA. Then Geoff spotted the man's briefcase on the desk. He fished out a sheaf of papers and a plastic bag full of thumb drives and shoved them all into the backpack.

When they were finished, Marcus asked his deputy if she could walk.

"At this point, shouldn't we better be running?" she asked.

"We should, but can you?" Marcus pressed.

"I'll do my best," she insisted.

"All right, then, let's move." Marcus shouted to the SEALs that they were coming out and asked Geoff to help Kailea limp into the hallway while he grabbed his M4 and took one last look around the room.

That's when Marcus spotted the Libyan's cane on the floor in the corner by the door. The president had asked for Abu Nakba's scalp. He hoped this beautifully carved wooden cane—Walid Abdel-Shafi's most prized possession since he was wounded in Gaza by an Israeli airstrike—would suffice.

Holstering his Sig Sauer pistols, Marcus grabbed the cane and his M4 and stepped into the hallway. Before he headed to the stairwell, he radioed the team and ordered everyone to prepare for evacuation. The men who had piloted the minisubs used by Blue and Gold Teams would now race back to their landing positions, suit back up in their scuba gear, and get the ASDVs running again and ready for departure. All SEALs still functioning would join them, taking as much equipment as they could. The dead and wounded, however, would have to be driven off-site to the private airstrip about twenty miles away. Marcus and his CIA team would handle their extraction.

First, though, they had to fight their way out of the building.

Blue Leader radioed that their side of the building was quieter and might be safer. From his vantage point in the main administration building, Gold Leader concurred with that assessment. Marcus agreed and asked Gold Leader to send two men in two SUVs to the rendezvous point. Then he asked Pete and Noah to commandeer the SUVs parked out front of the dining hall and bring them, as well. Four vehicles ought to suffice, he figured, with him, Geoff, Pete, and Noah driving. Then he asked Geoff to help Donny Callaghan bring Navarro's body to the SUVs. They would drop off Callaghan by the canal so he could pilot the third ASDV back to the *Maine*.

Everyone raced to execute the plan. When they reached their rendezvous point behind the dormitory, the SUVs had arrived. They quickly loaded the body bags containing their fallen comrades into one SUV, and Kailea and the other wounded into another. Then they heard a roar. It was coming from the direction of the pharmaceutical plant. They turned and saw at least a hundred men pouring out of the doors, screaming some sort of war cry at the top of their lungs and racing across the south lawn toward them.

89

If they didn't move now, they were all going to die.

Marcus ordered Geoff and Noah to jump into the driver's seats, head for the bridge, and not stop until they got to the airstrip. Annie confirmed over their headsets that their G5 was inbound and should be wheels down in fifteen minutes.

The moment Geoff and Noah roared off, Marcus ordered everyone else into the remaining vehicles. Only then did he realize that Pete should have driven the SUV with Kailea and the other wounded. But there wasn't time to change things now. Callaghan and Pete, who were standing right beside Marcus, opened fire on the approaching mob. They took out some, but the mob just kept coming.

"Pete, there's no more time—take the wheel," Marcus shouted over the gunfire. *"Donny, ride shotgun and give him cover. I'll be right behind you guys."*

Donny fired off two more bursts, then wheeled around and got into the passenger seat. Pete started moving toward the driver's side door, but a surviving Kairos operative stuck his head out a second-floor window and began firing at them. Startled, Marcus raised his M4 to return fire. But just at that moment, he was hit in the chest and sent sprawling to the ground, landing square on his back.

Terrified at seeing Marcus go down, Pete pivoted and fired his entire magazine into the window. The mob on the ground was less than a hundred yards away and coming fast.

"Marcus, talk to me—are you all right?" Pete yelled as he raced to his friend's side, only to find that while the wind had been knocked out of him, Marcus's Kevlar vest had prevented the rounds from doing any serious damage.

"I'm fine, Pete," Marcus gasped. *"Really, I am."*

But just then, the man on the second floor began firing again. Because Pete was kneeling over Marcus, they were both protected by the chassis of the SUV. But suddenly they heard Callaghan cry out.

Pete looked up to find the passenger side windows all blown out and blood splattered all over the windshield. Fearing another of his teammates had been killed, Pete jumped to his feet—enraged—and fired everything he had left at the second-floor window.

But it wasn't enough. The moment his M4 stopped firing, the Kairos operative reemerged and returned fire.

Now it was Marcus's turn to be terrified.

He scrambled to his feet, raised his M4, and emptied his magazine. This time, the rounds hit their mark, shredding the terrorist. As Marcus reloaded, he again ordered Pete to get into the vehicle and race for the bridge and the airport. But Pete didn't answer.

Marcus fired another burst at the approaching mob, then turned to find his friend lying on the ground, covered in blood. Pete had been hit. He was in serious pain. But Marcus didn't immediately see an entry wound, and there was no time to look.

Heaving Pete over his shoulder, he opened the back door and slid him onto the backseat. Then he slammed the door shut and jumped into the driver's seat. But the mob was already on him. They surrounded the truck and began rocking it. Marcus drew his Sig Sauer and fired ten shots out the front window, dropping several PLA operatives to the ground. Then he turned and fired two more shots out the blown-out passenger window, taking out two more.

Just as he turned to fire out his own window, though, he and everyone else heard the antimissile battery nearby activate. An instant later, one of the missiles erupted from its tube and went streaking into the night sky in a blaze of fire and smoke. Then a second missile erupted from its tube and followed suit. Seizing on the momentary distraction, Marcus squeezed the trigger twice. As he was about to hit the gas and break free of the murderous mob, PLA operatives began reaching through the shattered windows, trying to get Callaghan's rifle.

Marcus turned, aimed the Sig Sauer, and tried to fire, but nothing happened. He was out of ammunition. Again, he was about to hit the accelerator and try to plow through this mob to save the lives of his friends. But suddenly, the SUV was rocked by a massive explosion. Marcus instinctively ducked down and covered his head. Then came a second. And a third. When he looked up again and glanced in the rearview mirror, he found the dormitory engulfed in a ball of fire and collapsing to the ground. To his left, he found the Chinese missile battery had been obliterated. All that remained was an enormous crater, a twisted heap of metal, and a raging fire.

Marcus finally hit the gas, peeled away from the reeling mob, across the north lawn, and onto the service road. Seconds later, three more massive explosions erupted close by, leveling the main administrative building. But the resulting shock wave also flipped the truck, sending them careening down an embankment and not coming to a halt until they were teetering on the edge of one of the canals.

90

Covered in blood, battling shock, Marcus just lay there for a moment.

In the wrecked SUV. Trying to catch his breath again. Trying to get his bearings.

At least a full minute passed before Marcus thought to ask Pete if he was still with him. "Yes," Pete said. He had cuts and contusions all over his face and neck, but thank God, he was still alive. But was Callaghan?

Marcus had no idea. He reached over through shattered glass and checked Callaghan's pulse. It was weak, but it was there. Marcus tried to kick open the driver's side door, but it was jammed. He was about to try Callaghan's door but realized that would drop them right into the canal. The only way out was through the windshield. Grateful for his leather tactical gloves, Marcus ripped away the remaining safety glass and threw it into the canal. Then, grabbing Callaghan in a fireman's carry, he pushed the man down the hood of the truck onto the muddy bank.

Next Marcus lowered the front passenger seat until he could reach Pete and get a proper grip on him. He pulled his friend forward, eased him out the front window, down the hood, and onto the bank as well. Only then did Marcus crawl out of the vehicle.

He stood and looked back at all the burning wreckage behind and around him. It wasn't just the dormitory that was gone. The entire pharmaceutical plant had been obliterated. So had the dining hall. The main administrative building too. Most of the compound was a sea of raging, soaring flames and thick black billowing smoke rising into the early morning sky. He couldn't see them, but he now could hear the F-35s. They were circling, waiting to strike again—waiting, most likely, until he and his team were safely off-site.

His ears ringing, barely able to hear, Marcus tried to radio his team but got nothing in response. He tried to radio Annie but got nothing back from her, either. There were no vehicles left. Not even a golf cart. The Joint Strike Fighters had made sure that nothing and no one survived. It was a miracle, he now realized, that they had made it this far. But now what was he supposed to do? Neither Pete nor Donny Callaghan could walk, and the service road to the bridge was at least a mile away. Even if he wanted to drag them both, it simply wasn't possible. They were too big.

But then, through the haze of smoke and dust, he saw some sort of maintenance truck—a pickup—coming across the bridge and racing toward them. Reaching back into the wreckage of the SUV, he grabbed Callaghan's M4 and checked to see if it was loaded. It was but had only a few rounds left. Marcus told his buddies to play dead. It wouldn't be hard. Then he crouched down behind the SUV and waited. He only had a few shots left. He had to make them count.

But to his astonishment, Kailea Curtis suddenly pulled up and rolled down the driver's side window.

"Hurry up, old man," she yelled. *"Get those boys inside. We haven't got all day."*

Marcus was completely baffled. Where had she gotten the truck? How had she known to come back for him? Why wasn't she on the plane? If she had doubled back, where was everyone else? And wasn't she in too much pain to be driving? The questions kept coming, but there was no time to get answers. Nor did they matter. She was there. She had wheels. As wounded as she was, she could still drive. Everything else could wait.

Marcus hobbled over to Callaghan. Thank God, he was still breathing. Marcus picked up this hulk of a man with difficulty and set him in the bed of the pickup truck. Then he went back for Pete, who had just finished applying a tourniquet to himself.

"You good?" Marcus asked.

"Good enough."

Marcus got him to his feet, helped him over to the pickup, and put him next to Callaghan to tend to him as best he could. It was far from ideal, but it would have to do until they reached the airstrip. By the time that was all done, Kailea had slid over to the passenger's seat.

"Maybe you'd better drive," she said. "I'll call it in."

Marcus climbed into the driver's seat and began to turn the truck around. Then he saw the look of horror on Kailea's face.

91

"*Floor it, Marcus—now,*" she ordered.

"Why? What's wrong?" Marcus asked.

"*We've got company,*" she shouted.

Marcus looked from side to side, then in his rearview mirror, but saw nothing.

"What are you talking about?"

"Annie's watching the satellite feed," Kailea explained. "She says two trucks filled with armed operatives are approaching from the south."

Marcus hit the gas and got them back on the service road. But no sooner were they heading out of the compound than they saw the two SUVs emerging through the smoke. Marcus drove the accelerator to the floor, but he wasn't sure it would be enough speed.

"Can't one of the F-35s take them out?" Marcus asked.

Kailea relayed the question to Annie.

"Annie says no," she said a moment later. "The missiles are too powerful, and those guys are too close behind us. If our planes fire, they're likely to kill us all."

Marcus's mind was reeling, searching for options but finding none. His foot was flat on the floor. He was picking up speed, but the SUVs were still gaining ground.

Neither Marcus nor Kailea had enough ammunition left to protect themselves much less Pete and Callaghan from the terrorists bearing down on them. Marcus would fire everything he had to protect his friends. But he wasn't interested in some heroic but futile last stand. He didn't want to be remembered as a martyr. He wanted to survive. And the only way to do that was to outrun these guys. He had to get his friends to the airstrip. That's where the rest of their team was. Most of them were shot up pretty bad, but at least they would fight. They would never surrender. That was for certain.

Then Marcus heard something on the dashboard ding. Looking down, he saw the fuel light had just come on. *This can't be happening,* he told himself. *We can't be running out of gas. Not now.* He silently pleaded with the Lord for mercy—not for himself but for his friends—as he tore up the service road, through the jungle blurring past them, toward the front gate.

As they came up over a berm, he could suddenly see the single-lane bridge about three hundred yards ahead of them.

"That's it!" Kai shouted.

"What?" asked Marcus.

"The bridge."

"What about it?"

"The commander of Gold Team—when he gave me the truck, he gave me this," she said, pulling something from her pocket.

"What?" Marcus demanded.

"Never mind," Kailea shot back. "Just get us to that bridge and hold on. Pete, Donny, hold on to something—*anything.*"

Marcus gripped the steering wheel and silently begged God for more power. But every time he glanced in his side mirrors, the SUVs were rapidly cutting the distance between them.

"Forget them, Marcus," Kailea ordered. *"Just focus on the bridge. Nothing else."*

Marcus glanced over at her. He wasn't used to her talking to him like this.

"The bridge, Marcus," she said again, more calmly this time. "Just the bridge."

It was two hundred yards away.

Now a hundred and fifty.

One hundred.

Now fifty.

Suddenly they were there—and the moment they got halfway across, Kailea held up the remote-control device she had pulled from her pocket and pressed the button. An instant later, just as they cleared to the other side, an enormous explosion erupted behind them. The force was so powerful Marcus almost lost control of the vehicle. He was swerving all over the road, but finally he regained control.

As he did, he saw Kailea looking behind them. Glancing in the rearview mirror, Marcus saw what she did. The bridge was gone. So were the vehicles behind them. All replaced by a massive cloud of fire and ash.

But just as they all began to cheer, Kailea cut them off.

"Quiet—everyone, quiet. We've got a new problem," she shouted.

92

"What now?" Marcus asked.

"Hold on—I can't hear her. Say again, Blowtorch, say again; I didn't copy."

Marcus held his tongue as Kailea pressed her headset closer to her ear but to no avail, finally ripping it off her head in frustration.

"What's wrong?" asked Marcus.

"I think it's a short in the headset," said Kailea. "I can barely hear a word she's saying."

"What was the last thing you did hear?" Marcus pressed, and he continued racing toward the airfield and worrying about their lack of fuel.

"Something about a plane."

"Ours? One of the F-35s?"

"I have no idea."

Then Marcus remembered something.

"Kai, grab my backpack."

"Why?"

"Just do it."

"Where is it?"

"It's back here," said Pete. "I've got it."

Pete handed it forward.

"Open it," said Marcus.

"You've got another headset?" Kailea asked.

"No."

"Then what?"

"You'll see."

Kailea unzipped the backpack and pulled out a clear plastic evidence bag with a satellite phone inside.

"Whose is this?" she asked.

"Abu Nakba's," said Marcus with a wry smile. "It's one of the phones the Russians gave Kairos. Power it up and call Annie at the Global Ops Center."

"But this is evidence. Don't we need it for—"

"Kai, just do it," Marcus ordered.

So she did. The watch officer at Langley didn't believe it was Kailea Curtis, even after she gave her identification code and explained where they were and that they needed to talk to the deputy director immediately.

Marcus told Kailea to put the phone on speaker. "This is Marcus Ryker. To whom am I speaking?"

But the connection went dead.

Everyone in the SUV was dumbfounded.

"Did she just hang up?" Kailea asked.

"Yeah, I think so."

"So now what?"

"Call Annie's mobile number."

"But she won't have reception in the Ops Center."

"When she's in there, she rolls it through to one of the hard lines. When she sees the caller ID and knows it's me, she knows it's a personal call, not business."

Kailea dialed the number. This time Annie picked up. Not on the first ring. Not until the fifth and with no small measure of caution in her tone. But Marcus quickly explained the short in the headset and his decision to use the satphone.

"Fine, but we've got a new problem."

"What is it?"

"A large private business jet is heading to the same airfield where all your guys are and where you're headed now."

"And?"

"And there's no flight plan."

"And?"

"It's coming from Tehran," said Annie.

"Why aren't the Indians dealing with it?"

"Because the pilots cut their transponder about twenty minutes ago. It's gone totally dark. We only picked it up because we just happen to be monitoring everything going on there in excruciating detail right now."

"How do you know it's headed to our airfield?"

"We just do. I can explain later. The point is we have reason to believe it's Mahmoud Entezam's plane."

"The head of the IRGC?"

"Right—we think he's coming to meet with Abu Nakba."

"In the dead of night, without a flight plan."

"Exactly."

"How soon until it lands?"

"Eighteen minutes. How far out are you?"

"Ten minutes if we're lucky. But we're running out of fuel."

"Should we intercept the plane?" Annie asked.

"No, let it land," Marcus said.

"But if it's really Entezam, he'll have at least two dozen bodyguards with him."

"I know. But this is as good a shot as we'll ever have at him."

"Marcus, that's insane. I'll just ask the president to shoot it down."

"And he'll say no, especially if you don't know who's really on it. Look—you're going to have to trust me on this."

"I do trust you. Just tell me what you want me to do."

"Call Geoff and Noah. Tell them to grab four sniper rifles and plenty of ammo—plus headsets, night vision goggles, the works—and get up on the roof of that terminal immediately and without being seen."

"Okay, I'm on it."

"And radio the pilots of our G5 and tell them to take off immediately."

"Why?"

"If Entezam and his men see another jet there, they could get spooked and abort their landing."

"Okay, sure—anything else?" Annie replied as she relayed the orders to her staff.

"Yeah," Marcus said, taking a deep breath, "one more thing."

93

The fuel light on the dashboard was blinking red.

Marcus silently prayed they'd have just enough to get them to the airfield. He didn't want to imagine the disaster that lay ahead if they ran out of gas now. A few minutes later, he finally saw their exit and began to slow down.

Annie was still on speakerphone. "The mystery jet is six minutes out," she said as Marcus pulled off the highway and onto a side road. "And your plane just took off."

"Great," said Marcus. "And the guys are in place?"

"They are, but . . ."

"What?"

"They were spotted."

"By who?"

"A few people in the terminal," said Annie, "including the director of flight ops."

"You're not serious."

"Unfortunately, I am, but Geoff took care of it."

"How?"

"Let's just say he incapacitated them."

"How many?"

"Three."

"Permanently?"

"No."

"Where are they now?"

"Tied up, gagged, and in a locked closet," Annie said. "So Noah is now in the flight ops center, playing the part of the controller. Geoff just found a ladder to the roof."

"Why isn't he already *on* the roof?"

"He doesn't want to be spotted by the incoming pilots, who are just four minutes out now, so you guys had better get cracking."

"We're here, actually," Marcus said, driving around behind the terminal, where he parked and turned off the engine. "Stand by one."

He spotted Geoff by an access ladder on the side of the building and ordered Kailea to head to him immediately. He would bring Pete and let Callaghan rest in the pickup. The drugs Pete had given him had nearly knocked the man out already.

"You know, I took a few painkillers myself," Pete admitted as they hobbled over to Geoff and Kailea. "I really didn't imagine you'd need me. And I certainly never imagined this."

"It's okay," Marcus said. "I'm just glad you're here."

Geoff handed Marcus a sniper rifle, a box of ammo, a headset, and a whisper microphone, which Marcus put on immediately.

"I can see the plane," Noah suddenly said over the radio. "Wheels are coming down. I've given them permission to land."

Thirty seconds later, Noah again spoke over the radio.

"Okay, they're on final approach. Stand by."

Marcus closed his eyes, worked on slowing his heart rate and steadying his nerves.

"*Wheels down,*" Noah shouted, a little too loudly, and then a minute later. "*Okay, they're on the ground.*"

"Good, let's move," said Marcus. "You first, Geoff."

Geoff scrambled up the ladder, dropped his equipment, then helped Kailea up. She limped over to the end of the terminal, found a good position, and began setting up her rifle, scope, and tripod. Geoff and Marcus helped Pete up the ladder. That took a moment, and Marcus could see his friend wincing in severe pain. Still, he made it to the roof, and Geoff helped him take a position next to Kailea and set up his equipment.

"They're taxiing to the terminal," Noah announced as Marcus himself now worked his way up the ladder and took up a position between Pete and Geoff.

"Got it, Noah; now hold all traffic," Marcus ordered. "I need this channel for us."

"Roger that."

"Annie, we're in position," Marcus said. "But we're going to need some help."

"Don't worry—I'm already on it," Annie replied. "Just be careful. And know that I'm praying for each of you."

Marcus was pretty sure that line had never been spoken over the CIA's encrypted radio feed before. And everyone at the Global Ops Center and the White House Situation Room, including President Hernandez, and Martha Dell in Taipei, all of whom were now closely monitoring the operation, had heard it.

"Thanks, sweetheart," Marcus replied, adding, "I love you," because he simply couldn't help himself.

"I love you, too," Annie said back.

Pete turned and shot Marcus a quizzical look.

"Shut up," Marcus whispered with an embarrassed smile.

"What's that?" Annie asked.

"Nothing," Marcus said, shaking his head. "I was talking to Saint Pete."

"Hey, people, stay focused out there," said an unexpected voice through their headset.

It was Martha Dell.

"Yes, ma'am," Marcus replied, and everyone went quiet, refocusing themselves on the urgent mission before them.

Then Marcus noticed that the plane taxiing toward them wasn't a Chinese or Russian or even French business jet. Instead, it was an Embraer 175-E2, a small passenger jet built by a Brazilian company. His stomach tensed. Did they have this thing wrong? Was it possible this wasn't General Entezam at all—or anyone from the IRGC—but rather an actual group of businessmen or some sort of delegation? Then again, why no flight plan? Why turn off the transponder? None of it made any sense.

And then came another surprise.

94

A fleet of six black Range Rovers suddenly roared into the parking lot.

They immediately drove out onto the tarmac, stopping just twenty feet from where the Embraer was about to park. The drivers exited each vehicle and stood at attention, facing the plane.

"Are you seeing this?" Marcus asked Annie.

"I am," she said. "And the plot thickens."

The jet soon came to a complete stop. A moment later, two men came running out of the hangar—two men neither Marcus nor his team had known were there—pushing a set of metal stairs. When they got to the side of the plane, they positioned the steps properly, and someone inside the jet opened the door.

"Steady," Marcus whispered, glancing at the wind sock downfield and adjusting his scope to take into account a slight breeze kicking up. "No one shoots until I give the word. Clear?"

Everyone agreed.

Marcus was grateful for the size of the terminal. The main lounge downstairs had very high ceilings. But there was also a second floor. Marcus had asked Geoff about it while they were climbing to the roof. Geoff had explained that the second floor consisted of the flight operations center, a kitchenette, a restroom, and a small apartment where some of the staff apparently could rest during extra-long shifts. This put the roof a good thirty feet off the ground, well above the Embraer and the Range Rovers, and thus out of view of anyone exiting the plane.

And now here they came.

There was no question they were IRGC.

Six heavily armed men came down the stairs first and took up positions between the vehicles and the terminal. Next, six more men—just as heavily armed—followed, taking up their positions on the other side of the plane, effectively surrounding the Embraer with security. Marcus exhaled slowly, then whispered to each member of his team exactly which tango he wanted them to take out, moving left to right.

"Stand by, Blowtorch," he whispered, no longer talking to Annie personally but fully immersing back into his operational protocols.

"Standing by, Red Leader."

Just then, another IRGC commando popped his head out the door of the Embraer, scanned the situation, and began slowly descending the stairs. Then came another. And still one more. When they had finished descending the stairs and finally set foot on the tarmac, General Mahmoud Entezam emerged from the plane, stopped, and took in his surroundings for himself.

The moment he had the IRGC chief squarely in his reticle, Marcus didn't hesitate.

"*Now*," he ordered and squeezed the trigger.

Entezam's head exploded.

So did four others.

Then Marcus ordered his team to start firing at everyone they could. They were not using suppressors, so the shots—and their deadly effects—sent panic through the IRGC commandos. They had no idea where the rounds were coming from, so they began firing through the plate glass windows of both floors of the terminal while moving to take cover.

"Now, Blowtorch," Marcus shouted, ripping off his night vision goggles. "*Now, now, now.*"

Despite the noise of the firefight, every member of the team could hear Annie make her formal request to the commander in chief, as they ripped off their own goggles. They could hear Hernandez give the order. And Secretary of Defense Cal Foster relayed it forward.

Marcus and his team kept firing for another thirty seconds. Then, when Annie gave them the word, they ducked down, hugging the roof of the terminal, and covered their heads with their arms.

And then it happened. Somewhere above them, an American F-35 pilot fired. Two air-to-ground missiles streaked toward the earth at supersonic speed. Both smashed into their targets, dead-on. The Embraer and the center Range Rover in the convoy exploded upon impact, and the resulting fireball incinerated everyone and everything within a hundred feet.

Even over the roar of the flames, Marcus could hear the cheering in the Situation Room. And the Ops Center. He could hear Hernandez, Vice President Whitney, and Secretary Dayton joining the celebration. And Dell and McDermott, as well.

It was over. Marcus could hardly believe it, but it was really over. Abu Nakba was dead. Kairos was no more. The Cerberus virus had been eradicated. And in a development that none of them had imagined, much less planned for, Mahmoud Entezam, the mastermind of Iran's terrorist operations—the man who had put the bounty on Marcus's head—was dead.

The mission was a success. But Marcus could not celebrate. It had cost too much. He'd lost too many friends and come far too close to losing even more.

"Thank you, guys—thank you so much," he said, turning to Pete, Kailea, and Geoff, and knowing that Noah and Annie were listening too. "I couldn't have done it without you."

And then, as if reading each other's minds, they rolled over onto their backs, laid down their weapons, and stared up at the stars, knowing it would not be night for long. A new day was about to dawn. And they were going home.

95

Now came the ultimate test of the strategy Marcus Ryker had laid out for him.

President Hernandez picked up the phone from the console before him and waited for the NSC watch officer to patch him through. From the moment it was confirmed that both the compound in India and the head of the Iranian Revolutionary Guard Corps had been neutralized, Hernandez had been itching to make this call.

"Okay, sir, you're connected," the watch officer in the Sit Room finally said.

Hernandez nodded.

There was a hiss of static, and then Chen Guanzhong came on the line.

"President Hernandez, to what do I owe this honor?" asked the premier of the People's Republic of China.

Hernandez noted the dissonance between Guanzhong's light, almost airy, question and the thick tension in the man's voice.

"President Guanzhong, thank you for taking my call on such short notice," he began. "I'm calling to inform you that in a few hours, I will be making a live televised address to my nation, and to the world."

"Are you announcing your bid for your party's presidential nomination so soon?"

Hernandez shook his head in disgust. "No, Mr. President. I will be announcing that U.S. special-ops forces have just brought the most wanted man in the world—and your friend and longtime ally, Walid Abdel-Shafi—to justice."

"You must be confused. This name is not familiar to me."

"Well, of course, you're more used to his nom de guerre, Abu Nakba—the Father of Catastrophe."

Suddenly, Guanzhong was silent.

"He was shot and killed by U.S. special operations at a compound in the backwaters of Kerala, India."

Hernandez paused, but the premier remained silent.

"You will, no doubt, be getting a full report from the head of the PLA very soon. But I wanted you to hear it directly from me that the compound has been completely and utterly destroyed. The Cerberus virus has been eradicated, as have all the roughly two hundred Kairos terrorists and PLA operatives who were working there. We know exactly what they were working on, and I can assure you that I have all the evidence I need of your government's active and egregious complicity in declaring war on the United States of America and attempting to murder millions of our citizens with this ghastly virus."

Hernandez paused again, but there was still no reply. He glanced over at the watch officer to see if Guanzhong had dropped off the line or if there was some sort of technical glitch in the hotline. But after running a series of diagnostic tests, the watch officer assured the commander in chief that the Chinese head of state was still there and hearing every word Hernandez said.

"Now, I have not yet decided whether or not to lay this evidence before the American people or to introduce it in an emergency session of the U.N. Security Council. But I guarantee you, Mr. President, that if you do not immediately— and I stress the word *immediately*—cancel your plans to attack and invade Taiwan, then I will do both. You must stand down your missile forces, cancel the mobilization orders of your army and navy, and order your air force to stop buzzing American naval forces that are steaming at high speed to the East and

South China Seas and the Strait of Taiwan and other international waters in the Pacific. Otherwise, I will have no choice but to tell the American people and the world of the plot you and your generals have been preparing, and let me assure you, Mr. President, you will not care for the results."

This time, Hernandez left no room for his counterpart to speak.

"What's more, President Guanzhong, let me be crystal clear. If a single missile is fired at Taiwan, or if any hostile or warlike action of any kind takes place, then America's long-held policy of 'strategic ambiguity' with regard to Taiwan will immediately come to an end. Make no mistake: you will face the full and fearsome wrath of the American people—and that of every single one of our allies in the Pacific—in a manner that will leave your country's future unrecognizable.

"You came to Washington, you sat in my home, and you told me you wanted to lower the flames of rhetoric and embark on a new era of peace and cooperation. Yet all of it was a lie, and I must tell you that I don't respond well to men who lie to my face. So let there be no doubt: you have sixty minutes to stand down your forces—all of them—or I will act. Do not test me on this. Your plans to take Taiwan and cripple American supremacy in the Pacific are over. I couldn't care less if I ever stand for election again. I will defend my nation and my friends with all the power that I have at my disposal. Are we clear?"

Fifty-two minutes later, the evidence was in.

And it was indisputable.

Annie picked up the phone and speed-dialed the Situation Room. The watch officer answered immediately and connected her to the commander in chief as Martha Dell was patched in from Taipei.

"Well?" Hernandez asked.

"You did it, Mr. President," she replied. "Guanzhong didn't just blink. He has completely folded. To be sure, we're going to have to watch him like a hawk from this point forward. But I can tell you with full assurance that the PLA is, in fact, standing down. Congratulations, sir. I'm not sure who else sitting in that chair would have had the courage to make the decisions you have in recent days. The American people may never know what you've done, but I know. Marcus knows. Our teams know. And we are profoundly grateful."

"Sometimes the good guys win, Annie," Hernandez sighed. "Not often enough. But sometimes."

"Amen, Mr. President," Martha chimed in from half a world away.

"So how's your man?" Hernandez now asked Annie.

"He and his team are on their way home, Mr. President. They're approaching the Mediterranean, flying past Israel, right about now, sir. He's exhausted. They all are. But they're coming home."

"Well, they did a helluva job, Annie. You all did. And yes, before you ask, Martha did pass along to me your resignation letter, and Marcus's, and, regretfully, I accept. But give me a few days before we announce it. I don't want Beijing to read it the wrong way."

"Of course, Mr. President," Annie replied.

"When Marcus and Martha get back, let's sit down and hash out the details," Hernandez added.

"Thank you, Mr. President; we'd like that."

"Good. Now, Miss Stewart, go pop a champagne cork, kick off your shoes, and take a load off."

"Soon enough, sir, soon enough," said Annie. "Oh, but there is one more thing before I let you go, if I may, sir."

"Of course, what's that?" asked the president.

"Marcus and I would be deeply honored if you and the First Lady would attend our wedding. We'd like to have it out at the Air Force Academy in Colorado, to honor Marcus's dad. And we would really like it if you could be there and maybe even say a word or two at the reception."

"We'd be delighted, Annie," the president replied. "Nothing would please us more."

EPILOGUE

96

COLORADO SPRINGS, COLORADO—29 MAY

The day of the wedding had finally arrived.

It was a gorgeous spring afternoon. The sky was a crisp, clear cobalt blue, and there wasn't a cloud to be seen. One could still see snow atop Pikes Peak and crowning the other fourteeners. But on the grounds of the U.S. Air Force Academy the grass was green and freshly cut. There was a light breeze from the south, causing the American flags to flutter high atop their poles, and the temperature on this Memorial Day weekend was in the low seventies.

By the grace of God, the insistence of the White House, and a little extra money from the federal coffers, the extensive renovations of the iconic Cadet Chapel—underway for several years—had finally been completed just days before. Inside now sat the president of the United States, the First Lady, the vice president, members of the House and Senate, almost two dozen foreign ministers and foreign ambassadors, a half dozen Cabinet members, the chairman of the Joint Chiefs of Staff, the director of the Central Intelligence Agency, the director of the Diplomatic Security Service, and nearly four hundred guests.

No media had been invited or even permitted on the grounds. Even the cadets who studied there had been asked to vacate for the day.

Hermetically sealing the campus was a phalanx of hundreds of heavily armed Secret Service agents, DSS agents, and state and local law enforcement. Two Patriot missile batteries had been erected, one at each end of the grounds. Roads had been closed in every direction for ten square miles. The airspace overhead had also been closed to commercial and private aircraft for a hundred square miles. Flying CAP—combat air patrol—were four F-16 and four F-22 fighter jets, each armed with a full package of air-to-air missiles. Barely three months after the takedown of the world's most wanted terrorist and the destruction of the biological weapons plant being run by Kairos and Communist China, nothing was being left to chance.

"Hey, you okay?" Pete asked as he and Marcus waited in an anteroom just off the Protestant Chapel, located on the main floor of the historic landmark.

"Actually, no," Marcus conceded, looking a bit pale and pacing about the room.

"Why, what's wrong?" asked the best man, looking snazzy in his brand-new blue Armani suit, azure tie, and matching pocket square, though perhaps not quite as dapper as the groom, dressed nearly the same. "This should be the happiest day of your stupid, messed-up life."

"It is, Pete; it is. It's just . . ."

"Just what?"

"I just want everything to be perfect for Annie, you know? But this thing . . . I don't know, the whole thing has gotten so—"

"Nuts?"

"Yes."

"Bonkers?"

"Absolutely."

"Out of control?"

"Exactly."

"Well, that's the president's fault, and the First Lady's," Pete reminded him. "You never should have asked for their input. But, hey, what can you do?"

Marcus kept pacing, shaking his head.

"You know, I woke up thinking about your first wedding," Pete said after a few moments. "That was a beautiful day. Elena looked spectacular. She was practically glowing. You weren't horrible. But at least it was just family and a few friends. The entire White House and U.N. didn't show up with a couple of missile batteries."

"My point exactly," said Marcus, shaking his head. "Maybe all this hoopla was a mistake."

At this, Pete stopped Marcus in his tracks, grabbed him by both shoulders, and looked him straight in the eye.

"Knock it off, Ryker. There's nothing to worry about. The greatest girl in the world is madly in love with you. The commander in chief has secured the greatest wedding venue in the country for you—and, by the way, is paying for the entire reception himself, as a gift for all you've done for him and the country. All your friends are here. And all that's required of you is to go out there and say, 'I do,' and then give that girl a kiss that will take her breath away. Okay? For a man who's nearly been killed in combat more times than I can count, you really ought to be able to handle something that simple, right?"

Marcus exhaled, smiled, and nodded. "I'll do my best."

"I hope so," said Pete. "And I've got the rest. So just take a deep breath, enjoy the day, and send up one of your prayers for me that someday I get a day half as good."

Marcus laughed, gave Pete a hug, and slapped him on the back three times.

Just then, Pastor Jackson came in from the hallway.

"It's time, gentlemen," he said. "You good?"

Marcus looked at Pete, then back at his pastor. "Yeah, I'm good."

"Wonderful. Let's do this thing."

97

Pastor Jackson opened the door and led the way into the sanctuary.

Marcus and Pete followed.

Marcus was trying to slow his breathing, but nothing was working. The sight of hundreds of guests and Secret Service agents everywhere—including friends he used to serve with—didn't help. Seeing his mom and sisters in the front row to his right, dabbing their eyes with tissues, didn't help either. Even his brothers-in-law and nephews were getting all teary-eyed. Behind them was Maya Emerson with her daughter and niece. Beside them were Geoff, Noah, and Donny, all stoic as usual. And then, in the row behind them, Marcus spotted the Garcia family—Elena's parents and her sisters. He couldn't be more grateful for the reconciliation the Lord had brought about between him and the family, but especially with Elena's father, Javier. He could still barely believe they had come. It could not have been easy for them, and Marcus made a mental note to be sure to thank them in person at the reception later that afternoon.

Soon, two of his nieces—thrilled to be included in the procession—came down the aisle carrying small bouquets of Colorado wildflowers. After them walked Kailea Curtis, carrying her own basket of wildflowers.

As Kailea walked up the steps to take her position across from him, Marcus smiled at her, so grateful for her friendship to him and Annie over the past several brutal years. Then he looked to his left and saw Esther Dayton sitting in the front row. Seated beside her were President Hernandez and the First Lady and President Andrew Clarke's widow, all beaming with pride. Behind them were Vice President Whitney, Secretary Foster, Martha Dell, and Carl Roseboro.

Scanning the other pews, Marcus felt a stab of sorrow that Jenny Morris was missing. Not having Nick Vinetti at his side hurt deeply as well, though he was grateful that Claire had agreed to play the organ and that her girls had come with her.

The absence of former CIA director Richard Stephens didn't sadden Marcus in the slightest, given the overwhelming evidence that had surfaced revealing that Stephens had conspired with the Kremlin to have Marcus and Jenny assassinated inside Russia several years earlier. Marcus had invited Bill McDermott and his wife, over Annie's strenuous objections. She'd insisted that McDermott had played a key role in helping Stephens execute his plot. Marcus had countered that the evidence wasn't ironclad and that he couldn't imagine Bill would ever have been involved in such a thing. But nine days earlier, a federal grand jury in Washington had indicted both Stephens and McDermott on seventeen felony counts, ranging from attempted murder to conspiracy to commit murder to obstruction of justice. Those two men were likely heading to prison for a very long time.

When Claire began playing the wedding march, everyone in the sanctuary rose to their feet and turned their attention to the oak doors at the end of the long red carpet. Marcus gasped as the doors opened and he saw Annie for the first time. She wore a white Versace gown and could not have looked more beautiful as she came down the aisle on the arm of Secretary of State Robert Dayton. Annie never looked at any of the guests. She never turned to the right or the left. Though her face was covered in a lace veil, Marcus could see that she was looking straight at him and beaming every step of the way.

Marcus's eyes filled with tears. He could barely breathe. And then he, too, began to beam as a feeling of unstoppable and unspeakable joy washed over him.

Before he knew it, Annie was standing in front of him.

Secretary Dayton stopped just before the steps, lifted Annie's veil, kissed her on the cheek, and then turned to Marcus and put Annie's arm in his. Marcus gladly took it. Nodding his sincerest thanks to the secretary, he turned and locked eyes again on Annie, on those gorgeous, sparkling emerald eyes positively radiating her love and affection for him and him alone.

Pastor Jackson asked the congregation to take their seats.

Then he greeted the couple and their families before welcoming the First Family, the VP, and all the other dignitaries and honored guests.

Finally, he opened with prayer and began his remarks, speaking directly to the couple and effectively, though respectfully, ignoring everyone else in the hall.

"Marcus, Annie, we're finally here. The day you both have planned for, prayed for, dreamt of, and worried about, has finally arrived. Not everyone believed it was going to happen. Some of those present today were worried this day would never come. But here we are.

"Robert Frost once wrote, 'Love is an irresistible desire to be irresistibly desired.' Amen. How beautifully put. Homer once wrote, 'There is nothing nobler or more admirable than when two people who see eye to eye keep house as man and wife, confounding their enemies and delighting their friends.' I like that line, and I can't think of one that better describes the two of you—a couple who is continually confounding their enemies and delighting their friends.

"Many wise men and women have made insightful comments about love and marriage over the centuries. No one in history, however, has had a more profound or more beautiful or more accurate understanding of marriage than God himself. Jesus performed his first miracle at a wedding, thus affirming and sanctifying the very institution that he created from the beginning of time. What do we read in the very first book of the Bible? Before sin, before the fall of mankind, before the curse of aging and illness and division and death entered the world, God created a man and woman specifically for one another. He said it's not good for a man to be alone—"

"*Amen,*" Marcus blurted out.

This elicited a round of laughter, including from Annie.

"*Amen,*" Pastor Jackson bellowed. "Right, men? Can I hear you say, '*Amen*'?"

"*Amen,*" shouted most of the men in the sanctuary, to more laughter and now applause.

"That's right, y'all—amen and hallelujah! Look, some are called by God to singleness, and when it's of him, it's a wonderful thing. But for most people, God wants us to be married. He doesn't want us to be alone. He wants us to find the soul mate he's created for us. He wants us to find someone who loves Christ first and most and also loves us and is willing—eager, even—to give themselves to us for as long as we both shall live. And then, Lord willing, he wants us to be fruitful and multiply. This was God's plan from the beginning of time. The marriage of one man and one woman isn't the product of societal evolution. It's an institution ordained by God, and when God is at the center of that union, he will bless the two involved in it more than they can possibly imagine.

"There's a pastor and theologian that I've appreciated who has family dinners every Saturday night with his kids and grandkids. And every Saturday night he asks his grandkids, 'What's the point of the whole Bible?' His grandkids then respond in unison with these six words: 'Kill the dragon, get the girl.'"

Pausing, the pastor took a moment to look out over the entire assembly. "I love that," he said. "'Kill the dragon, get the girl.'"

He then returned his attention to the couple. Looking first at Annie, he then looked Marcus straight in the eye.

"When I think of that line, I think of you, Marcus. The world's first husband and man, Adam, had the responsibility to protect his wife from Satan. But we all know he failed. And what happened? Humanity fell into sin and death, which curses us all. As the Scriptures tell us, 'For all have sinned and fall short of the glory of God.' And again, 'We all like sheep have gone astray, each of us has turned to our own way.' But the good news is, 'The Lord has laid on Him'—on Jesus Christ—'the iniquity of us all.' That is, Jesus our Messiah came to earth and did what Adam failed to do. He went to the cross and took upon himself the sins of the entire world, becoming the one sacrifice for all of us. And when he rose from the dead, he defeated sin, death, and the devil and is thus worthy to take for himself, as his bride, the Church—in order to protect her, purify her, love her, bless her, and grant her eternal life with him in heaven for ever and ever. *That* is the story of the Bible. Jesus Christ came to kill the dragon and get the girl. And thus the central question each of us has to decide is this: Whose side do we want to be on—the devil's or the Savior's? There's no such thing as straddling the fence. We're on one side or the other. We either follow Christ and are one with him—are 'married' to Christ, if you will—and thus become part of his royal family and blessed with true love and safety and joy forever and ever and ever, or we reject God's offer of love and redemption and pay the consequences for ever and ever, with no way of escape.

"Marcus, you chose to follow Christ when you were young. And there are few men I know who love Christ as passionately and faithfully as you do. True, you're not a preacher or a pastor. You're not a monk or a missionary. But like King David—whom God called 'a man after his own heart'—the Lord called you to be a warrior, to risk your life every day to fight evil and thus protect our country and our freedoms and our way of life. And like David, you have excelled in following this calling. You have literally killed the dragon, and now the Lord has literally given you the girl. What a beautiful and fitting end to this chapter of your lives.

"Now you and Annie are about to begin a new chapter. As you both depart government service and begin your marriage and life together, you are display-ing to the world the beauty and the power of the biblical story, which culminates with Christ calling the church to himself as his bride. At the same time, I must both encourage and warn you: You are now engaging in a much larger war than anything you would have faced should you have continued in the employ of the American government. As the apostle Paul wrote in his letter to the Ephesians, 'You do not wrestle against flesh and blood but against the rulers, against the authorities, against the cosmic powers of this present darkness, against the spiritual forces of evil in the heavenly places.'

"The threats you will face now will not be physical enemies, but you will battle the lies of the world and the devil. And you'll have to fight your own sin, which is the most crucial fight there is. Marcus and Annie, as you struggle against your own sin in your marriage, may you remember the powerful truths of Scripture. The Lord says, 'I have loved you with an everlasting love' and 'there is therefore now no condemnation in Christ Jesus.' May you forgive each other as Christ forgave you. May you wake up each morning and immerse yourselves in the Scriptures. May you humble yourselves in prayer. May you ask God each morning to fill you with his Holy Spirit and suit you up in the full armor of God. May you fight the lies with the truth of God's Word. May you care for the poor and the needy and vulnerable with a heart of service and compassion. Freed of the restrictions of public service, may you be faithful in telling others about God's free gift of salvation and eternal life that can be found only in Christ Jesus, who told us, 'I am the way, and the truth, and the life. No one comes to the Father except through me.' May you lead people into his kingdom and make disciples of all nations. If the Lord blesses you with children, may you raise them to know your Savior and make him known. And through it all, may you truly cherish and serve and encourage one another, knowing and rejoicing in the fact that, 'He who began a good work in you will bring it to completion at the day of Christ Jesus.'

"Marcus and Annie, you have each been great warriors for your country, each in your own way. Now I urge you to be even greater warriors for Jesus Christ. And I pray that as you love the Lord your God with all your heart, your soul, your mind, and your strength, that you will love each other as you love yourself. And with such a great cloud of witnesses cheering you on, may you set your eyes on the finish line, knowing that the ultimate enemy's defeat is sure, and an even greater wedding feast is coming."

99

And then came the moment Marcus had been waiting for.

"Marcus, would you please repeat after me: *I, Marcus Johannes Ryker . . .*"

Marcus turned from Jackson to Annie and took both her hands. Despite his efforts, he felt his eyes filling with tears. But his voice was strong as he repeated the words he had imagined saying to her ever since their very first date.

"I, Marcus Johannes Ryker . . ."

"*Before God, my family, and my friends . . .*"

"Before God, my family, and my friends . . ."

"*Take thee, Annie Catherine Stewart, as my lawfully wedded wife.*"

"Take thee, Annie Catherine Stewart, as my lawfully wedded wife."

"*To have and to hold from this day forward—for better or worse, for richer or poorer, in sickness and in health, until death do us part.*"

"To have and to hold from this day forward—for better or worse, for richer or poorer, in sickness and in health, until death do us part, so help me God."

Annie was radiant. Her eyes, too, were filling with tears but Marcus had never seen her happier.

"Now, Annie, please repeat after me," said Jackson.

"Yes, sir," she quickly replied.

"I, *Annie Catherine Stewart . . .*"

"I, Annie Catherine Stewart . . ."

"*Before God, my family, and my friends . . .*"

"Before God, my family, and my friends . . ."

"*Take thee, Marcus Johannes Ryker, as my lawfully wedded husband.*"

"Take thee, Marcus Johannes Ryker, as my lawfully wedded husband."

"*To have and to hold from this day forward—for better or worse, for richer or poorer, in sickness and in health, until death do us part.*"

"To have and to hold from this day forward—for better or worse, for richer or poorer, in sickness and in health, until death do us part, so help me God."

Annie squeezed Marcus's hands, and he squeezed hers back. Then Pastor Jackson asked Pete and Kailea to present the rings. Only then did Marcus and Annie let go of each other and wipe their eyes.

Marcus went first.

"Annie, I give you this ring as a symbol of my love and my vow to honor and cherish you with all that I am and all that I have, in the name of the Father, and of the Son, and of the Holy Spirit."

With that, he slipped the gold band onto her left hand until it was snug against the diamond ring he had given her on the porch of her Outer Banks beach house.

Then it was Annie's turn.

"Marcus, with all of my heart I give you this ring as a symbol of my love, my devotion, my purity, and my sincerest vow to honor and cherish you, to adore and support you, and follow you and take care of you with all that I am and all that I have, and always to do so. In the name of the Father, and of the Son, and of the Holy Spirit." Then she slid the gold band onto Marcus's ring finger.

At this, Marcus almost lost it. But suddenly, from behind him, Pete's hand emerged with a clean handkerchief. Surprised and grateful, Marcus took it and dabbed Annie's eyes, then his own, then wiped his nose as discreetly as he could, meaning not at all with hundreds of people looking on. This elicited chuckles from the crowd. Embarrassed, he shoved the handkerchief in his suit pocket and looked back up at Annie.

"All set?" Jackson asked to more laughter.

Marcus nodded and blushed.

"Very well, then," Jackson replied with a smile.

He led them to the altar behind him, where they knelt, took communion together, and then prayed together out of earshot of the congregation. Next, they lit a unity candle, and then Jackson led them back to where they had stood before. Asking everyone present to bow their heads, he prayed a benediction over the couple before closing with the words everyone had been waiting to hear.

"Marcus and Annie, inasmuch as you have pledged your love and loyalty to one another before God and these witnesses—and declared your devotion to one another by the giving and receiving of rings—I declare as a minister of the gospel of Jesus Christ, in the name of the Father, the Son, and the Holy Spirit, that you are now husband and wife. Those whom God has joined together, let no man separate. Marcus, you may now kiss your bride."

Marcus turned to Annie and gave her a long and beautiful kiss. The place went crazy. Everyone cheered. Marcus's team whooped and hollered. Then, fighting a losing battle to be heard over the din, Jackson said, "Ladies and gentlemen, it is my honor to present to you for the first time Mr. and Mrs. Marcus and Annie Ryker."

Again the place went crazy. Everyone was clapping and cheering and whistling and celebrating a moment few had been certain would ever really come to pass. As Claire Vinetti began playing the recessional, Marjorie Ryker, Maya Emerson, and the Daytons dissolved into laughter and uncontrollable tears.

And then Marcus and Annie Ryker walked down the red carpet, holding hands and laughing like children.

Waiting out front was the presidential limousine known as "the Beast." A Secret Service agent opened the back door, allowing Annie to get in first while Marcus helped her with the train of her dress. Then Marcus climbed in after her. In all their years in government, neither had ever been invited to travel in the lead vehicle of a presidential motorcade, and they were positively giddy. So much so that they didn't notice the silver bucket filled with ice and the bottle of Dom Perignon. Nor did they notice the exquisitely wrapped gift waiting for them on one of the leather seats. They were too busy kissing—that is, until the door opened again a few minutes later and the president and first lady joined them.

Soon the forty-vehicle convoy was racing them fifteen miles across town to the Broadmoor, the grandest and most beautiful resort hotel in the entire State of Colorado, where for the rest of the afternoon they would take a million pictures, eat, drink, dance to their favorite songs, mingle with hundreds of guests, listen to scores of toasts—and a few roasts—and watch videos friends had made from their childhood photos and home movies and videos. Both Marcus and Annie were grateful that Marcus's mom had offered to spring for a team of still photographers and videographers whom she knew from church. Because as glorious as this reception would prove to be, and talked about for years to come, neither of them would remember much. They were too delirious to think straight. They would barely even remember what any of the food tasted like. But they would savor forever the gorgeous photo album and especially the beautifully shot and edited DVD that Marjorie Ryker would present to them a few months later, watching it over and over and spotting new and wonderful details they had missed the times before.

100

Marcus thought he'd awoken first.

Then he heard the shower running.

Glancing at his watch, he smiled as he realized it was nearly two in the afternoon. He literally could not remember the last time he hadn't set an alarm clock or let himself sleep so late. After spending an all-too-short wedding night at the Broadmoor, he and Annie had needed to get up at four o'clock the following morning to get to the airport in the Springs by five o'clock. That allowed them to catch a 7:15 a.m. flight, the first of a series of flights to Denver; then San Juan, Puerto Rico; and finally to Cyril E. King International Airport on the island of St. Thomas, arriving almost fourteen hours after their day had begun.

Once on the ground, they picked up the SUV they'd rented from Hertz, bought some basic groceries at a local market, got some takeout from Wendy's, and drove to the private beachside villa they'd reserved. It was around ten o'clock that night when they finally unlocked the front door, dropped their suitcases in the vestibule, put away the milk and other perishables in the refrigerator, and raced to the bedroom.

Now, many hours later, Marcus slipped out of the king-size, hand-carved, mahogany four-poster bed, retrieved their suitcases, and unpacked them both. He put on a pair of navy blue swim trunks and a cotton T-shirt, then opened the plantation shutters and let the gorgeous afternoon sun flood the master bedroom. After this, he opened the French doors and stepped out onto the second-floor balcony.

As he gazed out over Magens Bay off to his left and the white sands of its stunning beach, Marcus soaked in the surroundings and drank in the sound of the gentle waves lapping upon the shore and the exotic birds flying overhead. Located on the north side of the island of St. Thomas, Magens Bay Beach was widely considered one of the most beautiful in the world. Neither Marcus nor Annie had ever been there before. Nor had either of them vacationed in the Caribbean. Yet now that he could see it all—the island, the bay, the villa—in the fresh light of day, he realized the honeymoon location was everything he had hoped for.

The temperature hovered in the low eighties. Sultry ocean breezes caressed his skin as white puffy clouds drifted through clear blue skies. Marcus couldn't wait to enjoy some fresh seafood and other local specialties. But for now, he headed into the kitchen to make coffee and prepare some yogurt, granola, and fresh berries for himself and his new wife.

Seeking privacy above all—not just for the sake of security but because all they wanted was to be alone—the couple had opted against staying at the Four Seasons or any of the other hotels or resorts on the island. They'd chosen instead this secluded and walled-off two-story villa. They'd rented it for three entire months, and Marcus could not have been more pleased. It was beautifully decorated. It had been thoroughly cleaned. It was located right on the water and had a gorgeous inground pool and even a hot tub overlooking the bay. He couldn't imagine a more perfect oasis to get away from all the chaos of Washington and the world and spend time alone with his bride.

After finding a bamboo serving tray in a cupboard and cloth napkins in a drawer, Marcus poured two mugs of freshly brewed Colombian coffee and set them on the tray, along with the two bowls of yogurt and two spoons. Then he brought everything back into the master bedroom, only to find Annie in a bathrobe, drying her hair with a towel out on the deck and savoring the vista that he himself had just enjoyed.

"Knock, knock, knock—room service," he said as he set the tray on a small table between two rocking chairs. "Thought you might be hungry."

Annie turned and flashed him the biggest smile.

"I am. For you," she said, tossing the towel aside, throwing her arms around him, and kissing him like she was never going to let him go.

She did, eventually, but in no rush. Then they sat down and sighed, overwhelmed by the view and by finally being completely alone with no one to answer to and no place to go for the very first time. No one could even reach them by phone. Marcus had locked up their mobile phones in a safe he'd found in a closet and unplugged the landlines he'd found in the kitchen and bedroom.

"Isn't it breathtaking?" Annie asked, her emerald eyes flashing with delight. "I honestly can't believe we're really here."

"I know," Marcus said. "It seemed like it would never happen."

"You're telling me," she teased, then looked down at her rings, the diamond sparkling in the sun. "The Lord is so kind to us, isn't he? I mean, he's certainly put us through an awful lot over the years. Neither of our lives have been simple or painless. But he promised to give us 'plans for good and not for disaster,' a plan to give us 'a future and a hope,' and he kept his word, Marcus. He really kept his word."

"He certainly did," said Marcus. "There were times, I have to admit, I wasn't so sure. But here we are."

"Here we are," Annie echoed, putting her bare feet up on a wicker ottoman and then picking up her mug that matched his and breathing in the aroma of the coffee before taking a sip.

101

There was a long silence as Marcus ate his yogurt and Annie drank her coffee.

"You know what I can't believe?" Annie finally said, looking out at the azure waters of the bay.

"What's that?" Marcus said, turning to her as he began to sip his coffee.

"That you really married me."

Marcus was caught off guard by the statement. "What's that supposed to mean?" he asked, trying not to feel defensive.

She shrugged, turning to him. "I've been in love with you since the day we first met on that tarmac in Kabul. At the very least, I had a massive crush on you from the instant I saw you. It was completely crazy, of course. You were almost engaged, and I didn't really know you at all. But I couldn't help it. Some people don't believe in love at first sight. But I was just immediately and completely swept away by your blue eyes, your strong jawline, your rugged good looks, and your shy and gentle smile. And then you, of course—you and Pete and Nick— your team went on to save my life that day. Well, Robert's and mine. And that was that. I was done for."

Relaxing, Marcus said nothing, just listened.

Annie paused, took another sip, and looked back out across the bay. "Of course, you went on to marry Elena—which you absolutely were right to do," Annie insisted. "You guys were high school sweethearts. You were in love. And I was a mess. A new believer. Not strong in the Lord like you. And then pretty messed up after that helicopter crash. In and out of counseling. In and out of rehab, trying to get myself off all those pain meds. It was pretty dark there for a stretch. But Robert and Esther were so kind. They never gave up on me. Nor did Carter or Maya. Nor did my aunt and uncle. Even if you had been single, you never would have given me a second look, nor should you have. But you weren't single, of course. Not really. And then you got married. You were happy. And then you had Lars and were raising him. And you weren't even in D.C. for most of those years, and there I was slaving away on the Hill."

Another sip.

"But the truth was . . . I loved you."

"Really?" Marcus asked.

Annie nodded. "Don't get me wrong," she quickly added. "I don't mean I would ever have done anything about it. It wasn't impure. It wasn't adulterous. I just had such a deep respect for you, and such an affection for you, and for most of those years, I guess you represented the type of man I *wanted* to fall in love with, the kind of man I *wished* I could marry."

With another sip, Annie finished her coffee but kept holding the mug.

"And then you guys moved back to D.C. All of a sudden, we were all going to the same church. And Senator Dayton and Esther and I were being invited over to Carter and Maya's house for Sunday dinners with you and Elena and Lars. Or I was seeing you guys at church picnics. And then Maya invited Elena to join the Tuesday night Bible study she was leading, the one I'd been in for years, and I got to spend more time with her and saw what a kind and strong and godly woman she was.

"I was devastated when she and Lars were killed—devastated. I wept for days. Weeks, actually. I could barely keep food down. Elena had become a friend. A prayer partner. A soul mate. And now she was gone. And Lars was gone too. It was a huge loss for you, but it was for me, too. I wept for you. Suddenly, inexplicably, you were all alone in the world." Annie's eyes were suddenly filling with tears.

"I was."

Annie wiped a tear away and looked over at him. They were quiet for a while, and then Annie asked him a question. "So, what happened?"

"What do you mean?"

"I mean, one minute you're shattered. And I'm sick at heart. And then you resign from the Secret Service as you slip into this terrible depression. And I'm trying to come out of depression and grow in my faith, but now I feel like the rug's been pulled out from under me. And I'm afraid I'm going to slip into drinking again, or taking pain meds, or both. But the next thing I know, the senator is asking me to call you to invite you to come on a Co-Del to Europe, to provide security for us or whatever. And our lives become really intertwined— not peripherally, not incidentally, but very intentionally. Now we're becoming actual friends. Not acquaintances. Not friends of friends through Carter and Maya or through the Daytons or even through Elena. Now you're a widower, and I'm . . . whatever; and now we're becoming actual friends. Traveling together. Working together. Having dinner together. Fighting bad guys together. And suddenly we're here. Married. I mean, really married. Staying in the same house. Staying in the same room."

"Yeah, that's what married couples do." Marcus laughed.

"So I'm told," Annie said. "But it's *us*. Not someone else. It's you and me. For crying out loud, Marcus Ryker, there was a long period of time when I wasn't even sure you were interested in being my friend. And now we're married. How in the world did that happen?"

102

"It happened because you asked me to that dinner," Marcus replied.

Annie said nothing.

"Remember, the White House Correspondents' Dinner?" Marcus added. "Any of this ring a bell?"

"Of course it does. You really think I'd forget that night?"

"Well, I'm just saying, that night changed everything."

"It did?"

"I'll say. I'll never forget walking up the steps of your brownstone. Or how stupid I felt wearing that Armani monkey suit I'd bought back in my days in the Secret Service. Or the rush of fear and adrenaline I felt as I rang your doorbell and waited for you to open the door. The perspiration on my palms. The jitters in my stomach. My heart pounding in my chest. And all the while I'm thinking, 'What in the world is wrong with me? It's just dinner with Annie. You know, Annie, whom I've known forever?' And suddenly the door opened, and you were standing there, and you literally took my breath away with that sleeveless, floor-length gown with that glittering silver bodice and matching silver purse. Your hair was pulled back. Your lipstick and nails were pink. And when you smiled—like you're doing right now—I thought I was going to melt.

"I'd always liked you, from the very first day in Kabul. I can't say I had a crush on you or fell in love with you. Of course I thought you were attractive. How could I not? And I was furious at McDermott for flirting with you so shamelessly. Not because I wanted you for myself but because it obviously embarrassed you, made you uncomfortable. But I really was head over heels in love with Elena. I wasn't interested in anyone but her. I didn't save your life that day out of chivalry. It was my job. It's what I was trained to do. And when that chopper went down and we came under fire by the Taliban, my training just kicked in, pure and simple. But I have to tell you how touched I was when you and the senator and Mrs. Dayton would send me a gift or a handwritten note every year or even call me—usually all of the above—every year on the anniversary of that terrible day, thanking me for saving your lives. And I know you guys also would call and write Nick and Pete and Bill and the others. That meant a lot to me. I've saved other people's lives, and they don't say boo every year.

"Then, yes, we eventually moved back to D.C., and I started working at the White House, and we started going to Lincoln Park Baptist. And we became close to Carter and Maya. And Elena joined Maya's small group and met you, and we really did all become friends. I liked that. And the more I got to know you, and the more Elena and Maya talked about you, the more impressed I became with you. With your heart. Your character. Your faith. With all the challenges you were going through. Obviously I didn't know the details. But I didn't need to. I just could see that Maya was so impressed with what the Lord was doing in you. So was Elena. And they would speak about you with great admiration and affection, and that touched me.

"But honestly, it wasn't until you asked me to come to that dinner—long after I lost Elena—and I saw you open that door and look so absolutely stunning that I ever thought once about you in a romantic way at all. But standing on your stoop, everything changed. It was like I went into freefall."

"Really?"

"Scout's honor. And when you and I bailed on that White House thing because being with all those politicians and paparazzi seemed like . . ."

"A nightmare?"

"Exactly—and I asked if you wanted to go get some dinner at that Marriott—"

"The Key Bridge Marriott."

"Right. And there we were in the corner, at the only table they had left. Sitting there having a candlelight dinner with you . . ." Marcus's voice trailed off.

"What?" Annie pressed after waiting too long.

"I was completely mesmerized. I mean, I did my best to cover it up. But it wasn't easy. I tried to make all kinds of small talk. But I'm not good at small talk. And it wasn't like we'd just met. You already knew so much about me. And you started asking about my mom and sisters. I'd forgotten that you'd met them and had dinner with them like a year and a half earlier, together with Senator Dayton. But you reminded me and said it had been a lovely night. And you joked that the whole thing had been a 'special op'—I believe that was the phrase you used—designed to keep the rest of the Ryker family, and my mom in particular, in the dark about what you called my 'extracurricular activities' in the CIA in Moscow and points east. Do you remember all that?"

103

Annie nodded and smiled and leaned toward him.

Marcus continued. "I can still remember the rhythms of the conversation," he said gently.

"Can you?" she asked.

"Absolutely—it was playful but discreet," he said. "We'd never done anything social like that. We'd gone out to dinner and movies and bowling and whatever—in groups, of course. And movie nights at the Carters' now and again. But we'd never been out to dinner alone—just the two of us, all dressed up, you in a gorgeous dress, and me in a tux—and there we were. Night was falling. The candle flickering. Two glasses of wine. And the more we talked, the more I began to realize that you were intimately familiar with so many more details about my life and my family than almost anyone I knew. Sure, you knew more than most about my clandestine activities because you worked for the Senate Intelligence Committee and had clearance above top secret and you had been read in on some of the most sensitive operations the Agency was running. But it wasn't just that. We didn't even talk about any of that. We just talked as friends who had known each other for nearly twenty years. Friends who had been in Afghanistan together. In combat together. Friends who had worked in the intelligence community together. And traveled to Europe together with your boss. We'd even been to Moscow together. To the Kremlin. We'd met President Luganov and Oleg Kraskin together. And of course, we'd gone to the same church together—for years. We had many of the same friends. Good friends. Dear friends. And suddenly, as if someone was whispering the idea in my ear in the candlelight, I realized that I didn't want to just be good friends with you. I wanted to be with you. To be honest, Annie, that very night—at that very table—I knew I wanted to marry you. And that thought scared me."

"Scared you?"

"Yeah."

"Why?"

"Because on the one hand, it seemed to come out of nowhere, so it blindsided me. But on the other hand, it seemed so normal, so natural. I mean, I wasn't on a blind date with a stranger. I hadn't met you on the internet or some dating app or whatever. You and I really were friends. We knew each other's character, theology, everything. So I realized that starting a romantic relationship with you wouldn't be starting from scratch. We had history together. Good history. Healthy history. But that scared me too, because I realized that if I really asked you out—if I really asked you to start dating me—the only reason would be to find out if God wanted us to get married. And I knew at that very moment that we could accelerate very, very quickly. And I certainly didn't want to scare you off."

"Well, you were a pretty cool customer that night," Annie said.

"I was?"

"Are you kidding?" she asked. "I had no idea all that was percolating inside of you. I thought you were just being a gentleman, or that you'd taken pity on me and said yes to going to the dinner because I didn't have anyone else to ask. I certainly didn't imagine that you had any particular interest in me."

"Well, I did."

"But I couldn't read you. You were friendly and all, but you didn't show your cards. And all the while I was terrified because I was in danger of losing all sense of control. I was in danger of abandoning years of carefully managed discipline around you. Here I was having this amazing dinner with you—just the two of us—and I was petrified of saying something, or doing something, that would scare you off forever."

"Oh, Annie, I wish you'd told me that night exactly what you were thinking," Marcus said, smiling. "You could have saved us a lot of time."

"I think the ball was in your court, my friend, not mine," Annie replied, blushing as so many memories came flooding back.

"Fair enough," said Marcus, taking her hand. "I take full responsibility for being so slow to realize how much I liked you."

"Good," said Annie. "I'm glad we got that straight."

"So what do you say, Annie Ryker?" Marcus asked, pulling her closer to him and kissing her on her cheek, her neck, her nose, and then gently on her mouth. "What do you say we make up for lost time?"

Annie never answered.

Not with words, anyway.

Rather, she just stood, took Marcus by the hand, led him back inside the villa, and closed the French doors and the plantation shutters to the sky, the sun, and the world beyond.

ACKNOWLEDGMENTS

Marry a girl who loves you enough to take big risks—a girl who believes in you and is willing to ride the roller coaster of life together. I did, and I'm a better man for it.

Lynn, I thank God every day that He brought you into my life, and that in some cosmic and counterintuitive moment I wasn't stupid enough to let you slip away. I cringe to think of what I would be if I hadn't married you. I cringe to think of how many jobs I would have been fired from if you hadn't patiently read and edited everything I've ever written, before I gave it to my editors.

The fact that you are such a wise, discerning, and sensitive writer and editor, as well as a great wife, mom, daughter, sister, daughter-in-law, and friend, totally astounds me. I could never have written this book, or any other—nor would I have wanted to—without you. This was true in 2002 when I wrote my first novel, *The Last Jihad*. It's even more true today as I complete *The Beijing Betrayal*. Thank you. Thank you. Thank you. I love you so much!

To our dear sons and their wives—Caleb and Rachel, Jacob, Jonah and Cassandra, and Noah—thank you for bringing so much joy into Mom's and my lives. Thanks for supporting me for so many years in this crazy career of being an author and speaker. It has not always been easy, but it's always been an adventure, and we love going on adventures with you all. Indeed, we love each and every one of you more than we know how to express.

To our beloved parents, Dad and Mom Rosenberg and June "Bubbe" Meyers, our wonderful siblings and their precious families, and the families of our dear daughters-in-law—thank you so much for all your love, prayers, and encouragement over the years! Lynn and I love and cherish you beyond measure.

To our dear OBX friends and kindred spirits—Dan and Susan, Edward and Kailea, Kelly, Jim and Sharon, Chung and Farah, Marcus and Tanya, Geoff and Jennifer, Tim and Carolyn, and of course "John Black John Black" (aka *Jacque Noir*, man of the night) and Doro, and all your wonderful, spirited, fun-loving kids—what a thrill to be in the race with you guys. Thanks so much for doing fun, faith, and fiction with us over more than two decades! We count each of you a great treasure and blessing that we do not deserve.

To our courageous and creative Israeli friends—Calev and Sheli, Sasha and Lilian, Victor and Etti, Meno and Anat, Wayne and Ann, Slava and Orna, Meir and Michal, Gal and Liah, Danny and Anne, Tal and Asaf, and so many others—we have been so touched and so blessed by each one of you and we are so grateful for you all.

To our true and faithful ministry allies here in the Epicenter and back in the U.S. and Canada—those with The Joshua Fund, Near East Media (All Israel News and All Arab News), TBN, and *The Rosenberg Report*—thank you for your friendship, your hard work and passion, and your deep and abiding commitment to blessing Israel and her neighbors in the name of Jesus. Thank you.

To our extraordinary friend, colleague, "air traffic controller," and prayer warrior, Nancy Pierce, may the Lord bless you and Pete even more richly in the next season of life than he has so far. For more than three decades, we have been so deeply blessed by you, Nancy, and we will never take it for granted. God bless you!

To my literary agent, Scott Miller, at Trident Media Group—why you took my first call way back in the spring of 2001, I'll never know. But I'm so grateful that you did. Over almost a quarter of a century, you've done a fabulous, relentless, tireless, brilliant job, and I am forever grateful. Thanks so much for your hard work, wise counsel, coolness under pressure, and friendship. You da man!

To my Tyndale House publishing team—Jeremy Taylor, Mark Taylor, Ron Beers, Karen Watson, Elizabeth Jackson, Andrea Garcia, Maria Eriksen, Dean Renninger, Caleb Sjogren, the entire sales force, and all the remarkable professionals who comprise the Tyndale family—thank you so much for your kindness, creativity, and professionalism. I am forever grateful for your passion to tell great stories.

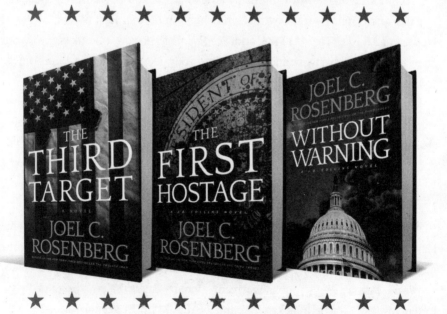

ABOUT THE AUTHOR

Joel C. Rosenberg is a *New York Times* bestselling author of eighteen novels and five nonfiction books with nearly 5 million copies in print.

Rosenberg's career as a political thriller writer was born out of his film-making studies at Syracuse University, where he graduated with a BFA in film drama in 1989. He also studied for nearly six months at Tel Aviv University during his junior year. Following graduation from Syracuse, he moved to Washington, D.C., where he worked for a range of U.S. and Israeli leaders and nonprofit organizations, serving variously as a policy analyst and communications strategist.

He has been profiled by the *New York Times*, the *Washington Times*, and the *Jerusalem Post* and has appeared on hundreds of radio and TV programs in the U.S., Canada, and around the world. As a sought-after speaker, he has addressed audiences at the White House, the Pentagon, the U.S. Capitol, the Israeli president's residence, the European Union parliament in Brussels, and business and faith conferences in North America and around the world.

The grandson of Orthodox Jews who escaped out of czarist Russia in the early 1900s, Rosenberg comes from a Jewish background on his father's side and a Gentile background on his mother's side.

Rosenberg is the founder and chairman of The Joshua Fund, a nonprofit educational and humanitarian relief organization. He is also the founder and editor in chief of All Israel News (allisrael.com) and All Arab News (allarab.news).

He and his wife, Lynn, are dual U.S.- Israeli citizens. They made aliyah in 2014 and live in Jerusalem, Israel. They have four sons, Caleb, Jacob, Jonah, and Noah.

For more information, visit joelrosenberg.com and follow Joel on X (@joelcrosenberg) and Facebook (facebook.com/JoelCRosenberg).